LITTLE BONES

NV Peacock lives in lovely Northamptonshire. She works full time and spends her spare time writing, reading, and running a local writers' group. She started her writing career with short stories in anthologies for publishers all over the world, before turning her hand to novels. After writing two YA supernatural series, she decided to indulge her dark side and write an adult thriller. As an avid writer, she spends every minute she can creating characters, drafting stories, and plotting. Nicky writes for her readers and appreciates every review she receives; without them, she couldn't do what she loves.

LITTLE BONES

BONES

N V PEACOCK

avon.

Published by AVON
A division of HarperCollins*Publishers* Ltd
1 London Bridge Street
London SE1 9GF

www.harpercollins.co.uk

A Paperback Original 2020

1

First published in Great Britain by HarperCollins*Publishers* 2020

ISBN: 978-0-00-843635-3

Typeset in Bembo by
Palimpsest Book Production Limited, Falkirk, Stirlingshire
Printed and bound in UK by CPI Group (UK) Ltd, Croydon CR0 4YY

MIX
Paper from
responsible sources
FSC® C007454

For you, the reader.

Prologue

Too many young boys are out tonight. Broken-voiced taunts and high-pitched laughter echo down the road to him. Crowds make him more careful. One boy alone is easy prey, but with packs of children roaming the streets, his actions need to be more careful, more considered and more inconspicuous.

To inspect the young faces on offer, he slips down to second gear. Crawling along the kerb, he hunts for the right one: the one all alone.

Emerging from a newsagent is a boy around ten years old with a plastic bag; wearing hand-me-down clothes, but sporting new white high-top trainers. For a moment, the boy stops. He looks down at his feet, eyeing his trendy footwear with pride, watching how the metallic embroidery catches the light. Happy, he almost skips forward, but then remembers his purchase. Rustling in the bag, he brings out a shiny packet of football cards, which steal his focus, so it takes a few seconds for him to notice the car creeping beside him.

Carefully, the driver rolls down his window. 'Can I give you a lift, mate?' he says.

Looking down at his cards, the boy keeps walking, albeit at a quicker stride now.

The driver glides the car along to keep pace with his prey.

'Don't be afraid – I'm a taxi.'

'You don't look like a taxi.' The boy stops and quickly adds, 'And I'm not afraid.'

'I'm off duty tonight, mate. Look, I have a kid about your age. I'd be worried if they were out this late, all alone.'

Smirking, the boy says, 'It's not late.'

'It's dark. You should be home by now. Your parents will worry.'

'I've spent all my money, sorry.'

'No charge.' He then whispers the next sentence like it's a secret only he and the boy share. 'Look, the streets are full of crazies. I'd hate to see your face in the morning paper. Didn't your parents ever warn you about predators who take little boys off the street? There was that kid who never made it home last week. You know the one.'

The boy narrows his eyes. A kid at his school did go missing a few weeks ago.

'All right. My dad said to get home before the street-lights come on, so you'd be doing me a favour.'

The man grins. 'No worries, mate. Hop in.'

The boy quickly slides into the back seat. When the man hears the slam of the car door, he knows he has his prize. It's like the snap of a jaw, the puncture of teeth, the squeal of an animal knowing its time has ended.

The boy's face will be in the newspapers, not the next

morning, but maybe the one after. The man sees it in his mind's eye and smiles. He's killed four boys now, and the police haven't connected the cases. Even if they had, no one would ever consider him a suspect. He lives with his happy family in a beautiful home. No one would imagine he has a dark blue room in that house. A room where each boy he has stolen gifts him his last words and final breath. A room where he hasn't bothered to wipe the blood off the walls, or even muffle his victims' screams.

He's the perfect man, the perfect partner, the perfect father. No one would ever see anything different. Monsters who kill little boys are evil and ugly and wear long dirty macs. Those sinister creatures skulk in the shadows while committing their dark deeds, ashamed of admitting the why with the how. When he looks in the mirror, he doesn't see a monster, but the smile of a man about to get what he wants.

'What's your name?' he asks his prey.

'Thomas.'

Chapter 1

The blade slices through the flesh, and a pink sliver falls down into a perfect curl.

'Cherrie!'

I look up at my name to see Mr Dawson, my boss, pointing towards a customer; a fifty-something woman with sharp features and an even sharper stare. Our eyes lock, and her fake fingernails begin clacking an impatient rhythm on my countertop.

Smiling, I stuff my hands into new plastic gloves, and then step towards her.

'Can I help you?'

'Five sirloin steaks.'

She narrows her keen eyes at me. I hate it when they stare; I'll probably drop all the meat on her beady-eyed watch. Carefully, I pull two steaks onto the scales. The cost is already at £13 but it doesn't seem to bother her. Reaching over, I grab a third steak.

Suddenly, the customer cocks her head and asks, 'Do I know you?'

I try not to react. Instead, I widen my smile and continue piling up her meat like a butcher's game of Jenga.

'I've seen you somewhere before,' she says.

'I'm here in the shop most days.' I nod, trying not to look her in the eye.

'Do you live on the Pine Holmes Estate?'

The moment the question leaves her lips, she realises how silly it is. I'm just a shop assistant, and the houses in Pine Holmes are worth more money than I'd see in three lifetimes.

'I wish,' I say and laugh, although it comes out more like a strangled hiccup.

Without bothering to tell her the final price, I quickly wrap up the meat.

'So, where do I know you from?' She's not even asking me now, just talking to herself.

Thrusting the package towards her, I throw her another smile, hopefully one that concludes our encounter. Still, the woman lingers. Looking down, I see her palm is flat against my clean glass countertop. As she moves her hand to collect the meat, she leaves behind a sweaty smudge.

'I've definitely seen you somewhere before. This is annoying.'

'Sorry, you don't know me. I don't think we've ever met,' I say, which is the truth, just not the whole truth. Daring to look her in the eye, I commit her face to memory so I can avoid her in future. She may not remember who I am now, but I might not be so lucky next time. Memories have a habit of snapping back into place like elastic bands.

'Can I get you anything else?' I ask.

With a blank face, the woman stares at me. If we lived

in a cartoon, this would be when I see inside her mind to watch the exhausted mouse on its wheel. I want to yell at her to give the poor rodent a break and stop her pointless interrogation but instead, say, 'Enjoy your steaks.' Life isn't a cartoon, not even close.

I turn away from her to continue slicing the ham. With my back to her, she loses interest and wanders deeper into the belly of the shop.

These encounters only happen now and then. Strangers who feel a tickle of familiarity when they look at me, and mentally chase their tails trying to figure out how I've crossed their paths before. Nowadays, people's attention spans are thankfully low. Usually, when I slip on the plastic cap and apron, no one bothers to look beyond them. It's why I love this job so much.

Grabbing a cloth, I wipe her parting smudge from my countertop. I wring my hands together, shut my eyes, and remind myself that that is all she is, a smudge on the surface of my day, nothing more. When I open my eyes, I realise she didn't even once say thank you. If Robin behaved like that, I'd have grounded him for a month.

'Hey!' Tracy steps out from the area behind the plastic curtains, where we sign in the meat deliveries. We affectionately call it backstage and the counter onstage.

'Where have you been? I'm onstage all on my own as a one-woman show.'

'Feel like having fun tonight?' she asks, avoiding my question.

'I can't go out tonight. Leo's buying a bottle of wine and we're watching *Strictly Come Dancing* together.'

'I swear Leo is the most boring boyfriend in the world.'

'Boring is underrated.' I smile.

'Look, I thought Gran was going to go with us tonight, but now she's told me that she already went with her mates from bingo instead. We need a fourth person.'

'A fourth person for what?' I ask.

'Come on, Cherrie, when are you going to join the rest of the world on Facebook? We've been talking about tonight on there for ages.'

'I'm a private person. I don't like strangers seeing stuff about me.'

Tracy lets out an exaggerated sigh. 'We booked a psychic, but she'll only see groups. We need at least four people. And I've been so looking forward to it.'

'Why?'

'I just want some hope that I have more of a life to look forward to than this.' She motions at a pile of sausages.

'I get the need for hope; just why four people?' I ask. 'It's not like some mystic number.'

'Because four people's money makes it worthwhile for her to get her psychic on,' Tracy replies with a sigh. 'Please come with us.'

'I've never been to a psychic before. What do they do?'

'Her name is Mariah. She reads tarot cards. Gran told me she predicted her little bingo victory last week, and her heart operation. It's only £25. A bargain to know your future.'

'Look, can I think about it and come back to you?' I ask.

I'm not sure I believe in all that psychic stuff, but if I'm wrong and this woman sees things in my past she shouldn't, it could be disastrous.

'I need to know now. Come on, Cherrie.'

My kneejerk answer is no. There is no win here. If this

fortune-teller is crap, she'll tell me nothing, and I'll be down £25 to discuss nonsense with a stranger. If she's good, she'll see my past. Not that I can tell Tracy my concerns. We may have been best friends for the past decade, but she has no idea who I am, or should I say who I used to be. I ought to say no. However, if I turn down this invitation, it could be months before the girls ask me out again. I could do with a night out, and as much as I worry about someone recognising me, it still hasn't happened yet. My name may live on the tips of the tongues of busybodies, but it is yet to be spoken aloud by those close to me. I can't let my past rule my present.

'Okay, I'm in,' I say.

Tracy jumps up and down. 'You're the best, Cherry Pie.'

She hasn't called me *Cherry Pie* in ages. A sudden warmth makes me grin back. 'What time and where?'

'Pick me up at seven. We'll go together. Wait.' She stops and narrows her eyes at me. 'You're not going to flake out on me, are you?'

'No, I promise I won't flake out on you.'

'Fab. Oh, and there are privacy settings on Facebook, just so you know.' With that, she disappears backstage.

It's Saturday, but the shop is quiet. Boredom affords me far too much time to think through what I've just agreed to. The worry of a stranger poking about in my past continually wriggles to the surface of my mind, like a worm in the rain.

On my break I text Leo that I'm going out with the girls tonight. His text back is *cool* along with an emoji my phone is too old to read. I still have an iPhone 4; emoji created after 2010 show up as an alien face. Leo says I need to update, as I'm only getting messages with half the information, but I love my phone. It was given to me at a time in my life when everything started to get better. It was the day I found out I was pregnant with Robin. Leo treated me. He wanted us to only ever be a fingertip away. I'm not prepared to give up on that solid, plastic daily reminder that I'm loved.

By the time five o'clock rolls around, I've served two more customers, and counted the chicken wings and stuffed olives twice. Tracy has already left to get ready for tonight. I'm alone. Almost.

As I put the lids back over the deli tubs, I see a young woman of about eighteen looking over her shoulder then back again at the pre-packaged meat. Shoplifter. I reach behind the counter and pick up our radio. It's our only security – it links us to the main shopping centre's lads in uniform. We call whenever we need backup.

I hesitate. If I catch a thief, it will mean hours of police statements and paperwork, which would equal an escape from the psychic encounter tonight, but it would mean no *Strictly* with Leo and Robin either, ruining my Saturday night.

The shoplifter raises her gaze. She holds my stare as her hand snakes out and grabs a chicken. A whole chicken. Without even looking away, she puts it under her coat. It protrudes like one massive knobbly boob. I've seen nothing like it before. Is this some gang initiation thing? Ten years in the job, and I've never seen anyone blatantly steal in front of me. Like a toddler who you've told no to, but does what they want anyway. Damn the extra time. Without breaking our staring contest, I lift the radio to my mouth.

'Security Team, come in.'

The radio crackles, and I smile at the girl. Robin went through bouts of both terrible twos, and the even more terrible threes; this shoplifter has no idea who she's dealing with. If she wants to act like naughty kid, then I'll treat her like one.

The girl purses her lips, blinks, and puts the chicken back. As she does, her coat flaps open, revealing her pregnant belly. The giant mound before her dwarfs her thin frame. When was the last good meal she ate? Who is looking after her?

An eardrum-pounding bleep sounds and Tim, the head of security, comes over the radio: 'Hey, Cherrie, are you okay down at Dawson's Food? Over.'

When you hold the radio, stealth is off the menu. In the past shoplifters have stampeded towards me when hearing it go off, but this girl looks as if she's about to cry.

I soften my smile. 'Everything is fine. Just wanted to say goodnight. Over.'

'Oh yeah, you part-timers only work until five on a Saturday now. Have a good weekend, Creeker. Over.'

'Thanks, you too. Over.'

She stares at me, mouth slightly open. Is she shocked I've given her a break, or waiting for the right moment to shove the chicken back under her coat?

Putting the radio down, I motion to the company sign hanging above my section and say to the girl, 'They call this place Dawson's Creek. After the TV show.'

'What TV show?'

'Never mind.'

Wringing my hands together, I make a decision. I pack up some meats, olives, and cheeses into a large package.

'Here, take this.' I wave the package towards her. 'And take some bread and milk.' I nod over at the shelves sitting parallel to my section.

'Why are you doing this?' she asks, yet walks up to take the food before I can answer.

'Looks like you need a bit of help. I know what that's like. Don't worry; I'll mark it all down as being out-of-date. We throw out a shocking amount of food here.'

'Thank you.' She looks down at the food package as if it's the most amazing thing she ever held; wait until she gets her baby in her arms.

'You're welcome. I'm here again Monday until five. Come around the back, and I'll save more *out-of-date stuff* for you.'

'The guy on the radio said your name was Cherrie. Is that right?'

'Yes. I'm Cherrie.'

'I'm Kylie.'

'Your mum used to watch *Neighbours* eh?'

'Huh?'

'Never mind. See you Monday, Kylie.'

She nods, takes a loaf of bread and a four-pint jug of whole milk, and then leaves.

The shop is eerie when it's empty, so I quickly check the tills are cashed up, then leave, locking the front door behind me.

It's five-thirty and already so dark I have to use the torch on my phone to light my way. Fortunately, I parked my car just down the street from the shop, so my time in the shadows is limited.

Climbing into my little Ford, I strap on the seatbelt

and then twist on the engine. It sputters out its anger at being disturbed, yet fortunately gurgles to life.

In the summer, I walk to work. I only live half a mile away from Dawson's Food, but in the winter months, when the nights close in quicker, I use the car. I don't much like the dark.

Opening my front door, I find a quiet house. I check my mobile and find Leo has texted to say they'll be late. He has included an emoji my phone can't read. I'm guessing it's supposed to be some sort of frustration face. They were at his mum's today, and she has a habit of making dinner later to keep them longer.

I pull off my boots and place them by the door, leaving space for Leo and Robin's shoes when they get in. I grab a microwave meal from the fridge, then pop it on. I run upstairs to see if I can change clothes before it's cooked. Pulling off my apron, top and jeans, I wriggle into a pair of corduroy trousers, and tug on a blouse and a jumper. I bound downstairs just in time to see three seconds ticking down on the microwave. It's a small life victory.

Clutching my meal, I plop down onto the couch, turn on the TV, and check the clock. I have over an hour before I need to pick up Tracy, so I can fit in an episode of *Grey's Anatomy*. Ever since I saw the medical series could be streamed, I've binge-watched it. I'm only on season four; it's comforting that I have at least another eleven seasons to spend with the feisty surgeons.

Reaching for the remote, I'm about to change the channel when I see a boy's face filling up the screen. He looks only a little older than Robin, and is sporting a chocolate-smeared grin and a Christmas jumper with a fat reindeer on the front. The caption reads, *Thomas Doncaster, age ten.* I want to change the channel over; I won't be able to see a full episode of *Grey's* if I don't, but my finger doesn't want to press the button on the remote. Something bad has happened.

Chapter 2

'Thomas Doncaster disappeared last night between the hours of six and eight. He was last seen outside the news-agent's on the Rosemount Estate in Northampton wearing a navy Adidas jacket, blue jeans and white trainers. If anyone has any information on his whereabouts, please contact the hotline number below.'

The local newscaster glares at the audience for a second longer than necessary, as if she knows the guilty party is watching and she can force her contempt at him through the screen. Suddenly, the camera angle changes. The news-caster twists around to a second camera, meets the viewers with a fake smile, and then proceeds to talk about the latest knife crime statistics.

Rosemount is only fifteen miles from my house in Oak Cross. A thought wrapped in a memory bobs up to the surface of my mind; I let it sit there a while before I mentally burst it. What could have happened to this little boy? His parents must be so worried, consumed with the worst thoughts in the world. What could be happening to him right now? Will they ever see his chocolate grin again, or give him a Christmas present?

I have to find out more about Thomas Doncaster's disappearance, but I barely get to sign in on my laptop when I hear rattling keys. My front door crashes open and in floods Hurricane Robin. He throws off his shoes, and they land like two little bombs on the floor.

'Mummy!' he yells, throwing himself at me.

Catching him, I pull his flailing body into my arms. As I do, his red Puffa jacket deflates, making a fart noise. He giggles.

A gush of cold air hits me, and I look up to see Leo closing the front door. A bottle of wine nestled in the crook of his arm.

'Hey, bloody freezing out there. You still going out tonight?'

'Yes, Tracy will kill me if I don't.'

'Okay, you better wrap up warm,' he says, and then walks into the kitchen.

I hug Robin again. He wriggles, but I hold him steady so I can whisper, 'You know never to accept lifts from strangers, right?'

'I'm eight years old. I'm fully aware of stranger danger, Mum,' he replies, pulling away from me.

'Even if there's another child with them. Never get into a stranger's car.'

'I get it. I won't.' Robin shrugs off his jacket. I can see he has eaten spaghetti at his gran's house; there are speckles of red all over his beige jumper. Leo's mum quite often leaves her mark on my son.

'Get changed into your PJs, sweetie,' I say.

Robin scrambles up the stairs.

'He was looking forward to us watching TV together tonight,' Leo states, lounging against the wall with a glass of red wine in his hand. 'We both were.'

'We watch TV together every night,' I say.

'But Saturday nights are special family time.'

I had been looking forward to sharing tonight's special family time.'

I wanted to tell Leo about Tracy's supernatural entertainment tonight; we could have laughed about it later. Right now, though, a twinge of guilt stops me. I should be staying in with my family. Spending my time with them, not gallivanting off to see some second-class sideshow. My future is obvious: sitting on the sofa holding Robin close, drinking wine and laughing with Leo. What more could a psychic say to me anyway? It's not like she could dig up anything about my past I don't already know. Just as I think this I get a text from Tracy: *Looking forward to tonight Cherry Pie*. With my best friend's hatred for grammar, I can't tell if it's a question or a statement; however, I do know I made a promise.

I text back: *See you soon x*.

Leo walks over to me and hands me his wine.

Looking at the half-empty glass, I go to swig the rest, but stop. 'Oh, you're sneaky, are you trying to get me drunk so I can't drive tonight?'

Letting out a playful laugh, Leo says, 'You can't blame a guy for trying. Tell you what.' He puts his arms around my waist and pulls me close. 'I'll leave a glass out for you for when you come back.'

'Deal.'

The lower level of our house is open plan with strategically placed kitchen units and bookcases separating the spaces between the dining room, kitchen, and living room. So, while I spend an inordinate amount of time doing my make-up on the dining table, I can still watch Leo loading the dishwasher in the kitchen, and hear Robin bumping about upstairs.

'How can putting on PJs end up such a noisy performance?' Leo asks after a particularly big bump.

'He's dancing. Practising the moves from *Strictly* with that teddy your mum bought him last Christmas.'

Leo grins. 'I hope the teddy isn't leading.'

It's only a night out with the girls, but I need to make an effort to look at least passable. I touch up my foundation, hiding the dark circles under my eyes. I pick out a new lipstick I bought last year; it's pillar-box red and claims to be kiss-proof. I gently apply it, pucker my lips then blot it with a tissue. Just as I finish up, Leo places a glass and half the bottle of red wine in front of me.

'Don't get excited; like I said it's for when you get back. It'll be waiting for you right here – that and this.' He lifts his jumper to reveal his distinctive hairy dad bod, then has the good grace to laugh.

'I can hardly wait. You know,' I say. 'This lipstick is kiss-proof.'

'That's a bold claim,' he replies sitting down beside me. 'Shall we test it out?' He leans in to kiss me but hesitates when there's a thunder of footsteps down the stairs.

Sitting back in his chair, Leo says, 'Hey, tiger, you excited for *Strictly*?'

Robin nods, then looks over at me. 'You look pretty, Mum. Just like one of the dancers.' He then grins. 'Dad told me to say that.'

'Oh, you were meant to keep that part secret and earn

brownie points with your mum.' Leo turns to me. 'He never lets me get away with anything.'

'And neither should he.' I get up to hug Robin, but Leo intercepts. He wraps his arms around my back and dips me into a Hollywood kiss. Soft lips and the taste of red wine overpower me. Only Robin's giggling breaks the spell. I wriggle out of Leo's embrace and quickly check my face in the mirror. I have visions of me looking like a clown-demon who crawled out of Stephen King's imagination; however, my lip line is perfect. It really is kiss-proof. Good to know not everything about my life is a lie.

'Are my lips as red as Mummy's lips?' Leo asks Robin, puckering his pout.

'No, your lips aren't red at all, Dad,' Robin replies. He turns to me. 'Is your lipstick magic?'

I reach out to Robin and kiss his cheeks, his forehead and his nose. He laughs at first, but quickly complains, so I let him go. There's not a single red mark on him. I look up at Leo to see he has vanished back to the kitchen.

'Mummy, you're so embarrassing.'

'That's a big word. And to be embarrassed there needs to be someone else here to see me kiss you,' I say.

My son wrestles out of my arms. 'Nostrom is here. He sees you.'

Robin has drawn Nostrom a few times; he looks like a red robot, all boxy with bright lights. It could be much worse. His imaginary friend could be a six-foot-tall man in a dirty rabbit costume like in *Donnie Darko*. Leo's mother doesn't approve of imaginary robot friends but I don't mind him. As long as he's good for my son, he's all right by me.

'Well, perhaps I should kiss Nostrom, too?'

'Robots don't like kisses. You can kiss me again instead.'
I tickle my son and kiss the top of his head.

'Hey, I see you just had a microwave meal, again,' Leo
says from the kitchen door. He reaches behind him and
produces a plate of chocolate biscuits. 'I know you're not
drinking tonight, but it can't hurt.'

We sit and eat together. Leo wolfing down the sugary
treats, while Robin takes his time sucking the chocolate
from the biscuit. Too soon, Leo says, 'Come on, tiger,
Strictly will be on any minute.'

Robin shoots off the chair and jumps onto the couch.
Leo gets up, bends down and kisses the top of my head.
'Have a good night and be careful,' he says, then follows
Robin.

As I go to leave, I hesitate. I would prefer to stay home.
I'm not even sure why I agreed to this psychic thing in
the first place. Leo looks up, winks and playfully lifts his
jumper again.

I grab my car keys and yell, 'Bye!'

Tracy is never ready on time and tonight is no exception.
I knock on her door and her gran greets me. Tracy has
lived with her since her parents died. My best friend never
talks about what happened to them, and I've never asked.
Our friendship has grown on mutual, unspoken boundaries.

'Aren't you seeing Mariah tonight?' Tracy's gran asks.

'Yeah, I'm not expecting much,' I say, checking my
watch. It's past seven.

'I've been to psychics and mediums all over the country;
she's one of the best. My sisters used to visit her up North.
I can't believe she moved down here.'

'What's the difference between a psychic and a

medium?' I ask, then realise it sounds like the set-up to a crude joke.

Tracy's gran doesn't hesitate. 'Well, psychics can see your past, present and future. Mediums talk to the dead. Mariah's both.'

The house suddenly feels warm. I undo my coat and shrug it off. 'I don't want to talk to the dead,' I mutter.

'Pardon, Cherrie?'

'Nothing, it doesn't matter. I might not even bother with a reading. Perhaps I'll wait outside, just listen to what she has to say to the other girls.'

'Oh, no, it's booked for four. You have to go in. Four bookings is the minimum,' she reminds me.

I'm about to ask about her visit to Mariah, when I hear Tracy coming down the stairs.

'Sorry for being late, Cherry Pie. Perfection takes time.' She smooths down her long, straight hair.

I put my coat back on and grab Tracy's arm. 'Come on, we still have to find Mariah's house. Who are we meeting there?'

'Our wayward Creeker sisters Shania and Gurpreet.'

'I'll text Gurpreet. Tell her we'll be late.' I fish out my mobile to fire off a quick text.

Once we're in the car, I ask Tracy for the address.

'Bramble Court on the Hackerwood Estate, Mariah's number seven.'

I turn off our estate and head towards the main road. There's probably a quicker route, but this is the only one I know, and Tracy's not offering any help. We get onto the A13. I drive until I see the Hackerwood sign.

'Did you hear about that boy Thomas Doncaster going missing?' I ask.

'No, but kids go missing all the time,' Tracy says staring at her mobile.

'Not really, not like this.'

'Like what? Are you just assuming something sinister happened?'

Carefully, I reply. 'No, I just think . . .' A stream of answers flood my mind: Kids can be taken, strangers want children for horrible things, and terrible fates can befall lone boys. 'I just worry, that's all.'

Tracy looks over at me and shrugs. She has no children, perhaps until she does, she won't understand my concern.

We drive on towards Hackerwood; a sinking feeling settling in my gut the closer we get.

'I saw what you did today,' Tracy suddenly blurts out.

'Huh?'

'The vagrant preggo. I saw you give her the food,' she says.

'I thought you'd already gone home.'

'Nah, I had to sort out some paperwork in Mr Dawson's office. Why did you help her?'

'She needed it. Her name's Kylie.'

'You know her?' Tracy asks.

'No, I only met her today. I gave her the stuff we would've binned or taken home ourselves.' I'm not sure I like Tracy's tone, maybe she's nervous about tonight, and if she's worried, perhaps I should be too.

'I'd already done the out-of-date stuff. I took it all home,' she says.

'Well, you missed some. Don't be mean.'

'I'm not being mean,' she replies, her childish lilt betraying her. Tracy then turns away from me to stare out her window. Now and then, she opens her mouth, yet no words come out.

I veer off into Bramble Court. It's a long, curvy road twisting around new houses built on the edges of an older estate. The fresh cream buildings look bright against the scarlet bricks of the old council terraces; they glow against the dark night like clean bones.

'Well, we won't be in business much longer if we keep giving food away,' Tracy finally says, fiddling with my heater.

'Kylie can't eat enough to put Dawson's out of business.' I laugh.

'Don't joke; I've seen the books.'

'What?'

'That's it, number seven, right there.' Tracy points at a new, beautiful detached house with a gravel drive. Bringing the car around, I park next to Gurpreet's Honda.

I twist off the engine and watch as Tracy struggles to find her seatbelt clip.

'Is Dawson's Food in trouble?' I ask.

She huffs at me, then gets out. 'Let's just enjoy tonight. I wonder how many dark, handsome strangers I'll have in my future.'

Heading to the door, we walk past an expensive black Audi sitting in front of a double garage.

'The psychic business must pay well,' I say, staring at the perfect paintwork and leather interior. It's immaculate inside. My car sports hundreds of sticky patches all in the shape of Robin's fingers.

'Come on, Cherry Pie.' Tracy grabs my arm, pulling me away from my car envy.

At first glance, the house looks every other on the

street; however, the source of the glow from the windows of this house is not electric but candles. Dancing flames beckoning you with their heat, until you get too close and you lose part of yourself in a bargain you never meant to make. I shouldn't be here.

Before I know what's happening, Tracy rings the bell. Quickly, the door opens wide, making us both jump, but instead of the expected clichéd clairvoyant, it's a man in the doorway. He's thin, of average height, and has a down-turned mouth; it clearly takes extra effort for him to smile, as he gives us a withering look.

We must have the wrong house. Does this poor man continually suffer random weirdos arriving on his doorstep expecting to have their fortunes told?

I'm about to apologise when he asks, 'Are you here to see Mariah?'

'Yes,' Tracy answers, stepping over the psychic's threshold.

As she pulls me in with her, I expect a melodramatic clap of thunder to ring out across the shadowy sky, but of course, it doesn't.

'And you are?' the man asks, fiddling with a clipboard like a mild-mannered doorman.

'Tracy Carter and Cherrie Forrester.' Tracy nudges me.

He drags his finger down the page. 'I've got a Tracy, but no Cherrie.'

My name's not down; perhaps I've successfully wormed my way out of this uncomfortable night. I can spend my money on a takeaway, eat the sinful snack with Leo, and stay up late watching TV programmes that wash over you like a lazy dream.

'Yeah, my gran, Donna Carter, had a reading the other

night instead. Cherrie has taken her place tonight,' Tracy says.

'Oh, I'll change it.'

He writes in my name, and the dream of an all-night TV and fatty food binge with my boyfriend evaporates in a scribble of biro. Oh crap, will Mariah sense I don't want to be here? You don't need to be psychic to spot a reluctant visitor. She'll think I'm rude, which could be the least of tonight's worries.

Grinning, Tracy pulls me further into the house. We walk down a thin, beige corridor to find a tiny living room with barely enough space for the two massive couches squashed into it. This house is like the anti-TARDIS, big on the outside and small on the inside.

On one of the couches are Gurpreet and Shania. Huddled together, they stop whispering when they see us in the doorway.

'See,' says Gurpreet. 'I told you she'd come.'

Clearly referring to me. I step forward, bend and hug Gurpreet, my defender.

Shania blushes when I ignore her, then says, 'That's not what I said. I said you're not normally *allowed out* on a Saturday night.'

Tracy plonks down next to Shania. I carefully perch beside her. The thought of being alone on the empty couch opposite is leaving me cold.

'Okay, ladies,' the doorman says, tentatively edging into the room.

I haven't even caught sight of Mariah yet. I hope it's not this weasel-looking guy in drag, and that he expects us to keep straight faces while he shuffles tarot cards, and digs around in our minds for our deepest, darkest, blood-soaked secrets . . . I shouldn't be here. I wriggle in my seat. Tracy rests a heavy hand on my knee.

The man squeezes past our sofa to stand before us. He's making little sounds beneath his breath, like an actor loosening his lips ready for a monologue. Are we paying for this too? If I had wanted Shakespeare in the living room, I'd have booked am-dram tickets, which I suspect might have been a better idea.

'My name is Jon. I'm Mariah's husband of fifteen years, and let me tell you, being married to such a talented psychic for so long is a huge feat. If I plan a holiday, she's already packed her suitcase. I try to organise a surprise birthday party, she arrives early to greet her guests. I buy her jewellery . . . well, she's a woman, so doesn't mind shiny presents.' He fake laughs while all four of us simultaneously sigh at his sexist joke.

Jon turns around to scoop up four clipboards off a nearby table.

'Fill these in, please.' He gives us each a clipboard, then leaves the room.

Tracy nudges me. 'What do you think?'

'I think if he were married to a real psychic, she'd have predicted all his jokes would be crap,' I say. Everyone giggles.

I look down at my clipboard and scan the questions. Nothing too intrusive, just the basics of name, address, age, and ticking a box to promise I won't have a heart attack mid-reading. However, I dither.

I look up to see Jon has appeared back in the doorway. He's staring at me.

'Umm, why do you need all this?' I ask him.

'Health and safety. Please fill it in if you want a reading.'

I want to scream at him that I don't want a reading, so taking my personal information isn't necessary. Then again, if I don't go through with tonight's entertainment, I'll prove Shania right, Gurpreet wrong, and Tracy will never let me live it down. We'll be old ladies shuffling along in the shopping centre; she'll look at me and say, 'Remember when you ran out on me at the psychic's house? Didn't see that coming.'

I must frown, as Jon scoffs and walks away. He'll be telling Mariah to give me a bad reading, which ironically could be useful. If this psychic is real, her laziness could mean she leaves my buried secrets untouched to rot.

'Fill it out. Go on.' Tracy pokes me in the ribs.

I pick up the pen. The form asks for my birth name, my address, date of birth, and my In Case of Emergency contact; I put down Leo. I tick the boxes, which say I don't have a disability and my heart is fine. I go to sign it. I hesitate again. *I declare all the information given is correct*, it reads in big black letters. There's one piece of information I've given that isn't one hundred per cent correct, but what sort of enforcement powers could this home-working sideshow have? I sign it.

As if he's been watching, Jon suddenly steps back into the room. He collects the clipboards. 'It's £25 each,' he tells us.

We all give up our money, which Jon rolls up in his hand. He disappears, shutting the door behind him. I can hear a murmured conversation. Closing my eyes, I try to make out the whispered words. Are they talking about me?

'I'm so excited about my reading.' Shania rubs her arms as if she's cold.

'Yeah? Not concerned she'll see you're dating a married man?' Tracy says.

'Shut it. What about you, Cherrie? Any skeletons in your closet?'

Swallowing hard, I choke a little and have to clear my throat.

'Oh, perfect little Cherrie does have something to hide.' Shania crosses her legs and nudges us all; our bodies knock together like the balls of a Newton's cradle.

I'm about to reply with a lie when the door opens.

'Welcome!'

I look up to see a thin woman in a black maxi dress, only a little older than I am. Her hair is short and dark, and her long nose is the most noticeable feature of her face. She's striking, with bright maroon lipstick teamed with thick black kohl-lined eyes.

'Hi,' Gurpreet mutters, perhaps expecting us all to say it at once.

'I'm Mariah. Thank you for coming tonight. I will choose my first reading.' She carefully looks at us all. I feel like a harem wife hoping her husband doesn't pick her for the night.

Mariah's stare rests on each of us in turn. I cross my arms over my chest and try to smile at her, although I fear I might just be baring my teeth. Tracy and Shania both shift in their seats.

Smiling, Mariah takes Gurpreet by the hand. 'You will be my first reading.'

The psychic pulls my friend off the couch and takes her away.

'How come she got to go first?' Shania complains.

'Yeah, I don't want to be last. Mariah will be knackered

by the end of the night. I'll get a crap reading.' Tracy makes herself comfortable in Gurpreet's vacant couch space.

'I don't mind going last,' I say.

It feels as if this evening will never end. When Gurpreet comes out, and Shania goes in, the whole show repeats.

In the living room, Gurpreet gushes about how accurate Mariah was in her reading. Apparently, she predicted her long-term boyfriend was going to propose on Valentine's Day next year. The psychic told her to say yes, that they would be happy together. I'm not sure I agree with that advice. Choosing your husband is a serious matter; it's why I haven't married Leo. He asked me once, when we discovered I was pregnant with Robin. In painful slow motion, he bent down on one knee, but he didn't have a ring ready to slip onto my finger. I said no. Although he often calls me his missus to his mates, he has never asked again.

Shania comes out. Mariah, in equally dramatic fashion, chooses Tracy, leaving me for last. Why would she do that? Has she secretly read me already and needs to build up to being in the same room as me?

'What was it like?' Gurpreet asks.

'Shit,' Shania says. She catches me smiling at her reply. 'Your lipstick is flaking. Shame. It was a great colour. A bold choice for a woman your age.'

'Thanks,' I say. I would typically throw out a comeback, but I'm far too relieved about Mariah's crappy abilities to care about a little dig.

Shania regales us with a blow-by-blow account of the cards' meanings and predictions. It takes so long to describe that, after a while, her voice sounds like white noise.

In the end, Gurpreet sighs. 'What a shame. Mariah was so accurate with me.' She leans across to pat Shania's knee.

'Oh, she was accurate all right; just didn't tell me what I wanted to hear.'

What? Didn't Shania just say she was crap! Does that mean she's good; that she's real? I gulp and look up to see Mariah escorting Tracy back into the room.

It's my turn.

Chapter 3

Mariah's hand is clammy and firm around mine. A silent gesture stating, *you're not going anywhere. I have you now.* Perhaps I'm misinterpreting it and it's more of a motherly, *everything will be all right* gesture. As if sensing my confusion, Mariah looks back at me with a broad smile. Although I don't have much experience with mums – mine never won Parent of the Year – I decide it's a nurturing gesture.

We walk down a hall the colour of curdled cream. It's tight due to a tin shelf jutting out along its length. As we pass, I see there's a collection of silver photo frames adorning the shelf. Each one shows a happy little girl about six years old. She has her mother's nose and her father's eyes. Their daughter. No doubt, they've confined her to her room while they work. Considering they have a kid, this place is almost spotless. I didn't even notice any toys. Perhaps girls are easier to entertain than boys. There's not a day that goes by that I don't trip over something of Robin's; usually his discarded shoes.

Mariah notices me admiring her photos. 'Sarah,' she says.

'She's beautiful.' Most mothers say this to one another regardless, but I mean it. Sarah has an easy smile and natural highlights in her hair, which catch the flash of the camera, giving her a perfect halo effect. I'm not sure why, but I feel more relaxed knowing Mariah and Jon have a child. I guess it's a kind of parental camaraderie.

The psychic leads me into another boxy room. This one is candlelit and smells of earthy frankincense. In the centre is a low, round table with a black tablecloth. A deck of cards sits on top. Surrounding the table are thin scatter cushions. I quickly scan the rest of the room and see a sideboard with several cups and saucers. In the low light, they look magical, like something from a Disney film.

'I do tea leaves too,' Mariah says, as if to justify their presence.

I nod and, as I move towards the table, bump into some plastic-covered clothes hooked over the door of a cupboard. Touching the plastic, I see a dark, elaborate outfit beneath and the hint of something white and glowing.

'Fancy dress for Halloween,' Mariah explains.

'Oh, that's soon, isn't it? Where does the time go?'

Moving the plastic aside, I count two costumes in the bag. It must be lovely to play dress up with your daughter.

'Ready?' Mariah motions for me to sit across from her.

My trousers are tight and it's uncomfortable, yet I manage to sit down and cross my legs.

'It's good to meet you, Cherrie.'

In an elegant gesture, Mariah offers me the cards. 'Please shuffle these, cutting them with your left hand, as it's your left hand that deals your destiny.'

I do as she asks, although the cards are large and awkward and slip from my grasp more than once.

'Have you travelled far tonight?'

'No, I'm about twenty minutes away.'

'The Rosemount Estate?'

'No, Oak Cross. By Dawson's Food where I work.' I'm rambling and giving too much away.

'The cards are ready now.' Mariah motions for me to put them down.

I place the deck on the table and cut them with my left hand.

'You're left-handed,' she tells me as if it's some amazing revelation. As if I will suddenly look down at my digits exclaiming, *Holy crap, that's why I've never been able to use regular scissors!*

'Yes. All my life,' I say.

'In the past, left-handed people were considered sinister.'

'All polar bears are left-handed.' A fact Robin read off an ice-lolly stick last summer.

'I didn't know that,' she replies.

'Perhaps that's why they're becoming extinct,' I add. 'Polar bears only have right-handed tin openers. They can't get into their cans of tuna.' That was the worst joke ever. What am I playing at? Wait a minute, I'm paying this woman – it's her job to entertain me.

'More likely we're ruining the planet,' Mariah says flatly.

I tap the top of the cards. 'Is that okay?'

'Yes, good. We will begin.' Mariah closes her eyes and waits.

I feel conspicuous now, and for some reason Thomas Doncaster's disappearance races through my mind. Hoping he is okay, strongly suspecting that he's not, I can't stand this anticipation. I should ask if she knows anything about Thomas.

'Mariah? Can I ask you about something?'

Opening her eyes, she gives a little nod.

'Have you had any visions of that missing boy – Thomas Doncaster?'

Mariah purses her lips and leans forward. 'I shouldn't tell you this, but his mother and brother came for a reading just after it happened.'

'Really?'

'People often seek out psychics when they feel the police are failing them.'

'How can the police be failing them? Didn't he only just go missing?'

She snorts.

'Did you see anything?' I then ask, wanting to end my question with the word helpful, yet deciding against it.

'Not at the time.' Mariah moves closer to me. 'I did see him this afternoon, though.' She then looks around us as if someone is watching. 'He had lost his shoes and was coughing on car fumes.'

'What the hell does that mean?'

She whispers, 'I fear he is no longer with us.'

I was expecting a lazy response of, he'll be found safe soon, not some ominous death prediction. I want to ask more questions about Thomas, but Mariah cuts through my thoughts with a clap of her hands.

'Now, before we begin I need to clarify how this works. I will deal you five cards. One represents the past, which still affects your present. One is your present as it is today. One is your future as it will be if you continue on your current path. The remaining two are messages from the spirits.'

'Oh, I think I'd prefer to just stick to the past, present and future. No spirits, thanks.'

'You get both. In life, sometimes we get things we don't want along with the things we do. I can't control what I see. I simply pass the information along in the hope it helps.'

At Dawson's Food, the customer is always right. Clearly, Mariah doesn't care about that in her line of work. A wave of defiance rolls over my manners, so I ask, 'Did you tell Mrs Doncaster you think Thomas is dead?'

Mariah coughs and grins at me. 'Do you have issues with the dead, Cherrie?'

'I have issues with the living and the dead,' I reply.

'Death hangs around you, like black smoke on your bones.' There's a rasp to her words that makes me want to run. It's icy in this room. Cold and dark. Last time I felt like this I was eight years old and hiding under my dad's workbench listening to the knocking coming from the cupboard . . .

'Are you ready?' Mariah asks.

This isn't real. It can't be. People like Mariah don't exist in reality. She's hustling me, and that's okay. *Hustle away, lady. I've dealt with worse.*

'Yes,' I say.

'Excellent.'

She takes the cards and deals out five. I know little about tarot cards. Only what I've seen in films and the opening credits of *Tales of the Unexpected*. I do realise there's one card I'd like to avoid. Mariah flips the first over – it's Death. I lean back, hitting my shoulders against the wall behind me.

'I'm sorry; I should have told you about the Death card

35

before I began. Clients are often taken aback by this card, but it's not as grim as it appears. It represents a new beginning. The end of something hurtful. Nevertheless, this card sits in your past. What does it represent?' Mariah raises an eyebrow.

I almost blurt out that she should know what it means, yet bite my tongue. I have to keep reminding myself she's not in touch with some cosmic energy; she can't see my past. Who I am. I mean, who I used to be.

'My parents died when I was eight,' I say. It's partly true, so perhaps it's enough to keep her fake spirits quiet.

'So, you went to live with another member of your family?'

'Yes,' I lie.

'That will be it. You've not quite come to terms with what your parents did.'

'Pardon me?'

'Leaving you so suddenly. They didn't mean to; it wasn't their intention.'

This woman is full of it. I slump back into her uncomfortably thin floor cushions.

'Actually, I think they did mean it.'

She looks a bit taken aback, but quickly shrugs it off. Mariah's not a real psychic, but she is a professional.

The next card is a picture of a small, smiling boy riding a white horse.

'The sun. This is your present. There is a child around you.'

'Oh, that's my son Robin.' I instantly kick myself for giving her both his gender and name. I'd be terrible in one of those hard-core police interviews.

'He's lovely, your little bird. He makes you so proud.' Her lips lift into the practised smile of a mother.

'Yes, he's great. He's the love of my life,' I say, wishing I'd stayed home with him.

Narrowing her eyes, Mariah gathers her lips into an unflattering grimace. 'His father; I see a lion, Leo.'

'How did you know his name?'

'Leo is a challenge. Set in his ways. It's his mother's fault. The woman panders to him, making him need lots of attention.'

'Yes, I guess so.'

She closes her eyes. I edge towards her.

'Men rarely grow up. Trust me. Jon has a habit of making everything my fault. He then makes it his business to fix it. Is Leo like this?'

'Kind of. He can be annoying at times; but he loves me. There's nothing he wouldn't do for me.' Even as I say this, I realise that there might be at least one thing he wouldn't do for me.

'Annoying, yes. That's what I meant.'

I'm not sure it was, yet she pulled Leo's name out of thin air. It's not as if he is a Chris or a Bob. She didn't even say *I see the letter L*, to entice me to offer the name. Mariah said it as if she just knew.

'What should I do about him? Does he get better?'

'They never get better, just easier to handle. Let's see if he's in your future.'

The next card is the Ten of Wands. It shows a lone man dragging a mass of tall tree branches.

'What does it mean?' I ask.

'Someone is working against you. This future is almost immediate.'

'You think Leo is plotting against me?' I say, knowing it's absurd.

'I don't think so. It could be, though. Be wary.'

Knowing she can't mean Leo, I ask, 'Um, could you give me more on the person I need to watch out for?'

Mariah sits up straighter. 'Apologies, I have no further information to give. You'll know them when you see them.'

Helpful.

The psychic looks down at the two remaining cards. These are the messages from the spirits. I've been lucky so far; she hasn't uprooted any buried secrets. Will my luck continue?

With a quick flick of the wrist, she turns both cards over. The first shows a dark-cloaked figure standing alone. The other depicts a heart with three swords piercing it from different angles.

Mariah mumbles something I don't catch.

'What? Tell me, what do they mean?'

Pointing to the cloaked figure, she says, 'This is the Five of Cups. The spirits are telling me there is a dark shadow around you. The other is the Three of Swords. You will be hurt, not once, not twice, but three times. Deep wounds.'

I'm about to question who would hurt me when I remind myself this is only a bit of fun. Everything she's said has to be guesswork. I've watched Derren Brown; he would have been able to read me even better than her, and he definitely doesn't have paranormal powers. Perhaps Mariah has found fear works better than hope in her readings and is dishing me up a big dollop of it, so I go away thinking hard about her dire predictions. If your mind marinates too long on anything you'll make it happen like a crazy self-fulfilling prophecy, but she did get Leo's name.

As she moves the cards around the table, I watch her fingers, with their chipped black nail varnish, dance over the pictures.

'Your son is in danger.'

'What?'

When I look at the cards, I see only meaningless images. What has she seen?

'You can't tell me that,' I say, my voice getting higher and louder on every word. 'You're just mean.' It takes a lot not to swear at her. A stray *fuck you*, paces behind my lips like a caged tiger.

Suddenly, she launches herself across the table and grabs my wrist. 'Please, you must believe me. Robin is in danger. A dark shadow haunts him. You must take heed of this warning.'

'What danger?'

Her chipped black nails are digging into my skin. I try to pull my arm away.

'The spirits will not say, but they are giving you a warning. Take the warning. Guard your son.'

'You're hurting me!'

Looking confused, Mariah releases me.

'Unfortunately, our time has ended.' In a swift motion, she gets up and heads to the door. Reaching out, I try to stop her. I have to know what she saw about Robin. Unfortunately, I've been sitting on the floor for so long, my legs have almost atrophied. I have to push my palms against the small table to stand up.

'Wait,' I say to her, but it's as if I've ceased to exist. Ignoring my pleas, she rushes from the room.

Great. She just told me Robin is in danger but didn't bother to tell me anything else because my £25 worth of her time has run out. You'd hope a real psychic would have dug deeper if she believed in her words. Mariah has to be a fraud. None of what she said is real – it can't be. If she was genuine surely she would have seen my past, and wouldn't have ignored it; no one can ignore it.

I follow her back into the living room.

Now our business has concluded Jon spirits us out the house as quick as he can. It's ten o'clock, so maybe Sarah can come down to watch TV with her parents. After all, it is Saturday night. Robin loves it when we stay up together; it's his special treat for being good. For this reason alone, I don't mind him hurrying me down their thin cream corridor, and then practically launching me through the front door like a bottle of champagne towards a new ship.

Once outside, we all hug and start to say goodbye. Although not sure I should, especially as I can't guarantee Mariah can be trusted, I tell them what the maybe-psychic said about Thomas Doncaster.

'Good grief,' Tracy says. 'How morbid.'

'What a bitch,' Shania adds.

'Do you think she said anything to Thomas's mum? I mean, do we ring the hotline and give them this info anyway?' Gurpreet, apparently the only one of us who received a favourable reading, is now a stone-cold believer in psychics. I guess you'd have to be to ensure the good predictions come true.

'No, kids come home eventually. I've concluded that Mariah is full of shit.' Shania bumps me with her hip. I nod; I think it's the first thing we've agreed since we met.

Gurpreet asks us all to go for a drink, and Tracy surprises me by declining the invitation. She must have seen my face after the reading; her curiosity is outweighing the need to punish her liver.

Tracy climbs into my car and we set off. We're quiet at first. I'm still trying to make sense of everything. Mariah got Leo's name without hesitation, yet went off on a scary tangent about the safety of my son, which can't be usual, or good for business. I turn off onto the A13. The long straight road of the dual carriageway gives me the latitude to twist my thoughts into speech. 'What did she say to you?' I ask.

'I got the Death card,' Tracy replies.

'The Death card means a new beginning.'

'This time, it meant death. She said someone close to me would die soon.'

We're both thinking the same name: Gran.

'I'm not sure we should put much faith in her readings,' I say. 'Did she get anything right for you?'

'Yeah, some stuff. That I worked with food and my parents died when I was little. It was eerie. What about you?'

'She said some weird stuff.' I turn off the A road and sweep onto the roundabout that leads to Tracy's estate. As soon as I'm on a straight road again, I ask, 'Did you talk about me with her?'

'I didn't pay £25 to talk about you, Cherry Pie.'

'So you didn't mention Leo's name to her?'

'No, why would I?'

'She knew Leo's name.'

'Didn't you put him down as your ICE contact on her form?'

'Son of a bitch. I did.' Tracy's right. 'Wait, didn't you say your gran went to her too?'

'Yes, Gran gave me Mariah's details; hang on, yes. I bet she spilt my dead parent beans, and where I worked.'

A mixture of anger at Mariah's fakery and relief that the grim predictions are bull sinks into both of us.

'Well, what a waste.' Tracy laughs. 'We should have gone for a drink.'

I indicate to turn around. 'What pub?'

'The Hazel Tree. I'll text them, let them know we're coming.'

'Just you. I'll drop you off. I really have to get home. Leo left me half a bottle of wine to polish off, and I think, after tonight, I'm going to need it.'

'Sure thing. Hey, maybe we should set up a psychic business. You'd be pretty good at it.'

'I don't want to tell people about imaginary disasters.'

'You won't have to. You can be a nice psychic who only gives good predictions.'

'Predictions are a numbers game. Odds are higher for something bad to happen than something good.'

I pull in at The Hazel Tree. Tracy pops her belt and leans across to hug me.

'Think about it, like I said, we should go into business together, you and me. No more Dawson's Food,' she whispers, raising her eyebrows.

'What does that mean?'

But my friend doesn't answer me, she just wriggles out of the car, then disappears into the pub.

A few doors down from the pub is the Drunken Schooner, a fish and chip shop who use beef dripping to cook its goodies. It's now half past ten; I shouldn't, but I pull the car in to park in front. I deserve a treat.

The moment I open the car door, the smell of the most popular chips in three estates hits me. Tonight was long and pointless. I deserve deep-fried goodness. I buy a large bag, then all but sprint back to the car.

Driving home always takes longer when you can smell chips drenched in salt and vinegar. I'd have eaten a few while driving if their wrapping was loose enough for me to steal a chip or two.

At home, I find Leo and Robin have already gone to bed, so I grab a plate, settle down in front of the TV with my wine and watch a couple of episodes of *Grey's Anatomy*. The chips are the best thing about tonight.

As I watch the fictional surgeons have inappropriate sexual encounters and pointless arguments, I mentally push out everything caught in my mind today. Tracy's weird comments about Dawson's Food, Mariah's obvious con job, and Thomas Doncaster's disappearance; then let it all go, like a fisherman who already has his catch and is releasing the rest back into the ocean to be trapped in his nets another day.

It's past midnight before I'm tired enough to go to bed. To avoid waking my family, I wash and clean my teeth in the downstairs toilet, then climb the stairs. I stop by Robin's door. Mariah's words of danger clatter through my mind. I should check in on him.

I push open the door. Instantly, I see my son is not in his bed.

Chapter 4

My hand shoots out, groping for the light switch. The bright flash shatters the darkness, stinging my eyes.

I rush forward and drag back Robin's bedcovers as if it would somehow make him magically appear. I check under his bed. Nothing there but shoes and toys. The wardrobe. One door is protruding. I bound towards it. I reach for the handle, but hesitate. Do I hear knocking? I fling the door wide then push and pull at the clothes inside. Hangers slide and drop as I frantically grab at the wall of clothes before me. He's not in there.

Panic grips me; its clammy embrace making each rushed breath sticky and sore. Bending over, I put my hands on my knees. Perhaps Robin went to the toilet. I stagger towards the bathroom; yet even from the hall, I can see the door is open. No one is in there. I burst into my bedroom and am about to yell at my sleeping boyfriend when I see my son's body curled up on my side of the bed. I clutch at my chest and ease my breathing down. I'm an idiot.

'You all right?' Leo asks sleepily.

'I was scared when I didn't see Robin in his bed.'

'Tiger missed you, so I let him kip in here till you got home. It's late.' Leo looks over at our red neon clock. 'Are you only just back in?'

I could admit to getting back earlier, but don't bother. I'm too tired to launch into tonight's epic tale.

'Yeah, the girls wanted to go to the pub.'

I pull off my clothes and grab my nightie from the dresser. As I crawl over Leo, I accidentally knee him in the stomach.

'Cherrie,' he complains.

'Sorry,' I whisper.

Robin stirs, but doesn't wake up.

'You smell like chips.'

'I went to the Drunken Schooner.'

'So you ladies were living it up in The Hazel Tree, eh?' Leo whispers.

I don't want to lie anymore, so I neither confirm nor deny his deduction.

Leo turns towards me. 'Oh, I really fancy chips now. Give us a kiss.' He moves in for a smooch, but I turn away.

'I cleaned my teeth, no chips here, just minty freshness.' I huff on him as proof.

'Urg, why did you do that? Salt-and-vinegar breath is hot.'

Laughing as quietly as I can I say, 'Go to sleep.'

We sleep in on Sundays, but Robin always wakes up early. I feel him twist around in the bed.

I grin.

'Did you have a nice time last night, Mummy?'

'It was good. How was *Strictly*?'

He tells me all about the dancers knocked out of the competition last night: what they wore, the songs they danced to, and the scores they got. My son has been entranced by the show ever since he saw his first episode. Between the music and the outfits and the sheer production, he unashamedly fell in love with it. Dancer became his first career choice, although lately it's been pop singer and robotic scientist – I'm not sure whether he means he's the robot or he works on them.

All too soon, our whispers wake up Leo. He turns around and grabs us both in a big-armed hug. To get to Robin, he squeezes me a little too tightly. What would a passive observer see in this Sunday morning scene: a boy beloved by his parents, a loving husband, and a lucky wife?

Leo gets up and makes breakfast: runny scrambled eggs and bacon burnt around the edges. Robin bounces around the living room trying to find where the lingering scent of chips is coming from.

Watching my family on a morning like this warms my heart and makes me so grateful. There's a mother on the Rosemount Estate waking up without one of her sons. A son who right now could be barefoot and lifeless, if you believe in psychics.

'How's your breakfast?' Leo asks.

I stare down at my untouched plate. 'Great, thank you.'

'You'd be hungrier if you hadn't eaten all those chips last night.'

'Can I have your bacon, Mum?'

Smiling, I slide my plate across to Robin. He raises his fork, ready to stab at the food.

'What do you say?' I prompt.

'Thank you!' Robin brings the fork down to skewer a rasher.

'I have some paperwork to do today; can you entertain the bacon-snatcher for the morning?' Leo asks.

'It's Sunday. Like Saturday night, isn't that special family time too?'

My snide comment earns me an eye roll.

'Well played,' Leo says. 'But my boss is putting pressure on me to seal the deal for the new housing estate up by Hackerwood.'

I narrow my eyes at him. The new estate is already there. It's where Mariah lives. 'Oh, Tracy told me it's already been built on.'

Leo flops bread into the toaster. I watch him pull the slices down into the glowing red metal. 'Yeah it is, but there's room for more houses. They built them small. I want to secure the extra land.'

Thinking back to Mariah's tiny rooms, it makes sense. I'm not sure why I tried to catch him in a lie.

'Okay.' I look over at Robin. 'How about we go to the park?'

'Sounds good,' Robin replies, his words muffled by bacon and eggs. He stuffs a crust of toast into his already full mouth. With chipmunk cheeks, he rushes upstairs to get dressed.

Since I have a few minutes, I grab my laptop to check out what's happening with Thomas Doncaster. Maybe he's home already? It wouldn't surprise me; Mariah was royally full of crap. It would be the icing on the cake for the boy to make it home safe; shoes still on his feet, and his lungs clean of car fumes.

Leo nudges me out of his way. 'I need to borrow your laptop. Left mine at work. It'll be free when you get back in.'

'I'm ready!' Robin yells from the hall.

Leo leans across as if to kiss my cheek, but instead sniffs me.

'What are you up to?' I ask, moving back from him.

'Just checking if you still had the Schooner's whiff.' He laughs.

'That sounds like a godawful perfume. Ooh, you're not leading up to a joke about seamen are you?'

'Bye, Dad!' Robin yells, reminding me it's time to go.

'See you, tiger,' Leo yells back, then leans in and kisses my cheek. 'Take care in the park. It's colder than a witch's nip out there.'

I grab my thickest coat and meet my son at the door.

'Which park are we going to?' Robin asks.

'Let's not drive today; how about we go to Black Friars?'

Robin's hand jumps into mine, and we walk towards the park. Black Friars is a massive urban expanse connecting the surrounding estates. I remember it from when I was Robin's age. Dad used to bring me here. He'd pack cheese sandwiches and Tab. We'd pretend we were explorers in a mysterious land, bringing back pinecones and conkers as our trophies. There are rumours there was an old monastery on the land hundreds of years ago. I've heard Robin and his friends telling ghost stories about headless clergy who push you on the swings, and monks who chase away little boys if they come to the park after dark.

As we enter Black Friars, I notice how bright the sun is; its warm lustre strikes a glaring contrast to the cold morning air. I can imagine this place is foreboding when the sun goes down. All twisted trees and jagged bushes, yet in the Sunday morning light, it's beautiful.

As soon as we're beyond the park's tree line, Robin lets go of my hand to run ahead. I quicken my pace to keep him in my line of sight, but he's too fast, and I have to jog a little to keep up. He disappears around a bend in the path. I run faster.

'Look at me, Mum!'

Around the bend, I see Robin swinging from a tree branch like a monkey. Laughing, he flops onto the ground.

Another little boy emerges from the trees. Seeing him, Robin gets up and darts across to say hello. They begin to play together.

There's an old wooden bench, so I sit down to watch them laugh and run. I scan the park for the boy's parents and quickly see the mother puffing up the path. We give each other the secret parent nod that can make friends from strangers, and she staggers over to sit with me.

'I'm getting too old for this,' she says.

'Nice bright morning, though,' I say.

'Too cold for me.'

'Yes, cold,' I say back, glad that Robin wore his warm Puffa jacket this morning.

I nod and continue watching our sons play; chattering and sprinting about as if they were fireworks made of flesh and giggles. Their breath spirals through the air like the tails of rockets.

The woman shivers and pulls her coat tighter about her neck. 'Did you hear about the Doncaster boy?'

'Yes, how awful.'

I consider telling her about Mariah's prediction of Thomas Doncaster. I'd love to erode the psychic's words with mockery and gossip, but this woman is a stranger. What would her reaction be? Intrigue? Repulsion? Suspicion? I'm also now almost one hundred per cent sure Mariah is full of crap, anyway. I don't need a stranger's reassurance.

'Look, Mum, look!'

Following Robin's outstretched finger, I squint and see he's pointing at a grey squirrel. The fluffy creature inches out onto a branch, oblivious it is now starring in a one-squirrel show.

'Look, Mum!' shouts the other boy.

His mum smiles. 'Wow, good spot, Declan.' She turns towards me. 'Declan is such a good little boy. I don't know what I'd do without him.'

I nod. 'Yes, I know the feeling. Kids are so precious.'

As she watches our two sons play 'spot the squirrel', an uncomfortable silence falls between us. Unsure as to whether I should say something, I get out my phone and begin to text Leo that we'll be back soon.

'What do you think happened to that missing boy?' she suddenly says, making my phone leap out of my hands and onto my lap.

'I don't know.' I retrieve my phone and put it away before I drop and break it.

'Oh, where are my manners, I'm Kristine. With a K not a C. Everyone gets that wrong. I don't know how many Christmas and birthday cards I've returned because of rogue Cs.'

'Cherrie,' I reply. 'With a C.'

'What an odd name. Were your parents foreign?'

Kristine sees my eyes widen but mistakes the look for surprise rather than anger. 'Oh of course you're not foreign.

With that skin and hair, you're another English rose. Our kind are few and far between now.'

I glance over to Robin in the hope he is having as bad a time with Declan as I am with the mother, but they look so happy. I don't want to drag him away so, trying not to encourage further xenophobia, I ask, 'What have you heard about Thomas Doncaster?'

'Poor boy. I blame the parents. Letting their child roam the streets at all hours, bound to attract the attentions of a wandering pervert.'

'Excuse me? It's not the parents' fault their boy is missing. How dare you say something like that.'

Kristine shifts in her seat. 'Kids don't disappear when someone is watching them properly.'

I open my mouth to protest, but a saying rattles through my mind instead: even a broken clock is right twice a day. This woman may be horrible, but that doesn't mean she's wrong. If left alone for any length of time, children can be abducted by strangers and bad things can happen to them; I know all this as fact. The thing is, you can't watch your child twenty-four-seven.

'And anyway, it's not like it hasn't happened before,' she says with a smug smile. 'There was that bloke, now what was his name? Mr something. Now what was it?'

'You know, Kristine. It's people like you who victim-blame and spread rumours that should be . . .'

'Victim-blame! How dare you!' Unbelievably, she clutches her bag to her chest, expressing her hurt.

'I was just saying . . .' But I don't get to finish my sentence.

Jumping off the bench, she yells, 'Declan!' at her son who instantly stops mid-chase of Robin. 'We. Are. Leaving!'

Without another word, Kristine with a K gets up and strides off. Her little boy waves goodbye at a disappointed Robin. The strangers then walk away from us, further into the park.

'I liked Declan,' Robin complains as we go to leave; fortunately in the opposite direction.

'I know, sweetie, but his mum was simply awful,' I say.

Robin laughs, grabs my hand, and as we walk home he tells me how nice it is not to have an awful mummy.

Home smells like roast lamb. Leo has started lunch. I find him hunched over the kitchen sink carefully peeling too many potatoes.

'How was the park?' he asks.

'It was nice.' I walk over and wrap my arms about his waist. 'Oh, there was this horrible woman there though.'

'Yeah, I'm not surprised, I hear the park attracts them.' He grins at me.

'Very funny.'

'Robin have fun? He barely spoke to me when you came in.'

'He was excited and wanted to tell Nostrom about his squirrel sighting.'

Leo stops peeling and turns to face me. 'You mean you left Nostrom here with me? Why didn't you tell me? I've had his imaginary robot eyes on me all this time?'

'Why does that bother you? Have you been up to no good?' I joke.

'You don't know what I get up to when you're not here.'

'Paperwork and making roast potatoes, very naughty.'

We both laugh. Leo puts down the peeling knife and

hugs me. 'Relax. I'll finish lunch,' he says. It's the most romantic thing he's done for me in ages.

Curious to see if there is any news on Thomas Doncaster, I use my bonus time to turn on my laptop. Kristine has to be wrong about an abduction. Mariah is definitely wrong about a murder; he's probably already been found and is home safe and sound.

I sit at the dining room table and look for information on his disappearance. I type his name into the search engine. Several recent articles come up. He is still missing.

Most of the articles say the same thing just in different tones, depending on its newspaper's political leaning. Thomas disappeared while out with his older brother, who he left alone to visit the newsagent on the Rosemount Estate. No one has seen him since. Police checked the shop's CCTV, but the camera was at an odd angle, so recorded no valuable footage.

One article mentions a case from the early 1990s, the serial killer William Hendy. However, Hendy is now in prison. It asks, *could a copycat killer be picking up little boys?* My eye twitches at this wild statement. Thomas is missing, not dead. In the case of William Hendy, or Mr Bones as the media dubbed him, he killed boys, and for some sick reason known only to himself, he removed their flesh so he could use their bones to create macabre artwork. Innocent lives were nothing but grotesque art materials to him.

There's a link in the article highlighting the killer's name so, without thinking, I click it and a new search reveals thousands of results about Mr Bones. I scan the first three articles and see something odd. There's a link to a new podcast called *The Flesh on the Bones*. I click through to find it has aired two episodes already – the latest uploaded only yesterday afternoon. I read the podcast's summary:

Welcome to The Flesh on the Bones. *This Northamptonshire-based podcast aims to flesh out the bones of the story behind one of the worst serial killer cases in the UK's history: Mr Bones. How much did Mrs Bones know? Wendy Hendy, ten years the senior of her serial killer husband William 'Billy' Hendy, committed suicide two days before the trial of her toy-boy husband. No one knows if she was an accomplice in the deaths of eleven boys, or whether she simply ignored her husband's bloodthirsty nature. In light of Thomas Doncaster going missing, we have to ask, is his case connected to Mr Bones? And if so, is the connection surface, or bone-deep? You decide.*

I scurry off and grab my headphones. I shouldn't. No good can come of it, but I have to listen.

Chapter 5

'Welcome one and all to the very first episode of The Flesh on the Bones. I'm your host Jai Patel and it's my job, nay duty, to seek out the truth, no matter where it is hidden. To dig up the facts, no matter how dirty. To put the flesh on the bones of this story. Here in Northamptonshire we have had our fair share of weird and crazy, and just when you think you've heard it all, someone comes along and snatches the new normal right out of your grasp. Today's podcast will look at the current case, the disappearance of Thomas Doncaster, and will also cover the 1990 child murders committed by the infamous artist Mr Bones.

'Now, why would I pick such a gruesome case as Mr Bones for my first ever podcast? Well, I grew up with it in Northamptonshire with the legend of a bogey man that was real enough to stand trial and be convicted. I know people who lived through those dark years when Billy Hendy freely stole boys, then boiled them up for their bones. I even saw a photo of one of the alleged pieces of art he created. Stark white, and jagged edges where he had broken limbs to match his sick artistic vision.

You would never think that such a picturesque place as Northants would breed such a monster, but it did.

'I remember when I was young. My friends and I would hang about the streets, joking, having fun and enjoying the small taste of freedom it allowed. But this was after Mr Bones was caught. Like there could only ever be one monster, and when he was behind bars, we were all free to enjoy ourselves again. Well, as poor Thomas Doncaster just found out the hard way, there are many more monsters out there. Monsters who lie in wait for boys walking home alone without their older brothers. I'm sure if I looked back over the missing children's records for this region, I'd find others too. How many, who knows. Well, one person would know, the killer who has been taking them.'

Jai Patel both writes and narrates *The Flesh on the Bones*. As I listen on, I find the first episode is a regurgitation of the rumours in the press at the time of Mr Bones' trial. He loosely links historical facts of the case to Thomas Doncaster, then backtracks, then vomits up another theory.

As host, Jai has a soft unassuming voice that masks the salacious undertones of his commentary. I'm stunned he can get away with openly claiming Thomas is dead. There is no evidence of this and surely if the Doncasters were to hear this they would be mortified. His assumptions remind me of Mariah. Perhaps in a future episode he'll claim to be psychic too. I'm so angry that I almost stop listening – almost.

Leo appears in my line of sight. He motions for me to take off my headphones.

'Your lunch is getting cold. What are you doing?'

'I'm listening to this thing about Thomas Doncaster,' I say.

'Who?'

'The little boy who's missing,'

'Oh, the one from Rosemount. Have they found him yet?'

'Not yet.'

'Poor little guy. You want me to bring your lunch out here so you can keep listening? I can eat in front of the TV.'

'That would be lovely, thank you.'

Leo scoots off into the kitchen and comes out holding a plate with a slab of roast lamb, mint sauce, all the trimmings, and a cup of tea. I'm half expecting this good deed to be cold when it lands on the table in front of me, yet it isn't. I smile up at him, and he bends down to kiss the top of my head.

'Robin is eating with Nostrom upstairs. Apparently robots love lamb.' Leo strolls across to the sofa. I watch him pick up the remote and flick through various channels. The flashing screen lights up his face as he finds something to watch while balancing his lunch on his lap.

I put my headphones back on and continue listening.

Jai likes to travel around town while he records his podcast. It gives his soundtrack a distinct feel of urban reality as if he's in the middle of the story; there as it happens. I eat my lunch and half-heartedly listen to him condemn Thomas, berate the Hendys, and sensationalise the needless deaths of eleven boys in the 1990s.

I'm too busy eating roast potatoes to realise the first episode has bled into the second. I simultaneously don't want to hear it, yet feel like I should.

It's not until I hear Jai say *Leigh-Ann Hendy*, that I stop eating.

I hold a mulch of minted peas in my mouth as still as I can, so I can hear what he says next.

'*The only daughter of the Hendys, Leigh-Ann, was eight years old when her father was arrested. Mr Bones used Leigh-Ann to lure young boys into his car. Any child seeing another would assume their safety. Leigh-Ann, who the papers dubbed Little Bones, is now thirty-five years old and lives in the Oak Cross Estate under the new name of Cherrie Forrester.*'

I yank off the headphones. My hand shoots to my chest to check my heart is still beating.

How does he know my name? What gives him the right to broadcast it! It's not his secret to tell. My new family has no idea about my time as Leigh-Ann Hendy; no one currently in my life does. Everyone knows me as Cherrie Forrester, and to be fair, I've now lived longer as her than I did as Leigh-Ann. I changed my name when I was seventeen years old. I wanted a new beginning as someone else, someone who wasn't nicknamed Little Bones by the media.

Tentatively, I put the headphones back on.

'*She got a new life, a fresh start; which is more than can be said for the young boys her father butchered. Leigh-Ann has a family and works at a local independent retailer in the town centre. How much does she remember . . . ?*'

I check how many people have listened to the podcast. This episode only came out on Saturday afternoon and it already has over two hundred subscriber downloads. Subscribers who could be anywhere: UK, international, local . . .

Slipping off my headphones, I stumble back from the table, knocking over my chair behind me.

'Cherrie, are you okay?' Leo asks from the sofa.

I push down the top of the laptop, stagger towards the sofa, and throw myself into my boyfriend's arms.

'What's up? Tell me: what's wrong?'

Should I tell him now and get all my dirty laundry out? Let him realise who the mother of his child is? Tell him my dad would wait until after sunset, then drive the county's streets luring young boys with lies. All the while, I would sit in the back seat, my innocent smile giving all his victims a promise of safety. A promise never kept.

Could there be another killer out there? Was the Doncaster boy offered a lift by a kind man with his little daughter in the back of his nondescript grey Ford? Is he now suffering the same fate as all those my dad snatched off the streets? Knowing my family's skeletons, Leo could believe I had something to do with Thomas Doncaster's disappearance.

Growing up in foster families all around the UK, this was their train of thought. A train that would repetitively follow the same tracks back and forth. All of them were certain Little Bones was Mr Bones' apprentice. I was evil by association. Leo could think it too; could believe I could hurt a child. That I could harm Robin.

'Cherrie?' Leo says, still staring at me.

'It's fine. This whole Thomas Doncaster thing just has me rattled,' I say. It's not an out-and-out lie, but the words still make me shudder enough to wriggle from Leo's arms. He wasn't holding me tightly anyhow.

'The kid will probably come home tomorrow. Don't worry about it. You know what little boys are like.'

I do know what little boys are like. I watched so many of them accept a lift from my father. Worse, just take his hand on the street and walk towards their death without hesitation.

'What are you doing for the rest of today?' Leo asks me.

'I want a PJ couch day. How about you?'

'I need to get a bit of work done on the extension. I'll join you and Robin on the couch after. We can watch the new film with Dwayne Johnson in. Robin loves that guy.'

'Yeah, sounds great.' Then, for some unknown reason, I add, 'Thanks.'

Leo smiles at me before getting up and jogging upstairs. He's been working on our extension for about two years. It's a proper room now, with a ceiling and four walls; still, Leo wants it to be perfect for his grand opening, so neither Robin nor I can set foot in it until the official red ribbon cutting. He's working hard. I hear him in there at all times, even in the middle of the night when he can't sleep. It should be ready in the summer; perhaps we can have a barbecue; on the other hand, would anyone turn up if they all find out who my father is, and that he is not dead like I told them, but alive and serving multiple life sentences in prison? Will I even be here for the extension's grand opening? Leo could throw me out of my own home; take Robin from me – no judge in his or her right mind would award Little Bones custody of a young boy.

I need to stay ahead of this. I go back to my laptop and set up a Google Alert for *Cherrie Forrester*. If anyone else mentions me online, I'll see it.

Upstairs in my bedroom, I find Leo changing into some old jeans and a cream jumper. I grab my PJs and go to change in the bathroom.

'I've seen you naked many times, Cherrie.'

Blushing, I look over at him. There's paint splattered all over the back of his jumper.

'I can get the paint off for you. Just put it on top of the hamper when you're done.'

Leo looks up at me and smirks. 'I'll just chuck it out. You'll never get dark blue paint off a cream jumper.'

Chapter 6

Right now, two hundred strangers know who I am. They hold the dark secret I've been hiding. These random people now know me better than the people I love.

I'm not sure why I take so long to think about it – I need to report Jai Patel to the police. As I pick up my phone, I realise my police contact will have retired by now. I can't even recall his name. I do remember he looked an awful lot like Magnum P.I. When I was little, I kept imagining him in a loud Hawaiian shirt on an even louder speedboat – the wind whipping through his moustache as he barrelled towards criminals. Without Magnum P.I., there's probably no one left who remembers Leigh-Ann Hendy. Well, there's one person who will remember me, but I haven't seen my dad since I was eight years old.

After Robin goes to bed, I open the laptop and check *The Flesh on the Bones* subscribers. Twenty more strangers now know who I am . . . I'm being an idiot again. No one close to me listens to podcasts. I have to weather this new-media storm until it passes. As soon as he realises that he's not in trouble, Thomas Doncaster will come strolling home. After that, Jai Patel and his *Flesh on the Bones'* wild predictions will curl up and die; wither into digital dust. Jai will have to move on to a new crime and conceive different twisted lies to cash in on online with morbid rubberneckers.

Leo is working on the extension, so I absent-mindedly watch TV. I'm about to change channels when there's a knock on the door.

Four panes of thick mottled glass make up my front door; through it, I see two shadows lingering on my doorstep. I open the door, leaving the chain off. Which I instantly regret. Standing before me are Mariah and Jon.

'Um, hi. Did I leave something at your house last night?' I ask.

'No,' Jon says, smiling at me.

Mariah is wearing the same black dress as yesterday, only now over the top of it is a chunky black jumper.

'Okay, so why are you here at my house?'

'Can we come in?' Jon asks, but doesn't wait for my answer. Gently, he pushes the door open so Mariah can walk inside my home.

Letting go of the door, I step backwards. 'I guess so; quickly, though,' I say. Leo still has no idea where I was last night. If he comes out now and sees my impromptu visitors, I'll have to confess, and I already have enough on my plate.

'Sorry to barge in like this,' Mariah says, not looking at me. Instead, her eyes are everywhere, feasting on my family photos and assorted knick-knacks.

'We don't make a habit of surprise visits to clients'

houses. But, Mariah was so insistent we come to you.' Jon shuffles into my living room.

'I don't want another reading,' I say. 'I have no more money.'

'No worries. Consider this part of last night's reading,' Jon replies.

'I had another vision.' Mariah is looking at a photo of Robin on our mantel. In it, my son is wearing his school uniform and a goofy grin. 'Your little boy, you must be careful, the danger is closer. Shadows are closing in on you quicker. Shadows who will swallow him whole.' She looks pale. Her lipstick has all but rubbed away, so her lips now appear like flaccid grey caterpillars clinging to her mouth.

'What the hell! I don't want you here. I don't want you spreading your insane lies,' I yell at them. Both Jon and Mariah look surprised that I haven't greeted their dire prediction with open arms. These people are crazy.

'Mummy, are you okay?' I look up to see Robin inching down the stairs.

'I'm fine, sweetie. Go back to your room.'

'Who are they?' he asks.

When Mariah sees Robin, her face lights up. Her caterpillar lips morph into butterflies as she smiles. 'He's wonderful, Cherrie,' she says, putting her arms out to my son.

'Please leave. My boyfriend is out the back; if he sees you, he won't be happy. Please just go.'

Robin looks from me to Mariah. 'Who is this lady?'

'I'm Mariah; I'm a friend of your mum's.'

I want to correct her, but Robin wouldn't understand.

'Go back upstairs, Robin. Mummy wants to talk to her friends.'

Tightening his lips, Robin is about to argue, yet thinks better of it. 'Nice to meet you,' he says to Mariah and Jon, then, God love him, he curtseys.

'Nice to meet you, little bird,' Mariah replies smiling at him.

'I'm not a bird.'

'You must have been named after one,' Mariah says.

'No, Mum and Dad named me after Batman's best friend,' my lovely little boy says.

I can't help but smile; neither can Jon and Mariah. They chuckle and the atmosphere in my hallway almost visibly lifts.

'You're named after the superhero too.' I wink at him.

Now confident he doesn't just owe his name to a small red-breasted bird, Robin runs back up the stairs.

'So sorry; we shouldn't have come, but Mariah was so determined, and I thought what harm could it do? Better to give you the warning than something happen and we regret not saying anything. That's happened before.' Jon purses his lips as if to stop from telling me more.

'Thank you for your concern, but Robin is fine. I'm fine.'

Mariah grabs my hand and squeezes it. 'Be vigilant, please.'

'Okay. I will.' It's an easy promise. Robin is everything to me. I'd kill for him.

As his wife starts her journey down my drive, Jon turns to me. 'I'm sorry about all this. Here, we want to give you a refund for your reading.' He gives me £25 and walks out the door.

As I look at the money, I realise it's his way of telling me that everything Mariah is saying is rubbish. She's not psychic, just chock full of doom and gloom. I feel sorry for their daughter. What kind of life must she lead?

'Come along now,' Jon says as he holds out his hand for his wife. Mariah slips her hand in his, and they both get into their posh car.

Before I go to bed, I check *The Flesh on the Bones* podcast page one more time; only two more strangers know my name now, but maybe one is all it will take to shatter my new life into a billion sharp shards. Like six degrees of Kevin Bacon. A stranger listens to the podcast and blabs to their friend, who passes it along to another, and another, until all the people I care about have learnt who I am. I slump down onto the bedroom floor. With that way of thinking, how long before even Kevin Bacon knows I'm Little Bones?

Is this Mariah's predicted threat? That my past is moving between my present and future and casting a dangerous shadow, like an eclipse of reality? What am I doing? I'm falling into her trap by dwelling on what she said. Mariah is not psychic. Robin is not in danger.

Leo is still beavering away in the extension. I leave him to it. He finally comes to bed after midnight. He's happy and smells of fresh-cut wood and paint. He kisses the top of my head yet my mind is too tied up to allow my body a reaction. I pretend to be asleep. He tries to wake me one more time, and then gives up.

Chapter 7

When I look at the clock, I see it's only 2 a.m., so spend the next couple of hours thinking through my options. I could come clean about who I am and what my dad did – hope my friends and family love me enough to let my lies slide. Of course, it's not just the lies about my past; it's the knowledge I was there. At the time, it was all over the papers, rumours of how involved Little Bones really was in the murders. A little girl whose dad included her on his hunts to collect prey. A little girl shown how to clean and break human bones.

Dad exposed me to darkness at an early age; criminology books all agree it can stain a young soul, driving them to commit equally dark deeds. Back then, once people knew their new schoolmate or foster daughter was Leigh-Ann Hendy they treated me differently to the other children. Little Bones was watched with a keener eye.

I lied about my mum too; telling everyone she died in an accident. I know it was a lie because I was the one who found her. There were three empty bottles of sleeping pills scattered on the bathroom mat, which I used to wipe my wet feet. She was in the bathtub; her head submerged. Her features should have been peaceful. They were not. My mother's mouth was slack and falling to one side. Her glassy eyes were painfully wide. She had struggled at some point, perhaps regretting her decision. The water magnified that expression, while forcing her pale, dyed-blonde hair out around her like a limp sea creature. In that moment, I hated her. I hate her still.

At around four o'clock, I force my mind to be as still as the waters that surrounded my mother. I repeat the mantra, *sleep don't think. Sleep don't think*. What would I tell Robin about his grandparents? What would happen if they never find Thomas Doncaster, or if they find only his bones? What if some sicko has decided to follow in my dad's footsteps? This thing could blow over or blow up. Most of the worries about my past are just that, worries. They never happen and, in hindsight, they caused more damage in my mind than they ever did in real life, but my luck can't hold. What if Mariah does have a gift, and is right about Robin being in mortal danger? What if he's in danger because of me? What if everyone deems me an unfit parent and the courts take him from me? What if – the worst way to start a question.

At six o'clock, out of sheer exhaustion, I roll over and close my eyes. I'm asleep for an hour before the alarm goes off. Leo throws out his arm to hit the snooze button, slapping me in the face as he does.

'Hey,' I say, shoving him back.

He turns over and spoons me, his breath warm on the back of my neck. His arm then snakes through the gap my hip makes on the bed.

'Robin will be up in a minute.' I slip from his embrace and out of my warm bed. It's a cold morning, so when my bare feet hit the floor, I shiver. I reach for my fluffy pink robe and pull it on.

'I had a dream about you last night,' Leo says as he lazily rolls onto his back and scratches his hairy belly.

'Yeah, what was I doing?'

'I can't tell you; you'll take it the wrong way.'

'Just tell me.'

'Well.' Leo sits up. 'You were wearing this long black see-through nightgown.'

'Bit cold for that.' I laugh.

'Wait, that's not all. You were straddling me.'

'Really?' I blush.

'Yeah, you were smothering me with a pillow. One of the nice memory foam ones we bought last week.'

'What?' I stare at Leo.

'You were trying to kill me. Do you think there's any meaning to it?' He comically raises an eyebrow.

'Why would I kill you? There's no life insurance to collect,' I say and try to laugh.

Leo smiles. 'Yeah, I'll put life insurance on the shopping list for next week.'

'Pop new pillows on the list too.'

'Ha, ha, very funny. Yeah, I can just imagine you as some black widow serial killer.'

I want to respond with something witty, yet only manage to stammer out, 'I, I, I need to get Robin up for school.'

Looking thoughtful, he falls back down against his pillow. 'Probably means nothing, eh?'

★

Robin bounces around the kitchen while I make him cereal. He asks me about my friends who came round last night. I tell him they are new friends, and that they wanted to check we were all right. As subtly as I can, I ask my son not to tell his dad about my friends, saying that he'd be upset he didn't get to meet them. I feel awful saying this, but I don't know these people and what their intentions are towards my family.

'Of course, I don't tell Dad everything. But it was nice of them to come and see us,' he says spraying milk and half-chewed Coco Pops across the counter. Instantly, his little hand jumps to his mouth. I grab a cloth and clean up the mess before he can shove the escaped cereal back in. It's his favourite chocolatey breakfast treat, and I know he wouldn't want to waste them; three-second rule be damned.

'Yes, it's nice to look after the people in your life.' Although I say this, I really don't mean it; Mariah and Jon don't know me well enough to care that much about my son's safety or mine.

Robin nods and then grins. 'Mum, Halloween is a few weeks away, and the school is letting us get dressed up for the day. Can we buy my costume soon? Nostrom told me that good outfits sell out quick.'

'Nostrom is oddly knowledgeable about the retail sector.'

'He's a robot – he knows a lot about everything.'

'What do you want to go as?' I ask as I butter a piece of toast.

'How about a skeleton? They're cool. My bones could glow in the dark. I can dance and it'll look crazy.'

He carries on talking about how they are learning about the human body at school, but I can't take in any further facts. He's Mr Bones' grandson, and without knowing, the same thing that enthralled Dad fascinates him.

'No,' I snap. 'No skeletons, they're too creepy.'

'It's Halloween; creepy is the point,' Leo says from the doorway. I'm not sure how long he's been watching us, or how much of our conversation he heard, but he's grinning at me.

'Yeah, Mum, creepy is good!' Robin jumps off the kitchen stool, and runs around the counter to tickle me.

'All right, we'll see. You'll be late. Go grab your school stuff.' I twist my son around and nudge him towards the living room.

'Bye, Daddy,' he sings before he disappears to fetch his bag.

'Bye, tiger.' Leo looks at me. 'Why don't you want him to dress up like a skeleton?' He takes a piece of toast off my plate and rams it into his mouth.

'It's just weird. There are so many things Robin could be. What about one of The Avengers? Thor might be fun; get him interested in myths and Viking gods.'

'That's a good idea. Perhaps we can swap Nostrom for Odin.'

I'm not sure if Leo is taking the piss or not. It's only when he smiles I realise it was a joke. I force out a chuckle to appease his ego.

'Mummy!' Robin calls from the door. 'Nostrom's worried we'll be late for school. Hurry up.'

Leo waggles his eyebrows at me. 'Odin's looking pretty good right now, eh? I bet he wouldn't bother about tardiness.'

I drop my toast onto my plate. As I do, Leo swipes it up and eats it.

'Actually, I think robots are kind of cool,' I say, grabbing my coat. After pulling on my boots, I head for the door.

I unlock the car, and Robin runs for the passenger seat. It's not worth the argument to make him sit in the back seat, so I let it slide. Also, while he's next to me, I can keep a better eye on him. As soon as he's in the car, he pulls off his shoes.

'Robin, you need to put those back on.' As I buckle up, an image of poor Thomas Doncaster's shoeless body flashes in my mind. Quickly, I shake it off. Mariah has no idea what she's talking about; I wish I'd never asked her about it.

'Can I keep them off; just for the car ride? I promise I'll put them back on again when we get there. Please?'

I start the car and pull off the drive. 'Okay, just remember we'll be there in less than ten minutes.'

'Lovely,' Robin says, wiggling his socked toes as if he is on a sun lounger at the beach.

Leo must have driven my car yesterday, as he's left the radio on an Eighties station. We listen to Shakin' Stevens' song about an old house. Robin chair dances to it, while I grind my teeth. When I hear the opening beat of Duran Duran's 'Hungry Like the Wolf'. I can't take it anymore, so switch it off.

'Mum, why'd you do that?'

I don't have a good answer for him. I can't tell him Dad would listen to Eighties pop music while he worked in his art studio. Sometimes, when he let me work with him, we would sing along while painting bones; bones I often held against my own limbs to see if they were similar to mine.

'Mum, please can I listen to the wolf song?'

When I don't reply, Robin reaches over to turn the radio back on.

'I'm sure this song was on *Strictly* once. The couple I like danced to it.' He hums the melody and then sings, 'I'm on the hump down after you, sense is a pound, it's in lost and found, and I'm chunky like the wolf.'

I laugh at him. 'Those are not the lyrics.'

'I like mine better.' He then sings, 'Cause I'm chunky like the wolf.'

After a brief argument about shoes, I drop Robin off at school.

My shift is from 9 a.m. to 5 p.m. today. I can see Shania is already on my counter, a runaway cleavage poking out of her top. Smeared across her face is a distinct look of disappointment.

'Thought Tracy was in today,' she says.

'Me too,' I reply and carry on walking to the staff room to hang up my coat and stow my bag. I hope Shania wanders off early in the shift; perhaps to stock the cheeses. She's bound to want to talk about Saturday night, and I'm not sure I can take another discussion about Mariah's night of doom and gloom. I still have a tangled garden of thoughts to weed through, and I always do my best thinking when I'm cutting meat alone.

I wrap my clean apron around my waist and, as I reach into the pocket to retrieve my nametag, see an errant spot of blood on the material. Sometimes the aprons are hard to clean, especially as Mr Dawson only puts them through a domestic washing machine. It's just a small drop of red, but I still don't feel comfortable. Dad was always so clean in the studio. Any stray drops of red were instantly cleaned up; clothes and aprons taken outside and burnt. I open Tracy's locker and quickly swap it out for one of her clean ones.

Shania forces a smile at me as I approach.

'So what did you think about Saturday night?' she asks.

Feeling my shoulders sag, I look around us. Annoyingly, the shop is lacking in customers, again. I can't feign helping someone, so I'm stuck regurgitating Saturday night with one of my least favourite people.

'Mariah used our health and safety forms for information,' I say, air quoting *health and safety*.

'Yeah, I figured. Shame, I needed to hear some good news.' Shania stares at her feet.

'So, she only gave Gurpreet a good reading, eh?'

'Well, if you call getting married a good thing.' Shania laughs.

Nodding, I peek out backstage to see if the deliveries have arrived. No such luck.

'How are you and Leo getting on?'

I'm not friends with Shania, but we're not strangers either. We know basic information about each other's lives. She's a single mum with a son about Robin's age, and she has a reputation as a boyfriend-stealer. She knows I'm with my son's father, and that we're not married. She's seen Leo around a few times. I suspect she fancies him.

'Pretty good. Leo is still building that damn extension, though.' I give her this much, any more and I'd feel too exposed.

'Yeah, I hear he's pretty handy. When is it going to be ready? Any chance of a party?'

'Sure,' I say, and realise I now have to invite her.

'Cool. Us Creekers need to stick together.' Shania bumps my shoulder with hers.

'Is Gurpreet in today?'

'Only till eleven – she's on the till. I'm taking over from her when she goes.'

'I'm on my own here?' That's odd. Usually, there's at least two of us on the deli counter.

'Yeah, Mr Dawson is cutting shifts.' Shania then whispers, 'Is it true?'

What is she talking about? Could she be one of the 221 people who now know who I am? Is my new life at an end?

'Is what true?'

'Dawson's is closing. How much redundancy pay would we get when it does?'

I almost breathe a sigh of relief that Shania's not talking about that bloody podcast, until I realise she's just said I'll soon be unemployed. Tracy said something similar on Saturday night.

'Where did you hear that?'

'I saw Mr Dawson's diary. He has the accountants coming in twice this week. That never happens, and we've been thin on the ground lately. Not too many deliveries either. It doesn't take a genius to add it all up.'

'You shouldn't say stuff like that. Rumours have a habit of becoming self-fulfilling prophecies. What if the customers hear you and decide to shop somewhere else?'

'What customers?' Shania raises her voice and spreads her arms wide.

She's right. It's dead. Usually, there's a few mothers shopping after the school run, or at least a bunch of elderly

75

people who wander around for hours, then only buy sweets, yet today there's no one.

'The delivery will be here soon. Why don't you have a tea break before you go on the till?' I suggest.

'Sure, I'll prepare myself to get rushed off my feet,' Shania replies with a smirk.

I busy myself with cutting ham; all the while, the podcast weaves between my thoughts. If everyone discovers my past, there will be a synchronised shunning. It'll be as if I'm wearing my dad's bloody deeds strapped to my chest; like a character in Hawthorne's *Scarlet Letter*. I'm not melodramatic; growing up it happened too many times to Leigh-Ann. People look at you differently when they assume they know what you are capable of doing.

Two hours of serving the odd customer, and wrestling tortured thoughts later, the delivery of fresh meat arrives. The driver is an unfamiliar face; I've barely seen the same one twice. He helps me move the meat towards the counter. That way, I can unpack it, yet keep an eye out for customers at the same time.

I'm too busy deciding if I will buy a chicken for tonight to notice the man by my counter straight away. He's only the fifth customer of the day, and it is past 4 p.m.

When I do clock him, I see he's in his late fifties, tall and handsome. Typically, customers barely look up to acknowledge me. They are too busy drinking in the meat, picking their choice cuts, yet this guy is looking straight at me. Not smiling. Not talking. Just staring.

'Can I help you?' I ask him.

'Two pork chops, please.'

I reach down to fetch the meat. I'm supposed to give

customers the older cuts, but instead give him the fresh ones delivered today.

'These are good for at least four days. It'll be £3.30. Is that okay?'

'That's fine, thanks, Cherrie.'

'Hey, how do you know my name?' I ask.

'You're wearing a nametag,' he replies.

As I wrap the chops, I watch him. His expression is the same; it hasn't changed throughout our entire interaction.

'Oh, sorry. It's just weird hearing a new customer say my name.' I give him the pork chops. 'Enjoy.'

'Thank you, Cherrie,' he mutters, and then saunters towards the cheese counter to stare at some prewrapped Stilton.

'You okay?' asks a familiar voice.

I focus to see Kylie at the counter, her baby bump straining out of her shoplifter's massive coat.

'Yeah, I'm all right.'

'You don't look all right. You look pale.'

'The guy over there.' As she turns her head, I quickly whisper, 'Don't look.'

Casually, Kylie looks down at the meat, then slides a glance towards the man. 'What about him?'

'I'm not sure, he's just weird. He called me Cherrie.'

'That is weird. Although, that is your name.'

'Yeah, but my nametag doesn't get used much. I mean you didn't notice it, right?'

Kylie narrows her eyes at me. 'No, and I'm still not noticing it. You're not wearing a nametag.'

Chapter 8

My nametag is still in the apron I left in Tracy's locker.

I fumble for the radio.

'This is Dawson's Food, over.'

It crackles, far too loudly. Security responds, 'What's the problem? Over.'

I look up to see the man has disappeared from the cheese counter.

'Did you see where he went?' I ask Kylie.

Quickly, she steps sideways to get a clearer view of the aisle. 'He's not there. I can't see him.' She walks up to the cheese and lifts up his two chops. 'He left his dinner, though.'

'Dawson's, are you okay, over?' comes the voice on the radio.

I press the button. 'There was a tall man, mid to late fifties, good-looking, just here, over.'

The radio hisses. 'You want us to find him so you can date him?' security says, and laughs without saying over.

'No, he was acting suspiciously, over.'

Silence.

'Okay, we'll check the town's CCTV, over.'

I hook the radio back on my jeans. I feel hot, as if someone is smothering my body with a thick, scratchy wool blanket.

'You should sit down.' Kylie moves behind the counter and helps guide me backstage.

'Have you seen that guy before?' she asks.

I think about it for a moment. He looked familiar, but I can't place him.

'Not sure,' I reply.

We both sit down on a crate of tinned tomatoes. My thoughts swirl around and around like oil on water. Could he be working with Jai on the podcast? Maybe he was going to ask for an interview, then lost his nerve? Which was a good thing; if he'd asked, I'd have belted him round the head with a leg of pork.

'Was he a shoplifter?'

'I don't think so. He didn't take the meat.'

'If he were, I'd have tackled him for you.' Kylie grins.

I can't help but laugh. 'Need I remind you how we met?'

'Yeah, but you're my friend now, right?'

Kylie's eyes are wide, waiting for my response. Pregnant and alone, she must be so desperate for friendship, and who am I to be choosy? Serial killer's child is way worse than young pregnant shoplifter.

'Of course, we're friends.'

Heaving up her baby-filled belly, Kylie exhales loudly. 'I'll be glad when this little bugger is out.'

'Boy or girl?'

'Boy. He's trouble too. Just like his dad.'

I shouldn't ask, but I have to. 'Where is the father?'

'He got on the wrong side of the law. I'm not allowed to see him for a while.'

'So, you're not with him?'

'No, not right now. I had to leave. It's why things are a bit tight. I don't normally make a habit of stealing food.'

Funny, she's not mentioned free food yet, and that must be why she came back.

'My shift is over in ten minutes, but I need to get this delivery away before I go,' I say.

Smiling, Kylie nods. 'I'll stay and walk you to your car. If we see the creep again, I'll push my bump at him. Baby boy here will gut-punch that stalker for you.'

'Thanks, but foetuses don't really punch people. They lack the upper body strength.'

'We'll see.' She winks.

To my surprise, Kylie lifts up one of Tracy's discarded aprons and ties it around her enormous bump. After washing her hands, she helps me square the rest of the delivery away. If Mr Dawson walked in now, I'd have some explaining to do, but I doubt he will. I've probably seen him three times in the last month; each time was to cut my hours.

Once we've put everything away, I do a quick super-market sweep, picking up items for Kylie. Shania is still on the tills. After serving an old man, who spends the entire transaction staring at her boobs, she comes over to us.

'I didn't know we had a new start,' she says, eyeing Kylie with suspicion.

'We don't. Kylie is helping while we're short-staffed.'

'That's nice,' Shania says. 'You should liberate a few

packs of new-born nappies while you're here. They go through them like you wouldn't believe, and cost a small fortune.'

'Thanks.' Kylie rubs her belly as if she's also channelling her son's gratitude.

'Wow that is nice of you. What have you done with the real Shania?' I joke.

'No biggie. You gotta make hay while the sun shines.' With that odd pearl of wisdom, Shania smiles and settles herself back behind the till.

Food going out of date is one thing – nappies are entirely different. I'm not sure how I will explain the missing packs on the next stocktake, but if Shania and Tracy are right about Dawson's dangling off the insolvency precipice, it won't matter. Also, Kylie should get paid for helping me. I get that he's trying to save money, but Mr Dawson shouldn't have us working on counters alone; that weird man could have attacked me – grabbed a knife and slit my throat. He could have yanked me upside down like a piece of meat to bleed me dry. My bones could have been adorning his bedroom walls by now.

It's already dark when we get to the car park. A cold wind is fingering the fallen leaves in vivid swirls. It's more than a little eerie, and I'm glad Kylie stayed with me.

At the car, I offer to drive her home. She says no, as she lives in town.

When I get home, I find Leo playing Xbox with Robin on the couch. I kiss them both, before heading to the dining room table.

I want to tell Leo about the man in the shop, but he's never been the protective type, so it feels pointless to pass on my worry. It was probably nothing anyway. I need to stop thinking everything is all about me, but it *could* be all about me.

My laptop is still on the sideboard where I left it yesterday. I open it up and look at the podcast. There are 230 downloads. Hardly the roaring sensation I bet Jai Patel thought it would be, but it still sends a jolt of worry skipping across my brain; especially as there's now more information on the podcast's web page. There's even a photo of Jai. At least he's outing himself too. He is painfully average-looking, yet it doesn't stop him from uploading a myriad of selfies in different poses, as if he's on some novice-reporter dating site. I click around the page and am about to give up when I remember I still have half of an episode left.

I put on my headphones, and press play.

'William "Billy" Hendy was a failed artist who married into money. The Hendys had a comfortable life . . .'

It carries on describing how my mum inherited her family fortune at thirty-five and quickly married my twenty-five-year-old dad after only dating for a month. Which is something I didn't know. I'm not sure where he found all the information. I don't have grandparents; both sets died before I was born. I don't have aunts or uncles either; both my parents were only children. It was why disappearing into the new identity of Cherrie Forrester was so easy.

How does Jai Patel know so much about my family?

'Billy Hendy became the infamous Mr Bones when police found the skeletal remains of eleven young boys in the artist's studio at his home on the Pine Holmes Estate. Billy would drive the dark streets of Northamptonshire looking to abduct the sons

of this county, boil their poor bodies in peroxide, and then manipulate their bones into sculptures for his sick amusement.'

I remember the nose-jarring smell of peroxide in our house. The way it made the air burn with each breath. Mum used to tell me it was for Dad's art, that as his family it was our job to support him. Surely, she knew what he was doing; no one can be that naïve.

Jai continues.

'In later years, prison psychologists would describe Hendy as suffering from an extreme case of the eccentricity effect, where an artist of mediocre talent believes eccentricity will increase perceived artistic skills and the appreciation of their work . . .'

'Mummy!'

I look up to see Robin; a peanut butter smear on his face and a crust of bread crumpled in his fist.

'Guess what? I saved you a bite of my sandwich.' He thrusts the crust at me.

Pulling off my headphones, I take the sticky bread. 'That's very nice of you.'

I look around for Leo. 'Where's Dad?'

'He went out to the chippie for you. He says you like chips, but everyone likes chips, don't they?'

'I've never met anyone yet who doesn't like chips,' I admit.

'Maybe chips could unite us all?' Robin looks thoughtful. I love him so much. He's trying to solve the world's problems with deep-fried potatoes.

'You might be onto something, sweetie.' I wrap my arms around him, pulling him to me.

'What are you listening to?' Robin picks up the headphones and tries to slip them over his ears, but I catch them and pull the wires away.

'Nothing fun,' I say.

'I've been drawing. Want to see it?' His face is all shiny with happiness.

'Sure, sweetie.'

Robin runs upstairs. Moments later, he's back, a white piece of paper flapping in his wake. 'Look.' He shoves the paper at me, covering my laptop.

A sharp intake of breath almost chokes me. My son has drawn a child's hand without the flesh – it's just little bones.

'What? Why did you draw this?' I yell.

My son's eyes widen, tears suddenly glazing them. 'I thought you'd like it,' he whimpers and backs away from me.

'It's horrible. It's a skeleton.' I grab his arm and pull him back. 'Explain this.'

Robin can't be like my dad.

'I told you, we're looking at the skeleton at school. We all drew him to make a whole one. The teacher made me draw a leg bone.' He sniffs. 'Leg bones are boring. I wanted to draw the hand, but Davie got one hand and Anya got the other. I only wanted to draw the hand, Mummy. I drew it for you. Please don't be mad.'

Worst. Mother. Ever. I lunge forward to hug him. He doesn't know what bones mean to me. He has no idea of his grandfather's deeds.

'I'm sorry, sweetie.' I stroke his hair and feel his body relax into mine. 'Don't worry. I get it now. You're such a good boy.'

'Sorry, Mummy. I didn't mean to scare you with the bones. We all have them and we kind of need them,' he says.

'That's okay.' Just as I say this, the front door opens. Leo steps in with a plastic bag carrying the unmistakable smell of fish and chips.

'Who is ready for the delights from the Drunken Schooner?' he asks, lifting them up so I can see them better.

I let go of Robin, so he can run for the bag. Leo side-steps him, strides into the kitchen, and begins to unwrap everything. I follow.

Leo offers me a mound of greasy paper with a plate. 'What's all this about?' I ask.

Robin rummages through the bag until he finds his usual sausage and chips. He reaches up for a section of kitchen roll. It takes two tries for him to separate it from the roll.

Leo grins at me. 'Just thought we could all use a treat.' He leans in to kiss me. His breath smells of salt and vinegar. I take my plate and follow Robin as he charges towards the couch.

We sit together, watch mindless TV, and eat. All the while, I think about how my wonderfully dull life is in danger from Jai Patel's thorough research, and what I can do to stop it.

After Robin goes to bed, I have sex with Leo. It's more for comfort than passion. The act reminds me I'm loved and wanted. The whole thing takes less than seven minutes to go from grunting to snoring. As I lie awake listening to his rhythmic wheezes – I remember Leo's dream, the one in which I murder him. Each rattling breath knocking around his chest, like a pinball machine, makes me realise that, to get some peace and quiet, I could merrily smother him with a pillow. Just not a memory foam one – they are too expensive to waste as evidence in a murder trial.

Even though I don't have a shift today, I get up early to take Robin to school. The faint aroma of fish and chips still lingers in the kitchen; it makes me grin. Before Robin comes down for breakfast, I open the laptop to check the download figures of *The Flesh on the Bones*. It's still at 230. Perhaps this whole thing will blow over without knocking me down.

As Robin eats his breakfast, I discover he's now utterly obsessed with Halloween. Thankfully, Nostrom has advised that it would be better for him to dress up like a robot rather than a skeleton. I think about the empty cardboard boxes at work and wonder how quickly I could paint them into a robot suit. I make him promise this is his last request for a costume, then plan how I'll make it.

After the school run, I nip in to Dawson's Food. I talk with Tracy about her upcoming date with a new guy from a dating app. She is happy and hopeful. Gurpreet finds me some empty boxes of various sizes, and tells me to buy poster paint from the cheap shop in town by the post office. It feels good to talk to my friends about mundane, frivolous things. Before I leave, I ask Tracy to look out for Kylie so she can give her the out-of-date stuff. Reluctantly, she agrees.

As I park up in town, I see scraps of yellow paper fluttering in the autumn breeze. They are everywhere. After paying for my parking ticket, I check one of the flyers. It's a missing persons poster for Thomas Doncaster. In the centre is the same grainy photo from the newscast; the copy is terrible and it's tough to see his features. In truth, it could be any boy's photo. There's a tip-line phone number on the bottom. I can't help but wonder how many of those tips are just bumf; and not just random stuff – information that takes the police off course. How many investigations are derailed by giving too much credence to the public?

I slip between two shops so I can come out by the pound shop. Gurpreet is right on the money; they're selling a rainbow of thick poster paints. I pick up a grey, a red, a black, a yellow, along with some red glitter. The woman behind the counter is sour-faced and rude. Smiling at her, I say, 'Thank you,' even after she unceremoniously shoves my paints into a flimsy bag that I didn't ask for.

Turning to leave, I notice there's another poster on the outside of the shop. This one isn't yellow but white. I walk towards it and see an enormous clown face splattered across the page in front of a whimsical animation of fairground rides. The clown is beckoning me to come to Crazy Clive's Fair, which has moved into Black Friars Park. Robin would love this. I take a photo of the poster with my mobile. It's in town until the end of October. I remember the money I got back from Mariah's poor reading. This is the perfect place to spend it.

As I'm checking the details, a shadow falls across the clown's face, giving him a sinister air. I turn around, but find no one. I seriously need to stop being so paranoid.

Back at the car, I see someone has put a fresh, yellow Thomas Doncaster flyer on every car's windscreen. I pull mine out from under the wiper, so I can stare at the poor boy's face again. I feel for the parents; I do, but I can't help them. This has nothing to do with me. My hand

87

goes limp. The wind takes the poster and spirits it away, out of my sight.

When I get home, I recheck *The Flesh on the Bones'* downloads and subscribers; they're still the same. There won't be a new episode until Saturday. I hope Jai will have given up on the whole thing by then. These low figures have to be soul-destroying.

As I make Robin's robot costume, I find the painting oddly soothing. The constant swipe of the brush coupled with the long thick straight lines of the paint hypnotises me. Even the smell is intoxicating. It takes me back to when I was young and painted with Dad, but not the dark crafts in his studio, the pictures we would paint in the park and by the lake; when I would wear one of his shirts and stand before an easel ready to capture light and beauty. All too soon, I'm lost in colours and glitter. I even cut out round discs for robot buttons. Carefully, I paint each one, shaking the glitter over the tacky paint.

Mum and Dad didn't make me costumes for Halloween. Why bother when I was already wearing enough masks as Leigh-Ann: daughter, student, artist's apprentice, serial killer's assistant.

I remember Mariah's Halloween costumes. It would be wonderful to have a little girl. To dress her up as a witch, a pirate, a princess – anything she wanted to be. I wouldn't change Robin for the world; nonetheless, I'd like a daughter. Someday.

Quickly I lose myself in the fantasy of having a second child; how much fun we'd all have together on summer holidays, birthdays and Christmas. The daydreams prove a wonderful escape, so it takes a while to hear the noise.

There's an odd sound coming from the extension. I stop painting and walk towards the door. It's soft, a sort of rustling. I edge towards the plastic-covered door separating the old part of the house from the new. Maybe Leo has come home early. Quite often, he gets straight to work on the extension, forgetting what shifts I'm on and that I'm home. Wait, he has a late meeting today; he won't be home until teatime.

My fingers hesitate on the door handle. If I go in and find nothing, it will piss Leo off that I saw his handiwork before he was ready to show it. But, what if something is wrong?

The muffled noise comes again. It sounds like crying. No, it can't be crying. No one is in the extension. I'm hearing things. But then again, I thought the noises from Dad's cupboard were in my head too.

My palms are itchy. Goose bumps prickle my skin. I hug myself, yet find no warmth. I walk to the front door, grab my coat off its hook and pull it on. I'm still cold. Slowly, I walk back to the extension door. I keep my footsteps light in case I hear the sound again. I don't hear anything. It's my imagination; it has to be, but what if it's not?

Fear scratches down my insides, clawing at my throat. I want to shout out; ask for help. I can't. I hear the noise again, and find I'm rooted to the spot like a dead tree; a tree that needs ripping up, but no one is here to dig me up. I close my eyes and ball my fists.

Trying to shake off the panic, I force myself to pace the length of my house until the fear shrinks back, and I can think again. I edge towards the door to the extension. My fingertips touch the cold, metal handle. It wouldn't take much to allow the weight of my hand to drag it down; the door would simply ping open.

Something is wrong. I feel it; like a stranger's fingers forcibly exploring my guts. Nausea crashes into me. I don't care; I have to know what the noise is.

I pull down the handle and find it locked. More annoyed than shocked, I hunt for Leo's keys in the kitchen drawer. Of course, he locks it. There are dangerous tools in there. Robin is a curious child; it is safer for the door to stay locked. The key is in the kitchen drawer with all the other random bits. Rustling around, I find the right one. As I push the key into the lock, I feel silly; there's no sound coming from behind the door now. I'm letting things get to me again. Worry is making me hear things, but I should check it, anyway. Just to be safe. Leo could have left a piece of machinery on; it could start a fire. I click the lock . . . There's a knock at the front door. My heart bangs, and I imagine the organ pushing against my yielding ribcage. There's a second knock.

'Coming!' I yell.

I shrug off my coat, throw it on the couch, and jog to the front door.

There's another knock.

'Calm your boots,' I say.

As I pull the front door open, I realise that, once again, I should have put the chain on.

Chapter 9

Instantly, I recognise him. The man on my porch is the weirdo from Dawson's Food. He's wearing the same clothes as yesterday and holding his face in the same blank, yet friendly, expression, as if he doesn't have a thought in his head. Eerily unreadable.

'Cherrie,' he says.

I go to shut the door, but he shoves his foot between it and the wall.

'Cherrie.' He says my name as if it's the only word he knows.

I feel hot. I've heard people talk about seeing red when they're angry – now I know what they mean. How dare this crazy man be at my home! Robin could have been here.

'Take your foot away right now. I will call the police if you don't leave!' I yell at him. Angry tears threaten to cloud my vision.

'Cherrie,' he says again.

'My husband will be back any minute. He's a bodybuilder.'

I'm not sure why I say this; it's just the first thing that comes to mind.

'No, he's not,' the man whispers staring at his shoe blocking my door. 'I need to talk to you.'

'You're stalking me. There are laws against that. You're breaking the law. Please leave.' I struggle again to close the door, although I'm not even sure that would help. With my front door being almost wholly glass, anyone who wants to get through it could easily smash my only defence into sharp smithereens.

'I need answers.'

For a moment, when he looks up at me, his face is no longer blank. There's a drip of sadness in his eyes. I feel his foot move a little in the doorframe, so I give it a more forceful push. His shoe slides backwards. I close the door. Both my mind and fingers are nimble through my panic. It takes milliseconds for me to lock the door and thread on the chain.

Silence.

His silhouette is still on my step. He's not moving or speaking. Suddenly, his hand is on the door, the palm pushed hard against the glass. I can see the white of his finger bones through his flesh. For a moment, I imagine what his skeletal hand might look like, its joints clinging together by stringy sinew and bloody flesh. The image in my mind is more intricate than Robin's drawing. It's hypnotic in its raw beauty. Raising my palm, I rest it on the glass, covering his hand. I wonder what his bones would feel like against my skin. What they would weigh. How much force I would need to break them in two.

His head bows to my door and, although muffled by the glass, I hear him say, 'I'm sorry I scared you. I went to the shop again and they told me you had the day off. I was about to go home when I saw you walk in to speak to your friends. I followed you home. I'm sorry. This isn't like me. I'm just; I'm just . . .'

'A stalker?'

'No, I just haven't been right since my son was murdered.'

'I'm calling the police,' I yell, but he knows I won't. I should, but I won't. I now know who he is and what he's doing here. I can also guess how he found me, that damn *Flesh on the Bones* podcast. I should leave him to it. Go back to making Robin's robot costume. Ignore him until he goes away; but I can't seem to take my eyes off the distorted shadow at my front door.

'I don't have any answers for you,' I whisper. 'I don't know why my dad killed your son.'

For over an hour, he lingers by the door of my home. I stare at him the whole time; as if he will do nothing as long as I'm paying attention. Just like the Weeping Angels made of stone in *Doctor Who*. When his shadow finally leaves, I race upstairs to Robin's bedroom window to watch him walk across the street. Twice, he looks back at my house, then gets into a dark car and drives away.

Exhausted, I fall onto Robin's bed. It smells of him, sweet kid sweat and Johnson's talc. Closing my eyes, I let it comfort me. I must fall asleep because the next thing I hear is the phone. It's Leo.

'How'd the meeting go?' I ask.

'Great. We have a deal. Just a little more bureaucracy and all's good. How're things there?'

'Nothing new here.' I might have to say something

about my stalker eventually, yet I need the point to be sharp enough for me to cut into the lies I've told. Maybe he won't even come back. Perhaps he will realise what he's doing will only dig up a carefully buried past. How can knowing why and how your son died help you move on?

'Cherrie?'

'Sorry, yes.'

'You went quiet on me. You sure everything is okay?'

'Of course.'

'Great. Mum called me; she wants to come to tea tonight.'

I want to say that it's not a good time, but don't have the energy for an argument.

'Sure, but it's only chicken for dinner. She'd better like it or she'll be the one who gets stuffed.' I chuckle at my joke.

Leo laughs. 'I'll let *you* tell her that.'

Picking up my paintbrush, I work a little more on Robin's robot costume. I even shake more glitter onto the red buttons; but it doesn't help. I'm no longer relaxed. The previous magic I felt has gone. If that man comes back tonight, how am I going to explain him away to Leo's mum?

I leave Robin's costume to dry, then check the download counter for *The Flesh on the Bones*. Still no new subscribers, yet there is now a 'contact me' button for Jai Patel. Righteous anger guides my fingers as they type a message to him:

Dear Jai,

How dare you expose my identity! I was only eight years old when I lost both of my parents. A victim's father is now stalking me, looking for answers about my dad that I can't give.

I'll now probably have to tell the people I love about my sordid family history.

What if someone you loved did something terrible? Something that, as a child, you had no control over? What if you'd worked hard to get past it and have a normal life, and then some jumped-up, wannabe reporter spreads that secret while weaving in more lies? My mother couldn't have known what my dad was doing. How dare you slander her name too!

I initially sign it: *Kind regards, Cherrie Forrester.* No, best to end with: *I will sue you if you don't end this harassment, Leigh-Ann Hendy.*

My fingers hover above the mouse. I want to press send but I can't stop repeatedly reading the email, as if I'm looking for an excuse not to send it. Maybe I shouldn't. I don't know this Jai. For all I know he might not scare easily and resent a threat. He could hit back even harder. Would he use my words; twist them into some damning quote? Am I starting a war? Should I take the high road and just ignore it all until it goes away?

I'm not sure how long I've been staring at my laptop, but my screen saver pops up three times; on the fourth, I look at my watch to see it's time to pick up Robin. Now or never. I press send.

As I pull up to the school gates, I feel a little better. Being passive might make for an easier life, but it's not a life to be proud of. Jai Patel is bullying me with his accusations. If someone bullied Robin, I'd tell him to stand up to the thug. They'd soon find another target.

Perhaps I'll do this to my stalker too. Shout threats and beat my metaphorical chest until he leaves me alone.

*

Robin is always the first one out of the school gates. He bounces down the path and tumbles into my car. Quickly, he straps himself in, and then twists around in his seat to grin up at me.

'I got an A on my math test!' He holds up the test paper to prove it.

'That's wonderful. You are a clever little thing,' I say, leaning over to hug him. As I do, someone behind me in a BMW honks their horn. I wave at them, start my car, and move out of their way.

'Nostrom helped me,' Robin says. 'That's not cheating, is it?'

As I pull away from the kerb, I consider his question.

'No, that's not cheating.' Of course it isn't. Nostrom is in Robin's head. Whether the answers come from him or his imaginary friend, it's all good.

'Being a robot, Nostrom is great at maths.' Robin slips off his school shoes, dropping them into the footwell. 'And science. He loves science too.'

'Well, Nostrom will be pleased; I made your Halloween robot costume today.'

'You did! That's awesome! I can't wait to see it.' He waves his little socked feet up and down.

As we drive, I keep an eye on the streets we pass. It's a dusky afternoon and there is a mass of dark cars around, but I don't see my stalker lurking near any of them.

I pull up into our drive. Robin climbs out of the car; leaving his shoes behind in the footwell. Just in socks, he makes a run for the house. I lean across to scoop up his shoes.

Once safely inside. I lock the front door and loop the chain across it. I place Robin's shoes next to mine by the door, leaving a gap for Leo's.

With the flourish of a tired magician, I reveal Robin's costume to him. Part of me expects him to be frustrated it's home-made. Another part of me knows my son better. A grin spreads across his face, and he shakes his little hands in delight. The paint is still a little tacky, yet somehow that makes him even happier, until he sees the glitter on the big red buttons lining the front.

'Nostrom says glitter's for girls.'

Smiling, I kneel in front of him. 'Well, maybe Nostrom is just jealous because his buttons are un-glittery.'

'Un-glittery isn't a word, is it?' Robin pouts.

'No, it's probably not, but it's fun to say.'

He laughs. 'Un-glittery.'

'Hey.' I take out my mobile phone and scroll to the photo of the fair poster. 'Would you like to go?' I show him my screen. His face lights up brighter than the artificial glow of my phone.

'When?'

'How about Friday night?'

'Can I wear my costume?'

'No, sweetie. That's for Halloween. It won't be a surprise if you wear it before.'

'Okay,' he mutters.

As I peel carrots, Robin flutters about the kitchen, trying to help me, yet ultimately getting in the way. He knows his gran is coming to tea, which makes me wonder if Leo prearranged this impromptu visit on Saturday, and only disclosed it to me now.

Suddenly Robin appears beside me. 'A surprise for who?'

'What?' I then realise he's been thinking about wearing

his costume to the fair this whole time. I love how kids' minds work. Things stick in them like bubble gum.

'For everyone. We all like surprises at Halloween.' It's a rubbish answer, but it's been a long day so it's all I've got left.

I've almost set the table when Leo texts to say he's stuck on the M5, and will probably be late. He finishes his update with an emoji my phone can't read, so all I see is an alien face. I text back to drive safely, and that I'll leave him a plate in the oven if he's home too late to eat with us.

A moment later, I get another text. I hope it's from Leo to say traffic is moving, but it's from Tracy. *Fed your stray x*, it says. She means Kylie. I text back, *Thank you*, and I get back, *You owe me dinner*.

Leo's mum is always early, so I'm not surprised when she knocks on the door half an hour before she's due. It's as if she's trying to catch me doing something wrong.

In a rush to let her in, I forget about the security chain, so the door jars when I try to open it.

'Sorry,' I say to her fumbling with the chain. It's not a great start. The one time I manage to put the chain on makes me look as if I can't even open a door right.

Mrs Duffill looks a lot like Joanna Lumley's character from *Absolutely Fabulous*. Her pale blonde hair is coiffed to perfection, and her make-up is delicate yet prominent. Unfortunately, she's not as much fun as the character in the Nineties TV show. Every time we're together, she slips into conversation that I'm not good enough for her son. She has never offered for me to call her by her first name, let alone 'Mum'. Robin calls her Gran; I address her as

Mrs Duffill. She loves Robin, though. When she steps through the door, the old woman grimaces at me, but swoops in to give Robin a massive hug, and a smile, which creases her perfect eyeshadow.

'Gran! Come and see the costume Mum made me!' He yells at her, dancing on the spot. He then offers his arm and escorts her towards the cardboard robot parts piled up in the dining room. My son, the little gentleman.

I veer off to set the dining table. As I do, I flip on the laptop to check out the podcast. It's just paranoia, but as long as it remains at two hundred odd, it's okay; I can continue with my lovely, boring life and everything can go back to normal.

As the page appears on the screen, I have to look twice. There are now over one thousand subscribers. I refresh the page, but find, as I do, the counter goes up two more. What the hell?

'Dinner smells more than ready, Cherrie. Are you dishing up now?' Mrs Duffill asks, loitering at the head of my dining room table. She sits down, and rearranges the cutlery beside her placemat.

I can't breathe. Over one thousand subscribers! This can't be happening. I look down again at the screen.

'Should you have your computer out? We are about to eat. Hopefully,' she says.

Robin bounces into the room. 'Do you need help dishing up, Mum?'

'No, no, sweetie, that's okay. Sit down and keep your granny company.'

I slam down the lid of the laptop and quickly move it to the sideboard. I then remember I haven't put the roast potatoes in the oven. They will take at least forty minutes to cook. I grab the bag of potatoes from the vegetable drawer, then look for the peeler. It's missing. As I fetch a small knife, I realise I need to heat the oil first, so spread two tablespoons over a baking tray. I bend to put it in the oven.

'What's taking so long, Cherrie? You knew I was coming tonight.'

I open the oven door to see there are already burnt potatoes in there.

'Why are we waiting?' Mrs Duffill sings with Robin.

Come on, Cherrie, you can get through this without stabbing that horrible, haughty piece of work in the heart with a spatula. Wringing my hands together, I imagine how much force it would take to push a piece of plastic through a person's ribcage; quite a bit. I pull out three plates.

I burn myself four times retrieving the chicken from the oven. The potatoes are cold by the time I have the bird carved. The carrots are still hard and my peas are so soft they might as well be mushy. With no visible lumps, the gravy is my only redeeming culinary act. I bring in the plates, then sit down. I'm not hungry, and the act of eating dinner feels even more of a challenge than cooking it.

Mrs Duffill bows her head and recites grace in the most sarcastic manner I've ever heard. Usually, I'd say something, but right now, all I can think about is that one thousand strangers know my secret. Mrs Duffill could have heard it. No, it's doubtful she'd have sat on that killer-nugget of information much past stepping over the threshold.

I listen to Robin's voice while picking at my food. I don't take in what he's saying, but the sound of it is soothing.

'So, what do you reckon?' Mrs Duffill asks me.

'Um, about what?'

She tuts and rolls her eyes. 'The fair. I could come with you on Friday night.'

The fair is my treat to spend time with Robin. 'We only have two tickets,' I lie.

'I could buy another one.'

'They're sold out.'

'Oh, well, that's a shame. It would have been fun to go to the fair with a robot,' she says winking. Robin lights up as if he'd just seen Santa playing Nintendo with the Easter Bunny.

'He's not wearing his costume to the fair,' I say back. 'It won't last until Halloween if he does.'

'Well, that's what happens when mummies make costumes out of old boxes and don't buy proper ones.'

My blood is boiling. It is red hot and bubbling. I go to open my mouth but stop in case I cough and splatter red all over Mrs Duffill.

'Mummy did a great job. My costume is awesome.' Robin smiles at me. I love him so much.

'Of course she did,' Mrs Duffill says.

I want to explain we don't all have the money to buy pre-made costumes, but I'm still worried about speaking; I could easily transform Mrs Duffill from a regal Joanna Lumley lookalike into Carrie at the prom. It's a ridiculous thought, yet I still can't bring myself to open my mouth.

The look on my face makes her change the subject. 'Did Leo tell you I'm buying a second home in Spain?'

I shake my head.

'Does Robin have a passport?'

'Of course I do, Gran!' Robin slips off his chair and

runs upstairs. He knows where we keep all our passports, nestled together in the drawer next to my side of the bed. I hear him thump around, and then he thunders back down again to show her his passport.

'Well, isn't this wonderful. Spain can be your first stamp,' Mrs Duffill says, looking at me with a sly smile.

How dare she point out I can't afford to take my son overseas for holidays right now. And say it in front of him. Casually, I twist my dinner knife around and around. The weight of the stainless steel steadies my thoughts.

'Mrs Duffill,' I begin.

Fortunately, the front door opening interrupts me. There's a bang. Damn, I put the security chain on, again. Leo swears. I rush over to unhook it.

'You trying to tell me something?' Leo taps the chain. He sees his mum at the dining table and smiles. 'Hey, Mum. How's the chicken?'

Mrs Duffill pokes a piece of meat. 'Dry and cold. How are you, my darling?'

I go to fetch Leo's plate of food from the oven; the plate I'd promised, but it's not there. Didn't I dish it up? Quickly, I pull together some leftovers and shove them into the microwave. I deliver Leo his dinner.

'Great stuff,' he says. 'Thanks, babe.'

He only ever calls me *babe* in front of his mum. Smiling, I slink back into the kitchen area to tidy up. As I move pots and pans around, I listen to my family laughing and eating without me. Robin talks to Leo about his maths test and his costume. Mrs Duffill complains I'm too distant and a crappy housewife.

Still, all I can think about is all the people who have heard my name, and figured out where I work. It's like a vice squeezing my brain. Each new person cranking it tighter until my mind implodes. I have to tell everyone now. One thousand is too many people, and this grisly revelation about my family is better coming from me than someone else.

I look down at the chicken carcass on the kitchen counter. Its chest splayed out where I cracked it open to retrieve the stuffing. The bones are stained and broken. I want to throw it away, but I can't stop staring at it; imagining it clean. How beautiful it could look, if I'd just taken the time to . . .

'Everything all right in there, babe?' Leo's voice breaks my weird chicken spell.

'Yeah,' I reply, then bundle up the old bird's bones and throw them in the bin.

As I go back into the dining room to clean up the dishes, I notice Robin has eaten everything but his carrots.

'Eat your veg, sweetie,' I whisper to him.

'I don't like them,' Robin whines.

'He doesn't have to eat them if he doesn't want to,' Mrs Duffill states.

'Yes he does, he needs to eat his vegetables.' I place a hand on Robin's shoulder. 'Don't you want to grow up big and strong?'

'I'm sure he'll be fine as he is,' Mrs Duffill adds, then looks over at my son. 'Why don't you go upstairs to play?'

I stand at the back of Robin's chair so he can't get up. How dare she! This is my house, my son, my carrots. She's setting herself up as a hero in Robin's eyes – the granny against vegetables.

I see Robin is looking up at me, so I bend down and

say, 'How about we put some cheese on them; would it help?'

I hate this, but sometimes to be a good mum you have to play the bad guy.

'Or, how about the cheese spread you have in sandwiches?'

He nods at me.

Throwing Mrs Duffill a sour look, I fetch the cheese spread along with a knife. I want to plant the dull blade deep into her chest, but I don't do that. The bloodstains would never wash out of my tablecloth. I scrape off a massive dollop of spread and smear it over the now-cold carrots. Robin picks up his fork, stabs a carrot, and then stuffs it into his mouth.

'You're such a good boy.' I give his shoulders a gentle squeeze.

I look up to see Mrs Duffill raising an eyebrow – not in the funny Dwayne Johnson way that Robin likes to imitate, more in a threatening, defiant way. Leo has been oddly quiet throughout the exchange. Usually, he would chime in on his mum's side. I guess his silence is pathetic support for me.

Watching Robin force down his vegetables, I feel a wave of anger and guilt. It's a familiar feeling, yet it still metaphorically knocks me on my arse. Muscle memory kicks in before anyone notices my odd staring, and I clean up the rest of the table. After putting all the dishes in the sink, I slide down onto the linoleum floor of the kitchen to dissect my problems. Carrot-gate aside, I need to find out why *The Flesh on the Bones* has unexpectedly become so popular. I need to tell my family who I am, just not now. I'll be damned if I prove Mrs Duffill right tonight, confirm that I'm not good enough for her only son; that I'm a terrible person because my dad turned out to be a senseless serial killer. Mum, at best she was weak; at worst, a killer too, but eight-year-old Leigh-Ann wouldn't have known the signs. It's only now as adult Cherrie I have my doubts about Mum, albeit doubts I hide deep beneath my memories that are just for me.

Mrs Duffill leaves after her second cup of tea. While Leo puts Robin to bed, I get out the laptop and see there have been another three hundred subscribers to *The Flesh on the Bones*. I check the site and the links. How has this happened? I open my emails. There's a reply from Jai Patel.

Chapter 10

The email is oddly professional. Jai apologises for outing me, yet claims the case of Mr Bones has never been more relevant due to the disappearance of Thomas Doncaster. He asks for a comment he can use on his next show. He also includes a link: a local newspaper has written a story on *The Flesh on the Bones*. They do not name me, yet the headline reads: *Is there a serial killer among us, again?* The article quotes the podcast in several places.

'I'm just going to do a little work on the extension. You okay?'

I look up to see Leo. My lovely innocent boyfriend who I've lied to and hidden my past from. What was I thinking? For what I did, I don't deserve this life, I shouldn't have any happiness. Leo and Robin have done nothing wrong – they deserve better. 'Yes, but I need to talk to you about something important.'

Sighing, he comes over. 'Mum is lonely. When Dad died, she went into hermit mode. It's good she wants to go to the fair with you.'

'That's not what I want to talk about.'

I put the lid down on the laptop.

'Did you really only buy two tickets? Do you even buy tickets in advance?'

I snort and shake my head.

'Not the most convincing lie you've ever told.' Leo laughs.

If only he knew the true extent of my lying skills. I want to tell him everything; just unload it all like a massive, vomitus mixture of truth and secrets. Maybe he'd understand. Probably not. My mouth opens ready for my confession to come tumbling out.

'Don't worry about it. Hey, nice robot costume. Another job off the to-do list for this year, eh.' Leo doesn't wait for a response, instead he walks away. With a clunk, he unlocks the extension door and disappears. I should have said something. My chance to come clean passed me by. I need to try harder; it's just this secret is like a solid ball that's lived in the pit of my stomach for years, and trying to cough it up could choke me.

Years ago, when the full realisation of my father's crimes hit me, one question stung my little mind: why? I didn't want to know about other killers, just why my dad did what he did. Perhaps he wasn't a monster, just sick. And when you love someone, you care for them when they are sick. I go upstairs and rummage in the back of my wardrobe. Hidden beneath a pile of old jumpers is a box. Most people hide porn and sex toys in secret boxes, but in mine, there are criminology textbooks. I haven't looked at them since I met Leo. I didn't have to; I know each one by heart. For years, I collected them, looking for answers. Why my dad? Why these crimes? Why include me? But, as fascinating as they were, there were no chapters on men who create artwork from children's bones. No sentence revealing even a hint of what could be wrong with my dad. Not long after he was sent to prison, psychologists published their diagnoses; but they didn't live with him, hunt with him. They didn't create art with Mr Bones.

I flip through the first book, the familiar dusty smell of the pages taking me back to when I first bought it from a second-hand bookshop. All the major personality types are covered. I stop at the chapter on Narcissists. Those who think the world exists for them alone. I've come across a few – I'm sure everyone does. They spare no thought about who their actions hurt. Wait, will telling Leo only help me? Would I be hurting him for no reason other than a selfish need for him to help shoulder my burden? No, I shouldn't tell Leo anything. This storm could still leave me unscathed. Why ruin my life unless I have a reason to? If I did, I'd be a self-indulgent narcissist, just like my dad.

As I carefully place my books back into the shadows of my wardrobe, my mobile beeps. I look down to see an email; it's a Google Alert. I click into it to see my name on a true crime blog. 'Cherrie Forrester' is now like a tiny digital spider with bloody feet, leading a scarlet trail back to my life. One or two footprints won't draw attention, but hundreds smeared across the internet will. The blogger talks about me as if I should be the number-one suspect in Thomas Doncaster's disappearance. *Like father, like daughter*, it says and even includes a horrific meme from a slasher film.

★

I don't hear Leo come to bed; I wake up with him snoring beside me. He smells of fresh-cut wood and has red paint speckles over his forehead. Not being able to sleep, I lie awake watching the sunrise.

When I finally doze off, I dream about my dad – something I haven't done in a long time. I blame that damn podcast, the missing Thomas Doncaster, my stalker, and Dawson's Food possibly shutting down. It's all swirling around in my mind like the perfect storm of guilt and worry.

In my dream, Dad is singing. He loved to belt out popular Eighties songs. In my dream, he dances in a sleek grey suit. When he offers his hand to me, I slap it away. I try to not dance to his beat, but I can't help it; I sway.

The surrounding landscape melts away; suddenly, I am in his art studio. Funny, it doesn't look like the place I remember with its midnight-coloured walls; it is more like our dining area. In the centre, a table supports a pile of bones from eleven young boys.

Humming, Dad works on his artistic creations; pulling out bones and sticking them together with superglue and coloured twine. I don't want to look, but I'm not eight years old anymore; I'm an adult. It's my responsibility to see what he's doing. I edge closer. He's grinning. My dad was never as happy as when he was working in his studio. I peer over his shoulder. The contents of the table morph into cardboard boxes painted to look like a robot. Fear floods my body.

With a wink, he says, 'Robin will love it.'

I wake up.

Lying in bed, I wring my hands together, and think through how much of my dream is my dark imagination and how much were regurgitated memories.

Dad never scared me. When they arrested him, I was convinced it was a mistake. He couldn't have really killed all those children. That wasn't my dad. The man who called me a host of endearing pet names, and who danced with me to pop songs. Finally realising all those little boys I'd met didn't exist anymore because of my dad was earth-shattering. Now it's easy to look back and see what was happening, but eight-year-old Leigh-Ann hadn't fitted all the pieces of the puzzle together yet. Hell, she didn't even realise there was a puzzle.

I shower early, so I can start breakfast before anyone else gets up. Frying eggs and bacon, I wait for Robin. He smells the food, and is down before I get the chance to recheck the laptop.

'Bacon, on a school day?' he asks.

'It's because of your math test yesterday.'

'Sweet,' he says and then shovels his breakfast into his mouth as fast as he can.

Leo strides to the dining table, kisses my cheek like a TV husband, then ruffles Robin's hair. How can a perfect family scene be happening now? I sit back to take it all in. This might be the last unspoiled family morning I get.

While Robin grabs his school bag, I check *The Flesh on the Bones'* subscribers. It's nearly two thousand now. Even more worrying, overnight it has given birth to a comments section. Scrolling down, I scan for mentions of both Leigh-Ann and Cherrie – neither is there. Most of the comments are talking about bringing back the death penalty for my father, and saying my mother did the right thing by killing herself. They also link Thomas Doncaster to Mr Bones. The more I read, the angrier I get. My blood is boiling again. How many times can my blood boil until it evaporates into nothingness, leaving me a limp sack of skin and bones?

'Ready, Mum,' Robin yells at me.

In the car, Robin flicks off his shoes and sits cross-legged on the front seat. I should tell him not to take his shoes off; remind him how dangerous it is to sit like that in a car, but at any moment, his happy little world could fall apart. His bloody lineage exposed for the entire world to see. I say nothing. Who am I to bring up the safety of little boys?

Switching on the radio, I find the DJ doing yet another Eighties throwback hour, so I quickly turn it off. I'd sooner not come across any more memory-soaked songs that remind me of Dad. Why can't people just leave the past alone?

At the school, I miss parking in front by just one car, so have to park further down the street.

'Bye, Mum,' Robin says and opens the car door to jump out.

I don't like the thought of my son walking anywhere on his own right now, so I say, 'Wait, sweetie, I'll walk with you.'

Scowling, he puts on his shoes and slips out of the car.

The large school gates are made of twisted wrought iron. They squeak when you push them, like the entrance to a haunted house in an old movie.

Once we're in the playground, I kiss Robin goodbye. As he bounces off, he doesn't look back at me. I'm proud of that. Two other kids cling to their mums. I hear one complaining that they're ill so don't want to go to school today. I take a minute to marvel at how great Robin is;

sure, some toys end up lying around for days, and there's the inconvenient dislike of wearing shoes, also of course, there's Nostrom; but he will grow out of all that. I'm a lucky mum.

Several metres away from me I hear a woman say, 'Have you heard about it?' Looking over, I know her face, just not her name. I do recognise the lady she's with: Sharon, a busybody who, each year, organises the Harvest canned food collection.

I rarely engage with the mums at the school gates, and I know I shouldn't eavesdrop, but I want to hear what they're talking about. What if it's the podcast? Unlikely.

'Yeah, who knew we have the infamous daughter of a serial killer in our midst?'

Oh no.

I sway a little closer to them so I can better hear their gossip.

'It's so awful, what's happening to the Doncaster family. Worse still that it happened in the county before. Do you think it's a . . . oh, what do they call them on those American police shows?'

'Copycat,' I say, knowing the term well from my criminology books.

They hear me.

'Yeah, that's it, a copycat. Hey,' Sharon says, moving to include me in their circle. 'You're Robin's mum, right? Robin Duffill?'

'Yes,' I reply a little too swiftly. Thank God, I gave Robin Leo's surname rather than Forrester. I offer no further info. There are so few Cherries around; I should have called myself Donna or Mandy. Maybe next time.

112

'Have you heard the podcast too?' asks the unnamed mum.

'Yes, I've heard it.' At least I can tell the truth on that.

'I remember when the Mr Bones thing happened here. I was about thirteen years old. It was the big, posh estate – Pine Holmes on the edge of town where the Hendy family lived, right?'

Our house wasn't that posh, but I nod anyway wondering how long I can stand here discussing my past with them. What is the etiquette for admitting that you're the topic of conversation?

'Oh, so do you think the daughter has the Doncaster boy?' asks the unknown mum.

Sharon looks at me, and I go cold. I do not have Thomas Doncaster, yet somehow someone saying it aloud that I might, ignites a searing guilt across my cheeks. A thick silence now lies between us; three women huddled together in a schoolyard, two stirring their cauldron of gossip, one thinking of how best to get the hell out before suspicion swings her way.

'Maybe, but more importantly, Wendy Hendy. Did the mum know?' Sharon asks.

I try to look thoughtful, but perhaps end up just looking constipated. My hands itch, so I hold them behind my back to stop from wringing them together.

'She knew. Who doesn't know what their husband is doing with his time? I mean, really,' says the mystery mum. What the hell is her name?

'Well, lots of wives have no idea what their other half is doing. Are you one hundred per cent sure where your husband is right now?' I say.

Sharon snorts. 'He's at work. He's an accountant.'

'Is he? Have you seen him with your own eyes today; sitting behind his desk and typing numbers into his Casio?'

'Well, no. He's there, though.'

'Husbands do all sorts of things when we're not looking. Mine locks himself away in our extension every chance he gets.' Lies, especially small ones, have a habit of piling up in conversations like these; I'm not married to Leo, but right now, they think I'm Mrs Duffill, and I must ensure that lie is maintained, even if sharing my almost mother-in-law's name makes me shudder.

'Yeah, no, I get that,' says the other mum. 'Man caves. They disappear all the time. Mine has an allotment.'

Sharon purses her lips. 'He grows nice carrots. Have you tasted her husband's carrots?'

They both burst out laughing. I chuckle at them, but not much of the laugh makes it past my gritted teeth. A strange, mischievous feeling builds in me.

'Allotments are great for burying bodies and . . .' I move closer to them to whisper, 'I hear veg tastes better when it's grown in human remains.'

Sharon nudges her friend and they laugh.

'Carrots in dead bodies – that's funny.' Sharon sighs, looking thoughtful.

'How many people are listening to *The Flesh on the Bones*?' I ask.

'I've no idea. I'm a complete addict of the show, though. I love true crime. I'm telling everyone about it on Facebook.' Sharon shows me her latest post on her phone about how shocked she is that child kidnapping and serial killings can happen right under our noses. 'So, do you think the daughter had something to do with the Doncaster abduction case?'

'More than likely,' says the other woman, grunting and wrinkling her nose. The very thought of me is making her sick. I want to yell at them that Thomas is just missing. There's no evidence of abduction – especially not by me, but I can't.

I feel hot. My coat is clinging to me in a clammy cocoon kind of way.

'Gotta go to work, ladies,' I say quickly.

'Don't forget the Harvest collection,' Sharon says. 'You do work at Dawson's Food, right?'

'Um, yeah. Bye.' Okay, so they remember where I work, but at least they haven't mentioned the name Cherrie Forrester. As Mrs Duffill, I'm safe, for now.

I leave the mum-huddle and almost run back to the car; it takes three attempts to unlock it before I realise I'm trying to open someone else's Ford. Mine is further down the road.

Finally, inside the quiet of my front seat, I scream and slam my hands against the steering wheel. How long do I have? How long before the police are knocking on my door about missing Thomas Doncaster, if they assume the serial killer apple doesn't fall far from the murder tree? How long before my bloody DNA loses me my family, my friends, my life? How long before rumours kill Cherrie Forrester?

There's only one answer. I'm surprised I haven't considered it before. If I find Jai Patel's address, I can pay him a visit. Threatening over email is one thing – face-to-face is different.

I grab my phone and search for Jai's details; an easy

task as he's listed his full information on the website. It's an odd address for a recording studio, but I tap in the postcode in my satnav, scream one more time, pull away from the kerb, and then head towards the A13.

It's time to talk with Jai Patel.

Chapter 11

I expect to pull up outside a stylish office building with a soundproof studio nestled inside, everything bought with blood money and the ruination of innocent people's lives. Instead, I find a house in a quiet, picturesque village cul-de-sac; well kept with a flower-packed garden wrapping around its sides. A family house. It never occurred to me he could be a husband and a father. A new plan forms; maybe I can appeal to that side of him? Ask that he see things from a parent's point of view.

While I muster my anger, I wring my hands together. I'm here now, so I might as well try to get Jai to take the podcast down, or at least delete the bit about me.

I march up the grey gravel drive and knock on the door. An Asian woman answers; she's in her late fifties and wearing tan trousers, which perfectly match her floral jumper.

'Yes, can I help you?'

'I'm looking for Jai Patel,' I say.

'Jai is my son. I'll get him for you,' she replies, stepping aside to let me in.

He lives with his parents. My game plan to appeal to his father-ethics shrivels into nothingness.

Jai's mum goes upstairs. I hear voices. A minute later, a young man follows her downstairs. Jai is about twenty. He is wearing an old Cure T-shirt and has thick stubble manipulated into a devilish soul-patch with matching moustache. Grabbing him by his chin, his mum tuts. Wriggling from her grasp, Jai whines like a puppy. His mum gives me a withering look.

'Can I get you a drink?' she asks.

'I'm good, thank you.' I smile at her.

Jai's mum walks down the hall and disappears through a door.

'What can I do for you?' Jai stares at me.

I stare back.

After I stretch the silence between us as taut as it will get, I declare, 'I'm Cherrie Forrester.'

'Oh, snap!' He puts his hands to his mouth and steps away from me, almost falling up his stairs.

'I'm here . . .'

'You're finally here for an interview, right? Man, it would have been nice if you had called ahead; but, hey, a journalist's life is always busy like this, right? We can record it in my bedroom.'

He records here? How easy is it to start a podcast anyway? 'I've not come for an interview. I need you to take down your podcast.'

'No way, I'm getting too many subscribers. I'm probably gonna bag a job out of this. Something local, but it's a stepping stone.'

'I don't give a damn about your job prospects; you are ruining my life. I was just a kid when my dad did what he did, and my mum was never involved. I changed my name to escape the media shitstorm back then. I've now carved out a new life for myself. I have a son now. You need to delete any mention of me from *The Flesh on the Bones*.' I move towards him, and he backs away. Moving up on the first step of the staircase, he looms over me.

'Don't get all salty on me. You can't suppress the truth.'

'I'm not suppressing the truth; I'm stopping your lies. Your conjecture. You sensationalising a tragedy.'

'Yeah, it might help find Thomas Doncaster, though.' Jai steps down, pushes past me and goes into his living room. He grabs a bright blue laptop and fires it up. 'Look, I want to show you the new graphics for the website.'

'You think he's still alive? Thomas is long gone. Some kids never get found,' I yell at him, then realise that's the exact opposite of what I've been telling myself, and everyone else. Anger has forced out the truth.

Jai cocks his head. 'Is that what you believe? Or is it what you know?'

'What? Are you seriously accusing me of taking Thomas Doncaster?'

'Naw, man. Just reading the room.'

'What room? There's only two of us here, you bloody idiot.'

Jai drops his expression into a sarcastic smirk. 'Okay, dial back the salt; so you didn't take the Doncaster kid, but someone did. If your son was missing, you'd want me to raise awareness.'

'My son? How dare you. You've already endangered my life, and my son's life, with your bullshit. What do you think will happen to my son when people start talking?'

'People are already talking,' Jai says. 'That was the point of the podcast. It's the point of all true crime podcasts.'

'And most podcasts are great, hell some have even solved cold cases. But that's not what you're doing here. You're recording a dirty gossip-rag of a podcast.'

'No need to get personal, Leigh-Ann.'

'You already got personal. Now delete my name from your podcast.'

'I can't delete you. I'd have to re-record the whole second episode.'

'Oh no, one more hour of your life taken up. Whatever will you do?' I'm losing my argument through anger and sarcasm. I need to get back on track, maybe hit him where it hurts. 'I will sue you. Let's see how many newspapers or TV channels want you when you're being sued for libel and reckless endangerment. The police might even arrest you. Revealing my identity has to be against the GDPR law. Not sure how many podcasts you'll be able to record in prison.' I highly doubt any of what I just said is true, but lies got me here, maybe lies can get me out.

'Okay, okay. I get it. I'm sorry, okay.' He puts his hands up. I see biro scrawls creeping vine-like across his skin. Notes of something – is it the next episode? I strain to read them. Suddenly, he puts his arms behind his back like a mischievous child.

'Where did you get the information from, anyway?' I ask.

'Your social worker. I caught up with him a few months before he died. The guy had a mega file on you and your family. He'd retired before the big GDPR scare. I think he was a bit obsessed with you; said you'd changed your name to Cherrie Forrester. It only took a short internet search to find you worked at that food place in town. There was an article on your shop being the only independent family-owned shop left in the town centre. You were cited in the photo.'

I remember that day. Silly me, being excited to be in the newspaper for something good. I'd smiled at the camera as if my past was clean.

'Re-record the episode and delete the mention about me.'

'No, actually I won't do that.'

He knows I'm bluffing. I can't sue Jai or call the police. Also, if I try, I'd be revealing even more of my past, and giving him more exposure to boot. I was relying on his fear, maybe even his decency, to help me. Right now, I've cultivated neither.

Jai stares at me, fully aware there is nothing I can do to stop him, or his podcast's quest to ruin my life. It's not as if he has a boss I can speak to. Oh, but he kind of does. There's one more card left to play.

I push past him and head through the door where his mum is cooking in their kitchen. She looks shocked to see me, yet good manners demand she smile.

'Your son is ruining my life. I'm an innocent person, and he is ruining my life. I hope you know what sort of man you've brought into this world.'

If I'd heard those words about Robin, I'd be mortified.

'What? What have you done, Jai?' she asks, looking past me at the sheepish wannabe journalist.

'I'm speaking the truth, Mum. It's the podcast I've been working on.'

'Your son has broadcast my personal details to the world.

Thanks to this revelation, I now have a stalker. My family is in danger.'

'Oh, my.' Mrs Patel puts her palms up to her face. She walks towards me, takes my hands and cups them gently. 'I'm so sorry. He'll stop what he's doing. Won't you, Jai.' A testament rather than a question.

Jai lifts his hands to protest, but then nods instead.

'Thank you, Mrs Patel,' I say.

I push past Jai, continuing my momentum out of their front door. Behind me, I hear her yelling at him.

With any luck, the last card I played will be the one that wins me this game.

Chapter 12

Fortunately, I sweep into my usual parking spot just outside the school, so don't need to stand at the school gates. Robin jumps into the car, then fumbles his shoes off.

'What did you do today at school?'

Robin's grin grows as he regales me with what he learnt from each lesson, which of his friends ate what at lunch, and informs me that Nostrom has recommended he try out for the football team next week. Nostrom has a lot to answer for.

When we pull onto the drive, Robin suddenly stutters into silence. His lips disappear into a soft gummy line.

'What's wrong?' I ask.

'Anya at school found a flyer on her mum's car this morning and brought it in to show everyone. There was a missing boy on it. What happened to him?'

'I'm not sure, sweetie.'

'I hope he comes back soon. I bet his mum and dad are worried. You'd be worried about me, right?'

Tears sting my eyes. 'Of course, sweetie, but nothing will ever happen to you.'

Suddenly, I remember Mariah's words of warning, but quickly, I push them from my mind. I have more significant problems right now than a crazy fraud who reckons frightening people is funny.

I make dinner and Robin seems to forget about Thomas Doncaster. He plays with his robot costume and reads his science book aloud to Nostrom.

Leo comes home just before I'm about to leave for my shift. He hugs me, then − as if it isn't the most earth-shattering question ever spoken − he asks, 'Who does that dark car belong to, the one parked on the street outside?'

I rush to the window and see it pulling away. I should say something. Perhaps now is the right time to tell him about the dad who'd appeared on our doorstep, maybe even about my own father.

'Whoever it is, they're probably visiting the neighbours.' I regret each word as they fall from my lips. I should say something, anything just to start the painful task of unravelling the ball of secrets and lies I've created, yet I still can't heave out the right words. Perhaps, with my name deleted from the podcast, things could settle down. The gossiping mums at school will soon have another obsession. No one I love has mentioned the podcast or Mr Bones. Maybe the whole six degrees thing is crap. Kevin Bacon will never know.

'They must be good friends with the neighbours. That's three times I've seen that car around here. Nice model too. We should buy a new car when I sign the Hackerwood building contract.' Leo takes off his trainers and places them next to Robin's school shoes by the door.

'I need to get to work. I have the late shift.' I go to leave, but Robin grabs my hand.

'We're still going to the fair tomorrow, right? I told everyone in school we're going. Nostrom is really, really, really looking forward to it.'

'Sure, but I want to eat before we go out, okay?'

'But I'll still get hot dogs and cotton candy?'

'Yes, but only if you share your treats with me.'

Robin sighs. 'Let's shake on it.' He extends a hand out for me to shake as if he's just completed a business deal.

'Have a good shift,' Leo calls out from the kitchen.

Waving, I leave before I hear him moan about having leftover chicken for dinner.

Tonight, I walk to work, checking each street for the dark car driven by my stalker, but I don't see him.

The shop is busy for a while; I serve several customers in a row. Backstage, Tracy is slowly doing stocktake.

It takes less than an hour for everything to calm down. A big meat delivery then appears, so we both start to unpack it.

'Hey, did some guy ask about me the other day?' I enquire as casually as I can.

'Tall, good-looking and only slightly past his sell-by date?'

'That's the one.'

'Yeah, I told him you weren't in. Oh, is there something you want to tell me? Are you playing away?' Tracy waggles her eyebrows.

'No! Nothing like that. He's kind of stalking me.'

'What? Cherry Pie, you should have told me. I'd have radioed it in. Got his ass capped by security.'

'It's not like that. He thinks I can help him with something.'

'Then help him.'

'But I can't. He only *thinks* I can help.' Things would be easier if I could tell Tracy everything; blurt out about me, my dad, what he did, the podcast and the shit I've been going through lately, but I can't. She's my best friend, I need her, and I'm unsure as to how she would react if she heard the truth about me.

For a moment, Tracy ponders what little she knows. 'He probably just fancies you. Tell him you're happy with Leo.'

I stop lifting pork chops onto the counter. 'Please, if he comes in again, just don't talk to him. Can you tell Gurpreet and Shania too?'

'Okay. No worries. We'll go all Chinese wall. He'll get the message. Or, perhaps Shania can *help him.*' She waggles her eyebrows again.

I spend the rest of my shift chatting nonsense with Tracy. I'm tempted to at least tell her about Mariah coming to the house, but even those words jam in my throat. She'd probably let it slip to Leo the next time he picks me up from work, and right now I want this whole thing shoved under the rug, even if it makes an unsightly lump.

Mr Dawson arrives at 8 p.m. and helps us lock up. He looks beaten down, and this random appearance in the shop is unusual. Mostly, our boss lets us do everything on our own. We're a family here, and he trusts us. He claims he's at work because he's bored. Maybe his wife has dumped him and he's desperate to get out of the house;

that could be why we have auditors in. They would need to value the business if he was teetering on the edge of a divorce. Maybe I won't lose my job and everything will turn out fine after all.

I buy dinner for tomorrow and a care package for Kylie, only she's a no-show. I don't have her mobile number or address. Maybe she went into labour. I leave her bag backstage, and Tracy promises to give it to her if she sees her tomorrow. As I go to get my bag and coat, I notice my best friend putting a packet of nappies next to it.

Tracy drives me home; all the while, I watch for dark cars, but see none. The only vehicles on my street are the ones belonging to my neighbours.

By the time I get home, Leo has put Robin to bed and is beavering away in the extension. The noise I heard before stopped after Leo started work again; no doubt it was all in my mind anyway. I want to casually open the door to say hey; get a quick, accidental nosey at the fruits of his labours, but I don't — we should all be allowed a secret or seven.

I don't go to bed. Instead, I make popcorn and watch a couple of *Grey's Anatomy* episodes. Soon, my real-life problems blend with the flimsy imaginary ones of the ditsy doctor until everything feels trivial; that is until I turn off the TV and thoughts of reality wallop me over the head, reminding me the worst can and probably will happen.

Before going to bed, I check *The Flesh on the Bones*, but it's not there.

Chapter 13

I search for the podcast, but I can't find it. I stumble over a few cooking websites, a slightly disturbing blog about theoretical cannibalism, but there's nothing else. I go back to the local news article and try the links. They're all broken. Well, hooray for meddling mothers. You rock, Mrs Patel, for telling that selfish son of yours to act like a decent human being. She must have made him take it down. No more secrets, no more podcasts, no more subscribers. As long as my six degrees of separation only spread two or three degrees to gossip-mongering mums at the school gates, I'm home free. Everything should calm down now, my past digitally buried by the next scandal.

Logging on to my emails, I see I have something from Jai. I open it to find a short apology for revealing my identity. It's almost rude in its brevity. Still, it makes me smile. A sense of justice sweeps over me as I log off my computer.

Upstairs, I check on Robin. I watch him sleep for a bit. It's a little creepy, especially if he wakes up to find me staring at him, but watching the gentle rise and fall of his chest is comforting. It probably goes back to when he was a baby. I was so paranoid he'd stop breathing in the night that I barely slept at all.

Eventually, I go to bed. Leo is snoring and taking up more than his fair share of the covers, but I don't mind. Life is good. It is back to normal again.

Curled up on the edge of my bed, I fall into a deep, dreamless sleep.

Waking up, I look over at the clock. It's past eight; Leo has let me sleep in and has taken Robin to school. I turn over to see a note on the pillow. It's a drawing of a robot and a little boy standing in front of a big red Ferris wheel. The colouring escapes all the lines, and the smiles on the two subjects are too big for their faces. On the back, scrawled in red crayon, it reads, *Nostrom and me at the fair.*

I get up and take a shower. Maybe I should let Robin wear the robot costume tonight. What harm could it do? It might be fun to go to the fair with a robot.

Once dressed, I place Robin's drawing on the fridge. I grab a quick bowl of cereal, then watch another episode of *Grey's Anatomy*. My phone beeps and I find a text from Shania, but all it reads is *Kylie* and an unreadable emoji. I text her back to say I can't read what she's sent, so she tells me Kylie is at Dawson's Food and says thanks for her stuff. I text back that I'll see them both soon, but before the message leaves my phone, Shania asks if I've been to the fair yet. I tell her I'm going tonight, and I'll let her know how it is.

Robin won't need picking up until three, so I flip onto the news to check out the weather for tonight. I'm staring at a prediction of clear skies with a potential ground frost, trying to work out what the Fahrenheit is for the Celsius, when an urgent news story flashes onto the screen.

The police have found Thomas Doncaster's body.

Swearing, I turn up the volume just in time to hear the newscaster say, 'Police discovered the body early this morning in an industrial estate on the edge of town. He was bludgeoned to death. Although found fully clothed, his trainers were missing. The police are treating the death as suspicious.'

Rolling this new information around in my head, ideas like shadowy tumbleweeds begin to form. I feel awful for the parents, but at least they know the fate of their son and can look for the bastard who did it. There's no mention of bones, or anything remotely similar to my dad's dark deeds, so that's something at least. The police won't release all the relevant information to the press, but fortunately, the little they have freely shared makes me sure Thomas Doncaster has nothing to do with my family tree.

After making lunch, I settle back down in front of the TV. I try to get into the medical drama, but the image of poor Thomas Doncaster lying shoeless, covered with dirt and lorry fumes, clouds my thoughts. Over an hour slips by like this. An untouched chicken sandwich on my lap, a now-blank TV screen in front of me. I look at my phone and see three text messages. Tracy, Gurpreet, and Shania. They've all seen the news about Thomas's body. I then realise why I can't let this go: Mariah was right. She said that he came to her shoeless and coughing on car fumes. Does this mean she is for real? Could her prediction about Robin being in danger be real too? I look for her telephone number online and quickly find her website. I call. Jon answers the phone.

'Can I speak with Mariah?' I ask.

'Who is this?'

'It's Cherrie Forrester. You came round . . .'

'Yes, I remember you. Can we help?'

He's heard the news about Thomas; I can hear the righteous indignation in his voice.

'I just wanted to ask Mariah something about my little boy. She said he was in danger.'

There's a rustling sound. I hear Mariah's voice. 'Cherrie?'

'Yes, it's me. I'm sorry I was weird with you the other day, but I'm sure you've come across other people like me.'

'You're not alone. Many people are troubled with darkness.'

'Pardon? I meant I was sceptical.'

'Even sceptics can have dark and sticky clouds clinging to their future.'

'What?' I hold my breath waiting for her to explain. I don't like the image of something shadowy glued to my future. Who would? And I'm an expert in dark and sticky things. My dad made sure of it.

'You want to know what danger your son is in. You want to be forewarned so you can be forearmed?'

'Yes.'

'Come over to my house; bring your little bird Robin. I'll do a reading for you both. We'll get to the bottom of this danger. Unstick the darkness.'

That would cost £50. If Dawson's Food is really in trouble, I can't justify the cost.

Sensing my hesitation, she says, 'There'll be no charge. Your little bird is very special. Come over tonight.'

'Oh, damn. I promised Robin we'd go to the fair at Black Friars Park tonight.'

'Sarah loves fairs. I understand. Come tomorrow night.'

'Okay, thank you,' I say.

Mariah hangs up on me.

My dad is locked away. He's not guilty of Thomas's murder, but there could be another killer out there – one just as wicked as him. A terrible creature looking for another boy to take back to his lair, and what if he has his sights set on Robin? What if this killer is the dark and sticky thing clinging to my future?

I text Tracy about my fear that Robin could be in danger, along with Mariah's kind offer of free readings. She texts back that she'll come with us to the psychic's house tomorrow. I feel better for that, for being proactive. While on my phone, I decide to set up a Google Alert for convicted sex offenders, and child kidnappers on my estate plus the two neighbouring ones. You shouldn't just rely on psychics when there is a wealth of information online. I realise the irony with *The Flesh on the Bones*, but quickly shrug it off.

While driving to school, I wonder if I should cancel tonight's trip to the fair. Wrap Robin up in a blanket, plonk him in front of the TV surrounded by his own weight in sweets and crisps; let him safely marinate in sugar and trans-fats until I get to speak with Mariah. Yet, when he gets in the car, wrestles off his shoes, and looks over at me with his face alight with joy, I realise cancelling is not an option. Anyway, the fair is just a short walk from the house. He'll be with me the whole time.

★

Dinner is a quick stir-fry. I watch as Robin eats the noodles and bean sprouts by wrapping them around his fork like spaghetti.

'Mummy, can I please wear the robot costume tonight?' he asks again as he takes his empty plate into the kitchen.

I think about it for a moment, then decide on a compromise. 'You can't wear the whole thing, it'll be too bulky for the rides, but how about part of it?'

I go to the robot costume and pick off one of the sparkly red buttons. Looking over at Robin, I say, 'How about having an on-off switch. You'll then look like one of those synthetic human androids.'

Robin gives me a suspicious look, but still runs across to grab the cardboard button. He picks up his red Puffa jacket, then slips the piece of painted cardboard into a pocket. He narrows his eyes at me. 'If I had an off switch, would you use it, Mum?'

I smile at him. 'Maybe. If you refused to eat your carrots, I could turn you off, open your mouth, and feed you baby-bird style. I'll even coat them in cheese spread so they slide down easier.'

'Ewwwww, gross.' Robin turns his back on me.

'What are you doing?'

Grinning, he spins back around. 'My button is in one of my pockets, but now you don't know which one it's in.' He pokes his tongue out at me, then carefully lays his jacket over the couch. 'This way, you can't turn me off and feed me vegetables.'

'Oh, you're too clever for me.' I chuckle.

We wash up the dishes and watch TV for a little while. I avoid putting on the news. I don't want to hear any more about poor Thomas Doncaster; I don't want Robin to see anything about it either.

Leo isn't back from work yet and hasn't sent a text to say he'll be late. Usually, I receive an alien face emoji accompanied by a short explanation. I shrug it off but take my phone off silent mode. It'll be loud at the fair and I don't want to miss Leo's text.

When it's time to go, Robin slips his jacket back on. It makes him look like a giant tomato. I can see the glitter from the makeshift robot button dotted around his left pocket.

Reaching for the door handle, I have second thoughts about going out tonight. Robin would eventually get over being disappointed and it's better safe than sorry. Even as I think it, I realise it's a terrible cliché. All I have to back up my craziness is paranoia and one vaguely correct prediction from a woman calling herself a psychic. Thomas's death could have easily been a good guess. Yet, the shoeless thing. But you hear stories all the time about so-called psychics playing the odds; she did spout a lot of nonsense too. She didn't even know who I really am, which would have definitely come up if she was for real. I'm being silly again. Just because something terrible could happen, it's still highly doubtful it will. I've spent years of worrying about my past, worries that never materialised into anything.

'Mum?'

I can't disappoint Robin on an unsubstantiated whim. 'Let's go, sweetie.'

As we leave the house, I look up to see a black car parked across the street. I blink at it. At six o'clock, I can only see by randomly lit streetlights. Not parked near any particular house, the car idles by the kerb. I squint. Someone is inside on the driver side; I can see their outline like a jagged shadow.

Robin grips my hand and tugs on it. He wants to get to the fair, but I need to find out if this is all in my mind, or whether it's part of Mariah's prediction. If I can just get a look at the person in the driver seat, see if it's my stalker or someone else . . .

I slip my hand out of my son's grip.

'Wait here by the front door,' I tell him.

He nods at me.

Striding across the road, I fortify myself to confront the dark car's owner.

Chapter 14

As I get within a few feet of the car, its engine roars. It pulls away from the kerb and aims itself at me. I stumble backwards out of its way. As I watch it speed up the road, I kick myself for not looking into the driver's window to see who was behind the wheel.

'Mummy!'

Robin stands by the front door, his hands on his hips, unfazed by what just happened. 'Nostrom says you shouldn't play in the road. We don't want you to get hurt.'

I should tell Leo about the car when he gets in. In fact, I should sit him down and tell him everything. Open up my secret past with its serial killer father, my present with a psychic who could be the real thing, and my future that might see our son in mortal danger. I look at my phone, but there's still no text from my boyfriend. Where is he? Leo said he'd be home by now.

'Mummy! Come on.'

'Okay, okay, we're going.'

I grip Robin's hand as we walk towards Black Friars

Park. Fortunately, he doesn't notice I'm clinging to him like a *Titanic* survivor to a life raft. He sings as we walk, and points when he sees the Ferris wheel in the distance; its lights make a slow, spooky glow against the dark, like a lazy sparkler. Robin's mouth opens at the sight as if he's about to say something, yet can't form the right words. It's weird, a colossal foreign structure has grown overnight in a place so familiar to us; I'm not surprised my son is overwhelmed.

I tug on his hand, and we stroll past the park's playground.

'Look, Mum, it's where I first met Nostrom. Do you remember?'

I'm not sure I do. In my mind, Nostrom has always been around. Not in a worrying way that indicated Robin has psychological problems, but in a comfortable childish way. Nostrom helps my son enjoy math and science. Every little boy should have an imaginary robot friend.

'Can we stop to play on the swings?'

I hesitate. It would be nice to linger a little; the sky is clear and there's only a slight chill in the air. I can hear the faraway beat of the music coming from the fair – although, the sooner we get there, the sooner we can get back home.

'Not right now, sweetie. We can play on the swings any time.'

My little boy's bottom lip trembles. 'Please, just for a little while.'

'Maybe tomorrow, eh? Crazy Clive is only here for a few days. Don't you want to go to the fair while it's still here?'

'That's a good point, Mum.' He dramatically points to

the lights of the Ferris wheel. 'To the fair!' he declares with a grin.

Laughing at my son, who seems destined to be an actor, we rush past the playground, the music from the fair getting louder the closer we get.

I keep vigilant for dark cars near the park. So far, I see none. Maybe the car before was nothing to do with my problems. The world doesn't revolve around me. Perhaps it was someone checking up on the neighbours. A jilted ex-lover, a worried spouse, or even a government benefits team waiting to catch the woman down the road without her walking stick.

The nearer we get to the fair, the calmer I become. It wouldn't be the first time a worry has festered in my mind out of all proportion. I will still tell Leo about the car and the stalker when we get in, just not about my past. His sound, logical mind will outweigh my crazy one.

Robin is so excited when we cross Crazy Clive's threshold that he bounces along beside me like Tigger. I feel it too. It's like stepping into another world. The smell of salted popcorn and sweet cotton candy suppresses the park's scent of nature. Overpowering pop music pulses through a massive speaker system, and the sound of laughter is everywhere. Scattered around us are several rides, but just one ticket booth. The line for the booth is fortunately short, which is good because I'm not sure my arm could take much more tugging from Robin. I get us ten tickets for five rides together. We decide to go on the Twirling Tea Cups first.

Running the ride is a teenager dressed in cropped cargo trousers and a ripped black T-shirt with goose bumps decorating his rail-thin arms. With the kind of boredom only teenage boys can muster, he waves us through. We climb into a chipped blue patterned cup on our own. The ride reminds me of Mariah's motley china collection that decorated her reading room. The cup is so large, even I feel small in it; it must overwhelm Robin. I look over at him, expecting a worried face.

'This is awesome!' Robin's smile is so big it reaches his hairline.

The teenager pulls down a creaking metal bar, which barely reaches Robin's lap. Before I can query it, he lollops off and starts the ride. Our cup spins almost instantly. My arm instinctively shoots out to hold Robin back.

Around and around we go. I quickly regret eating before we left. I haven't felt like this since I was pregnant with morning sickness. I should have let Mrs Duffill come with us. I could have sat on a bench and watched her swirled and pulled around until she primly vomited.

Somewhere in the heart of the ride, there is piano music playing; an old tune I've heard before, but can't remember. It's hard to listen to it through the squealing of the ride itself. I am so grateful when the whole thing stops that I laugh aloud.

'Again!' screams Robin.

'We can't ride again, sweetie. Other people want to have a go,' I explain, and we wait for the black-shirted teenager to pull up the bar, which bruised my ribs, and free us.

A dad with his young daughter swaps places with us. I make eye contact with him. We nod to each other with that unspoken parental camaraderie.

I have four more rides to go.

Just like his dad, Robin has an analytical mind; he

investigates all the nearby attractions before choosing the next ride; the Ghost Train. It's dark inside, and with the air cloaked in cloying dry ice it takes a while for my eyes to adjust. As the cart squeaks along the tracks, I spy fair workers dressed in Halloween costumes jumping out at the people in front of us. There are screams followed by laughter.

Movement. Someone is approaching our cart. I grip hold of Robin.

'Don't be scared, Mum. It's all make-believe.'

As we slow down, an errant skeleton in a top hat jumps into the back of the cart with us. Fear slams into my body, but I can't get out of the ride; darkness cloaks my surroundings. Grabbing Robin, I yank him over me to my other side, as far from the skeleton as possible.

Unperturbed by my reaction the skeleton asks, 'Are you enjoying the ride?' His accent reminiscent of The Count from *Sesame Street*, more vampire than skeleton.

'It's awesome!' Robin replies.

The skeleton looks happy; when he grins, his bursting toothy smile creases the sides of his mouth, cracking his white make-up mask.

The skeleton brings with him a sweet musky smell. A normal person with a normal past might be fooled into thinking this is what a decaying corpse smells like – it's not.

'What's your name, boy?' The voice is deep and the accent is even worse when he says more than a few words. He's dressed in a morning suit, with a top hat and frilly black trimmings, but you can see his painted white bones glowing in the dark beneath the clothes.

'Robin.'

The skeleton puts his head back and indulges in a long, slow laugh ending in a cackle. 'Good to meet you, Robin. Don't tell Batman I'm here. See you real soon.' He fist-bumps Robin and my stomach churns as they touch. I reach up to slap him away from my son, but he jumps back out of the way as the track veers towards the exit. 'See you soon,' he repeats and lifts his hat with a bow. Robin waves back, but I don't. Adults who dress up as something they're not give me the creeps. When dressed as someone else it gives you licence to act differently, almost as if it's not you anymore. As if you can leave your stray, uncharacteristic actions tucked in the pocket of the costume when you take it off at the end of the night.

'I told you skeletons were cool,' Robin says.

I grunt at him.

We stop between rides to eat blue and pink cotton candy. We take one of each and play blind taste tests with the different colours. Robin is convinced the blue is raspberry flavoured and the pink is strawberry. I suspect they are just different food dyes. During the taste test, he drops pink floss down his red jacket, making it sticky.

'Look, horses!' Robin points at the Carousel. Like the Tea Cups, it has its own music. The closer we get, the more we can hear its sharp, old-fashioned piano tune over the fair's pop music. It's an old ride. I remember Dad taking me to a steam fair where we both rode on a similar carousel. There's no queue, so we give up our tickets and climb aboard. I go to straddle a horse with Robin, but he pushes me away.

'I'm old enough to ride alone,' he whines.

The ride only goes round in a circle. He can't get off and no one can get on, so I let him ride his horse alone.

I climb up onto an angry-looking mare behind him. Its eyes are wild and its nostrils are large; as if it has figured out it'll never manage to go anywhere, and will never stop jumping up and down and going around and around, no matter how fast it gallops. I keep my eyes on the back of Robin's red coat. He's waving his arms about, talking to Nostrom. I see it from time to time. He has a brief discussion about something he's worried about and good ol' Nostrom steps in to fortify my boy's strength.

'Both hands on the horse,' I yell at him, earning a sour side-glance.

As the ride jolts forward, Robin yelps. I almost dismount to rescue him until I realise it's a noise of excitement rather than panic. He waves at the crowd gathering around the ride. I yell at him again, 'Hold on with both hands, sweetie.'

The music and motion of the ride are almost hypnotic. I close my eyes as my hair whips up in the artificial wind. I feel oddly relaxed. Mariah has to be wrong. Did I really think psychics were real? Everything is fine. I'm having a good time with my son. Opening my eyes, I see Robin is waving again. I'm about to yell at him when I see a flash of someone in the crowd. I can't tell who it is, or even what they look like, but for some reason I have a sinking feeling.

The Carousel rotates around again. I sit up on my horse, cup my hands over my eyes, and scan the gathered people.

'Both hands on the horse, Mummy!' Robin shouts back at me, and then giggles.

I laugh and then yell back, 'Quit looking at me and watch where your horse is going.' The ride repeatedly rotates until it slows to a stop. We dismount and Robin runs over to me. As my feet hit the ground, I feel woozy. With as much effort as I can muster, I check out the fair-goers around us one final time, but don't see anyone I recognise. Maybe I've eaten too many sweets and gone on too many rides. Your senses can only take so much.

'Where to next?' Robin asks, his eyes on a kiosk full of candy apples. I buy him a chocolate one; he devours it as if he hasn't eaten in a week, even eating the core. I have to stop myself from making him vomit up the apple seeds in case he's in danger of arsenic poisoning.

Walking back in the direction of the Ghost Train, we see people gathering for the Ferris wheel. We join the back of the line.

As we move to the front of the queue, I look up at the massive steel construction with its peeling paint and blinking fairy lights. My stomach drops, it looks like the very definition of a death trap. I want to back out of this ride, but if I do, I will disappoint Robin. The wheel stops and people move forward to fill each cart. As we get towards the front, my phone beeps. I look down. There's a message from Leo.

'Tickets!' shouts another teenage boy in yet another ripped black T-shirt; it must be their uniform. You'd think they'd wear something warmer.

'Hang on,' I say.

Robin insisted on holding his own tickets; secretly, I hope he's lost them and we don't have to go on this ride after all. Dashing my hopes, he passes his ticket over. While putting my hand in my pocket to retrieve my ticket, I glance at my phone. On the screen in capital letters, I see the words *MR BONES*.

My ticket flutters onto the ground. The family behind

me tut and huff. I grab Robin's arm, pulling him out of the queue.

'Mummmm,' he whines. 'I want to go on the wheel.'

I look back down to see my phone has flashed onto standby. I have to put in my PIN code to get Leo's full message back up.

'Mum!'

The dad from the Tea Cups is queuing too. He looks over at me and says, 'He can come with us if you like.' His little girl waves at Robin and blushes.

'Mum, no, I want to go with you.'

'Thanks, but it's okay,' I say to the dad.

My phone has a black screen again. I plug in my PIN and read the message.

I know about MR BONES. Why didn't you tell me?

'Mum!'

I look down at Robin. 'Will you be quiet for one minute!'

Robin gives me the stink-eye.

It's happening now. In the middle of a bloody fairground, the life I so carefully built is crashing down around me. It feels as if I'm in the centre of an explosion. Heat rises through my body, engulfing my limbs. I can't stand up straight. Bending over, I try to catch my breath. I can't have this conversation here and now on text. It has to be in person, so Leo sees I'm still Cherrie, that I'm not Little Bones.

I text back, *We'll talk when I get in. Please don't be mad.*

Leo texts back straight away, *I'm not mad, I just can't believe you never told me, Leigh-Ann.*

I'm not Leigh-Ann, I'm Cherrie. Please, understand; I was

only 8 when it happened. I lost both my parents; you don't know what it was like.

I look up to smile at Robin, but can't see him. A moment of panic grips me until I see the dad from before pointing up at the Ferris wheel. Robin's red jacket is in one of the carts. He went on by himself. I can't believe he did that.

I wave up at him. He tentatively waves back.

My phone beeps.

Do you still speak with him?

I text back, *No. He's in prison. I haven't seen him for over 25 years. He doesn't even know my name now.*

As I wait for his reply I wonder how Leo found out about me. The podcast may be gone now, but its damage was already done. What an idiot I was to think I was safe. I stare out across the fair at all the families having fun. There's even an elderly couple awkwardly throwing balls at coconuts in the next stand. Would Leo and I make it that far? We've been together ten years; there were only two other boyfriends before him. The first I treated like a rash – I got him, scratched him and got over him. The second guy was in my life for barely a month; I struggle to remember his name now.

At this stage of my life, could I go through it all again with someone else? Tracy is single; she puts on a good show, yet I can see deep down how unhappy she is. I don't want that. Leo may not be perfect, but I'm fully aware of those imperfections, and can handle them; but can he handle mine? He's the father of my child, and he's a great dad. What if he thinks Robin is in danger with me; that I could one day snap and hurt our child? Robin could so easily be taken away.

Looking back down at my phone, I see another text from Leo telling me we'll speak later.

No kisses, no weird emoji my phone can't read. Who am I kidding? I knew this day would come. I've imagined it so many times.

I watch Robin on the wheel. He can probably see for miles at the top; he must be so happy. I can't believe I'm going to wreck everything. He's a sensitive kid. Even if we don't explain what's going on, he'll realise something is wrong.

The ride slows down and I look for Robin. Kids begin to push past me; just my luck he will be the last one to exit. Making my way through the disembarking people, I watch as the last cart slows to a halt by the step. Catching sight of his red jacket, I push forward to hug Robin. When I finally get my arms around my son, I look down to see a strange boy's face. It's not Robin.

Chapter 15

The boy in the red jacket is my son's height, but his face doesn't have freckles or dimples. His eyes are a different colour to Robin's and he's looking at me as if I'm crazy; there's a mixture of embarrassment and fear slapped across his face.

'Have you seen my son? He's wearing a jacket just like yours.'

The kid shrugs, smirks, then runs off into the fair.

Could I have missed Robin coming off the wheel? Did he take his red Puffa off? I try to remember what Robin was wearing under his jacket, yet all I can see is the red. I rush forward and grab the fair worker's arm.

'Where's my son? Did you see my son get off the ride?'

'Hey,' he yells, pulling himself from me. 'What are you talking about?'

'My son went on the ride by himself; he hasn't come off. Is he still up there?'

'Okay, okay. Let me check.' He jabs at buttons like a monkey in a laboratory and carts slowly swing towards us. He checks them one by one. There are groans from the line of people behind me; I'm holding everyone up. I look across the crowd to see if Robin is hiding. Maybe he thinks I'll be mad that he went on the ride alone. I see the dad from earlier. He comes over.

'What's wrong?' he asks.

'My son, he's not here,' I mutter.

'Your son's missing?'

'No, not missing,' I say, yet instantly question what I've said. I don't know where Robin is – he is missing. 'He went on the Ferris wheel alone. Did you see him?'

'He wasn't in our cart. Did you see him, honey?' He looks down at his little girl.

'He was lining up with us,' she offers.

The teenager checks the last cart. Nothing.

'You sure he was on here?' the teen asks.

'Yes, I saw his red jacket. He was . . .' Was he? I saw a red jacket, but the other kid was wearing one too.

'Fuck,' I mutter, and get a disapproving look from the dad as he moves his daughter away from me. 'Robin!' I yell. 'Robin!'

'There's a stand for lost children at the back of the Coconut Shy; ask there,' the teen says, ushering fair-goers onto the wheel. New people are now crawling all over the last place I saw Robin, trampling crucial evidence I might need later. I shouldn't move away from the wheel, but as more people flood onto it, they push me back, so I head towards the Coconut Shy. Would Robin go to a lost child stand? Would someone be kind enough to steer my baby there for me to find? I turn in a circle to locate the Coconut Shy. As I do, I catch sight of a small caravan. The sign outside says, Fortunes Told. I think of Mariah.

She predicted Robin was in danger. How could I be so stupid? His hand should never have left mine.

In a daze, I stagger towards the lost child stand. Operating it is a skinny woman who looks about sixty; she's smoking and drinking from a pink-tinged bottle. I can't see any children. Are they concealed behind her tent, ready to pull out and parade before distressed parents as she croaks, *Is this your child?*

I walk up to her. 'Can you help me, please?'

'Who have you lost?' Her voice is calm as she stubs out her cigarette on the table; the last tendrils of the smoke twist outwards, reaching towards me.

'My son – have you found a little boy?'

'Yes, how old is your son?'

They have Robin. Thank God. I look around.

'How old is your son? Where did you last see him?'

'He's eight. His name is Robin. He was on the Ferris wheel. Can I see him now? Where is he?'

'Sorry, the boy we found tonight was by the Ghost Train. And he's no more than four. Let me put a call out, see if anyone else has found your son.' She picks up a radio and speaks quietly into it. The fair has a loudspeaker nearby; the music is drowning out her whispers. Would Robin go to a fair worker for help? I wish I'd had a plan; told him what to do if we were separated. I'm so stupid. This is my fault.

The woman lights another cigarette and moves towards me. 'No one has seen your son. They'll keep an eye out. Is there somewhere in the fair he wanted to go? Kids usually end up in the place they wanted to go to most.'

I think through her question. 'No, he was choosing the rides.' I shake my head.

I look out at the crowd again. Maybe I'll see his face. Perhaps this is all a massive mistake. I'll laugh about it later . . . The Ghost Train, maybe he went back there. He liked the dapper skeleton.

'The skeleton in the top hat in the Ghost Train. My son might go to him, maybe.'

'Eh?' The woman grunts. 'There's no one dressed as a skeleton in the Ghost Train.'

Chapter 16

Someone dressed as a skeleton has abducted my son.

I pull out my mobile and dial 999. My hand is shaking so much it takes two tries to hit the final number. I ask for the police, then, as calmly as I can, tell them I've lost my son.

The female operator asks, 'Where did you see him last?'

I will my voice to stay calm. 'By the Ferris wheel at Crazy Clive's Fair in Black Friars Park.'

'Where are you now?'

'I'm still there. I'm at the lost child stand at the back of the Coconut Shy. Can you send someone to help me, please?'

'Where is his dad? Are you still together?'

'His dad is at home. Yes, we are still together.' I hope.

More questions follow and my answers string together like beads on a heavy, ugly necklace.

'Has he ever run away before?'

'No, Robin is a good boy.'

'Did you argue with him today?'

'No, no, not really.'

'Not really?'

I cringe as I reply, 'He wanted to wear his Halloween costume to the fair, but I said no.'

'Do you live near the fair?'

'Yes, a ten-minute walk.'

'Would he go back home for the costume?'

My head is hurting. I drop the phone, and stumble around in a circle trying to catch a glimpse of Robin in the crowd. This has to be a mistake. Hearing the distant voice of the operator, I pick my phone back up. She speaks, but I understand nothing. I recognise the sounds, not the words.

'Please, just call the police. They need to come here,' I finally push out.

'I have already dispatched them. There's a unit on its way to you now. I'm recording this, so keep talking. Keep giving me information.'

'Okay,' I say.

'You're not married to the father?'

'What does that matter?'

'Most children are taken by people they know. Estranged parents, grandparents and the like.'

'Leo didn't take Robin.'

'Where in the fair are you now?'

'I already told you, I'm at the back of the Coconut Shy.'

Sirens. I head towards them, my phone hanging limply in my fist. I can barely hear the woman on the other end now. She asks, 'Has he ever run away before?'

'He hasn't run away; the skeleton has him. The skeleton!' I sound crazy. My voice is distant to me; it's as if it's not coming from me at all.

I'm about to drop my phone again when I see a policeman barrelling towards me.

'Cherrie Forrester?'

'Yes. My son is missing. Please help me.' I all but fall into this strange man's chest.

'It's all right. We're looking for Robin now. I'm DC Kimmings. Do you have a recent photo?'

I scroll through the photos on my phone. The last picture I took was one of Robin on our holiday in Devon over a year ago. He's wearing swimming trunks on the beach, stray sand dusts his hair, and he's wielding a red plastic spade.

'Ummm, is this okay?' I show the policeman my phone. 'It's from last summer.'

'Last summer?' He gives me an odd look.

'There are more photos at home,' I add quickly, although it's a lie. There are no other photos. Leo isn't a big photo taker either. I don't think he even owns a picture of me taken in the last four years.

'Your son's full name?'

'Robin Leo Duffill.'

'And the last time you saw him, was here at the fair?'

'Yes, I said that already,' I whine and have to stop from stamping my foot like an ill-tempered child.

'Where in the fair, exactly?'

I point over to the wheel behind the Coconut Shy; it's still slowly spinning around. Why haven't they stopped it?

'What were you doing?'

I was texting – that sounds bad. I wasn't watching my son. 'I didn't want to go on the ride; he went on by himself,' I finally push out.

'You saw him on the ride?'

'Yes, he waved at me.'

'So, you lost him after he went on the Ferris wheel?'

Did I see Robin? I saw the red jacket. Leo's texts distracted me. However, I've already told DC Kimmings I saw him. 'He never came off the ride.'

'What? He couldn't have gotten off, though. The ride doesn't stop.'

He doesn't believe me. 'I saw a red jacket, but when I approached the boy coming off the ride, it was someone else; it wasn't Robin. I waited for him, but he never got off the ride.'

DC Kimmings looks up at the Ferris wheel. 'Are you sure you saw him on there in the first place? If I ask the fair worker running it, will he be able to confirm your son got on the ride?'

'I think so.' I'm losing my credibility. I can't even get the pattern of events that just happened straight in my mind. Wait, the dad with the little girl – there was someone else who saw us in line. 'There was a man with his daughter in line near us. He can tell you.'

'Did you get his name?'

'No, I didn't get his name. I didn't know I'd need it later for a police interview,' I yell and notice everyone at the fair is now looking at us. Some have their mobiles lifted as if I am a special sideshow for their entertainment.

'Okay, okay. I understand. Do you live near here?'

'Yes, on Rockingham Drive; it's part of the Oak Cross Estate.'

He speaks into his radio and then turns to me. 'Let's get you home. Your son could be there already.'

'He's not at home. Listen to me. There was a skeleton on the Ghost Train. He was talking to us. The lady at the

154

booth . . .' I grab DC Kimmings' arm, and I drag him towards the chain-smoking fair worker. 'She claims they don't have a skeleton on the Ghost Train.'

The policeman allows me to push him towards the booth. 'Is this correct, ma'am? Did you say there are no skeletons on the Ghost Train? Could someone who doesn't work here gain access to your rides?'

The woman slowly puts out her latest cigarette. 'Our security is tight. Course there's skeletons on the Ghost Train.'

'That's not what you said,' I butt in.

'It's understandable you don't remember what I said.'

'My memory is fine, you condescending bitch.'

The skinny woman reacts as if no one has ever called her bitch before, all wide-eyed and flustered.

'Let's keep this civil,' says DC Kimmings. 'I want information on your security on the Ghost Train. If the skeleton isn't one of your workers, could someone break into your ride?'

'No one broke in. Why wouldn't there be skeletons on the Ghost Train?' She then lays her beady eyes on me. 'Come on, dear. You're in shock. Let us help you.' The woman reaches to pat my arm. I slap her nicotine-stained fingers away.

'All right. Calm down.' DC Kimmings stands between the booth and me. 'I've been called out on more cases of kids going missing than I've had hot dinners. They usually turn up. We need to get you home now.'

'They don't usually turn up. What about Thomas Doncaster? He didn't turn up. Alive anyway.'

He twitches at Thomas's name. 'I understand how you feel, but let's get you home, okay?'

'Home? I need to search the fair. Robin could still be here. What about the car park?' I rush past the policeman and begin banging into people as I sprint on rubbery legs towards the makeshift car park at the bottom of the fair.

As I get to the first line of cars, I see police blocking the exit. They are checking each vehicle as it leaves, but there are so few cars. Black Friars is in the centre of three neighbouring estates. Most people could have easily walked to the fair.

'Are you checking all the exits?' I ask the policeman as he catches up with me.

'Please, Robin is probably already at home waiting for you.'

'No, he's not. You have to believe me. The skeleton took my son.'

The DC nods and speaks into his radio. 'Search the Ghost Train from top to bottom. Talk to me about their security. Check how easy it would be for someone to break in.'

'Thank you.'

'It's just a precaution. I'm sure it's not as bad as you think.'

Yeah, sometimes, it isn't as bad as you think. Sometimes it's worse.

The police radio crackles. 'Ghost Train looks clear.'

'Secure the exits, just in case,' DC Kimmings says.

The whole park is one big exit. Each side bleeding into a different housing estate. They can't keep track of it all. The skeleton could have already slipped out, Robin unconscious over his shoulder. Shuddering, I imagine the growing grin across the abductor's face. Dad smiled when he would take his victims home; it was the only smile of his I tried to forget.

I need more help than the police can give. Even though I have no idea what I'll say, I have to call Leo. Picking up my phone, I scroll to my contacts, but stop. It feels like, if I say Robin is missing aloud to him, it becomes real. Yet arriving in a police car won't be good either. I text, *Is Robin with you?*

I stare at my phone, waiting for a reply. DC Kimmings guides me into the back of his car, like a criminal. People are looking at me as if I've done something wrong. But I have committed a crime, I'm a shit mother. My son is lost because I wasn't watching him. I was too busy hiding my secrets to stop someone taking my child. The worry of my exposed past now feels so trivial against losing Robin, it's laughable.

The car rumbles and we slowly edge out of the park. I imagine the ghost of a headless nun and an angry monk, looking on at me from the dark tree line, judging my loss. Then I remember what Robin said before the fair. He wanted to play on the swings where he met Nostrom.

'The play area of the park. We need to check it. Robin might be there.'

The police officer slows to park near a hedge. 'Okay, let's check the play area.'

Chapter 17

From the back of the police car, I can make out the eerie, motionless swings in the dark. As a reminder that kids shouldn't be playing at this time of night, the park is unlit.

DC Kimmings opens my car door and offers me a sizeable torch. It's heavier than I expect and I almost drop it. He flicks his flashlight on, illuminating me. I fumble for the button on mine, find it, then click it on.

Without speaking, we search the park. Instantly, I can tell it's a waste of time. There are no sounds of children at play, no squeaky swings, no laughter. No one is here.

After a few moments, DC Kimmings strides back to the car. I hear the muffled sound of radio chatter. He steps back out and fixes his light on me.

'They are sending a dog unit down here to sweep the area. We should leave now.'

I squeeze my eyes shut against the bright light. 'No, just a moment longer. Please. I haven't checked the bushes. I should look there, just in case.'

'Robin is probably home by now. We need to leave and let the other officers do their jobs.' He switches off his torch. Darkness envelops me, a sharp life reminder that everything can change at the click of a switch, the opening of a door, or the arrival of a text.

I look down at my phone. I want to see a message from Leo telling me Robin is with him, but my phone is stubbornly unhelpful.

DC Kimmings motions for me to once again slide into the back seat of the car. Quickly, I scan the play area one more time with the torch. Robin isn't here. I slowly slip into the police car.

It takes less than five minutes to pull up outside my house. The car has no siren or flashing lights, so slinks past the usual neighbourhood curtain-twitchers. DC Kimmings helps me out of the car. I walk up my drive. Put the key in the door. I step in and look down to where Robin's shoes should be. They're not there.

Leo strides across the living room towards me. He's about to say something but stops when he sees DC Kimmings.

'There was no need to call the police. I'm hurt about you keeping a secret from me, not what the secret was,' Leo says with a sigh.

'No,' I say. I slip down to the floor, finding the first step of my stairs to sit on. 'Robin, is he here?'

'He's with you, isn't he?' Leo moves forward, extending a hand to the DC. 'Leo Duffill.'

'DC Kimmings,' the policeman says shaking hands.

'Robin's missing,' I blurt out.

'What do you mean, missing? He was with you. How can he be missing?' Leo shouts.

'Let's calm down, Mr Duffill. Does Robin have a key?' DC Kimmings asks.

'No, he's too young to have his own front door key.' Leo locks his eyes on me. 'Why didn't you call me?'

'I sent you a text to ask if he had come home. You didn't answer it.'

'I didn't hear my phone. I was in the extension.'

'Then calling you wouldn't have made a difference, would it?' Bending, I take off my boots and throw them at Leo's feet.

Easily sidestepping my flying footwear, Leo says, 'A ringtone is longer and louder than a text tone, Cherrie.'

DC Kimmings interrupts our argument by radioing for an update. We all wait for the reply. I need to hear someone say Robin is safe; that this has all been a massive wake-up call; that my petty little worries mean nothing. My past doesn't matter. Robin is what matters and I swear I'll never forget it. Never.

The radio crackles. A voice comes over the static; they are sending people to check the house.

'You need to search the fair,' I whine.

'He's not home,' Leo tells DC Kimmings. 'I'd tell you if he were.'

Police cars pull up outside; these ones have their sirens whooping like angry primates. People in uniform fill up my open-plan living room; it's like watching dull, duplicate clowns flow out of a wailing Mini. A petite woman in a soft grey skirt suit follows them in.

'I'm DCI Jeddick,' she says. 'We are doing everything we can to find Robin, but you need to help us. Do you have an up-to-date photo? You said you had one here.'

'DCI? Why are you here? I thought DCIs were for

160

high-profile cases only?' They think Robin has been taken by the same man as Thomas Doncaster. Why else would they send the top brass?

She smiles at me. 'Popular misconception. I've personally been on more missing child cases than I care to mention. Most turn up in the first few hours.'

Leo moves forward and grabs a school photo from the mantel. 'It's just a month old, taken when he started Year Four.'

He gives it to DCI Jeddick, who passes it to another officer.

'Gov, I'm going to search upstairs,' says DC Kimmings.

When the DC disappears, my stomach twists up with a weird feeling of abandonment.

'We are going to search your house. You'd be surprised how many kids are hiding at home, scared they're in trouble. Are there any places where he could hide?' asks DCI Jeddick.

'No,' I say. 'Robin's not that kind of kid.'

'And I told you, he's not here. I think I would have seen him,' Leo says, his voice getting louder by the word.

'You're wasting time,' I add.

Leo shakes his head. 'This isn't happening,' he whispers.

The DCI crosses her arms over her chest. 'This is DC Steadman.' She motions to a broad-shouldered, heavy-set man who huffs and puffs as if he's one brisk walk from a heart attack. 'He will interview you now, and I need you to be honest. Honesty finds your son quicker. Okay, I'm going to leave you in his capable hands and get back to the station.'

DC Steadman's large hand snaps out towards me. I shake it, but it's sweaty and he grips me too tightly, so my fingers practically pop out of his professional gesture. 'Good to meet you both, sorry about the circumstances.'

Nodding, I fall back onto the couch. Leo sits beside me, no part of him touching me. His issues will have to be dealt with later. I can't concentrate on him right now.

'Is your son on any medications?' DC Steadman asks as he pulls out a thick-looking iPad covered in black rubber.

'No,' I reply.

'So there's nothing he needs to get back to take? Insulin? Inhaler?'

I shake my head.

'Has he ever run away before?'

'No, he's not like that,' Leo says.

How many times are they going to ask the same question? As if I will suddenly realise they're right on the thirtieth time they ask.

Leo huffs. 'Robin is a good boy. He'd never leave either of us.'

'Yet you told DC Kimmings he ran away from you to go on the Ferris wheel, and then went on it alone?' he asks me.

Leo's weighty hand suddenly presses down on my knee. Avoiding his stare, I look away. I can hear officers opening doors upstairs, rootling through my private stuff. What will they think if they find my box of criminology books tucked at the back of my wardrobe?

A policewoman comes up to DC Steadman and whispers something to him.

'Do you have the keys to your extension?' he asks Leo.

'He's not in there. I always lock it. He can't get in.'

'We'd like to check anyway.'

162

'It's still under construction and dangerous; I don't want people in there. I'll check it myself; your officer can wait by the door.' He gets up and strides across to the kitchen drawer, retrieves the key, then goes into his new room alone.

DC Steadman gives me an odd look. 'The notes say your son was wearing a red jacket, and you saw a child step off the Ferris wheel in a similar jacket. We're tracking down the other boy, along with the father and daughter you mentioned in the queue. It will take time. There's no CCTV in Black Friars Park, but there are plenty of cameras around it on the estates. We're doing everything we can.'

The police continue searching my house. They find nothing. All of them then leave, save for DC Kimmings who sits with Leo and me as we silently drink cold tea. I look up at the clock to see it has been four hours since I last saw Robin. Now, even his photo from the mantelpiece is gone. I've been sitting in the same cross-legged position for most of that time; my legs are numb. The dull ache of pins and needles is gripping them both from toe to thigh. I should stretch; instead, I accept the pain, welcome it. It's my only feeling.

A helicopter flies overhead.

'It's searching for Robin,' DC Kimmings says. 'You know, your name sounds familiar. Have you ever been arrested, Cherrie?' His eyes narrow, expecting me to blurt out I'm some sort of criminal mastermind.

'No, and shouldn't you have that in your files if I were?'

'Of course, I just can't shake the feeling that I've heard your name somewhere before.'

I can't take another round of *Guess Who*, not now. Clamping my mouth shut, I sink into the couch, my senses searching for the scent of my little boy. Only a few hours ago, Robin was here watching TV. The couch fabric still imprisons his essence. I bow my head and lose myself in a quick imaginary rewrite – we didn't go to the fair tonight. Leo came home early with a DVD for us to watch instead. Robin is in my arms; his face smeared with chocolate. His sweet breath laced with Haribo, and his tired limbs sprawled all over me.

The sharp trill of our house phone slices through my daydream.

Chapter 18

Leo reaches the phone first and presses the button to put it on speaker.

'DCI Jeddick here. We're still searching for Robin, but with the circumstances as they are we would like to set up a TV appeal right away; say first thing tomorrow. We've already circulated Robin's photo to media outlets, but if you are both strong enough to do the appeal in the morning, it could really help.'

'Anything we can do,' Leo replies, then hangs up.

Circumstances as they are? What the fuck does that mean? Is there something they're not telling us?

DC Kimmings edges closer. 'Cherrie, this is important. If someone has Robin, and that might not even be the case, but if someone does, it's important to show . . .'

I don't care what he says next. The Doncasters made an appeal for their son and all it got them was a shoeless corpse.

Did the murderer who stole Thomas's life take my

son tonight? Or is Robin's disappearance something to do with me? Is it because he's Mr Bones' grandson? At this point, I can neither assume, nor discount, anything.

I look over at DC Kimmings. 'My given name was Leigh-Ann Hendy.'

'Pardon?' DC Kimmings picks his iPad up again.

'My father was the serial killer Mr Bones. In the early 1990s, he murdered eleven boys. He used their bones to create sculptures for his private art gallery. I changed my name when I was seventeen.' My shoulders slump, and I all but fall back against the sofa.

Leo grunts. 'This better not be something to do with your sordid family history.'

Pursing his lips, DC Kimmings looks over at Leo. 'Go make another cuppa, will you?'

'This is your fault. No matter which way you cut it,' Leo whispers as he gets up.

'I knew I recognised your name. Okay, let's take this from the beginning.' DC Kimmings looks at me with a cocktail of concern and contempt.

'I was eight when they arrested Dad. I changed my name at seventeen. I've now been Cherrie Forrester longer than I was Leigh-Ann Hendy.'

'Does anyone else know about your past?'

'There's a podcast. It talked about my parents and told everyone my name; even hinted where I work. It was popular because of Thomas Doncaster's disappearance. So some people knew.'

'Okay, okay. Let me tell the gov. You should have told me from the start, Leigh-Ann. The more information we have, the sooner we'll find your son.'

'My name is Cherrie,' I mutter and watch as he walks into our dining space to call it in.

I don't wait for Leo to come back from the kitchen; instead, I put my boots back on, grab a coat and slip out of the front door.

The helicopter is still searching above me. On the road, I see a few uniformed police officers. I walk down every street Robin has ever walked; checking in bushes. I even knock on random doors. I find nothing. I don't want to go home, so I carry on across the estate to Tracy's house. I knock on the door. Her gran answers; she's crying and hugs me straight away. Her surprisingly strong arms pull me into their home. Tracy is in the sitting room. I slip onto the sofa next to her.

'Cherry Pie.' Tracy puts an arm around my shoulders and I lean on her. 'I just saw it on the news. I was about to call you.'

I can't speak; I just sit next to my friend, feeling her warmth and unasked questions.

After Gran makes a phone call, DC Kimmings arrives. He ushers me out of their house, then, in silence, drives me home.

'You have to be there, for when he comes back,' he tells me at my door.

I nod my head like a tree branch in the wind.

When they've finished taking statements and searching the house, the police leave. Finally alone, Leo grunts that it's late and he will sleep on the couch tonight. I don't care; I can't even open my mouth to acknowledge his mood, so just go to bed.

I sleep in my clothes. When I wake up, I have to remind myself Robin is missing and my sweet little boy might be, right now, in pain. Might be crying out to me to help him. Might be dead.

Morning comes. I hear a knock on my bedroom door. I get up and open it to see a strange woman standing in my home.

'I'm your family liaison officer, Patricia Falmer. I'm here to keep you informed of the case and to help you with all this. We need to do the appeal quickly, so it's happening in an hour. Can I help you prepare?'

I stare at her. She's about my age with dyed blonde hair and dishwater eyes. Patricia is not in a uniform but wears a smart pinstripe suit. There's a look on her face as if nothing I could do or say would faze her. Deep down, I don't take this look as comfort but as a challenge.

I close the door in her face. If it's in an hour, I have at least another fifty minutes of thinking time before I have to shuffle in front of the cameras and face the reporters.

After they arrested Dad, the press tried to interview Mum – Wendy Hendy, the steel-faced wife who never cried or commented about her husband's dark deeds. We didn't leave the house for a month. Every time we went outside, one of those parasites would shove a microphone or a camera in our faces and make up a news headline the next day: *Wendy Hendy – serial killer sidekick, or Mrs Bones?* Worse: *Are there more skeletons in the Hendys' closet?* She stopped speaking to me too. I was just a little girl. I did not understand what was happening. Dad was gone, and my mum became a recluse, taking me with her.

Consequently, reporters are not my favourite people, yet I have to do this appeal.

At fifteen minutes to the hour, I get up, lumber downstairs and say, 'Morning,' to Leo, DC Kimmings, DC Steadman, and Patricia.

'At least brush your hair, Cherrie,' Leo whispers.

'Fuck off,' I whisper back.

Now aware of my past, everyone is looking at me as if I am a World War II bomb, stuck in the middle of the house, which could detonate at any moment. They've forgotten I've been here all along – an explosion waiting to happen.

Patricia offers me a cup of tea. When I reach for it, the mug burns my hands. I let it fall onto the floor between us. The cup doesn't smash, but the tea blasts out over the wooden floorboards.

'I'll clean it up,' she says.

In an instant, Patricia is on her knees mopping the floor with my kitchen towels. She's sponging off my socked feet, all the while making a soothing, cooing sound like I'm a tantrum-throwing toddler, not a mother who has lost her child. I want to kick her in the face. How dare she come in here thinking she can solve all my problems. How dare she make me tea without asking me how I take it, and hand it cup first to burn me. How dare she use up all my good kitchen towel. It's the stuff that can be used again and again and she's throwing it away. I lunge forward and begin unfurling the discarded sheets of sucked-up tea. I squeeze them out in the sink, then carefully place them on the radiator to dry.

Patricia, who has seen it all before, has apparently never seen this. Under normal circumstances, a small part of my soul would have lighted up with pride at this. But today is anything but normal.

Leo stares at his watch. 'Time to go,' he says, walking out of the front door without looking back.

The police drive us to our community centre. I imagined being escorted to a hi-tech room stuffed with computers and gadgets covered with people in sharp dark suits; instead, I find myself in the dull place where we vote on pointless politics and cookie-cutter council members. The main room holds one long plastic table with a gaggle of reporters and news cameras stretched out before it.

'Bet you wished you'd brushed your hair,' Leo says, as he grabs my hand, just like a good partner should. This mood is unlike anything I've seen from Leo before, but I deserve it, and he deserves to be mad, so I say nothing.

We're ushered to the table. I look behind us and see there is a banner with Robin's school photo along with a tip-line telephone number. He'll be so embarrassed when he sees his photo blown up; I want to continue with the veiled hope that this is all a simple misunderstanding, nothing sinister. I want to be the person who thinks the best. Someone convinced her child will come home safe and sound. He could still be at any of his school friends' houses. Maybe he found a new little friend while waiting to go on the ride, and followed them to their house for a sleepover, not realising he would cause all this trouble. Now, he's too scared to come home. But I know better. Bad things happen. Eleven boys never made it home because of Mr Bones, and Thomas will not be sitting around the Doncasters' Christmas tree this year.

Dropping my body onto an empty chair, I have a sudden realisation — today could be the start of a lifetime of these appeals. All those social media have-a-go investigators could forever parade Robin's image as evidence. My son's destiny could be a link in a chain of dead boys, my dark heritage the knot to tie it all together. How many kids do they find after an abduction? I need to ask someone. As I get up, Leo pulls me back down.

'Don't you dare move, Cherrie.' His thumb presses into my wrist.

Patricia saunters up to us and sits on the table. She lounges as if she's flirting with her boss at the office.

'We need you to appeal to Robin at this stage. In most of these cases, the kids have simply run away. We need to tell him he won't be in trouble when he comes back.'

'He hasn't run away. How many fucking times am I gonna have to tell you?' I snap.

'Cherrie,' Leo says.

'Someone took my son. Shouldn't we appeal to them to let him go?'

'Not yet. I realise that this is hard, but you both need to emphasise you want Robin home now and he won't be in trouble. This is to gain trust. The trust of those watching the appeal to help us, and the trust of the press. Stick to the facts of what he was wearing, and where you saw him last. Did you watch the Doncasters' appeal? Mrs Doncaster was great. She spoke directly to Thomas. Even mentioned her other son Harry wanting his brother back in time for their football game at school. Very effective.'

'Got it,' Leo mumbles.

Did she just give me coaching tips on how to act during my missing child's appeal? I roll my eyes so hard I feel like my eyeballs could, at any moment, pop out of my skull and tumble around the community centre like squishy marbles.

Patricia smiles at me. 'Ms Forrester, you're giving me a strange look. Are you quite all right?'

'Sure,' I reply, forcing my lips into the smallest smile in the world.

Leo thrusts a hand out of sight under the table. I feel the warmth of his palm hovering above my knee, as if he's deciding whether to touch me.

'Okay, let's begin.' Pulling herself up, Patricia gives us a patronising smile, then fades into the crowd, leaving Leo and me to quietly seethe together.

DCI Jeddick sits down next to me. She has a trusty iPad clutched to her chest like a bulletproof vest. Looking up, she says in a firm, clear voice to the press, 'Please refrain from asking questions until after the appeal. Thank you.'

Leo looks over at me. Under the table, he squeezes my hand until it hurts. Does he want me to cry? Is this what today is about? Me, the wailing mother falling apart; him the strong father keeping his family together?

'My son, Robin Duffill, is eight years old. He will be nine in January. You're not in trouble, tiger. We just want you back home with us.' Leo squeezes my hand again when he's done.

'*Strictly Come Dancing* is on Saturday, and it won't be the same without you, Robin,' I say, earning another hand crush.

Leo continues, 'He was last seen at Crazy Clive's Fair in Black Friars Park with his mother, Cherrie Forrester. He was wearing a red Puffa jacket and dark blue jeans.

He's a lovely boy, so friendly . . .' My boyfriend glances at me, then falters. I can't do this anymore. I can't pretend Robin has any choice about where he is and whether he can come home. This is bullshit.

'If someone has my son,' I blurt out, 'you need to let him go unharmed before I find out who you are and come for you. Trust me, you will not like what I'll do if I get my hands on you.'

The DCI lurches across me to snatch the microphone. She adds, 'You're not in trouble, Robin. Please come home. Your parents are distraught. They just want you back safe.'

'Please come home, Robin. We miss you,' Leo adds.

'The police are seeking a child on the Ferris wheel who might have important information. He was wearing a red Puffa jacket and is about eight years of age. Mrs Duffill approached him last night at the fair. If this is your child, please contact the tip-line. Mr and Mrs Duffill need your help.'

I lean forward and say, 'I'm not Mrs Duffill. I'm Ms Forrester.'

'Questions?' DCI Jeddick says.

The room erupts and someone points at the loudest voice. The reporter stands up; he's a frail-looking young man, who seems as if he couldn't possibly have the most prominent voice in the room.

'You're not really Ms Forrester, though, are you? Aren't you Leigh-Ann Hendy, Little Bones?'

Silence. I have two choices. I can deny it and, when it comes out later, look like a liar. On the other hand, if I admit it I doom Robin to be forever chained to Mr Bones. What do I do?

DCI Jeddick coughs. 'A young boy is missing; please

keep your questions about his disappearance and how you can help get him back to his family.'

Fuck, I have to get this appeal back on track, humanise Robin. I snatch the microphone back and stare at the reporter. 'I made a costume for Robin for Halloween. He is looking forward to wearing it. Please help me get him home in time to go trick or treating.'

'There will be no more questions.' The DCI moves around the table to block me from the cameras.

I get up and as I do, see a familiar face in the crowd: Jai Patel.

Chapter 19

Pushing through the reporters, I head straight for him.

'If this has anything to do with your fucking podcast, I'm going to . . .' Grabbing his jacket, I pull him back and forth on the spot.

He puts his hands up. 'Whoa, please, Leigh-Ann!' Jai yells as loud as he can, looking around to see if anyone is coming to his aid.

The reporter from before hears him call me Leigh-Ann. He pulls out his mobile phone to take a photo. DCI Jeddick deftly intercepts him.

DC Steadman appears, yanks Jai aside, and says something I don't catch. Straightening his coat, Jai nods at the DC, he then steps back towards me. 'I'm sorry, but I came to help. As soon as I heard your name, I came to help,' he says.

I don't believe him. People you barely know don't help you. They're just vultures feeding off your sorrow. Wait, in my criminology books it says criminals often put themselves into investigations; they do it to see how close they are to being caught, and for kicks.

'If you have my son, I'll kill you,' I seethe at him, gripping his jacket again.

'I don't have your son.'

'You do, that's why you're here inserting yourself into the investigation like the clichéd criminal you are.'

'Snap, I'm no kiddie snatcher. Why would I?'

'To get more subscribers for that pathetic podcast of yours.'

'I took it down, remember? You told my mum on me.'

I let go of his jacket. The material rumpled by my fists gently expands back into its original shape, reminding me of Robin's red Puffa coat.

'Damn, salty really is your go-to flavour,' Jai says.

'Everything okay here?' DC Kimmings asks coming up behind us.

'He's the bastard who created the podcast that outed me.' I shove Jai in the chest.

'Ouch.' Jai stumbles backwards. 'I'm here to help. Let me help you, Leigh-Ann.'

'My name is Cherrie!' I go to push him again, but DC Kimmings grabs me, jerking me backwards.

'This isn't the place, Ms Forrester,' says the DC.

DC Steadman takes Jai by the elbow and leads him away. It was dumb to attack and accuse Jai; I realise this within seconds of seeing him look back at me, grinning. He's an asshole, but not a suspect. Where would he even keep stolen boys for long periods of time? His mum would have noticed something, and she seems the type to do what's right, rather than keep a secret.

Through the dispersing crowd, I catch sight of DCI Jeddick. She's giving me a look I've seen several times stamped on Mrs Duffill's face: disappointment. I've ruined

176

Robin's appeal. I threatened people and appeared crazy. Whoever has Robin will think they have done him a favour by taking him from me; who'd want to grow up with a psychotic mum?

The DCI makes her way to me.

'Well, I've never seen that reaction before,' she says. 'I've seen breakdowns, tears and pleas, but never threats.'

'So, I wasn't as good as Mrs Doncaster?'

'It's not a competition.'

'You still think Robin has run away, but someone has my son. A skeleton approached us in the Ghost Train. It can't be a coincidence. What if there's a Mr Bones copycat on the loose?' As soon as I say it, I shiver.

Cocking her head, the DCI narrows her eyes at me. 'A copycat is a serious theory, Cherrie. One we are looking into; however, there's just not enough evidence to support it at the moment. Thomas Doncaster's body was left where it would be found. The police only discovered your dad's victims when they raided your house.'

'It wasn't about the kill, he just wanted the bones,' I mutter.

'Now, copycats, well, they copy. There are few similarities between the Doncaster boy, your son and the Mr Bones murders.'

This information sinks in, yet still doesn't feel right. Serial killers have both signatures and modus operandi; they retain their signature, but can change their MOs. Only film and TV tell us they stick to a rigid pattern. A dual-servicing lie to give their hero a clue, and the audience hope that these monsters can be caught in the real world. The truth is, most are never found or punished.

'What are you thinking?' she asks.

'If there is no copycat, I've fucked up Robin's appeal.'

'That remains to be seen.' The DCI takes off her jacket revealing a colourful sleeve of tattoos on her left arm. 'You better get off home now. I'll deal with the reporters.' She leaves before I can study the images she deemed important enough to live on her skin forever.

Like a summoned genie, DC Steadman suddenly appears. 'I'll take you home.'

Patricia rushes over, Leo in tow.

'This appeal is already going viral. Maybe the threat will help?' she gushes.

'Cherrie was aggressive rather than tearful. She's probably killed my son.' Leo stares at me; his lips so tight across his face I'm surprised any words made it past them at all.

DC Steadman and Patricia take us home. Leo doesn't intend to stay. Instead, he packs a small bag of clothes. He then grabs a packet of crisps from the kitchen. As he goes to leave, I stop him at the door. I don't want him with me, but equally I don't want him to hear any news about Robin alone. He stares through me. The words I should say die in my throat.

'I'll be back in a day or two. I just can't stay here with you right now. You ruined the appeal. Robin might go to my mum's house. I should be there if he does.'

His mum lives a half-hour drive from us. Robin doesn't know the way, nor could he walk that distance. 'If you think Robin ran away then the appeal means nothing.'

He drops his bag. 'You still ruined it.'

'Thanks for the support.'

'Why should I support you? You lied to me for years.

178

And don't forget, you told my mum not to go to the fair. If she had, Robin wouldn't have been taken.'

'If you hadn't texted me!'

'I'm not fucking psychic, Cherrie. I didn't know you weren't watching our son.'

Psychic. Mariah. I have an appointment with her tonight. She might see something; give me a clue. 'Yeah, well, why don't you go and piss off to Mummy's house!'

Leo picks up his bag and walks out, colliding with Patricia as he does.

'Where's he going?' she asks.

'To his mum's house,' I tell her.

'Oh, that's a bad idea – you should stay together.' She then gets a panicked look on her face. 'Umm, I'm needed elsewhere. Are you all right alone?'

'What? Has another boy gone missing already?' Fuck, this could mean whoever took Robin is now finished with him and has a different toy to play with.

'No, no, not another missing boy. Just another case. I'm the only family liaison officer in this area. They are spreading us a little thin due to budget cuts. I have to leave you for a bit. I'll come back.'

'I thought you said we all need to stay together?'

'Sorry. Let me speak with Mr Duffill. I'll go to his mum's house with him.' Patricia runs into the street to catch Leo before he drives away.

'Knock yourself out,' I yell, as I slam the front door on them both.

I drop onto the couch and switch on the TV. I avoid the news. Instead, I click straight on to *Grey's Anatomy*. The next episode comes on. I try to clear my head; even if it's just for a few moments, but my mind refuses.

179

I keep imagining how scared Robin is right now. I hear him begging me to find him. Closing my eyes, I will my imagination to stop the torture. Barely ten minutes into the episode, I switch off the TV. How can I help? What can I do? Maybe the answer is in my books upstairs? I'm about to raid my wardrobe when my phone pings. I pull it from my pocket and see a notification of a Google email with 'Cherrie' on it. I don't want to look, but my finger clicks it before my mind has a chance to stop it. There are links to a freshly published newspaper article. Quickly, I scan it to find the piece says nothing too bad. It's the comments below that make me cringe.

Can't believe she'd ruin her own son's appeal.

Little Bones is back! She's already killed two boys. One her own son.

Is anyone safe with her around?

What if there's a Mr Bones copycat out there?

Like father, like daughter. Why don't the police just arrest her already?

Makes me wish we could pitchfork and torch the bitch.

Comment after comment, insult after insult, and lie after lie. Pitchforks and torches; what am I? A *Hammer House of Horror* monster to run out of town? I've lost my son. Mrs Doncaster didn't get abuse; she got sympathy. I wonder what dark deeds could be in her family's past. For all they know, her great-great-grandfather was Jack the Ripper.

Maybe I deserve it. Who was I to think I could just change my name and live a normal life? Cherrie Forrester's life was on borrowed time. I just hope Robin isn't paying for my naïvety.

I throw my phone onto the couch, then watch as it bounces onto the floor.

'Shit!' I retrieve it. I expect to see at least a broken screen, something to distort my view, but it's still intact.

The front door suddenly swings open. I look up to see Tracy with her gran.

'You shouldn't leave your door open, love,' Gran says.

As they walk in, I see Gurpreet, Shania, and Kylie behind them all carrying Dawson's Food bags. They walk in single file into the kitchen and start unpacking a mountain of groceries.

'Mr Dawson closed the shop this afternoon. He told us to bring you some stuff over,' Tracy explains. She lunges forward to hug me. I can't bring myself to hug her back, so limply accept her support.

'They're going to find him,' Gurpreet says as she puts the kettle on. 'I'll bet Robin's case has nothing to do with the Doncaster thing.'

'Yeah, people have a habit of making assumptions,' Kylie says, moving her pregnant belly towards me to hug me too. 'It's happened a few times to me.' When she lets me go, I see a familiar look on her face, guilt. Kylie has a secret too, but now is not the time to ask.

I feel awful. These are my friends and, apart from Tracy, none of them have been to my house before. If I had known they were coming, I'd have cleaned up. Looking down, I see a random pair of Robin's discarded shoes on the floor. I bend and pick them up, but once they're in my arms, I can't seem to put them back down again. I hold them close; their laces dangling down my chest.

Shania takes the shoes from me. 'He'll need these when he's back. You'll put mum smell all over them. That's what

my kid tells me; stop putting mum smell on my stuff.'
Her voice disappears and she offers a thin smile as she
gently places them alongside the other shoes by the door.

The girls make tea, then manoeuvre me back into the
living room. Gurpreet sits next to me, her arm around
my shoulders.

'That was nice of Mr Dawson to give you the time
off,' I mutter.

'Yeah, we Creekers stick together,' Tracy says.

'What's been on the TV?' I ask.

They all look at one another.

'They're saying you're the daughter of the serial killer
Mr Bones. Is it true?' Shania asks.

'Yes.'

Silence. We are at the point I've dreaded for years. This
is where all my friends abandon me – as my mother did.
Disgusted at my bloody DNA, they walk out on me. Yet
my friends don't. Instead of looks of disgust, I see a mixture
of sympathy and intrigue.

'I also ruined the appeal,' I add.

'You're kidding, Cherry Pie. You were a badass. You
looked right at the camera and threatened whoever took
Robin. I've never seen that before.'

'Yeah, I'd be surprised if Robin isn't carefully placed
back on your doorstep with a sorry note attached to his
jacket.' Shania snaps her fingers.

'The police weren't happy with me,' I admit.

'The police are idiots,' Kylie says.

'Yeah, it's not like they did much for the Doncasters
. . .' Realising what she's said, Tracy's sentence trails off.

Closing my eyes, I imagine Robin is playing upstairs.
He's safe. The thought doesn't last; an image of my baby

screaming superimposes itself onto it. I have to drop my stare to avoid the girls seeing my tears starting to gather.

Tracy's gran, with her motherly logic, steps in. 'None of that matters now. We need a plan to find Robin.'

'We made flyers this morning,' Gurpreet says. 'They're in the car. We're going door to door with them.'

'Won't the police be doing that?' I ask.

'I don't trust the police. I say we do it.' Kylie nods at me.

'Umm, can I say something horrible?' Tracy looks pensive. She's going to say what everyone is thinking. Whatever monster took Thomas Doncaster now has Robin.

'No, you can't,' her gran replies.

'Yes, but what about Leo?' Tracy continues regardless.

'What?' I say.

'Forgive me, Cherry Pie, he's lovely and all. Good-looking, great dad, but if he found out about your past, he might have done something silly.'

Could Tracy have a point? 'What do you mean? You think *he* took Robin?'

'Well, you're not married, and he could be worried about the Mr Bones thing. When did he find out?'

'He texted me asking about Mr Bones while Robin and I were at the fair. I don't know how he found out. I never got the chance to ask.' After what happened to Robin, my son was all I could think about, all my other worries faded into the background.

'Then Leo knew about your past. Who's to say he didn't find out earlier? Distracted you with the text and then took Robin.' Gurpreet puts her hands on her hips.

'Makes sense. Where is Leo now?' Shania asks.

'At his mummy's house,' I say.

'He could be keeping him there. Just for a little bit. Then suddenly, he miraculously finds Robin. You end up looking like a crazy person. Full custody for Leo ahoy.'

Tracy has a point.

'There are police at Mrs Duffill's house. Patricia went with him. She's not the brightest bulb in the box, but she'd notice if Robin was there. He's hard to miss.'

'Is there anywhere else he could keep him? Even if it's just for a bit, before he takes him to Granny's house?' Kylie asks.

My eyes drift to the locked door of the extension. He would not. He could not, could he? Robin might be just a few feet away from me. It makes sense. Leo didn't text me until I was at the fair; he deliberately distracted me so he could take Robin. He's never let me go into the extension. What could be lurking behind that door? What has he been working on so diligently for years? The only room the police didn't check, because he insisted that he check it alone for health and safety reasons.

I propel myself off the couch and run to the door, my socks sliding on the floor. I grab the door handle and shake it, but it won't open.

'Robin! Robin! Sweetie are you in there?'

The girls follow me. They put their ears to the wall to listen.

'Where's the key?' Gurpreet asks.

'The drawer, over there,' I say, pointing.

I hear her moving stuff around. 'There's no key in here.'

'Let me look.' Shania pushes her out of the way, and begins to shove the contents of the drawer around with more force. 'She's right; there are no keys in here.'

184

'Did he take it with him?' asks Kylie.

'He opened the door last night; he must have only just taken the keys.'

Did he go into the kitchen before he left? Fuck. I have to get this door down. I kick it, but it doesn't move. Tracy kicks at it too. Gurpreet pulls a bobby pin from her hair. She jams it into the lock.

'Robin!' I yell.

'Surely he'd answer you,' Tracy's gran says.

'Leo could have drugged him. Knocked him out so no one would hear him,' Kylie says. 'But probably not, right?' She instantly backtracks, but the thought is already out there.

'Get it open now,' Tracy urges.

'I'm trying, I've never done this before,' Gurpreet admits, as she wiggles the bobby pin around.

'Fuck it, let's look it up.' Shania pulls out her mobile and we all stare at a YouTube video about lock picking. If we were in a comedy show, it'd be hilarious, but this is reality, so it's just plain horrific.

Kylie puts her skinny arm around my shoulders. 'Is he capable of something like this?'

I want to say no, yet even after all these years, I still don't completely know Leo. Can you ever know anyone one hundred per cent? He can be childish and spiteful sometimes, like everyone else, but he's also gentle and caring. No, he loves Robin, he'd never hurt him, so the theory that Leo has Robin instantly becomes the one I want to hang my proverbial hat on. With Leo as the abductor, Robin is safe. It also explains why he left the fair. I'd told my son so many times not to talk to strangers. Warned him never to go off with someone he doesn't know. Leo taking him would make sense.

'Got it!' Gurpreet says, stepping away from the door. 'It should be you who opens it, Cherrie.'

I put my hand on the wood. It's warm and smells of fresh paint. Whatever is behind this door will change my life forever, no matter what I find. The realisation that my boyfriend could hate me enough to cruelly take my child away, could break me. And then there's another thought, one I haven't shared with my friends: what if Leo also took Thomas Doncaster and I'm the clichéd girl attracted to men just like her daddy?

I push open the door to find out.

Chapter 20

The smell hits me first, an artificial aroma of chemicals and paint. I squint. It's too dark inside to see anything, so I grope across the wall for a light switch. When I find it, I flick it on, and find I'm in a nursery. Painted all blue and green, and featuring happy woodland creatures along the walls. It's the last secret I would have guessed Leo was hiding.

Tracy pushes past me. 'Are you pregnant, Cherry Pie?'

'No.' I don't look at my friend when I answer. I can't seem to tear my eyes away from the painted, cheerful animals dancing around the walls. It's a perfect room; one that will be even more perfect when the covers come off the bay windows to let in the light. This was his surprise, the promise of another baby. A brother or sister for Robin.

I hear a squeak and look over to see Leo has left a window ajar. The cold breeze is pushing at a small, thin metal stepladder. That's the noise I heard the other day.

'Well, I don't know about you lot, but I now feel like a total bitch,' Shania says.

'Wow, I didn't realise Leo was so good at this building stuff. He could have his own show on TV,' Gurpreet adds, tactfully changing the subject from what we were accusing him of moments before.

The relief that my boyfriend is not just normal, he's planning our future together hits me like a punch in the jaw. I can't speak. It hurts so bad, I feel the pain down to the nerves in my teeth.

'Come on now, let's sit back down. We need a new plan.' Tracy's gran takes hold of my arm and leads me out of the nursery. As we shut the door behind us, I suddenly remember Robin is missing, and scold myself for being able to push a single thought past the mental block of my lost son.

'Let's do the flyer thing,' Kylie suggests. She downs the rest of her now-cold tea as if it's a shot of whisky and heads for the door. The others follow her.

'Oh, but I can't go. Someone has to stay here, in case Robin comes back home,' I say.

'I'll stay,' Tracy's gran says. 'This cold is playing havoc with my arthritis. I could do with a sit-down.'

I shrug on boots and a coat, then slip my mobile into my pocket. We march out together. As we do, I notice a group of strangers lingering at the bottom of my driveway on the public footpath. One, a middle-aged woman with frizzy dark hair rushes forward and thrusts a mobile phone into my face. 'Where are you going, Little Bones?'

A fit of familiar anger raises within me.

'We're going to poster the streets. You got a problem with that?' Kylie asks, her pregnant belly aimed at the woman like a weapon.

The other reporters stay back, watching their elected scout with keen eyes.

'Do you have anything to say to whoever has your son, Leigh-Ann?'

'Why don't you leeches fuck off and do something useful.' Tracy puts her arm around my shoulders. The woman dashes back to her group.

'This is private property. I'm calling the police. I suggest you all bugger off now.' Shania dramatically gets out her mobile to dial two nines.

As if they are of one hive mind, the reporters scurry away. They separate and climb into the cars they have haphazardly parked along my street.

Tracy steers me towards her car's boot. She opens it and a rainbow of Robin faces stare back at me. They'd printed the flyers on all different coloured paper. There's even a reward at the bottom for information leading to his safe return: £5,000.

'Where did the reward money come from?' I ask.

'We took up a collection at the shop this morning. Made enough for the reward as well as to print the flyers,' Tracy explains.

'We don't have a lot of customers,' Shania says, 'but the ones we do have are oddly wealthy. One guy gave us over four grand. Just handed it over in cash. Like he'd found it in one of his pockets on washing day.'

'That's so wonderful. I need to thank everyone,' I mutter. 'I can't believe a stranger would just give up four grand for someone else's son.'

'Come on, let's get to work.' Gurpreet grabs a wad of flyers and divides them up for us. She then points us in all different directions. Everyone starts canvassing, except

Shania and me. Clutching the flyers and rolls of tape to our chests, we stand together.

'Cherrie?'

'Shania?'

'My mum died when I was small too. Everyone told me growing up that I would end up just like her – a whore with a coke habit – but I didn't. DNA doesn't work like that. You're not your father's daughter. Just as I'm not my mother's daughter. We're good parents. This isn't your fault. Shit happens and it's horrible it happened to you. We're gonna find Robin.'

I hug her. Who knew we had so much in common.

'I'm not saying your dad was like my mum and into the booga–sugar or anything, although in the early Nineties it was all the rage.'

'Stop talking now,' I whisper.

We hug a little longer, then set off in opposite directions with our flyers.

I tape my son's face on lampposts, garden walls and the sides of houses. I knock on door after door. Everyone tells me how sorry he or she is and takes a poster to put up in their window. Part of me was convinced they would slam their doors in my face. Most are of an age to remember Mr Bones; some had probably referred to me as Little Bones. Odds are they listened to that bloody podcast, but it seems they have forgiven me the sins of my father, or are too polite to let slip their retrospective outrage.

As I move through the estate, I feel a tiny bit better. I'm actively doing something. It may not be a theatrical investigation akin to Sherlock Holmes; however, I am paying attention. Every time a door opens, I look for a young boy's shoes in the hall, and take a deep breath, searching for Robin's tell-tale scent to ignite my maternal brain.

It's not until I reach a tattered yellow poster of Thomas Doncaster that I waver. The hesitation feels like it lasts for ages, but in reality is only a moment.

I tape Robin over Thomas's face and move on to the next house. As I do, my mobile vibrates in my pocket. Is it Leo? Has he heard something?

Chapter 21

Looking down at my phone, I see it's not a text from my boyfriend, but another email from my Google Alert. I'm not sure I can take any more internet trolls digitally name-bashing me, but I have to look. I open it up to discover this one is not about me; it's the alert I set up for sex offenders and kidnappers in Northamptonshire. There's a name along with a news story. *Mr Oscar Greer last year accused of kidnapping and having sex with a minor.* The alert picked it up from a comment on a blog. Scanning the short blurb beneath the link, I see he lives on the Hallow's Gate Estate, only a twenty-minute walk from my house, and one of the estates that backs on to Black Friars Park. I drop the flyers. The autumn wind instantly sucks them down the street in a multi-coloured swirl, like dead leaves.

Oscar Greer could have my son. Hanging around a fair would not be out of character for the likes of him. Also, if he has restrictions on his bail about being around minors, dressing up in a costume to avoid being recognised would make sense. I want to find my son, but finding him in

Greer's house, seeing what he has done to him, it would break my heart. In turn, I'd have to break something of Greer's of equal measure.

I run. I'm not much of an athlete, but pain and terror propel me forward. Before I'm mentally prepared for it, I'm on his street. I don't know the house number, so I knock on doors and ask if anyone can direct me. I can remember a time when we all knew our neighbours' names, yet this street appears seriously ill informed, or just not bothered. Only when I catch an elderly woman taking her dog for a walk, do I get my answer. He lives at number forty-seven. It's a small bungalow with a front door made up of peeling navy paint and smeared glass panels. Flanking the door are two hanging baskets overflowing with dead plants. It looks like a haunted house, something that belongs in a fair. Somewhere a skeleton would live.

I charge up the driveway and bang on the front door. My plan is simple; when Greer opens the door, I'll punch him. To get him on the ground, I might have to hit him a few times, but that shouldn't be a problem. Once he's down, I'll search his house until I find Robin. If he's done something terrible to my baby, I'll hunt for the sharpest knife in his kitchen, then I'll slit his throat. As I watch him bleed to death, I'll cut off any part of him that touched my son. Greer is a dead man walking.

Waiting on the paedophile's doorstep, with this easy-to-action plan churning around my mind, I try to imagine any immediate drawbacks to it; nope, there's none. If killing Greer equals saving my son, and probably other innocent children, then it's a simple equation. One I can live with.

I knock again, this time louder. There's still no answer. To take in more of the house, I step a few paces backwards.

Four windows are facing out towards the street. I scrutinise each one, waiting for a curtain to twitch, or a face to appear. Nothing.

'Oscar Greer!' I yell.

No answer.

'You pervert! Open your door right now!'

No answer.

My shouting draws out his neighbours, a middle-aged man and a young girl of about thirteen.

'I'll call the police if you don't leave,' the man says.

'Do you have any idea who the fuck your neighbour is?'

The girl giggles at the word fuck.

'Oscar is at work,' the neighbour replies.

'He's a registered sex offender. He has my son.'

'I saw you on the news – you're sassy,' the girl says.

I turn to face them properly. 'Have you seen a little boy here?'

'No, I work from home, I'd have noticed. Oscar is quiet. He doesn't have kids.'

'Did he go to the fair on Friday night? Does he have a skeleton costume?' I sound like a madwoman.

'I'm not his personal assistant.' The man shrugs. 'You shouldn't be here. You should leave now.'

'He did go out on Friday night. I saw him leave the house,' the girl offers. She pulls out her mobile phone. 'When I leave school, I'm going to join the police. I could do with stakeout experience. Give me your number; I'll text you if I see anything.'

'Gemma! Don't give your number to this crazy woman. I remember Mr Bones. For all we know, she killed her son.'

'I love my son.' Before her dad can stop me, I grab Gemma's outstretched mobile and put in my number. Handing it back to her I say, 'Thank you.'

Walking home, I realise that I should tell the police about Greer. But what have the police ever done for me? And, deep down, a huge part of me wants to be the hero. The one who rescues Robin. It's a frivolous thought; what if keeping it from the police makes matters worse? Robin is missing, Leo has left me, everyone now knows who I am, and there is only one way things will get worse: Robin's body discarded by the side of the road, and, if I'm not careful, I could be the cause of it. That's exactly why I need to keep Greer's identity secret. Police have legal and ethical limits. I don't.

Tracy meets me at the top of the street. 'Guess where Kylie is now living?'

I don't answer. I hear the question, but all I can think about is Oscar Greer and getting a text from my new spy to tell me he's home, so I can push him in front of a speeding car.

'With Gran and me. I adopted your stray.'

'That's great,' I mutter.

'Kylie's fun to have around. Gran is looking forward to having a baby in the house. It's as if she's ten years younger. Like she's sucking the youth right out of Kylie's belly button. Not that it'll be forever. Her boyfriend wants her back. There's a legal thing he needs to sort out first, though.'

'That's nice,' I say.

When we get home, we find Tracy's gran in my kitchen. She's made a lunch of baked beans, sausage patties and fried mushrooms. It smells great, like my house is a home again, almost.

When everyone comes back without flyers, Gran dishes the food up. The girls chat as they eat. I want to talk to them about Greer, but they'd probably make me tell the police, and I'm not ready to let that information go just yet.

As if thinking about the police makes them appear, DC Steadman and Patricia knock on the door. They're checking up on me. Miraculously, Tracy's gran has made enough lunch for everyone, so both sit down to eat with us.

'What have you found out about Thomas Doncaster?' Kylie asks them.

'Yeah, is that case connected with Robin?' Shania adds.

DC Steadman chokes a little on his beans.

'I . . . I'm not sure we should talk about it,' Patricia stammers.

'It's a good question. You said you'd keep me informed of the case. So far, you've told me squat. Tell me this at least.' Surprising myself with my hard tone, I shove a whole sausage patty in my mouth to stop me from saying anything else.

DC Steadman clears his throat. 'We can see a few similarities between the cases, but also major differences.'

'That's good, right?' Tracy asks. 'In all the police shows on TV, they talk about criminals' MOs, which they don't change. It probably means the cases aren't related.'

'Two young boys go missing twenty miles and one week apart; they're connected.' Shania looks at me when she finishes her sentence, almost as if to apologise.

'TV isn't the best comparison here. We can't rule anything in or out at this stage,' DC Steadman says taking a bite of toast.

'Have you looked into the travelling fair?' Tracy's gran asks.

'We searched it and interviewed all the workers,' DC Steadman replies.

'Were they in town when Thomas went missing?' Tracy asks.

'No, they came here a few days later.' Patricia looks over at me.

They're discussing Robin's disappearance as if it's a reality show on TV. Like I'm not his mother, and not sitting next to them in gut-wrenching agony.

I want to yell at them to get out, so I can wallow in my dark thoughts alone while watching for a teenage girl's text about a known paedophile, but I can't do that. My friends came here to support me. They had the afternoon off work, yet came to help Little Bones. I served them a significant slice of my sticky past and they stuck around. Which is more than can be said for Leo.

After a few hours, the girls all leave together. Each of them hugging me as they go. Kylie's belly kicks out as she grips me to her. She mouths *sorry*, but I'm unsure if she's apologising for her foetus's violent outburst or Robin's abduction.

DC Steadman leaves too. I turn to say goodbye to Patricia but see her sit back down on my couch.

'Umm, you can go too,' I say.

'I'm supposed to stay with you. You'd be surprised at the silly things parents do in these situations.' She picks up yesterday's newspaper and begins flicking through it.

At least I'm not surprised at the *silly things* Patricia says anymore. Raising my lips into the best smile I can muster, I say, 'Don't you have another family to hassle now?'

I want this woman out of my house. I know she is supposed to help me, but right now, I'm itching to lash out, and she's gonna cop it if she doesn't get off my couch and do something constructive to find Robin.

'No. I told you I'm here for you.'

'I'm good. You can go. I'm sure you have a family of your own that you want to get home to.'

Patricia puts down the newspaper and looks over at me. 'You're going through something bad; it'll be okay, though. I've helped many other families through similar situations.'

'Were you with the Doncasters?' I move around to the couch, but I don't sit down. Instead, I deliberately loom over her.

'Yes,' she replies.

'Did you tell *them* everything would be okay?'

Standing up, she knocks over the side table to the right of the couch and swears under her breath.

'Please, just leave. I won't do anything silly. I just want to be alone and get some sleep.'

'Okay. Sleep is a good idea.' Patricia inches towards the coat rack. As she takes her coat, I look down to see she's still wearing her shoes; Leo, Robin and I always take them off by the door. Everyone who has been in my house since last night has kept their shoes on. All of them have dragged dirt through my home.

After I close the door on Patricia, I wring my hands together, then busy myself with housework to make the time go quicker.

★

Exhausted and covered in dust and muck, I sit down at the dining room table and stare at my phone. Two hours tick by. I get up to pee, but take the phone with me. I feel like a desperate single woman waiting for a date to call.

I should contact Leo. I'm not heartless, even though my heart isn't in my chest anymore. However, I have to remind myself that he's being comforted by Mrs Duffill; all the while, my monster-in-law will be drip-feeding him poison. If Cherrie Forrester wasn't good enough for her son, you could be damn sure Little Bones isn't. Shaking off my emotional instincts to call my boyfriend, I make a cup of tea, and resign myself to stare at my phone.

As night draws in, I fetch Robin's duvet, so I can curl up with it on the couch. It smells like him, like his hair and his skin; how long will that last? It's late and I need to rest. Exhaustion doesn't help when you're hunting a paedophile who has abducted your son.

It's hard to fall asleep when you're fully clothed. Every time I turn around, my shirt catches under my body, tugging at my torso, but I refuse to undress. At any moment, Gemma could text me; I need to be ready. I toy with the idea of just going over to Oscar Greer's house to try some stalking myself, yet my eyelids are heavy and the duvet is warm. Soon, I find myself drifting into an uneasy sleep. Quickly, I jerk awake again. Sleeping is a bad move. Waking to remember Robin is missing is like losing him all over again.

I hate feeling weak; like life is a game and my body is letting me down by succumbing to sleep. I remember when I was little and Dad used to play snakes and ladders with me. We played for hours until I'd win a game. He was so patient. I guess you have to be patient to be a serial killer.

I make a coffee and then sit back down on the sofa.

A vibration from my mobile startles me. I scramble to answer it without checking the caller ID.

'Hello?'

Silence.

'Is anyone there? Is that you, Gemma?'

Nothing.

'Robin?'

Laughter, low and grumbling, like a villain from an old film.

'Who is this?'

'You don't deserve a son. You should be in prison like your sick dad.'

I want my voice to rise up, to be hard enough to protect me from this crazy caller, but it doesn't; instead, it sinks to a whisper. This could be the person who has Robin. If I'm not careful, my temper could kill my son.

'Do you have my son?'

'You don't know me.'

'Do you have Robin?'

Silence.

'Who are you?' I ask.

'Pay attention, I said you don't know me.'

Something snaps deep in my brain. I say, 'I may not know you, but the police will. They're tracing this call.'

The line goes dead.

I scroll through my latest calls. They withheld their number. Fuck.

Quickly, I grab the house phone and call Patricia.

'Someone just called my mobile,' I tell her.

'Oh, I was just about to ring you,' she says.

'Did you hear me, someone just rang. They could have Robin.'

'Did their number come up? Did you recognise the voice?'

'No.'

'We'll look into it, but it's probably just a prank call. I wouldn't be surprised if someone targeted you after that appeal. There's been several hoaxers here too.'

'Wait, you said you were gonna call me? What's happened? What have you found?'

Chapter 22

'We need you to come down to the incident room.'

'What? Have you found Robin?'

'No, but we have found the boy from the fair. The one in the red jacket. We need you to come down to the station to identify him.'

Looking at the clock, I see it's now six in the morning.

'I'll give you time to get dressed. DC Kimmings is outside; he'll drive you.'

When I hang up on her, I realise I forgot about my appointment with Mariah last night. I hope that she will have seen the news and realises why I stood her up. Admittedly, I'm surprised she hasn't called. Maybe she's moved on to another vulnerable child. Perhaps she believes Robin is already lost. No, I have to hope that a woman so intent on helping me that she came uninvited to my home, would pick up the phone if she had any news, be it good or bad. She was right about Thomas Doncaster. Whether I truly believe in her abilities or not, I have to listen to her. What have I got to lose?

I don't bother changing my clothes from yesterday. I put on my boots, then throw on a coat.

It surprises DC Kimmings to see me emerge from the house so quickly. He opens the car door for me to climb into the back seat. Once again, I feel like a criminal he's caught. As if I've done something wrong. I did. I was selfish to want a new beginning with a new name, but would my life have been the same if I hadn't? Would Leigh-Ann have met Leo, had Robin, worked at Dawson's Food, and still made the friends who would support her through a crisis? Changing my name made me paranoid, secretive and ultimately distracted at the wrong time. Perhaps Leigh-Ann would not have lost Robin. Maybe the abductor would have stolen another boy, which would have been sad, but I could have lived with that. These are the thoughts that attack my mind as we drive to the police station. The same station where they questioned my dad. The same station they drove me to when Mum committed suicide.

Once parked, the DC frees me from the back seat, and leads me to a small room. Inside there is a little boy with a woman. With pity dancing behind her eyes, the woman looks up at me.

DC Kimmings speaks quietly with Patricia, then he beckons me forward.

'This is Mrs Gordon and her son Luke. Is he the boy you saw at the fair?'

Mrs Gordon heaves her son to his feet. He's about Robin's height and age, and he has the same hair colour; however, his face is not freckly like my son's. There are no dimples in his cheeks. His eyes are brown rather than blue. From a distance, he'd look like Robin, but up close, the differences are huge. It is the boy from the fair.

'Yes, I saw you in the red jacket.' I reach out to ruffle his hair, but DC Kimmings moves me back.

'I'm so sorry about your son,' Mrs Gordon says.

Patricia suddenly steps between us. 'Let's get a statement from little Luke.' She throws a weird look at DC Kimmings, who cups my elbow to manoeuvre me out of the room.

'Wait, I want to speak with them,' I plead.

'No, I need you to identify the jacket now,' he says.

We move to a smaller room. Sitting on the centre of a table is a red lump covered in clear plastic. DC Kimmings gives it to me. Peering into the bag, I move the material around in my hands. Why are they showing me this? I identified the kid. Why should I have to identify his jacket? As I move the plastic around, I notice a twinkle. I raise it up to the light to examine it. There are red sparkles dotted about the jacket.

I must get an odd look in my eye as DC Kimmings dives forward to take the bag from me. He doesn't make it in time. I rip into it; the jacket instantly puffs up as it hits the air. A waft of Robin's scent smacks me in the face, along with the sticky sweetness from the cotton candy he dropped on it on Friday night.

'Ms Forrester,' DC Kimmings pleads, reaching for the jacket.

I step away from him while I search the pockets. My hand stops dead when I feel a small circle of cardboard. His robot off switch.

'Where did you get this from? It's Robin's jacket. Where did it come from?' I screech, clutching the red coat to my chest.

'From the Gordon boy. He was wearing it at the fair. You saw him in it on that night.'

With Robin's jacket clutched to my chest, I bowl past the DC and burst back into the room with Patricia and the Gordons.

'How did you get my son's jacket? You little thief!' I yell at Luke.

The boy shrinks into his mum's side.

'Don't you dare yell at my son! We've been co-operating so far. We don't have to, you know.'

'This isn't appropriate.' Patricia gets up to try to turn me around; her fingers gripping Robin's jacket.

'Get away from me. And get the fuck off my son's jacket.' I pull it away, almost knocking her over. She maintains her grip on the red material. I pull back again, and we enter into a childish game of tug of war that I'll be damned if I lose. I lost Robin; I won't lose this small part of him, I can't.

'Cherrie, calm down,' Patricia says.

Yanking harder, my breath judders in my ribcage. 'Fuck off!' I push out.

'It was on the ground. I found it,' Luke yells out.

I stop moving but still keep my grip on Robin's jacket.

'Where?' As I ask this question, I attempt to disguise my voice in a more motherly, less insane timbre.

'It was by the Ghost Train's exit.'

'My son has done nothing wrong,' Mrs Gordon says.

'Tell me exactly where you found my son's jacket. Was it by the train? Was it on the ride?' My voice has surpassed a warm tone; it's now borderline crazy. Even I can hear it.

'By the train,' Luke whispers.

Mrs Gordon stands up to get in my face. 'I remember you from the papers, Little Bones. For a while, we went to the same school. You were crazy then and you're crazy now.'

'Well, perhaps you shouldn't mess with a crazy person,' I tell her, squaring my shoulders.

'Okay, please, Cherrie, just go back to the other room with DC Kimmings and let us get the full statement from little Luke here.' Patricia stares at me as if I'm a mental patient who's off her meds. I fucking hate her. From her patronising tone to the smile that doesn't make it past her mascara-clumped eyes. She is telling me what to do as if she understands what it feels like to have your son ripped from your arms.

'Please, Cherrie,' Patricia says again.

I unfurl my fists; I hadn't realised I'd clenched them so hard until my palms feel the relief of where my fingernails were digging in. Taking a breath, I give them all a sour look, and then walk out of the room. There's a sigh of relief from behind me.

Fortunately, I have all the information I need. If Luke found Robin's jacket at the Ghost Train, then it was definitely the skeleton who took my son; there's no imagining that, or chalking it up to a chance encounter. Someone deliberately dressed in bones and stole Robin. He knows me, who I am. This has to be a copycat of my dad. This is all that bloody podcast's fault. It unearthed the bones of my past and got dirt all over my son. If the abductor found out about Robin's granddad, taking him could be for some killer kudos. It was probably him who called me; laughing down the phone like Batman's Joker.

I wander outside towards the police car. Robin's red jacket is in my hands, my palm cupping the small sparkling disc I'd given him before we left that night; his off switch.

He doesn't have it anymore. Robin won't be able to turn anything off now.

DC Kimmings runs to open the back door of the car. I head towards the front passenger seat and wait for him to open that door; in one small action asserting I'm not a criminal.

'I will need the jacket back; it's evidence. You want us to find your son, right?' DC Kimmings reaches for the jacket. I let him take it back, while I slip the glittery cardboard disc into my pocket.

He opens the car door. I slide into the front seat, and watch him bundle the last thing Robin wore into another evidence bag. I begin to formulate a plan.

Dad never touched the boys he took; he only wanted their bones, but that's not to say the copycat isn't a sex offender, that it's not Oscar Greer.

They can have the jacket back; it won't make any difference. The police won't find the skeleton man. There's only one person who might know who the copycat is, or at least could give me a look inside the mind of someone who abducts and kills little boys; Mr Bones himself. But am I ready to, once again, breathe the same air as my father?

Chapter 23

By the time I get home, I've convinced myself that talking to Dad would be a mistake. I'm not in the right mental state to deal with him now. Instead, I explore my copycat theory and search online for Mr Bones sites. More results than I'd have liked to see pop up, including the top result, *The Flesh on the Bones* website, which links to that fucking podcast. Jai Patel has broken his word and breathed fresh digital life back into it. There's even a new episode entitled, *Cherrie and Leigh-Ann*. I resist the temptation to listen. I doubt it'll be anything other than nasty rumours and spiteful theories. It won't help me find Robin, or discover if there are any Mr Bones wannabes. Sticks and stones may break bones, but my past might kill my son if I don't dedicate every ounce of my energy into finding him.

I search through website after website and find many disturbing articles – nothing of use. I'm not even sure what I'm looking for. Would a copycat create a website? Would he be so obvious as to record his wicked thoughts in public?

Shit. Dad could shed light into the dark world of child abductors and murderers. I may not want to, but it could be the only way to find Robin. Even if he isn't aware of any adoring fans who have pieced together my connection to him, he might still have insight; a clue only a twisted mind can pull apart, then tie back up again. No, I can't. I'm not there yet. Dad's my last straw to clutch.

Slumping back in my chair, I close my eyes. I've made great strides in suppressing the memories of my parents, of growing up not needing love and guidance. Right now though, as weird as it sounds, I'd give anything to hug my dad, to let him tell me everything will be okay. After the conviction, my young mind separated out the two beings of Dad and Mr Bones. Dad bought me sweets. Mr Bones bought me knives. Dad played games with me. Mr Bones watched me play games with his victims. Dad baked scones with me. Mr Bones taught me how to remove internal organs without creating a mess. I didn't kill the boys, but without me, would they have gotten in Mr Bones' car? It took years for me to accept the part I played. Years of criminology textbooks and searching missing people websites. There were the boys I knew he'd killed, but what if there had been more? Victims he'd hunted alone? I searched, but there were no others. Eleven boys' faces used to haunt my thoughts; now it's only my son's face I see when I close my eyes.

Opening a new window on the laptop, I start searching for missing child statistics in the UK. Google tells me over 140,000 under-eighteen-year-olds go missing every year. Scrolling down, I see they find ninety-one per cent within the first forty-eight hours. Quick maths tells me that's over twelve thousand lost children. I look over at the mantel clock. Robin's been missing since Friday night; there are only a few hours to go before my son has been missing over forty-eight hours and becomes a darker statistic.

I check my phone; there are no new messages. When does Oscar Greer finish work? I should have asked where he worked. I could have then figured out what time he'd be back and laid in wait for him, rather than relying on the observations of a teenage police-wannabe. It's a rookie stalker mistake.

I wring my hands together and stare at my laptop. Slowly, I type in Greer's name. My screen fills with a myriad of irrelevant results; it's an oddly popular name. There's Facebook Pages, LinkedIn profiles and company staff lists, but without knowing what he looks like, the search is difficult. I add the word, *pervert* to the search parameters, which conjures up a few sites I'd rather not have in my search history. Wait, the Google Alert. I load up the email and click the link it coughed up. Something I should have done in the first place.

The link takes me to a blog by someone called *Concerned in Rosemount*. It's a new site, only live since last Sunday. It lists a few petty crimes, a missing garden gnome, a stolen bike, several cans of pop littering the path, and a speeding car, but mentions nothing about Thomas Doncaster's murder. With its digital birth just a day after they reported the disappearance in the news, you'd think a boy going missing would be of more concern than litter. Especially as he was murdered.

The longest post on the blog is about Oscar Greer. It links to his conviction notice online and even has a small photo, which I click on to enlarge. He's younger than I imagined; he looks just in his early twenties. In the picture, he wears a horrified look of sadness as he stares into the camera. If I didn't know what I knew, I'd feel sorry for him. He's standing by the side of his bungalow; I recognise the dead–plant–encrusted hanging baskets. Could Greer be the skeleton from the fair? Could he be a copycat? He has the build for it. The blogger has written a short sentence under his photo: *Shine a light! Do these monsters need to live in our estates?*

The blog doesn't reveal Greer's work or home address. I check out the hits; it's had quite a few. The irony of this whole thing grips my conscience; this happened to me. *The Flesh on the Bones* sensationalised the Thomas Doncaster case and linked it to my family. That is how my stalker found me, and I'm about to do the same thing to Greer. Fuck it. What has a high moral standing ever done for me, anyhow? The principle of not continuing this vicious cycle of online muck spreading isn't enough to stop me going back to Greer's house and confronting him; I'm not sure anything on this earth could.

Staring at Greer's photo, I scorch his image into my mind. All too soon, glaring at the bright screen makes my eyes sting. Blinking a few times, I look away. Artificial dots gather in my vision. They disappear as quickly as they appear. I'm tired and need to get some sleep, yet I can't do it right now. I have to be ready to take a call. Be it from a nosy teen neighbour or the police.

Closing my laptop lid, I imagine curling my fingers around Greer's neck. How much pressure would it take? He'll be strong; how could I subdue him long enough to choke the perverted life out of him? Drugs? No, not my style. Maybe stabbing. Blood loss and panic could weaken him . . .

As I make my way upstairs, I trip over one of Robin's books. I bend, scoop it up and place it back in his room. As I do, I sit down on his bed. I take in a long breath, which judders in my chest. No, I can't afford to be some clichéd grieving mother, not yet. Forcing myself up, I leave Robin's room. I don't want to get mum smell all over it.

I go to the bathroom and fill the sink with cold water, then dunk my head into it. The chill smacks my skin. I open my eyes under the water. A stray image of my mum floods my mind; her bloated mouth open in a silent scream. Tears distort the scene before me.

I flick my head up; my long hair sprays out in cold, sticky clumps down my back. If Mum had not taken her life, would she be here right now trying to help me? Comforting me? Doubtful.

Staring in the mirror, I examine my rough appearance. No make-up, little sleep, I'm all sharp features aching for a fight. My hand is on a hairbrush when I hear my mobile's ringtone coming from the dining room. I rush down the stairs and pick up my phone. There's no caller ID. What if it's that laughing asshole from before? Fuck it. I answer.

'Hello?'

'Cherrie? This is Gemma.'

'Oh, hi Gemma, what have you seen?'

'Approximately ten minutes ago, Mr Greer came back from work. Dropped off by the number three bus. He has bags of groceries from somewhere called Dawson's Food and another bag from a toy shop.'

He shops where I work. Could he have targeted me specifically? And toys make sense: Robin would be bored. Wait, if he has spent money on toys then my baby is still alive.

'I'll be right there,' I say and hang up.

Looking down at my feet, I realise I didn't take my boots off when I got home. I'm just as guilty as my errant visitors for dragging dirt through my home. I grab a coat and stride out of the house. I don't want to take my car. If any of those reporters swarm back, I want them to believe I'm still inside the house.

At the top of my street, I break into a sprint towards Greer's bungalow. I'm not in the best shape, so have to stop to gasp and hold my knees. I don't remember it being this far away before, but then again, I had put up flyers all the way along the street before I even saw the email.

Looking up, I see my son's face floating ghost-like on every lamppost, reflected in the windows of strangers' houses, staring back out at me. A smile playing on his lips. His eyes alight with mischief. A puckish lost boy daring me to find him. This gives me the energy I need to reach Greer's street, to get to his house, to walk up the paedophile's drive, to knock on his door. He has to be the abductor, and Little Bones wants to meet him.

Chapter 24

I'd planned to have at least thirty seconds to think through this confrontation before he opened the door, but it's as if he knew I was coming. The door swings wide open and I see Oscar Greer wearing a beige short-sleeve shirt and tie with moccasin slippers. An outfit you'd expect your granddad to wear, not a twenty-something.

'Can I help you?'

His voice is soft and familiar; could he be the man who called me, laughing?

Opening my mouth, I try to speak, but nothing comes out.

He looks down at my hands. What's he looking for? A weapon?

I expect a villain's cackle but instead he asks, 'Are you all right?'

I can't speak. My brain grasps for a well-constructed lie to get me through Greer's door, so I can search the house for Robin, yet the words stay trapped behind my gritted teeth.

Greer sighs. 'I've been expecting you.'

He is the copycat. He has Robin.

'Robin!' I yell at the top of my lungs.

'Hey, hey, what are you doing?'

Greer moves to close the door, but I ram my boot in the way, wedging it between the door and its frame, leaving me a small gap to yell, 'Robin! Mummy's here!'

'Shhhh. I don't have your son,' he says, gently trying to dislodge my foot.

'Robin!'

'I don't have your son!'

'Let me in. If you don't have him, you can let me in and show me.' I snake my fingers through the gap and clutch his shirt. I get a handful of his dangling tie and use it to pull his head towards me.

'Stop! What are you doing?' he screams.

I wind my knuckles around the tie, pulling him closer. So close, I can smell something sweet on his breath.

A feeling stirs inside me. Soft, familiar darkness I've ignored for a long time. It reaches up and through me.

'I'll kill you,' I whisper.

Greer's eyes widen as his hands claw at mine. I feel his fingers, but he has short nails, so can only paw at me with blunt panic. Images of him doing horrible things to Robin cut through my brain, cracking my logic into splinters. Sweet madness slips over my common sense and I grip harder. I'm moments away from having Robin back in my arms. If I have to, I will kill Oscar Greer. No one will miss him. The world will be a better place without him.

'I'll call the police!' Oscar screams.

The door opens a little more, so I inch my boot in further. I'm almost to Robin. *I'm coming, sweetie. Mummy's coming to save you.*

'Please, you must believe me,' he whines.

'Call the police,' I tell him. 'We'll see what happens. Will they help the sick kiddie fiddler or the mother rescuing her child?'

'What? No, please, just listen.' Looking down, he kicks out at my foot.

Sharp pain pulses up through my leg, but I don't move. I can take it. I pull harder on his tie, and his head plunges further forward, hitting the glass of the door. His ruddy skin squeezes up against it. I'm so close that I can see his gaping pores and stubble through the thick glass.

'You will let me in,' I seethe.

My voice is coming out different. I hear it and even register the change, yet can't seem to dial back the tone.

With one hand, he scrambles around behind the door while trying to hold on to his tie with the other.

'Please,' he says.

A flash of metal and I'm suddenly reeling backwards. The door slams shut. I stand on the doorstep bewildered, half of his tie still in my grasp. He cut it off. Who keeps scissors by their front door?

I bang loudly. 'Don't you want your tie back?' I say, throwing the limp material at the house.

His shadow lingers behind the glass of the door. 'Please leave me alone.'

'Give me back my son!'

'I don't have your bloody son. Go! Now!'

'Fuck you. I'm not going anywhere. I'll camp out on your front lawn if I have to. I'll find a way into your house, and if you've hurt Robin, I'll do the same back to you, only worse.' Laying my head on the glass, I laugh. 'I can imagine so much worse; I won't even make a mess.'

'I'm sorry about your son, but you're looking in the wrong place. I don't like boys. You need to leave now.'

'I'm not going anywhere.'

'Please. I've already spoken to the police. They came here first. They've searched my house.'

I take this new information in and roll it around in my head, yet it doesn't stick. Leaning forward, I place both my palms onto the glass.

'I'll huff and I'll puff,' I whisper.

There's something oddly familiar about this. I close my eyes. The bereaved father on my doorstep. I was in this exact situation with him; only I was on the other side of the door, scared and without the answers to give him. This is how it feels, hollow and desperate. I bang my fist once against the door, then amble down his drive. Turning back, I look at the house again to check each window for a familiar little face. I see nothing.

I reach my estate with no memory of the journey. As I walk down my street, DC Steadman pulls up. He gets out of the silent Panda car and patiently waits for me by my front door. As I reach him, he says, 'I had a call about you hassling Oscar Greer. Is that true?'

'You should know, you guys apparently hassled him first,' I say staggering into him like a drunk.

'Yes, we searched Mr Greer's house. There was nothing there.' DC Steadman puts an arm around my shoulders to direct me through my front door.

217

'*I* didn't get to search his house. I want to go in there myself.'

'You're exhausted and not thinking straight. You need to sleep. Consider this a warning; stop meddling in the investigation. You can't go vigilante on us.' He pushes me further into the house. 'Seriously, Mrs Duffill, get some sleep. Don't you dare go back to Mr Greer's house. I'm warning you,' he says and leaves, closing the door behind him.

'Ms Forrester!' I yell at the door.

He's right about one thing: I've hardly slept, and been mostly awake since Thursday night – the last time Robin was safely under this roof. That's over seventy hours awake. I slump down on the couch. Seventy hours is nothing; the interns in *Grey's Anatomy* were up for much longer, and someone gave them sharp instruments to cut people open. I understand it's a TV show, but they had medical consultants on set. Most of the episodes were based on truth.

My eyelids are sticky. After I rest, I'll go after Oscar Greer again. Wait, I frightened him. What if he wants to get rid of the evidence and kills Robin before I get there? He could end my flesh and blood just as easily as he extracted his tie from me, with a sharp flash of metal.

Itchy feet make me walk into the kitchen to put on the kettle. As I reach for the milk, I see the picture on the fridge, the one Robin made before the fair featuring him and Nostrom. Two smiling faces with the ominous Ferris wheel in the distance like some grim prediction made of crayon.

My mobile rings. I can't look at it. What if it was Greer who called before, and he now wants to tell me what he's done to Robin, or where I can find my baby's body? It rings out and then there's a beep for a text message. I fish it out of my pocket and look down to see the missed call was from Leo; after, he sent a text. It reads, *I'm* and an alien face. He's sent me yet another emoji my phone is too old to read. He could be anything: sorry, hurt, dead, a pile of poo, the list is endless and I, to be honest, don't give a shit what he is right now. My fair-weather boyfriend ran off to his mummy, leaving me alone to deal with our son's abduction. No doubt, they've spent their time lamenting on how I'm no good for him. How I lost our only child at a bloody fair. He's fully aware that I can't read most of the emoji he sends me, so why send them at all?

I ignore the text and put my phone on to charge. Dragging myself around the kitchen, I grab some food. Crackers with gherkins and instant mash with baked beans. I sit back down on the couch, stuff a cracker into my mouth and chew. In time, with my stomach reeling from the bizarre meal, I close my eyes.

That night, I get about two hours' sleep, in which there are no dreams, and the moment my eyes open, I realise Robin is still missing. Sitting up, I brush stray pieces of cracker from my jumper. There's a godawful smell; it's me. I go upstairs, strip off and get into the shower. I wash my hair, and as the steam fills up the bathroom, I notice Robin's Matey Bubble Bath. The little plastic peg-leg pirate stares at me, judging me with his one good eye. I bend down and twist him around, so he faces the bathroom tiles. As I do, I see letters forming on the mirror by the bath. I squint at them. It reads:

Nostrom. No doubt written by Robin the last time he was in here.

As I step out of the shower, an unusual blast of cold air smacks my skin, bringing goose bumps in its wake. The front door is open. Someone is downstairs.

Chapter 25

Wrapping a towel around myself, I quietly pad to the landing. There are whispers. I crouch down by the stairs, my hair dripping over my shoulders, and try to make out who has come into my house uninvited. I can't hear words, yet there's movement. A rustle here, a footstep there.

'Cherrie!'

I sigh. It's Leo, but who is with him? Please, God, don't let it be his mum.

'I'm upstairs,' I yell, feeling my heart fall back into its familiar rhythm.

I hear him coming up the stairs. As he appears around the landing, I can see he looks just as exhausted as me. Shadows lurk beneath his blue eyes and he has more stubble on his chin than usual.

'You opened the extension?'

No, *hello*, no, *how are you doing?* Definitely no, *sorry to abandon you at such a horrific time of need*.

'I had to open it,' I say walking back into our bedroom. I throw off the towel and am about to pull out clean underwear when I hear him follow me into the room. He sits on the bed.

'Why would you open it, and how? I took the key.'

I can't tell him the real reason. 'There was a weird noise in there.' I step into a no-frills pair of knickers and pull them up. I thread my arms through a mismatched bra, then snake my hand around to hook it up.

'There was?'

'Yeah, you left a window ajar. The wind was catching on a stepladder.'

'Oh, so you saw my surprise, eh?' Leo doesn't look at me when he speaks; his focus is on a dust bunny that has gathered on our bedroom floor.

'Fancy getting the hoover out while you're here?' I say and kick the dust clump for emphasis, breaking his concentration.

'Please, don't start. Hey, did you get my text?' he asks.

'You mean the one you knew I wouldn't be able to read?'

'You could update that bloody phone at any time.'

'And I told you, I don't want to. I've bigger things to worry about right now.'

'Cherrie, this is your fault. Nothing about this is on me,' he says, watching me dress.

I pull on a jumper and sit down next to him to wriggle into a pair of jeggings.

'It could easily have happened to you, Leo. I swear I was paying attention. Robin was on that fucking wheel. There was nowhere for him to go but around and around.' I motion a circle with my arms.

Quicker than I thought he could move, Leo grabs my wrist mid-spin and pulls me to him. 'He didn't get on that ride though, did he; some bastard in a skeleton costume grabbed him. Dumped his jacket for Luke Gordon to find, and you watched little Luke go around and around while ignoring the abduction of our son.'

I snatch my arm back. 'Oh, now you believe me, eh?'

Leo thrusts his fingers through his hair. 'Yes, I believe you. Doesn't really help us, though, does it. There's not even one viable suspect.'

'I'm working on it, Leo!'

'Oh, you're working on it are you? I see, well let's allow the police to get on with another case, just as long as you have this whole thing in hand.' He gets up, walks to the edge of the door, and yells, 'It's all right, Patricia, you can go now. Cherrie is drawing up a suspect list and has everything under control!'

Most people can't yell and sound sarcastic at the same time, but Leo nails it.

'What was that, Mr Duffill?' Patricia calls up the stairs.

'Fuck you! I feel the ache of not having Robin in my arms. I can't sleep without thinking about what could be happening to him. I feel it so deep I can barely breathe,' I admit.

'Maybe that was what the parents of those boys your dad killed felt like? How many did he kill again? You can't believe a skeleton taking Robin is a coincidence. This is all on you. You didn't just drop the ball, you kicked it out into the cold and closed the door behind it.'

'Get whatever you came here for, and then fuck off back to Mummy. I don't need you, and I won't need the nursery you made downstairs. Oh, and building a nursery downstairs? What the hell were you thinking?'

223

'You don't want another child?' Leo's voice raises several octaves, as if I had broken a promise to him.

'Of course I do, but we would have needed the room next to ours. You can't have a kid downstairs on their own, you moron. How would we get up in the night to feed and change them?'

Leo bursts out laughing. 'Shit, I didn't think that through.' He covers his mouth, laughing through his fingers.

I can't help it: as much as I want to punch him in the face, a laugh escapes me.

'Two fucking years, I built that nursery. You're right; it should have been upstairs. I should have built it over the garage.'

'Did you just admit I'm right about something?' I ask him.

'Don't rub it in.' He shuffles his feet like a child.

It feels wrong to laugh without our son, but Leo and I are still a family, even with a big Robin-shaped hole punched through both of us.

A question, which seemed so pointless before, slips from my lips. 'How did you find out about Mr Bones?'

'It's stupid.' Leo purses his lips. 'Doesn't really matter now.'

'It matters to me.'

Leo huffs and says, 'One of the guys at work. His wife was talking about a podcast on Facebook. He listened to it and heard your name. Told me about it the day Robin disappeared. It took me hours to build up the courage to text you.'

'That fucking podcast. Have you listened to it?'

'No, I just googled Mr Bones. There was plenty of information online.'

It took three degrees of separation for my secret to find Leo. Just three.

'Cherrie . . .'

'Why are you here?' I ask him.

'I live here, remember?'

'You left.'

'I shouldn't have gone. I was scared of what I'd say, and what I'd do if I stayed. I can't stop wondering – would I be going through this if I wasn't with you, with Little Bones?' He reaches out to touch my face. His fingers are cold and rough against my cheek.

'I understand; I do. I was *her* for seventeen years, remember? I'm not ready to talk everything through, and I don't have the time or energy to keep defending myself. I have things I need to do,' I try to explain, but my words are coming out strangled.

'Miles to go before you sleep,' Leo mutters.

'Something like that.'

'I'll get some stuff and head back to Mum's house. I'm coming home, though. Whatever you're doing, you have to tell me about it. I need Robin back too. I miss him. I miss his hugs and his smell.' Tears gather in my boyfriend's eyes. I've never seen him cry; I don't want to see it now.

'Well, melancholy is not going to get Robin back. I refuse to mourn our son, until I have no other choice. Are you with me?'

Leo sniffles but nods. Turning, he grabs a bag from the wardrobe and fills it with clothes. I watch him the whole time. As angry as I am about the blame he is laying on me, I still don't want him out of my sight until I have to let him go. Even knowing this, I must remember to keep him at arm's length. Leo isn't my knight in shining armour;

he never has been, or said he would be. I need to slay the dragon alone; because with slaying comes consequences. Robin will need at least one parent out of prison to raise him after I kill Greer. It won't be difficult; killing is in my genes. All I need to do is peel off the carefully constructed layers of Cherrie to reach Little Bones.

Finished with his bag, Leo slowly walks downstairs. I'm about to follow him when I hear a noise in Robin's room. Relief floods my body. Thank God, he's back home! Safe and unharmed. This nightmare has all been a massive mistake . . . I fling open his door, but instead of my lost son, find Mrs Duffill clutching clothes she bought for Robin's last birthday.

'What the hell are you doing?' I ask.

Shock widens her eyes, then her usual mask of superiority slips over her face. 'I came over with Leo and that officer.'

'No.' I shake my head. 'What are you doing here, in Robin's bedroom?'

'I'm picking an outfit.' She places the pile of clothes on a nearby chair, then lays a sweatshirt, jeans and a pair of socks on top of the bed. It looks as if the boy wearing them vanished leaving a material echo behind. Sighing, she steps back to look down at her selection, almost tripping over her large handbag. That's when I realise she's not choosing clothes for Robin's return, she is deciding his funeral outfit; the last thing he'll wear; the shroud that will cover my son's corpse and hold together his little bones.

'Get out.'

Mrs Duffill looks up at me.

'Get out.'

'Cherrie, I . . .'

'Get. Out!'

Grabbing her bag, she hurries from the room.

As I stare down at the empty clothes, I imagine Robin on his bed, laughing and reading. As much as this is Mrs Duffill's handiwork, I can't bring myself to tidy anything away.

After shutting the bedroom door behind me, I trudge downstairs to say goodbye to Leo.

'Where is your mother now? Rifling through my knicker drawer?'

'She's in the car with Patricia.' Leo kisses my cheek, heaves his bag over his shoulder, and walks to the doorway. He looks back at me. 'When this is all over, maybe we can all go to see Mum's new house in Spain.'

'We can give Robin the first stamp in his passport.' I smile at the thought of the three of us laughing in the sunshine, even if Mrs Duffill is there, then remember Leo's text. 'What emoji did you send me earlier?'

'A house. I was telling you I was coming home.'

'I got an alien face. For all I knew you were telling me aliens abducted you.'

'For future reference, I wouldn't text you if I was taken by a flying saucer. I'd text—'

'Mummy, right?' I instantly regret it. We'd been doing so well. For a brief moment in time, we were partners; not back to where we have been, but close.

'Actually I was going to say I'd text The Men in Black,' Leo says, then leaves.

It's not until I hear the car door slam I realise I should have made a joke about wanting Will Smith's telephone number. It would have made Leo laugh, and that would have been better than a parting shot at his mum.

From the window I watch all three of them drive off together. At least they are out of the way, for now. Looking at the shoes by the door, I see Robin's pair are gone. Mrs Duffill must have taken them. Busting in on her wardrobe raid, I didn't give her time to find my son's dress shoes; the ones he hides under his bed.

There's an awful lot of plotting I need to do to sort out Greer. The police have him on their radar; does that mean they're watching him? Hell, they don't even have enough money for two family liaison officers, it's not as if they have budget to mount a massive surveillance operation . . . and I'm being stupid again. I'm putting all my hopes on one suspect. What if Greer doesn't have Robin? He said he doesn't even like boys. Can I believe a word he says? After all, if he is a true Mr Bones copycat, surely little boys have to be his preference.

I sit down on the couch and fall back against the cushions. I need help, but not the regular kind the girls, or Leo, or even the police could give me. God help me, I do need my dad. I need a killer connection. I need to find out if any weirdos have been writing him fan mail, especially ones called Oscar Greer. Or if anyone has said anything to him about resurrecting his past, or making art from dead kids' shoes rather than their bones. The image of a bony tree decorated in tied-together trainers flashes through my mind. How many boys would it take to bring that artwork to life? More than the eleven my dad murdered.

If the police searched Greer's house and found nothing, maybe he is innocent, although Gemma said she saw him with a bag of toys. Why, if he has no kids, would he have toys? He also had a bag from Dawson's Food, but it is the nearest supermarket.

None of this is simple. In books and movies, they make it look easy. Just follow the trail of clues to find your answer. In real life, you don't get all the clues; you get fragments that don't fit together. Like a jigsaw puzzle where the pieces never matched in the first place.

As I pull myself off the couch, I hear my stomach growl. I make a smoky-bacon crisp sandwich. It gives off a satisfying crunch as I cut it in two. I sit at the dining room table with my laptop. I can't help myself; I click on to *The Flesh on the Bones*, more out of habit now than actual want. Jai has now threaded his Twitter feed through the website. A disturbing hashtag keeps appearing #fakecherrie. Yet more trolls looking to make his or her life more interesting by attacking me. I've never used social media. I was always scared in case someone recognised me, which means I have no established profiles to use to retaliate. Just like when I was a little girl, I will have to suck it up and take their half-arsed lies on an already fragile chin.

'Sticks and stones may break my bones,' I say to myself, but there's no conviction in my words. Just like there was no conviction in them when I repeated the same childish rhyme to myself at school. Every day my so-called school friends would dance around me singing their crude song. I still remember it:

Little Bones lives in a home,
With eleven thin little boys.
Each night they moan, for their own headstone,
As their bones are now her toys.

Imaginative little bastards.

I tried to ignore their silly chant, a song that didn't even rhyme properly, but I couldn't. As when my foster family and teachers looked at me, I knew they only saw the daughter of a serial killer. Born of murder and drawn to death. I was so careful of the stories I wrote in English class – nothing too dark. And how I acted around everyone – never too sullen. I went mad on the inside. God forbid I showed it on the outside.

It wasn't until I hit seventeen, changed my name, dyed my hair, and moved back home to Northamptonshire that I carved out a life for myself. No one looked at Cherrie Forrester as if she was about to pull out a hatchet and go nuts. No one thought Cherrie Forrester was dangerous to have around his or her children. No one crossed the street when they saw Cherrie Forrester. For a few years, I had a life; an identity truly mine, not some bloody hand-me-down from my dad. Now it's all over. Cherrie Forrester is #fakecherrie and forever linked to Little Bones. Not the biggest problem I have right now, but I still feel it – like a sharp knife slicing curls of tender flesh from my life. Cutting until there's nothing left but a stark, greasy bone.

I click off *The Flesh on the Bones.* I can't put it off any longer. I find the details of Dad's prison. Quickly, I discover the process of seeing him isn't what I imagined. I can't just pop in and surprise him. Dad has to request a visiting order for me. Fuck. I'll need to contact him first. I wasn't ready for this interaction so soon. I was hoping I'd have a train ride and a taxi journey before having to deal with him for the first time in so long. TV makes visiting prisoners look easy, as if you can just rock up to the gates whenever you like. Should I be doing this at all?

I search for what to expect when you visit a prison. I scan each page of each website. Is it as complicated as it looks?

Logging off the computer, I check my phone: nothing. I make a cup of tea. My fingers itch at the sight of the knives in the cutlery drawer. I can bear this, I can.

Greer is a good, solid suspect. I don't need my dad to give me any serial killer clues or advice . . . but perhaps I do need him. I loved him when I was little. He was always there for me. Mum took little interest in her only child. She only loved her husband. Losing him was why committing suicide was as easy as abandoning me. I was just an everyday reminder of the man she lost. She bought all those pills. Filled up the bathtub; swallowed the tablets one at a time with a glass of water. It would have taken a while for her to do it all. I remember that day. Mum left me watching TV. She hadn't even loved me enough to take me with her.

No, I do need Dad now. I pick up my mobile and call the prison. I need my dad, but this time I also need Mr Bones.

Chapter 26

The phone rings. I haven't seen my dad since I was eight years old, and he hasn't contacted me. What will I say to him? He doesn't even know he has a grandson. Do I just blurt out about Robin being missing, and tell him I've only now reached out to ask about his fanboys? I haven't thought this through. I should hang up.

The phone stops ringing. I hear an automated message about the prison. They will record this call and so on. The message stops as suddenly as it started.

'Can I help you?' comes a woman's voice on the other end of the line.

'Umm, yes, I hope so. I want to speak with a prisoner, William Hendy.'

'I can't just put calls through to inmates. They need to call you. Please hang up and . . .'

'How can he call me when he doesn't have my details, or know I need to talk to him?'

The woman sighs. 'Don't hold your breath; Mr Hendy doesn't do interviews.'

Is she insinuating he won't see me? 'Well, thanks for your fucking help.'

'There's no need for foul language.'

'I'm sorry. I really need my dad right now. Can you help me?'

'Your dad? You're his daughter?'

'Yes, I'm Cherrie, I mean Leigh-Ann Hendy.'

'Well, yes; okay, there's an online email system.' She gives me the address. 'You can use this service. You email and we print it off for the prisoner the same day.'

'Thanks,' I say and hang up.

I go to the site and follow the instructions, then stare at a blank email for the next hour. What do I write? Somehow, this is even harder than thinking through what I would say face to face. Do I tell him the truth? I begin typing about Robin, how great he is, and that he has an imaginary friend called Nostrom. I tell Dad I need his help, but I'm not specific as to why I need it. I press send before I can change my mind, or liberally redraft the email with swear words.

Now, I have to wait.

The sun flutters through the dining room window. I close my eyes. In its bright warmth, I imagine Mrs Duffill's house in Spain. Robin playing in the sand. Leo wearing surfer shorts, which billow in the water as he swims. Me in a bikini, sipping cocktails on a sun lounger. Mrs Duffill drowning in the nearby pool. Her damp bouffant hair slowly dragging her, head first, towards the tiled bottom. That's awful. I need to stop being so mean.

Perhaps Mrs Duffill and I are fuelling this cycle of hate together, one giving the other cause to react. Maybe I should extend an olive branch; especially now. She loves

Robin almost as much as I do. She'll be feeling his absence just as much.

I make another crisp sandwich that I don't eat, then check my email for the Visiting Order. It's not there. Would Dad ignore my pleas for help? It's not essential I speak to him. The police now have all the details of my past, so have probably already spoken to him. I might be putting myself through this all for nothing. My dad might have some Hannibal Lecter-style unique insight into what's going on, but it's not as if he's psychic . . . Though I know someone who is. Shit, I should have done this sooner.

Driving to Mariah's house on autopilot, my mind twitches with questions. I realise that her gift isn't easy to interpret, and there will only be vague answers; but ambiguous answers are better than nothing. After all, she did predict Robin's abduction and Thomas's death, so there has to be some insight she can give me. I should have listened to her from the start; if I had, maybe I'd be curled up on the couch right now with Robin and Leo.

Pulling into her drive, I see her car, so I know she's in. I jog to her front door and knock. No answer.

'Mariah!' I shout through her letterbox.

The door opens. It's Jon.

'She's with Sarah,' he says. 'Can I help you?'

'I missed my appointment Saturday night. I'm so sorry.'

'We saw it on the news. We tried to warn you.' He gives me a sympathetic smile, with undertones of *I told you so*.

'I know you did, but I need her help now. Will she help me? I'll pay her anything you ask.'

Jon purses his lips and looks behind me as if someone in the street is watching. 'Okay. Come in.'

'Thank you.'

He smiles awkwardly as if he'd prefer anyone but me at his door, but he stands aside to let me pass. As I enter the house, I smell their dinner. I look at my watch and realise I've interrupted their teatime.

'Oh, I'm so sorry about barging in like this. Has your little girl eaten yet? I'm not disturbing her dinner, am I?'

'She's upstairs playing now. Sorry about the mess, I was just tidying up the dishes.' Jon walks me into their kitchen. Like all their rooms, it's a small, yet strangely sparse space, holding just the basic kitchen appliances and a little dining room table and four chairs. Three used plates sit on the table. It's not exactly what I'd call a mess.

The house feels so different compared to when I came for my first reading. Then, it was cold with a musky scent, but today it's warm and smells like a home.

He moves to clear the dishes, and I jerk in front of him to help. I put my hand on one plate and my finger touches something soft. Looking down, I see cheese spread on a stray piece of carrot. I almost burst into tears, yet manage to hold it together. I can't have a breakdown in their kitchen over cheesy vegetables.

'You do this for Sarah too?' I ask.

'Yeah, kids hate veg; it's all we can do to get her to eat them. We also add whizzed-up carrots and broccoli to gravy and sauces.'

'That's a good idea. I must try it with Robin . . .' I say, my voice trailing off with his name.

'I'd introduce you to Sarah, but Mariah doesn't like her

speaking with the clients. You understand. It's nothing to do with . . .'

'Sure.' I help him put the dishes in the dishwasher. After, Jon sits me down in the living room with a cup of weak tea.

'I'll see if Mariah can see you now.' He sighs. 'I'm sorry about your son.'

I want to say it is okay; it's a natural knee-jerk response, but I can't seem to push it out. Probably because it's not okay.

Sipping hot, tasteless tea, I wait for Mariah. As I do, I hear little Sarah bumping around upstairs playing.

I've almost drained my drink when Mariah sweeps into the room. She's wearing a pink dress and a fuchsia shrug. Her hair is messy, and her make-up is heavy, although not as perfect as when I last saw her here.

'Do you have good news for me?' I ask her.

I hear the faint voice of Jon telling Sarah to be quiet because there's a visitor downstairs who needs their help. Mariah notices me eavesdropping so explains, 'She likes to play tag with her dolls. It can get pretty noisy.'

It's an odd game. I'm guessing Sarah likes to win at things; she can't lose when dolls are chasing her.

Mariah leads me to the reading room. Wordlessly, she gives me the cards. I shuffle them, cut them with my left hand, then give them back to her.

Drawing only one card, she looks up at me. 'We only need help tonight, only the advice on what you should do.'

Wiggling her fingers over the card like a magician performing a trick, she smiles at me.

A big bang sounds upstairs and she blushes. 'Sorry about

that, Sarah is in one of her moods tonight. It was supposed to be family time.'

'Oh, I'm so sorry for just barging in. I could talk to her, tell her how important you are?'

'No, that's okay. I can't vouch for her attitude, and you've had enough abuse recently.'

Wow, Sarah sounds like a right little madam. 'Okay, thanks again for doing this,' I tell her. 'I really appreciate it.'

Smiling, she flips over the card: the Wheel of Fortune. It looks like the bloody Ferris wheel.

'Hmmm, the cards are saying you have to go back to the fair.'

'Back to Crazy Clive's?'

'Yes, a man from the fair took Robin. He still has him. Your little bird never left there.'

Robin's still at the fair? Wait, what? 'How can that be?' I ask. 'The police checked the fair.'

'He's a clever man. This is not his first time, but his first did not go as he planned. It frustrated him, made him act sooner than he would have liked.'

'Has he hurt my son?'

'No. Robin is safe. For now.'

'Is he a copycat?'

'Pardon?' She looks at me, her eyes narrowed.

'The fair worker, does he want to be like another killer?'

Mariah closes her eyes. 'Yes, I think he does.'

One more question. 'Has the abductor made contact with me?'

The psychic takes a deep breath and then says, 'I cannot answer that. I do not wish to go any deeper into this disturbed man's mind. You understand this, don't you?'

I do understand. More than I'd care to explain. I nod. 'But Robin is safe?' I ask again.

'For now.'

Most psychics tell you what you want to hear, but Mariah has proved herself anything but that type of psychic. She told the truth to Tracy, Shania and hopefully Gurpreet too. I hope I'm hearing the truth now; Robin is safe and he's where I left him. It's why the CCTV didn't pick anything up; he never left the fair. The man who has him is echoing my dad, why and how much of Mr Bones' MO he's copying, who knows. Robin can't end up chalky sticks of art. I won't let it happen. I need to hear his laugh again. The world needs to have him in it to make it a better place.

I get up and hug Mariah. She pats my back. 'Go to the fair,' she whispers.

But what about Oscar Greer? If Robin's still at the fair he can't be at Greer's house. 'There's another man,' I say to her. 'His name is Oscar Greer. He's a registered sex offender. Are you sure he doesn't have Robin?'

Mariah looks back at the cards. 'Hmmm. He's a horrible man. Awful, but it's not him.'

'How much do I owe you?' I say.

'Nothing, Cherrie. I look forward to seeing you here again, with Robin. He's such a good boy, your little bird.'

'Thank you. Perhaps he and Sarah could play together.'

Mariah quickly covers her mouth. 'Oh, that would be wonderful. Your little bird and my little angel. They'll be such great friends.'

I make it to the door in time to see Jon. I thank him too, before getting back into my car with a new plan of action. It was someone at the fair. It sounds so obvious.

Why didn't the police think of it? Should I say something to them? No, I doubt they would believe where I got my information from; the other side isn't their typical informant.

I need to get back to Crazy Clive's Fair and search it properly. I didn't do it on Friday night because I wasn't in the right frame of mind. I was too busy trying to remain calm and answer the police's fantastic array of useless questions. I'm not sure why I even trusted the chain-smoking freak at the fair. It was stupid to think a stranger would be honest and help me. The police took me away before I even made it back to the Ghost Train.

At home, I sit at the dining room table with my laptop. I need to check out how long the fair will be in town. When I log on, I see there's an email from the prison. Dad has replied.

Chapter 27

Dear Leigh-Ann,
You changed your name . . . a rose by any other.

I'm a granddad. I'd love to see you and Robin, if that's why you're contacting me. Has he asked about me? Does he know what I did?

Anyway, please find attached the VO form. They have told me you need to bring your passport as a form of ID, and a pound coin for the locker. I've never had a visitor who wasn't a solicitor or a policeman.

I'm looking forward to seeing you both.
Dad
X

Dad thinks Robin's coming too. Like I'd ever put my son through a prison visit. But, if I do something terrible to the skeleton copycat for taking Robin, I'll end up in prison too. Would Leo let Robin come to see me there? I shake off these thoughts. Even though Mariah has given me a lead to replace the need to see Dad, I still print the

Visitor Order form off. Holding something in your hands feels good. An email attachment is nothing. It doesn't really exist. You can't touch it, or rip it up into confetti.

Online, I search for Crazy Clive's Fair. I find their website, which features several towns announcing where they'll be pitching up next. Grabbing some paper, I make a timeline of their stops and google the towns they've already visited plus the words *missing child*. Nothing. Perhaps they are so sneaky that no one has pieced it together, or could Mariah be wrong? Yet she was right about Thomas Doncaster. I quickly check to see when the fair arrived in Northampton, but it doesn't coincide with Thomas's disappearance either. They came here three days after Thomas went missing and had travelled from Scotland. Wait, Patricia mentioned this, or maybe she didn't. I can't remember.

I smack my forehead with my palm as if my brain is an engine needing a jolt to get it going again. The fair opens at seven; it'll be too busy now, so I need to get there tomorrow before it opens, that way the workers will be busy with their preparations, and there'll be no crowds to spot me lurking; hunting the copycat.

My stomach grumbles. I pull away from the laptop, all the while suppressing the urge to whack the uninformative machine across the table. There's cereal in the kitchen cupboards, so I pour out a massive bowl and cover it with milk. I eat on the couch. While I do, I flick on the TV and start an episode of *Grey's Anatomy*. When the bowl is empty, and my belly full, I fall asleep listening to the sounds of oversexed doctors.

Something touches me. It's like little fingers holding my nose. I gasp awake and see a message on the TV asking if I'm still there, if I want to watch another episode. Switching it off, I check my mobile. Like magic, it rings as I touch it, making me jump.

Right now, I can't take another unknown caller. Fortunately, when I look down, I see it is Patricia.

I answer with, 'Have you found Robin?'

'Umm, no, but we have CCTV footage that has given us more to go on.'

'You're calling me at . . .' I squint at the clock on the mantel. 'Three in the morning to tell me you found CCTV footage? What the hell is on it?'

'Well, umm. Perhaps I should come over. I know Mr Duffill wants us to leave you alone, but it's my job to help you through this.'

'Help me through this!'

'I'm sorry, that didn't come out right.'

Silence.

As calmly as I can, I ask, 'What was on the footage?'

'Mr Duffill has already identified Robin in the picture.' She pauses, then pushes out, 'He's holding the hand of a man dressed as a skeleton.'

This is not news to me. I want to scream at Patricia to catch up. Remind her I've already told the police about the skeleton.

'Both leave the fair. They head towards . . .'

'Pardon? They didn't leave the fair.'

'What do you mean? The camera clearly shows them leaving the fair.'

Is Mariah wrong? Maybe they left and doubled back? 'Okay, where did they go?'

'It's hard to tell – not all the cameras work. At some point, they get into a car.'

'What kind of car?'

'It's parked at an angle so we can't see the number plate, but it appears it's a dark car.'

A dark car. Just like the one I saw here. Just like the dark car that belongs to the man who was stalking me. Wait, it makes a twisted sort of sense, a son for a son. Mr Bones took his little boy, so maybe he took mine. Not so much a copycat, but a vigilante out to even the score.

'Patricia, there was a man who listened to that fucking podcast and found out my name and where I worked. He stalked me; went to Dawson's Food, and came to my house.'

'Did anyone else see him?'

'Well, I didn't imagine him! Oh, sorry, yes. Kylie was there. She saw him.'

'Kylie who?'

'I'm not sure of her surname, but she's staying at my friend Tracy Carter's house.'

'Yes, we have Tracy's details. I'll send someone over to speak with Kylie. Why didn't you report a man stalking you at the time?'

I sigh; not wanting to admit to Patricia that it scared me people could find out who Cherrie Forrester used to be. 'He is the dad of one of Mr Bones' victims. He wanted answers I couldn't give him. He could have taken Robin.'

'Okay, okay. Keep your phone on. I'll keep you updated.'

'Thank you,' I say to her.

'This is a horrible thing that has happened to you, Cherrie. I read about your past. I've looked into the Mr Bones case. You don't deserve to lose your son over something your dad did.'

'Thank you, but I haven't lost my son yet,' I tell her and hang up.

I roll this new revelation around my mind. Too many suspects and not enough time. My stalker! I can't believe I didn't think of it before. It makes sense. He has to be my priority now, then the copycat fair worker, then, pervert Greer. How am I going to discover the bereaved father's name? Maybe the shop will have footage of him. I text Tracy and ask her to look up the recordings for the day he lingered around the cheeses. She texts back that she'll check.

There might be a quicker way to identify him. My dad. If he wanted answers about his son badly enough, he'd have gone to the source first. Requested to see Mr Bones in person. This settles it; I have to go to the prison. I need to speak with Dad.

The morning creeps in around me like insects edging towards a fresh corpse. I will myself to sleep, but I can't. I will see my dad today. I'll be in the same room as him. Be breathing the same air. I wished I'd told him Robin was missing in the email. I'm not sure how I can say it to him face to face. I'll cry and he'll try to comfort me. He was always that sort of dad. I'd fall over, he'd pick me up, then clean my wound and put a cartoon-character sticky plaster on me, whether or not I needed one.

The last time I saw Dad was in the courthouse during the trial. Social workers wouldn't let me go into the hearing. Instead, they sat me with a bored-looking guard in a room next door. The walls were thin, and I could hear other people on trial talking to their solicitors, crying and pleading. My dad's barrister gave me a book too young for me. I remember flipping through the pages staring at the illustrations and trying to picture my dad and me in them. Imagining us anywhere but at court.

At that time, I was desperate for him to be found innocent, even though I knew he was guilty. It was selfish, but I needed him. I'd just lost my mother; he was all I had left. After just a few hours, his barrister told me they had found him guilty. Years later, I read the details of the case in an old newspaper; the judge had wished the UK still had the death penalty so they could exterminate my last remaining parent.

The accompanying grainy black and white photo showed my dad forcibly dragged towards a police van. His oddly calm face captured forever amid a jeering crowd. That was the day I bought my first criminology textbook, a scary-looking volume entitled *Diseases of the Sick Mind* by Dr Hawk. Thinking back, it was just as much to explore the reaction of the crowd as it was to delve into my father's mind.

To kill some of the morning, I go online and book my train to the town nearest the prison. Without meaning to, I gravitate to *The Flesh on the Bones*, and download the latest episode with my name on to listen to on the train.

Before I go, I text Leo what I'm doing, then switch off my phone. I don't want to see a shocked emoji face, or worse another alien face I can't read. He knows my plan; that's good enough for now. I have to keep my mind on track, no matter what scary place it leads me.

Picking up my keys, I am about to leave the house when I remember the VO form. I go back in and grab it. I'm in my car before I think of my passport.

Swearing, I run back into the house and up the stairs.

I reach across to the drawer by my bed and fumble around in it. I pull out the passports. Odd, there are only two in there. I check them, just Leo's and mine. Where is Robin's passport? I pull the drawer out and shake the contents onto the bed. Sifting through the stray documents, I quickly see there are no more passports. Robin's one is missing. When did I see it last? I perch on the end of the bed and close my eyes. He was showing it to Mrs Duffill at dinner; perhaps he didn't put it back?

If I don't go soon, I'll miss my train. Normally, I would leave an alert on my phone to remind me of something like this, to search for the missing passport when I get home, but I can't bring myself to put my phone back on, just in case Leo has sent a text to talk me out of going to the prison, or to ask if he can come with me.

The train station is about a fifteen-minute drive from my house. All too soon, I'm parking the car, collecting my ticket, then standing on a platform in the cold. I'm wearing a pair of dark jeans, a pink jumper and my raincoat. I must look a complete mess as I get several looks of disdain from other commuters. Perhaps they recognise me from my not-so-appealing TV appeal. Worse, there could be more about me online, maybe even photos now. I need to listen to the podcast.

A strangled-sounding announcement informs me the train is running ten minutes late. As I groan about the delay, my stomach echoes it. There's a McDonald's by the station, so I run over. I order nearly everything from the breakfast menu and a cup of coffee. I get back to the platform in time to see the train pulling up. I climb on and check my ticket to see where I'm sitting. G4 is my reserved seat. I walk through the carriages to find it, but discover someone is already sitting there, a lady about my age. There are other seats free, albeit ones facing the wrong way.

My food is getting cold. I should just sit down, yet I can't let the seat-stealing woman get away with it. Too much has been stolen from me already. Carefully, I place my food and drink on a nearby table, then bend down and whisper to her, 'Excuse me, you're in my seat.'

She narrows her eyes at me, and her face wrinkles like a Shar Pei dog. 'There's plenty of room.'

'I bought this seat because it's facing in the right direction.'

The woman stares out of the window, ignoring me.

Cherrie Forrester would have let the seat-stealer get away with it. She would have backed down out of embarrassment, but not Little Bones. It looks like I'll never escape my heritage, so if it's Little Bones they want, it'll be Little Bones they get. I position my face in front of the woman so she has to see me. 'Get up now.'

'Or what?' The seat-stealer grips her handbag to her chest as if it'll protect her from my wrath. It won't. I reach out to grab her elbow. She grunts and tries to pull away from me, but I have a steady grip, and don't care if I hurt her.

'Get the fuck up and sit somewhere else!' I yell.

Everyone turns around to stare at me. Every face wears a matching shocked expression. I pull up the seat-stealer – she lets me. She stares into the distance as I push her up the aisle of the carriage. I'm waiting for her retaliation, an accusation, or a swear word. Nothing. Red-faced, she bustles down the train and leaves the carriage. Feeling deflated, I sit down in my seat. I wanted a fight. I needed to punch and kick her until I saw blood and bone.

The smell of my fast-food breakfast hits my nostrils. All I want to do now is stuff my face with fatty goodies. I open the paper bag. Groans from the other passengers quickly reach me. It must be some unwritten rule that you don't bring stinky food onto a train. I don't care. I'm hungry. If someone complains, I'll handle him or her. I'd welcome a complaint. Anger floats like a bloated corpse just below my smile.

I eat until my stomach hurts. Eventually, my jaw aches too much to chew, so I stop and stare out of the window at the flashing scenery. The train slows as it reaches towns and their stations. Greenery morphs to urban houses; graffiti-covered walls, along with blocks of flats too close to the train tracks to afford their occupants any kind of decent vista. With my luck, as the train ambles by, I'll see a murder. A limp body, empty of fight, shoved out of a window to explode in a dollop of blood and sinew by the tracks.

No, I have to stop thinking like this. Not everything in my life belongs in a horror film. My friends are supporting me: Cherrie, not Little Bones. I still have Leo. And, as long as I can get to him in time, I'll still have Robin.

Closing my eyes, I listen to the clickety-clack of the train and let my food go down.

No one checks my ticket. With the absence of a conductor, I feel cheated having spent money on something I apparently could have gotten free.

Becoming bored, I switch my phone back on to find I have ten unread texts from just about everyone: Tracy,

Shania, and Gurpreet, several from Leo. I scan them to see they are all messages of support. Not a single emoji on any of his texts. It's a record for my boyfriend.

There's still at least an hour of travelling before we get to the station, so I put on my headphones to listen to the latest *The Flesh on the Bones* episode. As ironic as it sounds, at least I'll be able to block out the rest of the train journey now. Have something to concentrate on other than my fellow passengers who seem intent on giving me the stink-eye like customers waiting in a queue.

This new episode is more professional than the last two. Jai now has sponsors, an insurance company along with an estate agent. He dutifully introduces them at the start. Glad to know it's not just Jai profiting from my family's misery.

'This is the third episode of The Flesh on the Bones,*'* Jai says. *'If you haven't heard the others, where have you been?'* Pause for laughter. *'Today we will be talking about Little Bones. Only daughter of the serial killer Mr Bones, she changed her name at seventeen from Leigh-Ann Hendy to Cherrie Forrester, which I exposed in a previous podcast.'* Pause for admiration. *'However, to add a twist to the events surrounding my story . . .'* His story? *'Last Friday night Robin Duffill, the son of Leigh-Ann Hendy, disappeared at Crazy Clive's Fair in Black Friars Park.*

'This raises several questions.' Pause as he rustles papers. *'First, could Robin's disappearance be linked to the Mr Bones case of over twenty-five years ago? Could it also be connected to the abduction, and subsequent murder, of Thomas Doncaster?'*

That's only two questions, hardly what I'd call several, and both of which I've considered myself. I'm hoping the police have too.

'Was poor Robin abducted at all? I've found many cases where mothers black out and kill their children.' What the fuck? 'One particular case in 1945 in Florida, USA, tells of a mother of three, Mrs Irene Baker, who drove a car, filled with her young children, into a lake. In a daze, she freed herself, swam to the shore, and then walked three miles in the midday sun to a general store. Seemingly coming to, she yelled, "Someone has taken my children!" It took weeks for the police to dig up the truth, so this brings us to the question: did Leigh-Ann Hendy kill her son?'

I stop the podcast and shove half a leftover chocolate muffin into my mouth to stop from swearing.

'Unbelievable fucker!' I say, the muffin doing nothing to defuse my F-bomb.

I would never hurt Robin, yet Jai's now officially put this idea in all those eager listeners' minds. What motive would I have? Plus, I was in public the whole time during the abduction. I was the one who called the police. Could I sue him for defamation of character? Probably, still, it'd cost money; money I don't have, and if Dawson's Food is in trouble, I can't go putting expensive legal costs on a credit card. All Jai is doing is sensationalising gossip to gain a following. He has no evidence to back up his claims. No evidence, because I didn't hurt Robin.

I finish my internal rant, yet feel obligated to listen to the end of the podcast. Knowing what they're saying is better than being in the dark, for Robin's sake.

'Does murder run in the family? There's scientific evidence that serial killers' brains work differently than the rest of us ordinary folk. Children can inherit this brain damage.' How could he say something like that? When Dad introduced me to his *art*, I was an innocent child. It's your parents who teach you right from wrong. I had no innate inclinations to kill other children. I was a good girl and did what I was told.

'Let's look at the evidence. Leigh-Ann took her son to the fair alone. I've canvassed the fair, and the people I spoke to all said she looked jittery and worried. One even claimed she was in a daze when he saw her. Most of them don't remember seeing her with her son at all. Could Leigh-Ann have killed Robin and then claimed she lost him at the fair?'

People at the fair would have only noticed me after Robin was taken; so of course, I looked frazzled.

'Let's go back to the case of the Florida mother. Mrs Baker just switched off, killed her children like a murderous sleepwalker. Leigh-Ann Hendy could have killed her poor little boy, stuffed his body somewhere, anywhere in that vast park, which was local to her, so she knew it well, and called the police after she awoke from her trance. I've met Leigh-Ann. She accosted me at my home after the second episode aired. I'd already agreed to take everything down, yet she attacked me at Robin's appeal, even though I went there to support her.'

He didn't go to the appeal for anything other than a story. Jai is a liar, and the worst kind, saying I could have blacked out. Wait; is there a gap in my timeline? I don't remember. I was texting Leo the whole time. I swipe the podcast off to look at the texts between Leo and me on Friday night. My texts to him are close together, all under a minute, until the last one; there is a two-minute gap. Nowhere near enough time for me to . . . Jai has no evidence, but it's never seemed to matter. He's turning everyone against me. My stomach rolls at the thought; it feels as if it has dropped through the floor of the train onto the tracks; my entrails dragging between the grinding metal below.

The rest of the podcast is dripping in even more loose conjecture, along with a few wild theories about a cult sacrificing young boys to an ancient god. In the end, he wraps up by thanking his new sponsors for their support. Although my name is the title of the episode, he jumps from topic to topic without even a hint of consistency. His bullshit is neither written nor produced well, making me madder.

The train slows. I look up at the digital board to see I'm almost at my station. Quickly, I text Leo about this episode of the podcast. He comes straight back to tell me he'll listen to it and not to let it bother me.

As we pull into the station, I rise and make my way down the aisle. There's a loud squeal, then a blast of cold air as the door opens. I step off, minding the gap, and walk towards the station's exit. I'm sure I can hear whispering around me as I do. Let them talk. I've heard worse.

The prison is nowhere near the station, so I have to find a taxi. I see one lingering near the bus stop with its light on. I open the back door and slide inside. When I give the driver the prison address, he looks back at me with a mixture of pity and worry, like I'm about to rob him, or burst into tears, or maybe both. As we drive, he makes eye contact with me a few times. Each time he must think better of speaking as we just sit in silence. I'm glad of the break. I wasted the whole train ride on Jai Patel when I should have been working on what I will say to Dad. I need quiet time, but my mind continues to marinate on that bloody podcast; the origin of my misery.

We pull up at the prison gates, and I pay the driver.

'You all right?' he finally asks me in a thick Eastern European accent.

'Not really,' I reply.

'You want a lift back?'

I look at my watch. 'If you could swing by in an hour and a half, that'd be great. I need to get back to the station for the three o'clock train.'

The driver smiles at me. 'I'll be here.'

The prison is massive. Made up of several buildings all with the same matching grey paint job. It's not what I expected; the other buildings around it are commercial offices. Ordinary people a stone's throw away from sick criminals. I was picturing more of an Alcatraz vibe. Rolling spotlights and barbed wire fences surrounded by man-eating-shark-infested waters. I guess a Bond villain isn't running this prison.

I walk to the visitors' entrance and knock on the door. A guard ushers me inside. There's a line of people handing across forms and passports to the front desk. Looks like I'll have time to think through everything after all.

After ten minutes of standing in the queue, my legs start to ache, but I have a plan. I'll ask Dad if he's talking to anyone about abducting little boys. If he has murderous fans who live near the Oak Cross Estate, or in Northants at all. Shit, it sounds so ludicrous; then again, it's all I have. That, a pervert and my stalker. What would Sherlock Holmes ask? Probably very little – his powers of perception would have already found Robin by now. Hell, even Batman would have saved his sidekick within the first few hours. I'm neither a superhero, nor a detective. I'm just a shit mum who took her eye off the ball.

There's a soft nudge on my thigh. I look down to see a liver-spotted spaniel. Its sparkling black, soulful eyes stare up at me. I bend down to stroke it. Its tail bobs up and down while its tongue finds the leftover McDonald's grease on my palms.

'Excuse me, miss.'

A tall guard with a scratchy-looking ginger beard steps towards me.

'Yes?'

'The dog is working; please refrain from touching him.'

I look down at my new furry friend.

'Sorry, he came up to me,' I say, scratching the spaniel behind the ear one last time.

'You wouldn't pet me if I searched you for drugs now, would you?' Ginger Guard winks.

I nod; despite nothing he said making sense. He then waves me through to another part of the line. A female guard comes over to pat me down.

'Pay no attention to him,' she says smiling. 'Too much testosterone in here, love.' She checks my passport and VO form. Upon seeing my dad's name, her smile vanishes.

'You're the first visitor *he's* had in a long time.' She checks my passport and confirms my date of birth and ID. With a wave of her hand, I'm steered towards another door and told to put my personal items into a tall, thin metal locker. I place the pound coin in the slot, then heave my bag and coat into the awkward space. Wait, I need my phone to show Dad a photo of Robin, so he can see the face of his grandson. The boy he'll save if he helps me. I sneak a sideways glance at the other visitors; they seem to have all done this before. They move in smooth, robotic motions. Bags heaved into a locker. Locker locked. Key in pocket. Out the next door. It's as if we're on some weird conveyor-belt production line.

My phone is old and big, it will be hard to smuggle in, and what if my furry friend is on the other side of the door and sniffs it on me. I'm stupid; dogs can't smell phones, can they?

It's not worth the trouble. I put the phone in my locker and join the other people as they move to the next room.

I open the door and, I'm not sure what I was expecting, but it looks like an airport lounge. Vivid-coloured plastic seats with Formica tables all bolted to a bright, patchy carpet. It's a vast room. I hesitate. Where am I supposed to sit? The whole hour could tick by without me finding Dad at all in this space.

'Park yourself,' says a woman next to me. 'The prisoners come to you.'

I weave my way through the plastic maze and find a table by the door. I hope, from this vantage point, I'll be able to recognise Dad as he comes in.

The chair is uncomfortably cold. There are no arms and the back is hard against my spine. I've already forgotten my plan. My hands are sweaty, and I'm hungry again.

Hearing a little boy laugh, I twist around to see kids playing in the corner of the room. Who'd bring children to a prison? I can't imagine letting Robin come here.

Prisoners dressed in matching grey tracksuits with red sashes walk in single file into the room. It's like the world's worst beauty pageant. All of them look forlorn until they spot their visitor.

I try to watch them without looking too crazy, or desperate. Even though each second that ticks by feels as if it's burrowing into me, germinating seeds of worry. What if Dad doesn't show up? What if he's punishing me for not visiting him before, or for changing my name to start a new life? What if he doesn't recognise me? What if . . .

The flow of prisoners slows. I wring my hands together as I lock eyes with a parade of deviant criminals. Where is my dad?

Chapter 28

'Leigh-Ann?'

Suddenly, there he is. Greyer and thinner than I remember, but still my dad. I'm shocked at how close he is to me now. He's not even wearing handcuffs or a Hannibal Lecter mask. He looks normal apart from the grey Converse-style trainers pulled together with Velcro, no laces. He'd have never worn anything so dull when he was free.

'Hi, Dad,' I whisper and get up, not sure what prison etiquette is for a daughter who has ignored her father for decades. Lifting my arms, I lean in to give him a slight hug, but see a guard move to stop me, so quickly sit back down.

Dad picks a chair across from me and sits, his sharp blue eyes, just like Robin's, never leaving mine. The smile I tried so hard to forget getting bigger by the second.

'I wasn't sure you'd come,' he says.

'Funny, I thought the same about you.' I almost laugh. 'Where else could I go?'

'How'd you recognise me?'

'You grew up pretty. It's like looking in a mirror.' He chuckles and adds, 'So, Leigh-Ann, lots to catch up on.'

'I changed my name to Cherrie, remember? I'm sorry,' I blurt out. Why did I just apologise?

'That's a lovely name. I used to call you Ma Cherie, do you remember?' He leans forward for my answer.

'Oh, um, I didn't remember that.' Now I do though.

'May I ask why you changed your name?'

'I couldn't take the taunting anymore. Did you know everyone called me Little Bones?'

'No, I didn't. I'm sorry. It must have been awful. I never did like Mr Bones either. I wish I'd picked my own nickname.' He looks down at the table, then beams a killer smile up at me. 'I'm a granddad now. Isn't that something?'

'Yes, it's why I'm here. I need your help.' I wanted a little benign small talk before I launched into why I'd come for my first-ever visit, yet I can't afford to wait. We only get an hour, and Robin could need every minute.

'Ma Cherie, if I can do anything to help you, I will. You know that, right? I am always here for you.'

'Here,' I say. 'In prison. Yeah, and you were always there for me, except when you were butchering eleven boys.' I instantly regret my anger. I need to keep him on my side. Robin needs him.

Sighing, Mr Bones sits back in his chair. 'You have every right to be cross, Ma Cherie. I understand.'

'Why did you do it?' I should have waited to ask that until after he'd told me everything he knew about Robin's abductor, yet that question has been burning a hole in my brain for so many years, it was bound to shoot out.

'The why was never important,' he replies. 'But, you need not worry about that now.'

'Oh, you're a changed man?' I'm fucking this up.

Dad inches his hands across the table, bringing our skin closer together. He looks over at the guard staring at us and winks at him.

'Don't be mad at me, Ma Cherie, I am the same man. If they let me out today, I would drive the streets again seeking new bones to make my next masterpiece. I have decades of ideas I'm desperate to work on. Ones that would fit smaller bones.' Leaning in, he whispers, 'I just won't get caught again.'

A gasp almost chokes me.

Grinning, he whispers, 'Breathe, Ma Cherie. Breathe for Daddy.'

I'm an idiot; why did I come here thinking he'd help, that he'd even know anything I could use to find Robin? I'm grasping at serial killer straws.

I bend down to pick up my bag, but realise it's not here, it's in the locker. His hand shoots out across the table and grabs my wrist. My head snaps up towards the guard, but he is now watching another table.

'Never be frightened of me. You are the best piece of art I ever created. You're beautiful and strong down to your bones. I never hid who I was from you, but you were too small to understand. I'm sorry. Looking back, which I've done a lot, I can see I was cruel to you. I didn't mean it. Please, how can I help you now?'

I stare into his eyes and I'm eight years old again. My father, the only person who truly cared for me, as flawed as he is, wants to help.

'Robin is missing,' I whisper.

'What? When?'

'Last Friday night, we went to a fair in Black Friars Park and someone took him.'

'Who took him?'

'We don't know; it's why I'm here. The abductor was dressed as a skeleton.'

Dad leans back, releasing my wrist. 'Understood. What can I do to help, Ma Cherie?'

'I need to find out if what's going on is to do with the Mr Bones case. Has anyone sent you letters, a fan perhaps?'

Dad laughs. 'It's not like in films. Someone reads our post before we see it. They weed out anyone talking about murders or crimes. All I see are marriage proposals from desperate women.'

Just because Dad's not seen any letters from the copycat, doesn't mean there were none; but, if they were weeded out, surely the police would have them. There's also my stalker, who I haven't seen since Robin's disappearance. If he tracked me down for answers, then he'll have tried to contact Dad.

'Okay, so some asshole started a podcast about our family and the murders.'

'What's a podcast?'

'It's like an independent radio show. In one episode, the host revealed my identity along with where I work. The dad of one of your victims started stalking me.'

'Which one?'

'That's the thing; I don't know. He never told me his name, or the name of his son. Has anyone tried to see you?'

Closing his eyes, Dad shifts in his seat. 'Some of the

parents tried, but I never granted them VOs. One tried more than once. His name was Lawrence something . . . Lawrence Edwards. I was tempted to see him. I remember his son; wonderful cheekbones. I thought perhaps his father had them too.'

Before I can stop myself, I say, 'Fuck sake, could you at least try to act like a normal person?'

'I didn't bring you up to use such foul language,' he says.

'You didn't bring me up at all, remember?' I bite my lip to stop anything else coming out. I need his help. This family reunion isn't for me and my psychological issues, it's for Robin.

Before I can apologise with a lie, Dad holds up his hands.

'Did you get the name, Lawrence Edwards?'

'Okay, thank you.' I make a mental note of the name, intending to save it on my phone later.

'Are there any other suspects?' asks Dad.

'I found a paedophile living down the street.'

'Lowest form of life. Did you confront him?'

'Damn right, I did. But he wouldn't let me in.'

'This may be cold comfort, but those monsters take kids to keep them for as long as they can, and then pass them on to others as they age.'

My eyes glaze. I need to be quicker. What could be happening to my baby right now? How many tears has he already cried? If Oscar Greer has done anything to my son, he's a dead man.

Seeing my hesitation, Dad says, 'You'll find him. You're strong, I can tell. More like me than your mother. I'm sorry she left you alone. If I'd known what she was planning . . .'

'You were already locked up and awaiting trial by then. There was nothing you could have done.'

'Ma Cherie, I'm so sorry for leaving you. I despised your mother's weakness, yet I always knew who she was. Tigers don't change their stripes. I loved your mother, but she loved me so much more. I should have known she couldn't be alone.'

'Mum wasn't alone. She had me.'

'You were never enough for her, but you were always my special girl. My protégée. The pieces we made together were some of my best creations.'

Sitting very still, I realise now what the clichéd shiver down your spine actually feels like. It's so horrific, it makes me wonder if it's the same sensation that all those other people felt before. Surely not, for the saying to be bandied around so carelessly. I can't seem to move. My whole body is rigid and cold. Suddenly, I'm a little girl measuring an ivory stick in my hands, wondering how something so light could hold up pounds of flesh, sinew, and pints of blood; even for a body as young and small as mine.

Mr Bones smiles, his icy blue eyes warming by the second. 'Tell me about Robin,' he says, his tone even warmer than his eyes.

My mouth won't open.

'Is he a good boy?'

When I still don't answer him, his smile widens. 'Please, Ma Cherie. Tell me about your life. You're a mother.'

My neck cracks as I look down at my watch and realise I still have over half an hour left. It would embarrass both of us if I left midway through the visit.

'I'm so proud of you,' he says with a hopeful smile.

Fuck it, I tell him about Robin, Leo, and even Mrs

Duffill, whom he laughs at and tells me he used to have a crush on Joanna Lumley. Something to do with the TV show *The Avengers*.

He is too easy to talk to. I share more than I intend. He laps up the facts of my new life like a hungry cat, smiling and laughing in all the right places.

When the hour is up, I nod at him. 'Bye, Dad.'

'See you soon, Ma Cherie. I'll think about Robin. If I come up with anything, may I call you?'

'Yes. Thank you.'

Moving around the table, he lunges forward to hug me. Before I can escape, he catches me in his arms. He smells of soap and toothpaste; I feel his stubble graze my skin as he gently kisses my cheek.

'Hey, stop that. It's not allowed!' yells the guard.

'It's easy to kill someone,' he whispers in my ear. 'You just need a good reason and a way of disposing of the body. Without a body, it's harder to charge you.'

The guard pulls him away from me. Laughing, Mr Bones puts his arms up.

'Sorry, mate. I haven't seen my little girl in decades. I just wanted a hug.'

I leave before I see, or hear, any more. I have a name now – Lawrence Edwards. Out of the three possibilities, I want it to be him. When I looked into his eyes, he was no killer, just a miserable man whose sadness had crept into his soul and set up shop. Oscar Greer is terrible; God help him if he has Robin. An unknown copycat could be a different story altogether, especially one who travels round the country with a fair as Mariah predicted.

After I retrieve my stuff from the locker, I text Lawrence Edwards' name to Leo so he can pass it on to Patricia.

He comes back straight away and asks what it was like to meet Mr Bones. I ignore his question.

As I go to leave, I give my mobile number to the front desk for Dad to call.

Outside, I find my taxi waiting.

'Thank you,' I say to the driver, scrambling into the back seat.

'It go okay in there?' he asks me.

'Time will tell.' I slump back, my eyes aching and stomach growling. How can I be so hungry again?

The taxi drops me off at the train station. I tip the driver a twenty. He passes me his business card, in case I come back. I throw the card in the bin outside the station.

There's half an hour before my train, so I buy an inordinate amount of food from the station shop and sit with it in the cold waiting room.

While thinking through my next move, I eat a bland sandwich. Leo will have now told the police about Lawrence Edwards; they'll find him. Nevertheless, I can't rely on it being Lawrence. Robin has more of a chance if I check out Greer, and hunt down more suspects; dressed up, the skeleton could have been anyone.

While I wait, I'm surprised at how many times my thoughts rewind to Dad. We spent just one hour together and I have already remembered a thousand things I want to tell him. However, as much as he was helpful, he was also incredibly creepy. He may have been sorry for leaving me, yet he wasn't sorry for making eleven mums and dads lose their sons. And for what? Art, which only us and a handful of police officers would see? After he created his first sculpture, he redecorated a back room in our house for his private exhibition space. He bought expensive

264

lights; I helped him position them, to better show off the colours and curves of the piece. Sinfully, I enjoyed it; so much so I forgot what I was highlighting, where it came from, and that I had played with its owner just days before.

I'm glad I could just walk away today. Leave Mr Bones locked up where he can't hurt any more little boys.

Looking down, I see my whole sandwich has disappeared into my belly. I'm about to rip open a bag of crisps when my phone rings. It's a number I don't recognise, which is happening a lot now. It's like some grim caller lottery. I don't have the luxury of ignoring it; it could be news on Robin.

I answer.

Chapter 29

'Cherrie?'

'Who is this?'

'It's Mariah. I had a vision. I need to tell you something important about Robin.'

'What?'

'I told you Robin is still at the fair, but in my vision, they were packing up. They are leaving soon and if they do, you'll never see him again. You need to get there now.'

'I'll pay them a visit when I get back home.'

'Promise me?' There's a weird tremor in her voice.

'Yes, I promise.'

'The Ghost Train. Check the Ghost Train.'

'Okay, I'll check it.'

'Do the police have any leads?'

'Not really.' I toy with the idea of telling her about Lawrence Edwards, but if she has real powers, surely she knows about him already.

'Good luck, Cherrie. Thank you for listening to me now.'

Hanging up, I think of how Mariah has helped me. Gratitude is difficult for me at times; growing up, there was little to be grateful for, so it was a skill I learnt late in life. Right now, I'm grateful for Mariah. Whether I believe her or not, I can hear an urgency in her voice. She believes in me; believes that I can find Robin.

I hear my stomach growl, so shove half a chocolate bar into my mouth. Sitting across from me is a man giving me an odd look. Usually, the weight of his stare would crush my confidence and make me leave the cold room to wait on the colder platform. Today, I flip him the bird. Shocked, he looks down to stare at something interesting on his shoes.

I finish my chocolate in time to see the train slither and sigh its way into the station. I gather my things, then make my way onto a carriage. Fortunately, there's no rogue passenger in my designated seat this time. Sitting down, I close my eyes.

I don't sleep; just sit in an almost stage. The chasm in between sleep and rest. As much as I need the peace, my brain won't switch off. Thoughts slam around my head like bumper cars. Each one denting my mind's eye, distorting its clarity into warped shards. Do I trust my dad? Does Mariah have powers? Am I wasting time on the wrong suspects and damning my son to pain, fear and death? A hot flush of nausea rolls over me. I run to the toilet and throw up everything I've eaten in the past couple of hours; heaving until my stomach is sore, and my throat aches. I slide down onto the dirty toilet floor, and put my back against the door. The toilet may smell like sick, but at least it's my sick.

Help me, Mummy, is the voice in my mind. *Help me.*

Pulling myself up, I splash water on my face, and then glare at my reflection.

'I'm coming, Robin. I'll find you.'

Once I'm back in my car, I look at my watch – it's six o'clock. The perfect time to sneak into the fair. Mariah clearly believes Robin is there, and she's been right before.

Once at Black Friars Park, I leave the car two streets down from its entrance and walk the rest of the way. Looking down at myself, I wished I'd worn darker clothes. What is the right outfit for breaking into a travelling fair? It's not exactly the essential fashion trends advice you see in *Cosmo*.

It's dark now, and the streetlights are highlighting everything in an eerie glow. There are kids already roaming around the park. I want to yell at them to go home where it's safe, but I can't draw attention to myself. They are some other mother's problem.

Ducking behind a tree, I scan the entrance to the fair. There's no music on yet; the rides appear dull and still. It's like something out of a *Scooby Doo* cartoon. An empty fairground filled only with memories of past fun, and teeming with fake ghosts and monstrous men wearing masks.

Mariah told me I needed to start my search on the Ghost Train, which makes more sense than I'd like to admit. I close my eyes and remember where it sits in the fair. It was on the left, towards the edge of the park, near the Ferris wheel. I sneak around the side of Black Friars and slip between the Tea Cups and the Carousel. I kneel by an empty cotton candy stand, drinking in the scene before me – there are scattered fair workers throughout;

men in overalls tightening screws on rides along with women cleaning seats. They talk, laugh, and seem oblivious that they played a role in Robin's disappearance. If they hadn't come to town, if I'd have never shown Robin the poster, he'd be safe at home right now.

I wait for a moment, then sprint across to the Ghost Train. No one is near this ride; it's as solitary as a haunted attraction should be. They haven't locked the back door, so I step inside. Trespassing is far too easy. Part of me is happy about this; it's made my breaking and entering less breaking and just entering. However, another part of me is pissed it was this easy. If they don't lock the ride, the skeleton could have easily gotten in and lain in wait for Robin and me. Jumped into our cart to have that first important introduction before stealing my son. Everyone else was far too busy oohing and aahing over glowing paintings of scary creatures to recognise the real danger.

It's dark, so I get out my mobile and switch on the torch. I stumble my way along the ride, moving around stationary carts, checking for signs of . . . I'm not sure what I'm even looking for. I'm here because Mariah told me to come. I didn't listen to her once before and look what happened. I guess I'm here for peace of mind, to prove she's a good guesser rather than a psychic; however, that would mean what she said about Robin still being alive is false hope. No, he's alive. If he'd died, it would have been like a cosmic claw across my chest. I would have suddenly crumpled to the floor into a pile of useless flesh and sobs. It hasn't happened yet, so he must still be alive.

As I move further in, I realise what little attention I paid to the ride the last time I was here. Along the edges of the tracks are various tableaux made up of wax dummies. My torch highlights one of a boy dressed in a bright white T-shirt and dark tracksuit bottoms lying on the ground with blood smeared over his wax lips. When I get closer, I see someone has written *Thomas Doncaster* on his white T-shirt, and removed his shoes. I gasp and almost drop my phone. What bastard has done this? Do people think it's funny that a boy was brutally murdered? Trying to wipe the letters off the dummy's shirt, I rub the material so hard the ink blurs its lines, but the name is still recognisable. I can't erase the wicked joke.

'I'm sorry,' I whisper to the wax boy, and then carry on walking up the tracks.

As I move, I hear muffled voices coming from around the bend. I inch as close as I can and use my free hand to cover the torch on my phone. Darkness engulfs me, yet it somehow improves my hearing. I make out two male voices. One younger than the other.

'I don't want to,' says the younger one.

'You'll love it,' says the older, deeper voice.

'I should go home,' the younger one whines.

'Don't be a chicken. No one likes a chicken.' I hear shuffling.

People talk about a mother's instincts as if they are some superpower. As my mum was less than instinctual about her care of me, I never believed in them; until Robin was born. Right now, my instincts are flaring like the snout of a bull ready to charge. Something horrible is about to happen – at least I'm here to stop it.

Chapter 30

I rush forward. Round the bend of the track, I see two shadows struggling. The taller of the two slaps the other. The sound of flesh striking flesh echoes through the dark. Sprinting towards them, I body tackle the tall shadow. We topple over and hit the ground at an awkward angle. Looking down, I see his jeans are around his ankles; it's why he fell so easily.

The smaller shadow – a young boy – cowers against the wall. I shine my torch on him. He's barely twelve. The one beneath me struggles. Scrambling up, I kick him hard in the stomach. He gulps for air and tries to roll away from me. I turn to the younger boy.

'Are you okay?'

'I didn't want to. He was going to make me.' Even in the weak light of my mobile, I can see the boy is shivering.

The man on the ground is probably in his late twenties, with a short bushy beard, which makes him look older. He's hugging his chest and gasping for air.

'I shouldn't have come here,' the young boy whispers.

A surge of anger rides my body. I step forward and kick the man on the floor again, this time in the groin. As my boot connects, he yells out in anguish.

The young boy tugs on the back of my coat. As I turn around, he throws himself into my arms. I hold him and, while patting his back with one hand, I dial 999 on my phone.

'What's your emergency?' the voice on the other end asks. Suddenly, I'm catapulted back to Friday night, to the last time I made a similar call. Shaking my head, my brain clicks into place. I'm about to tell them to send someone to the fair when the boy in my arms shakes himself free.

'Please, don't tell. I'll get in trouble for coming here. I don't want anyone to know about this.'

Sighing, I say, 'Sorry, false alarm.'

'Are you sure, ma'am?' comes the operator's voice.

'Yes, so sorry. I'll hang up now.' I disconnect the call, and put my phone in my pocket. Darkness drapes over us, a darkness broken only with the intermittent glowing, red eyes of a nearby plastic zombie.

I place my palms gently on the boy's shoulders; smiling I say, 'It's okay. You're okay.' As I turn away, my smile fades. The bastard on the ground needs to pay for what he tried to do. He could have done it before. No doubt, he'll do it again. The next boy might not be so lucky. Wait, could this squirming sicko holding his junk be the skeleton from the Ghost Train? Could he be a viler version of Mr Bones, a copycat with an added twist?

Moving forward, I kick him in the face. Warm wetness splashes out into the surrounding dark.

I bend down to whisper in his ear. 'Did you take my son?' My voice is unrecognisable. The anger dripping from the words has tainted its tone, as if a demon has possessed me and my head could spin around at any moment.

The man on the floor writhes. Taking out my phone, I highlight his face in its torchlight. He looks scared. Good.

'Was your son the one that went missing?' the younger boy asks me.

I look over at him. Although he's stepped back a few paces, I'm surprised he's still here, watching. In the dark, I can't tell whether he's frozen with fear, or fired with vengeance.

'Yes, my son is Robin,' I say. 'Have you seen him around here?'

'No, I'm sorry.' He looks down.

'You should leave now,' I tell him, but he doesn't move. Vengeance it is then.

The bastard on the ground is moving too much. He keeps shifting parts of his body out of my spotlight, so I place my boot on his chest to steady him. I press down a little and he groans. He could easily push me off if his hands weren't protecting his vulnerable boy-bits; fortunately, he doesn't seem to realise this.

'What's this fuckwit's name?' I ask the young boy, nodding to my prisoner.

'Not sure. I only met him last night on the Ferris wheel. He works at the fair. He said he had gin, and he'd share it with me if I met him tonight before the place opened.'

I put more pressure on the would-be rapist's ribs. His face screws up in pain.

'You should go now. Get home where it's safe.' I look over at the young boy who nods at me.

'Will you be all right with him, here, in the dark?' he asks.

'I'll be fine. Go home. Now.'

Giving me a weak smile, he walks backwards for a second, then turns around to run up the tracks. I see a flash of light as he reaches the end of the Ghost Train, and escapes into the bright lights of the fair.

At some point, this jackass on the floor will get a hold of his fear and figure out he can overpower me. I'm not a trained assassin, or an enforcer. I have never even taken a self-defence class, yet deep inside the pit of my stomach my instincts have taken over. There's a primitive knowledge ingrained in me. All I have to do is channel Little Bones.

Slipping my mobile back into my pocket, I bend down to cover his mouth with one hand; with the other, I grab his nose between my thumb and forefinger. The moment I do, he bucks beneath my boot, so I push all my weight down to hold him in place. He's struggling to breathe. It's dark, so I can't see his eyes; the red flashing lights only afford random snapshots, but I'm betting they're glassy like a wild animal caught on a busy road.

'You will tell me where Robin is, and God help you if you've hurt him,' I say.

I let go of the man's nose and he gasps for air. 'I don't know what you're talking about. Let me go, you crazy bitch!'

'Oh, I'm not crazy, I'm a mother, and there's nothing I wouldn't do for my son. Even if that something involves gifting a timely end to a child sex offender.'

'I didn't touch your kid,' he whines.

I pull out my mobile and shine the torch back onto his face. 'Why did you dress up like a skeleton? Do you know who I am? Do you want to be the next Mr Bones?'

He gurgles. 'I don't know who the fuck you are. I don't

dress up as a skeleton. I don't even work on this fucking Ghost Train. Who the fuck is Mr Bones?'

Suddenly, his hand shoots away from cupping his balls. He grabs my boot resting on his chest, and tries to pull me off balance. In doing so, he's left a vital piece of anatomy exposed. I step back and out of his weak grasp and take another swing kick at his groin. I feel the impact up through my leg. He doubles over again.

'Please.' He dribbles, his hands shooting back to his balls.

Adrenaline builds in my body along with a pleasant, just feeling. I'm about to kick him again when there's a metallic crunching sound. All around me, the Ghost Train cranks to life. The fair must be open now.

'Please, let me up. I swear I never touched your son.'

I look down at him. 'How many young boys have you raped and killed? Did you kill Thomas Doncaster?'

'No! Fuck, no! You've got this all wrong.' He waves at me. Realising he's left his groin exposed again, he quickly covers it back up.

'Bull. Shit.'

I can now hear the fair's tweeny-bopper pop music, along with the creepy sounds of the Ghost Train. Puffs of dry ice begin to surge around us. Any minute now, there will be a cart full of kids chugging around the bend. And they will see a live action tableau they'll never forget.

'Tell me a number. If you're honest about it, I'll let you go.'

'None.' He splutters and quickly adds, 'Two, I promise, and they were drunk, but I never killed them. I swear.'

Visions of my son with this asshole jolt across my mind like electric shocks. I scan the nearest gothic diorama for a makeshift weapon. In the dark, I see a hefty-looking shape. Grabbing it, I raise it up over my head, ready to slam it down onto the rapist's skull.

'Please, no. I'm sorry I touched them; but I never killed anyone. I've never met your son. Please stop.' He moans.

Mid-swing, I stop and look up to see I've picked up a fake headstone. An echo of that bloody children's rhyme rattles through me, *Each night they moan for their own headstones.* Dropping my weapon, I carefully place my boot back onto his chest to hold him still. I bend down to stare at him. The snivelling little fucker may be a rapist, but he does not have the attitude, or the eyes, of a killer – I know what they look like.

'You gave alcohol to minors. That's your excuse. Did you give alcohol to my son?'

'No!'

'Which caravan out there is yours?'

'It's the one with the green door.'

'If you do this again, I'll know. A psychic told me where to find you, so if you ever even think about hurting another kid, she'll tell me, and I'll come back. Only next time I'll be more prepared with knives and peroxide and . . .' My mind clouds as if I'm coming out of a daze. I shake it off and lift my boot off his chest. Shivers rack my body. Stumbling back, I put my hands to my face; my fingers are so cold and numb that they no longer feel like they're mine anymore. I run for the exit.

As the doors open, I bend over, put my hands on my knees, and puke. A group of teenagers point and laugh at me as if I'm some wimp who can't handle a Ghost Train.

What did I just do in there? It was like another world;

a world where I could get away with torturing a man in the dark.

Scanning the fair, I spot the workers' caravans. I check each line until I see a green door.

I climb the small unsteady metal stairs and knock. There's no answer. I reach down to the handle; it's unlocked.

I open the door.

Chapter 31

The smell of alcohol and old junk food smacks me in the face, making me wince.

'Robin?' I yell. 'Sweetie, are you in here?'

I want to find my son; I just don't want to find him here.

The caravan has all the essentials: a kitchen, a dining room table, a shower, a toilet, and a large flat-screen TV with a DVD player. There's even a bookcase labouring beneath hundreds of shamelessly unhidden porn DVDs.

I check everywhere a sick bastard could hide a young boy. Nothing. I sit down on the edge of his bed and close my eyes; when I open them, I feel numb again.

I stagger out of the caravan. I shouldn't have hurt its owner but perhaps he'll think twice now, when he looks at another young boy with hungry eyes.

As I walk, I check in all the other caravan windows. No signs of Robin.

Strolling back through the fair, I get a few odd looks. I don't slink into the shadows, as I should. Instead, I walk, head held high. Carefully, I watch the fair workers to gauge their reaction to my presence. Some of them recognise me. They have the decency to look sad and concerned. After all, Robin went missing on their turf. Some sneer at me, though, as if they realise what I've just done.

Quickly, I look around the Carousel and the Ferris wheel, yet find nothing. Mariah is wrong. There's no evidence Robin is here now, or even that he was ever here with me on Friday night.

By the time I get back to the car, my legs hurt, and my body has used up all its adrenaline. I fall into the driver's seat, but can't force my feet to put any pressure on the pedals. I want to cry. Nothing comes out. With shaky hands, I scoop up my mobile. I text Leo where I am and ask for help. I'm not even sure he'll come. While I wait, I text Patricia that a man in a green caravan at the fair is hurting young boys, that they should investigate. I expect her to text back and ask if I've done something silly, but she doesn't. Instead I get an, *Okay, we'll look into it*. It's a risk; the rapist could easily tell them of my attack, but my conscience can't leave him free to hurt any more young boys. Never will I make that mistake again.

Twenty minutes later, Leo is tapping on the window. He opens the car door. I slide out.

'What are you doing here?' he asks.

'You know what I'm doing here.'

Silently, he manoeuvres me into the passenger seat. We drive home in silence.

I open my front door to the smell of chips.

'Thought you'd be home straight after seeing your dad, so they're cold now,' Leo says.

I follow my nose to the Drunken Schooner bag. I open

it and stuff a handful of greasy goodness into my mouth. My boyfriend watches me fill my cheeks with cold chips like a chipmunk.

'I'm suing Jai Patel,' he blurts out.

'Really?'

Leo motions for us to sit at the dining room table.

'I tried to get the police involved. Robin's disappearance is an open case; this *The Flesh on the Bones* thing jeopardises our son's safety. However, apparently, there are no regulations for podcasts. He can say whatever he wants, so I contacted a solicitor who Mum plays golf with at her club. He says we have a case.'

'Will that work?' I grab another fistful of chips and ram them into my mouth. Even cold, they taste great; the salt, vinegar and beef dripping are all congealed and clinging to the fat slices of potato.

'Probably not. I'm just hoping the threat will stop Jai. After all, he is sort of telling the truth.'

I stop mid-chew to let the contents of my mouth fall out onto the table so I can speak. 'What did you say?'

'He's just going over your dad's case. I mean he was convicted and has been in prison for quite some time now.'

'He's talking about my mum and me too. He accuses me of hurting Robin in the latest episode!'

My boyfriend takes a huge bite of fishcake. After an impossibly long time he looks up, into my eyes. 'Last night, I dreamt about you again,' he says, shifting the subject.

'Was it like the last dream when I tried to kill you with a pillow?'

'No, Robin was in it. We were on the beach playing in the sand, but we couldn't make the sand stick together to make castles. We'd fill a bucket, turn it over, and the bloody stuff would just keep falling out. You then turned your red buckets on me and buried me up to my neck. This time the sand held together like cement. Mum says it's just my frustration about you losing Robin manifesting.'

'Your mum the psychologist eh? Tell me, did she get her degree at the country club?' I say popping a cold chip into my mouth.

'She's just trying to help, Cherrie.' Leo huffs and looks away from me.

How is throwing out wild theories villainising me helping? 'You know, that's the second dream you've told me about in a week.'

'Huh? What? I can't tell you my dreams?'

'You never have before. I don't remember you ever telling me about your dreams. In the first, I'm smothering you with a pillow from our bed. In the second, I'm building a sandcastle around you up to your neck. It's odd, that's all.'

'Maybe I'm just annoyed you're not doing what you said. You told me you'd fix this, that you'd find Robin.'

'I'm trying, but I don't have all the clues. Have the police said anything to you?'

'Not really. Patricia is supposed to update us on everything, but I've barely seen her since she swanned off to another case. They've only told me stuff when I've pushed for it.'

'At least I got the stalker's name,' I say.

'Lawrence Edwards.' Leo puts his head in his hands. 'Is this all your fault? Some random stranger targeted Robin because you come from a serial killer dynasty?'

'I don't come from a family of serial killers. My mum did nothing wrong.'

'Shit, Cherrie. She must have known what he was doing. You can't live with someone and have no clue what they're up to.'

'I had no idea what you were doing in the extension.'

'Well, that was different.'

'Was it?'

'I don't need your lip now, Cherrie. Against my better judgement, I came back to check on you.'

'Well, you can indulge your better judgement again and fuck off.' Getting up, I walk towards the door.

Swearing under his breath, Leo follows me. 'My subconscious has you all figured out. My dreams were right about you.'

'Good, perhaps in your next dream I'll be repeatedly kicking you in the balls.'

Flinging open the door, Leo stalks out into the night. He doesn't look back, just gets in his car and drives.

After slamming the door shut, I sit back down at the table. I can't bring myself to eat any more chips, so I get a big bowl of cereal instead. Leo says he trusts me, but he can't help exposing his true doubts; they're like a wound beneath a bandage destined to fester. Dad had those levels too, only his burrowed deeper. On the surface a loving father, yet dig deeper and there was evil. He destroyed memories of ice cream, late-night films and shopping trips with child abductions and grisly murders. He said today that why he killed wasn't important, but it is. I put my cereal to one side and try to recall the memories I still have of my dad. It's tough; imagination frays the edges of memories. It blurs them until what's left could be a regurgitation of a film, or a twisted thought.

I have an idea. I grab my laptop and log in to my Amazon Prime account; I find a playlist crammed with Eighties hits and press play. Not every song will trigger a memory, yet maybe the music can somehow take me back, make me remember something important that could help Robin now. Mariah meant well, but her prediction of the guilty fair worker was a bust, so my suspect list is back down to Lawrence the stalker, Oscar Greer, and worst: the unknown copycat.

Eighties pop music fills the house as I ransack my mind for a useful memory. I remember dancing with Dad to one particular song, my mum looking at me with a green-eyed stare as he taught me how to twist and waltz. He was a good dancer . . . Wait, there was a cat. Trumpton. It belonged to the elderly couple next door. It was friendly, so I always played with it. Of course, I didn't know Dad had taken him until after I'd helped the neighbours search the entire estate for the wayward feline.

Days later, Dad called me into his art studio and showed me what he was doing. By the time I got there, Trumpton was dead. He looked like one of my cuddly toys, all fluffy and still. I thought that he must have been hit by a car, we lived on a busy street, but there was no blood. Later, Dad admitted to poisoning him. Death was just the beginning; it took hours to skin Trumpton. All the while, I watched Dad work in silence, never daring to ask the obvious question. Carefully, he placed Trumpton's skinned body into a vat of peroxide and covered it up. We then watched a cartoon together: *Tom & Jerry*.

When he took Trumpton's body out of the vat, it wasn't clean. There was no helpful bone-cleaning information on the internet back then; so, next morning, he visited the library to check out a book about hunting. We found out that you have to leave the body outside for a while first, let it decompose. After, you use the peroxide. That afternoon, he buried the cat, and unearthed it a few months later; like some bizarre reverse funeral. Dad then dumped Trumpton back into the vat.

I remember when he pulled off the lid. The smell was like pale hands reaching down my little throat, choking my senses. Once clean, he finished the cat bones off with a dip in the biological washing powder we used on our clothes. He dried the carcass off with a bathroom towel. The cat suddenly smelled like us. Its skeleton was beautiful; bleached indestructible bones that would last forever. He showed me each white piece of Trumpton, all the while he sang that old song, *Dem Bones,* but the words were warped and disjointed, the wrong bone connected to the wrong bone. The song is now so vivid in my mind that I sing the last line aloud: 'Now hear the word of the Lord.'

He is an evil man, but he's still my dad, and part of him is in me whether I want it there or not.

Just because a copycat hasn't contacted Dad, it doesn't mean one isn't out there. In prison, Mr Bones said someone checks his correspondence, perhaps this new killer's letters didn't make it beyond the prison guards. And as I thought before, surely the police would have those letters already. Perhaps they're holding the copycat's existence back from the public to ensure they don't cause a panic. Surely, they'd tell me though, if there were any real leads.

It took Dad the dry run with Trumpton to perfect his method, maybe Thomas Doncaster was this killer's dry run. Was there any real damage to that poor boy's body other than the head wound? Perhaps there are things the police are not telling me about how Thomas died. Killers always have a vision of their murders; a reality to live up to their fantasy. If this killer is the same, his routine takes a while, so I still have time to find Robin. Maybe I need to look deeper into the Doncaster murder. If Thomas was this killer's Trumpton, I should look into the little boy's life – find out who was around him.

I stop the playlist. Who knew music could be such a Pied Piper to the past. I guess it's easier to resurrect something still lurking just below your facade. Bad memories are like tea bags; they taint the water around them, then defiantly bob to the surface.

Dad killed Trumpton because of his proximity to our house, which could mean Thomas lived near his killer on the Rosemount Estate. Wait a minute, wasn't the blog highlighting Greer's name called *Concerned in Rosemount*? I log on to check it. There's no author name on the blog, and I'm not technical enough to trace ownership, although it doesn't stop me poring over all the whining posts about missing garden ornaments, and neighbours who play their music past eleven at night. There are even some photos with each post, ones taken by the blogger, but nothing jumps out. I'm useless; the only thing I notice is the same annoying expression of exasperation: *shine a light*. I've never heard that before, not around here anyway.

It's also odd there's still no post about Thomas's murder on the blog. He went missing from the Rosemount Estate. I should speak to Mrs Doncaster. Would she even see me? Thanks to Jai, she probably thinks I killed her son as well as mine.

I give up, flop down in front of the TV and switch on

Grey's Anatomy to clear my mind. I finish the gloopy bowl of warm cereal while watching the overly good-looking doctors argue and have inappropriate hospital sex. However, the whole thing feels frivolous. My head is full and my heart is empty. I turn it off, then curl up on the couch in silence.

A weak guilt washes across me. I hurt someone today. I left him writhing in pain on the tracks of a Ghost Train. He was awful and deserved it, but it still shocks me I am capable of such violence. Guess it's not surprising the cruel songs sung in the playground about Little Bones would turn out to be true.

It's night now, and I want to sleep. My body is crying out for it, yet every time I close my eyes, I see Robin's face and any meaningful rest eludes me. Time is running out. I'm guessing Thomas Doncaster's mum did nothing when her son went missing. I can't do nothing in case my son ends up like her boy, used and discarded, shoeless and lifeless on the roadside. His soul sinking into the asphalt, his lips never to form the word 'Mum' again. That will not happen to Robin. I keep saying I'll kill whoever took my baby, but today I found out I'm capable of delivering on my threat.

My dad took the lives of young boys for his own sense of self. His art was always a passion for him; one more attractive than his family. I will take whatever seed of murderous evil he passed on to me and forge it in the fires of my anger. I'll use it as a weapon to protect my family.

Just as I start to drift off to sleep, my phone rings. Looking at the clock, I see it's 7 a.m. If this is that laughing asshole from before, he'll wish he had never been born.

'What?'

'It's Patricia. I'm just checking in with you. Mr Duffill said to give you an update.'

'What is it?'

'We traced the harassing phone call you received. It's nothing, just some teenagers who watched the appeal and thought it would be funny.'

Teenagers don't cackle down the phone, hell they don't even call anymore.

'You're wrong,' I say. 'I mean, how'd they even get my number? Why would they bother?'

'Not sure how they got your number. Teenage boys can be oddly resourceful.'

'I want to speak with them.' It's the only way I can be sure the police are right and the call was not connected to Robin.

Patricia sighs. 'Cherrie, we can't do that. Don't worry, we've just interviewed them.'

'Are you with them now? Are they at the station?'

'Yes, but . . .'

'Then I'm coming down there.' I go to hang up.

'No!' Patricia yells.

'Then you tell me what they said.'

'They listened to that podcast, okay. They were subscribers from the start. Thought they'd investigate you, which for lazy teens meant they got your number and called you to see your reaction.'

'So, the call is a dead end? Nothing to do with Robin?'

'I'm afraid so. We've cautioned them. They won't do it again. Do you want to press charges?'

Do I want to make this a legal thing? There's already so much on my plate. 'No. What about Lawrence Edwards?'

'We have looked into him. He lives locally on the

Rosemount Estate. We've sent a car to pick him up for questioning. This is a good thing, Cherrie. I feel like we're close . . .'

I stop listening to her. The Rosemount Estate? Could Lawrence Edwards be the copycat rather than a son-for-a-son kidnapper? Could he have murdered Thomas Doncaster? You hear stories about victims becoming predators – is it so far-fetched? I could be wrong about what I saw in him. Sad eyes easily hide rage. He could have taken Thomas as a dry run for Robin, as Dad did with Trumpton.

'Cherrie? Are you still there?'

I look at my phone.

'Cherrie?'

'Yes, I'm here.'

'As I was saying, we are looking for Lawrence Edwards, and when we find him, I'll call you.'

'Wait, Patricia. I'd like to speak with Mrs Doncaster. Can you arrange it?'

'I'm not sure it's a good idea. She's grieving right now.'

I hear a knock at my front door.

'Hold on,' I tell her.

Once again, I answer my door without latching the security chain. Silently, I stare at my visitor.

'Cherrie?' Patricia's voice is distant.

I put the phone slowly back up to my ear and say, 'I know where Lawrence Edwards is right now. Here, standing on my doorstep.'

Chapter 32

The faint voice of Patricia tells me she's sending a car to my house. Slowly, I hang up on her; my eyes never leaving Lawrence.

After at least a minute ticks by with us locked in a staring contest I ask, 'Where's my son?'

'Can I come in, please?'

'Where's my son? Is he with you?'

'I don't have your son, Cherrie.' He puts his arms up and steps forward. I move aside to let him into my home.

'Why should I believe you?' I say. 'Did you take Thomas Doncaster? Are you some crazy Mr Bones copycat?'

'Christ, no! I've felt your pain. I'd never do that to someone else. I'm sorry about your son, but I didn't take him or Thomas Doncaster.'

I firm up my stare. Narrowing my eyes, I watch as his shoulders sag and his fingers dance by his sides. He looks like a little lost boy; Peter Pan grown up. His pain is easy to see; it's carved into his bones. He lets me stare at him. Not defending himself. God help me, I believe him. I mean, why else would he be here, standing before me? What would be the point? But, if I think that, it takes my suspects back down to the monster Greer and random copycat who I might never be able to track down.

'Why are you here?' I ask him.

'I knew I'd be a suspect, so I wanted to clear myself. That way, the police could concentrate on who really did take your boy. I have an alibi. On the night Robin went missing, I was in Wales on a work thing.' Lawrence reaches for my hand. 'I've been stupid in pursuing answers to my son's murder. I shouldn't have followed you like that. I didn't mean to scare you. I'm sorry.'

I look past him. The police will be here any moment. Our time together is limited.

'I'm sorry about what happened to your son, Lawrence.'

I put my hand out to shake his in a hopeful act of solidarity. Instead of taking it, he hugs me.

'Find Robin, and soon. I've studied a lot of missing child cases over the years. The longer they go on, the lower the odds of seeing those kids again.'

I look up at him. 'I had a suspect, but the police cleared him.'

'The police were useless with your dad. Did you know they interviewed him after he took my son?'

'What?' Mr Bones could have been caught? How many young lives would have been spared? It could have even spared me.

'A group of boys spotted his car in the area that night. As they'd seen him before, they reported it to the police. Even gave them a number plate.'

'I had no idea that happened. I don't even remember him going to the station.'

'You are brought up to believe the police are above human, that they can do things ordinary people can't. That's bullshit; they're as human as the rest of us.'

'It's why I'm trying to find Robin myself.'

'You've called the police, right? You were on the phone when you opened the door to me?'

'Yes. When they get here, I'll tell them you're not the one.'

'That won't matter. Don't worry, I'll co-operate. The police will rule me out quickly. Who is your suspect?'

'A sex offender called Greer.'

'Yes, Oscar Greer. I still check the court listings. He lives up by Hallow's Gate.'

'I went to his house, but he wouldn't let me in.'

'Like you wouldn't let me in.'

'Sorry.'

Lawrence claps his hands together. 'We need to get into Greer's house. He's on the sex offender register, and just like your dad, he's a local. He knows the area. He has to have Robin. Are you with me?'

Technically, I was there before him, but I nod yes.

'I'll meet you there at seven tonight. We'll find your son. I don't want him to end up like mine.'

Sirens wail and DC Kimmings is suddenly lumbering up my drive. 'Stay where you are, Mr Edwards.'

Lawrence puts his hands up.

'He's okay,' I say. 'It's not him.'

'We need to take him in. Will you come quietly, sir?'

'Sure.' Lawrence moves to follow DC Kimmings outside. Abruptly, he stops and turns to me with a wistful look. 'I wish I had been there at the fair that night. You never know, I might have been able to save Robin.'

That strange thought of a stalker stopping an abduction makes me smile. I nod as the DC shoves him into the back of a waiting police car.

Leo would come to Greer's house with me. He'd do anything for Robin, but then we'd both be in trouble. Trusting a stalker seems like one of those silly things Patricia warned me against; however, I'm pretty sure it's sillier to break into a paedophile's house and confront him alone. Maybe it's time that I trusted more people around me. Mariah has been trying to help, and if I'd trusted her sooner, then maybe . . . No, I can't keep thinking like that. The past is behind me; the present is what I need to deal with now, and if Robin is to have a future, I'll need all the help I can get. Lawrence said it himself; he has felt my pain. When this is all over, I'll make sure Mr Bones speaks to him. Dad said he'd help with whatever he could, and Lawrence will have earnt it. He will get the answers he needs.

When the sirens fade into the distance, I close my front door and wander into the dining room to look at Robin's robot costume. It feels like a million years ago when he asked to wear it to the fair. Now it sits there, a collection of poorly painted cardboard boxes waiting for a child to bring them to life.

I need to straighten everything out in my head, focus on what I believe. Is Mariah right? Is Robin still alive? If there is a spirit world, I haven't felt my baby ripped from my chest, so he must be. I have to believe it, but Mariah has been wrong about so much. She's been using health and safety forms as cheat sheets. Maybe even telling every mother who visits that her child is in danger. After all, she'll be right at some point, and when she is right, she'll look like a rock star, and that's when she milks money from the family. But, she hasn't asked me for more money; Jon even gave me my £25 back. Wait, isn't it what all good con artists do? Reel you in slowly, like a fat fish?

My mobile goes off. I don't recognise the number. My stomach rolls over. I answer without saying 'hello' and find it's just the clerk at the prison. He checks my identity and asks if I'm willing to receive calls from William Hendy in the future. He knows who my father is. The disdain in his voice is palpable. Nevertheless, he goes through the motions of data protection and other legal issues. It's mindless bureaucracy I could have done without right now. Once I agree with everything, he unceremoniously hangs up.

I collapse in front of the TV and put on the news. It's something I haven't done this whole time for fear of what people are saying. I learnt early on in my life as Little Bones that it was easier not to hear the rumours. Ignorance is bliss, but it only gives you half the picture.

The news is talking about global warming and some member of parliament who grabbed his secretary's bum. Nothing to do with Robin, or me. Even Thomas Doncaster has fallen off their radar. I grab my laptop. The local news sites still feature stories about missing boys. They mention Mr Bones and the significance of it happening in this county again.

There are links to *The Flesh on the Bones*, and I find there's a short bonus episode. Hating myself for clicking on it, I listen.

'*Come back for some more juicy* Flesh on the Bones *eh, listener? Well, your secret is safe with me. So, in the previous episodes, we've tackled a few of the theories about the missing* boys of Northamptonshire, but today's bonus episode is all about you, the listeners. You've sent hundreds of questions to me about the Doncaster and Duffill case, along with queries on Mr Bones. So let's get to them.'

I dread to think what kind of people have sent questions and what is on their minds.

'Okay, we have a question from Terry from Rushden. He asks, who is more dangerous now, Mr Bones or Little Bones? Well, good question.'

It's a shit question. It reduces me and Dad down to some childish 'Who'd win in a fight?' debate.

'I've only been face to face with Little Bones, and let me tell you, that woman is nuts. You can see it in her eyes. Years in prison might have mellowed Mr Bones, so I'd say Little Bones is the most dangerous right now. I wouldn't want to get stuck in a lift with her!'

Jai should meet my dad; he'd soon change his mind.

'Lorraine from Corby asks, what gives you the right to . . .' He trails off, obviously not having read the question in full before he started recording his bonus episode. A click signifies that after a quick edit, he amended the end of Lorraine's question to: 'comment on these cases? Well, Lorraine, I've been a true crime connoisseur for a number of years now. I've looked into the Mr Bones case, some might say, I'm a bones expert.'

Referring to himself as a 'bones expert' is enough for me to turn off Jai's bonus episode and carry on my internet search, but I find nothing else related to my son's case. I was hoping to see Robin's smiling face. To be reminded he's still out there somewhere, but there's nothing. The media has left Robin in the dust, just like someone did to poor Thomas Doncaster.

Fuck it. I'm going to go door-to-door. Knock on every household in the Rosemount Estate. I didn't cover that area with the flyers; Gurpreet did, and she wouldn't have been using it as a sneaky clue-finding session as I did in Hallow's Gate. I yank on my coat and am just about to get my shoes on when I realise that I don't have the excuse of the flyers. Grabbing my phone, I text Tracy to ask if she could have more printed. She comes back with, *I'll bring some round.*

With nothing else to do, sleep attacks my senses; still, it's fretful rather than restful. I'm always just on edge, like a mother with a new-born baby.

I open my eyes. The rays of the mid-morning sun are lighting my room. I lie still for another hour, thinking through my plan for tonight. With Lawrence eliminated from my suspect list, Greer has to have Robin. Dad said paedophiles are the lowest form of life. As a judge of character he should know. My instincts shouted Greer the minute I learned of him; that counts for something too. Now, what do I need to bring tonight, and how will Lawrence and I split up the search? Perhaps he should handle Greer, so I could be free to explore the house. Paedophiles swap kids with one another to keep off the police's radar. What if Greer has done this with Robin? If he has, I'll kill him, just not before I torture him for the address of where he sent my son.

The doorbell rings, so I slide off the couch. My whole body aches and I bang into the side table as I make my way to the front door.

It's Tracy. Her eyes are red and she is clutching her mobile to her chest.

'What's wrong?' I ask.

Thrusting her free hand out, she slaps me on the shoulder. 'You never answered my texts. I thought they must have found Robin. Or you were dead, or something.'

Stepping aside, I let her in. I don't remember seeing any more texts from her; they must have arrived when I slept.

'What were the texts about?' I ask as we sit down on the couch.

Tracy's worry dissolves into a sheepish smile, one I've never seen on her before; somehow, it frightens me more than her worry face.

'What's wrong now?'

'No, it's okay. Have the police said anything more about Robin?'

Her face is too pale and I realise this is the first time in ten years I've seen her without make-up.

'Seriously, what's up? I could just read the text, you know.'

Crossing her legs, she inches over the couch, away from me. 'Have you seen Facebook?'

'I'm not on it, remember?'

'Yeah, it's probably for the best.'

'What the fuck is going on?' My patience feels frayed so deep that its edges are dragging across my last nerve.

'People have been hassling Dawson's Food employees. Gurpreet, Shania, Mr Dawson, his wife and me. Even the Saturday girls, whose names I can't be bothered to remember, are being cyber bullied. It's that fucking podcast. Its judgemental listeners getting everyone riled up with their shit questions and crazy theories.'

The questions after Lorraine must have gotten worse. 'Theories about my past?' I ask.

'Yeah, they're saying you're a killer like your dad. That you helped him murder those boys. That we're accessories to murder if we keep being your friends. Even Gran's bingo buddies have disowned her until she admits you killed the Doncaster kid and Robin.'

She won't look at me. Instead, Tracy picks at the edges of her cardigan, pulling out loose pieces of wool.

'I'm sorry,' I say.

'It's not your fault. Hell, we've all gone on there to defend you, even Shania. Kylie's been comment-bombing threads too; telling everyone not to make assumptions on crap they know nothing about.'

'That's sweet of her.'

'Apparently it's not her first Facebook war. She went through the same thing with her boyfriend after she found out she was pregnant. I'm assuming it was to do with an ex-girlfriend kicking off; didn't like to press for details.'

'You, not press for details? What have you done with the real Tracy?' I laugh.

'Oh, she's still here. I'm saving all my energy for you, Cherry Pie.'

My friends are all still defending me. Shit has hit the fan, and they could lose parts of their own lives staying in my corner, but they don't care. Tears threaten to fall. I inhale deeply and suck them back up. I haven't cried yet; I don't intend to start now.

'Thank you.' I reach across and hug my best friend, patting her back.

'Are you feeling which of my bones you want to take?' She giggles.

'Why would I want your shitty, old bones?' I laugh.

Tracy pulls away. 'You smell bad.'

'Showers are optional now.'

Smiling, she holds me at arm's length. 'They're not. They're not optional at all. Go upstairs and sort yourself out. I'll hold down the fort.'

I look down at her bag and see flyers poking out; bless her, she brought them straight over.

Nodding, I trudge upstairs. I don't understand why I'm so smelly. Maybe it was the dry ice in the Ghost Train. Shit, I've been lazing around with the evidence of an assault all over me.

I take a brief shower and wash my hair. Not bothering with a hairdryer, I just put a brush through the tangles and towel it off. I dress in a pair of jogging pants and a sweat top. A throwback outfit from the days when I thought doing yoga would be cool.

As I trot downstairs, I see Tracy holding a plate of toast. 'So, I'm not the best cook in the world, but I can do toast.'

I look down to see two brown slices devoid of butter. If I were feeling jovial, I'd point out that without the butter she can't do toast either. Taking the plate, I sit on the couch.

Tracy goes back into the kitchen. Seconds later, she sits beside me with two mugs of tea.

'Robin wasn't even covered on the news last night,' she says.

'They've forgotten him already.' I take a sip of tea and it scalds my lips.

'Leo says you went to see your dad in prison.' Although a statement, she's really asking a question as she looks away, ashamed of her curiosity.

'When did he tell you?'

'Gran and I went round his mum's house. Did you know she's planning to go to her Spanish holiday home this week? Abandoning you?'

'Doesn't surprise me.'

'Gran called her a heartless bitch and told her to go fuck herself.'

'Your gran is the best.' The look on Mrs Duffill's face would have been priceless after hearing the F-bomb from a pensioner. I wish I'd been there.

'Leo is coming home soon, right?'

I take another burning sip of tea. 'Yeah, we haven't split up or anything. He's just giving me some space.'

'Cherry Pie, are there any leads at all? Any hope?'

'I spoke with Mariah. She told me to look at the fair again.'

'You believed her this time?'

'I don't exactly have much else to go on. And she's gotten some stuff right.'

'You mean shoeless Thomas Doncaster?'

'I went to her house again,' I admit.

'How much did that set you back?'

'Nothing.'

'Nothing so far. Okay, so the fair is all we have?'

Putting my steaming tea down, I stare at my feet, then wring my hot hands together. I can't get my best friend involved in my plan with Greer and Lawrence. She deserves legitimate deniability.

'Mariah said he's still at the fair.'

'Well, you better look quick, the fair is packing up today.'

'I went yesterday; I didn't find anything.'

'You look weird, Cherry Pie. Are you sleeping?' She strokes my wet hair.

'I'm sleeping as much as I can.'

'Did your dad help at all?'

'Kind of, but not really.'

'Well, don't give up hope. I'm rounding the girls up for a search party at Black Friars Park this afternoon. The police will be there too. Will you come?'

It'll look weird if I don't. 'Yes, of course. Thank you so much for your help.'

'That's okay, it's the least we can do. Get some sleep.'

'Okay.'

She pulls me into an uncomfortable embrace. I'm lucky to have her; but this isn't what I need right now. Tracy is Cherrie's friend, not Little Bones' friend. I need to be Little Bones if I have any chance of finding Robin alive.

Tracy leaves after making me promise to text her later. Apparently, the searchers are meeting at the park entrance at five o'clock. The fair may be packing up, but the police told them they couldn't leave until after one final search. Odd that Patricia didn't mention this to me. Probably doesn't want me to make another scene, like at the appeal.

I pick up my mobile and see an alien face emoji from Leo. I don't reply. I call Mariah. She doesn't pick up. My call goes to an answerphone, so I leave a message.

In the kitchen, I open every drawer looking for a weapon for tonight's visit to Greer's house, yet I only find butter knives, a vegetable peeler, and one dull bread knife I'd have to use like a saw. We've kept little in the way of sharp cutlery in the house in case Robin got into the drawers. This is ridiculous; I need something heavy and sharp that can cut down to bone.

I grab the flyers, put on a coat and trainers, then drive to Dawson's Food. I go in the back door and see Shania serving a customer. She waves at me as if she wants to talk. Waving back, I slip backstage to find my favourite long, professional butcher knife. One that I've used a thousand times to gut fish. I manage to slip it into my pocket just as Shania steps through the plastic curtain.

'You okay?' she asks.

'I'm all right, thanks. Just thought I'd . . .' Oh, I haven't constructed a lie about why I'm here. My brain is fuzzy, so all I can think to say is, 'I came to give you some extra flyers and thank you for coming out later, to search.' I pass a handful of fresh Robin flyers towards her.

Taking them, she says, 'Sure, what are friends for, Cherry Pie.'

Weird to hear my pet name coming from a woman who two weeks ago was only an awkward acquaintance.

I grin back at her, the stolen butcher knife feeling heavy in my coat.

'Hey, Mr Dawson is in today; you should go see him.'

For days, I've had shifts here that I've not clocked in for. Work hasn't even once crossed my mind. A sinking feeling floods my body. I step around the counter and walk to the office like a child being sent to the headmaster. I'm probably going to get a warning in my work file; the first since I became Cherrie.

I knock on his door.

'Come in.'

The moment he sees me, he plasters a fake smile across his face.

'Cherrie, or is it Leigh-Ann?'

'I legally changed my name – it's Cherrie.'

He motions for me to sit down; I don't. If I do, the knife could drop out of my pocket.

'I just want to say Dawson's Food is behind you.'

'That's lovely, thank you.' I turn to leave. 'I should go.'

'Cherrie, you must know that things are not going well for us here.'

Facing Mr Dawson, I say, 'It's quiet.'

'That's an understatement. Your friends feel your troubles too, but I need you to take a step back from work. I mean, you want to, right?'

Where is this going? 'I'm sorry I've missed my shifts.'

'Completely understood. But, I can't pay you for being off work. You understand.'

'Yes.'

'And you might not want to come back,' he says getting up from his desk. 'When your boy is found, you'll want to spend time with him. It's completely natural and understood.'

He keeps saying *understood*, yet I don't quite understand anything he's saying.

'It's best you perhaps take a permanent step back from Dawson's Food. I'll miss you, but it's . . .'

'Understood.'

He shrinks under my gaze like a time-lapsed recording of a waterless plant. The man, who has been in charge of me for a decade, now looks so small to me that all I can do is turn my back on him and leave.

I stomp back through the shop that I've worked at for years, yet today it doesn't feel familiar.

'Did you catch Mr Dawson?' Shania asks as I waft ghost-like past her counter.

'He fired me.'

302

She stares at me for a moment, the knife in her hand hovering above a slab of cooked flesh like a hesitant bird of prey. 'Oh, um, why would he let you go?'

'You tell me.'

'Look, customers were complaining. Said they'd heard you killed Robin. It's crap, I know, but you know how people love to talk. The shop can't afford to lose custom.'

'Yeah, I'm painfully aware of what people are like.' It doesn't surprise me that the undying support I felt at first has been eroded by rumours. 'So, Shania, I'll see you later today, for the search party?'

'Yeah, I wouldn't miss a party.' Pausing she adds, 'Sorry, that came out wrong. You know what I mean.'

As I go to leave, I hear the radio on her hip crackle. The voice of one of the security team comes through. 'Has Little Bones left the building? Over.' Sniggering, they click off.

'Really?' I say to Shania.

'It wasn't meant like that.'

'Not many ways it could have been meant.'

The radio crackles. 'Baby, are you there? Over.'

The voice belongs to Tim, the head of security, whose wife runs the coffee shop in town.

Shania has the decency to blush. I guess Tim is the married man she's screwing. The one she hoped Mariah would tell her was going to divorce his wife and run away with her. What a dumb bitch.

Looking her square in the eye, I say, 'I thought you understood. I guess once the daughter of a serial killer always the daughter of a serial killer, right? Just like once the daughter of a whore, always the daughter of a whore, eh, baby?'

Shania's lips twitch. She looks at the radio. With a steady hand, she clicks it. 'Tim, Little Bones is still here, over.'

'Fuck you,' I say.

Marching out the front door, I pat the knife inside my coat. I feel justified in taking it now. It's my severance package.

In the street, I call Leo. I tell him about Mr Dawson firing me. He tells me not to worry. Apparently, his business hasn't taken a hit, even though he shares a child with Little Bones. I suggest we add this to the lawsuit against Jai Patel; after all, the rumours about me killing Robin started with him.

Hunger rattles my belly, but rather than go home, I head to the Rosemount Estate. I put up flyers and knock on doors. This time, I get more doors slammed in my face. It appears Jai has spread his lies thick enough to infect both social media and the more traditional doorstep neighbour gossip.

Frustrated, I decide to check out the newsagent where the media said that Thomas Doncaster was last seen. It looks like every other newsagent: cramped and selling too much variety. I remember when these shops were for newspapers and mix bags of sweets. Now they sell anything they can buy in bulk. Rather than the giggles of schoolchildren, there is the hum of industrial fridges chock full of out-of-date food. Approaching the man behind the counter, I smile and give him a flyer. He doesn't speak just nods as he places the flyer beside the till.

'You that Robin's mum?'

I look behind me to see a boy about twelve years old, dressed in a dazzling white tracksuit and a baseball cap two sizes too big for him. In his hands are a bag of crisps and a can of pop.

'Yes, I'm Robin's mum.'

'Thomas was my brother.' This revelation comes out more like one-upmanship, rather than an attempt at empathy.

I look around the shop to see where his mum is. Surely, after losing one son, she wouldn't let this one out alone in the same place, but there's no one else here.

'Where's your mum?'

'At home. She's a wreck. Spends all her time staring at her laptop.'

'I know that feeling, but you shouldn't be wandering the streets alone.'

'It's the middle of the day, I'm good.' Shrugging, he puts the bag of crisps back on the shelf. With an excessive amount of change, he pays for the can of pop.

'Do you live near here?' I ask.

'Yeah, we're on Dale Street,' he says, pointing as if we could see his house from here. He looks down at my hands. 'Gimme some flyers. I'll take them down there for you, if you like?'

'That's kind of you. Can I give you a lift home?'

'Thanks, yeah,' he replies, and walks out of the shop.

I follow Thomas's brother outside. When he stops for me to catch him up, I notice a Tasmanian Devil temporary tattoo on the back of his right hand, and that his jacket pockets are bulging with unknown stuff.

'Where's your car, Robin's mum?'

'I'm just there,' I say, pointing to my Ford.

'Sweet.'

I walk him over and open the car door. He slips into

305

the passenger seat and, just like with Robin, I have to remind him to put the belt on. When he does, I start the engine.

'What's your name?' I ask.

'Harry. You can call me Hazza.' He shifts his feet, and I notice the sparkling white trainers he's wearing. They remind me of bones, all chalky and just between dirty and clean; if it were Robin next to me, they would have been in the footwell by now. Choking back the memory, I start the car and our journey falls into an uncomfortable silence. The route I'm driving to his house is jerky due to my lack of knowledge of the estate.

As Harry casually looks out of the window, I realise I've just abducted this boy. I could drive anywhere: my house, an abandoned building, or even a sinister art studio, which stinks of peroxide. Harry trusts me when I say I'll take him home, or maybe he doesn't care if he makes it back or not. I don't remember too much about Dad's child abductions, just that I'd see those boys merrily go with him, disappearing forever. I'd like to say that I thought it was some weird game, but even at that age, I wasn't dumb enough to believe it. It's easy to look back with an adult's eye, and question why I didn't stop him. They asked Leigh-Ann Hendy that many times. My reply was always the same, because he's my dad. Present tense. He's my dad; Mr Bones was always, and will always be, my dad.

I hear a rustling and look over to see Harry opening a bag of crisps. He smiles at me as he crunches, daring me to realise he didn't pay for them. I've seen this behaviour before; he's acting out, seeking attention. Focused on Thomas's funeral, Mrs Doncaster is ignoring Harry. I can't stand shoplifters, yet right now, I have bigger things on my mind.

'Can I have one?'

Harry offers me the bag and I slip a crisp out. When I bite through it, there's a loud crunch. He grins at me and keeps eating. Then, with a mouthful of half-mashed salt and vinegar, he says, 'What happened to Tommy hasn't happened to your son. I'm not one hundred per cent sure, like. I just don't think it has.'

My heart jumps into my mouth, but I manage to push out, 'That's kind of you to say.'

'No biggie, Robin's mum.'

'Harry—'

'Hazza.'

'Hazza, you know you shouldn't get in cars with strangers, right?' I pull the car into his street, and he gives me a look of disdain, one that belongs on a teenage face.

'Now, you tell me!' He laughs, pointing at a house. 'I'm over there.'

Parking in front of his house, I half expect to see Mrs Doncaster lingering on their front step, waiting for her only son to return. She's not there.

'Thanks for the ride, Little Bones,' Hazza says.

Before I can react, he's out of the car and swaggering up his drive.

It's only as I'm driving home that I realise Hazza didn't take the flyers as he had promised.

A quick bowl of cereal in front of the TV and I'm out of the house again. I want to arrive at Black Friars Park before the rest of the search party. I'm not sure why, but it feels like I should be the first one there. The host of the party.

For some reason, the afternoon air feels crisper in the park than in the streets. I sit on a bench by the car park with my coat pulled tight around me and stare upwards. Clouds like twisted white animals made of smoke dash across the dusky sky. The longer I stare, the more intricate the animals appear. One is like a charging elephant, another a zebra with fur-frayed stripes. Robin would love them.

I'm dreading the next couple of hours. What if the search party finds a piece of bloody clothing? I couldn't bear it. Would I then still meet Lawrence to search a paedophile's house? Probably. I have a knife in my pocket, and just because Mr Dawson made me redundant, it doesn't mean it will be too.

I should have slept before I came out. How many hours of sleep have I had in the past week? I don't even remember. What damage could it do to my health or mind? I need to be in fighting form right now. Not falling down a rabbit hole of sleep-deprived insanity.

Patricia pulls into the car park. I get up to greet her.

'I'm glad to see you here. Trust me, you'll feel better for doing something,' she says.

I want to punch her in the face. She thinks I've been sitting on my bum all day waiting for news. Hang on, isn't it her job to keep me informed? Where was that professionalism when she neglected to tell me about today? I wouldn't have known about the search party at all if Tracy hadn't told me.

'Everyone will be arriving soon. We need to mark quadrants on the map to ensure we all search the whole park this time.'

'This time?'

'Well, yes, the police searched it on the night Robin went missing, but . . .' Her voice trails off in a potential lie.

Lawrence is right; I can't trust the police. If they didn't even search the park properly, what else have they not done?

Passively, I wait for over an hour while all the other people arrive. I see Tracy and her gran, so wave at them. They come over and offer me a flask of tea along with a doorstep cheese sandwich.

'Shania told you what happened?' I ask them.

'Ignore her,' Tracy replies.

'Easier said than done,' I echo back a cliché that even I cringe at saying.

The night is now sneaking in around us. A creepy holler from an owl makes my best friend jump.

'Bloody wildlife,' she mutters.

More searchers pull up.

'There'll be over a hundred. Gurpreet called the PTAs of three schools,' Tracy's gran explains.

'Hundreds of people are coming to help me?' I say.

Tracy shakes her head. 'Sorry, Cherry Pie. They're not here for you, they're here for Robin.'

As everyone arrives, I can feel something strange lacing the air. If I didn't know better, I'd say it was excitement. Not the same innocent child-like enthusiasm that laced the air here on Friday night, but morbid excitement. Imagine the attention someone would get if he or she were to find my son's body. They'd change their social media status to 'heroic finder of dead boys' and tweet endlessly about how it both strengthened and damaged their superman-psyche. I already want to kill them.

Finding Robin's body will mean a clue for the police, but the end for me. I won't be running on maternal need anymore, just vengeance to find the one responsible. If it's a copycat, he will get his fondest wish to be close to Mr Bones, I'll bury his corpse for a few weeks; then dig him up so I can pop him in a bath of peroxide. I'll dunk the leftovers in the washing powder I used on Robin's clothes. I'll crack the bones and mould them into a human costume for a robot.

'You look weird. You okay, Cherry Pie?'

My mouth twitches. 'I'm plotting.'

'Thinking about the future is good,' Tracy's gran says and hugs me. As she does, I have to use one hand to hold my knife away from her stomach.

Once the park is full of have-a-go heroes, Patricia steps in to divide them all into groups. They are all gifted flashlights. I don't join in a group. Instead, I let Tracy and her gran go on ahead. I linger by the entrance to people-watch. My criminology textbooks talk of cases where murderers insert themselves into the investigation. It was this thought that had me in Jai's face at the appeal, and although that didn't pan out, I can't completely dismiss the theory out of hand. Robin's abductor could be in the park right now.

People deliberately look at me as they walk past in their groups. They don't all do it obviously, yet they all stare for as long as they can get away with it. Sly glares, quick glances. I use this time to watch them back. I didn't see how tall the skeleton was; he was sitting in the cart with us on the Ghost Train; but I would recognise his build;

thin and weasel-like. I discount all the women at the search party and focus on skinny men. Being winter, it's hard to tell their builds due to a plethora of padded jackets, but I still mentally survey the thin-looking men; none I recognise, apart from Mr Dawson whose guilt from firing me has morphed into catering the party. He has set up a table covered in drinks and biscuits. What a lovely man, still supporting the killer ex-employee who is sullying his business.

I see Leo in the crowd. He doesn't look at me. Instead, he stands with Mr Dawson. I hope he's using his new moody skills as a force for good by giving my ex-employer a piece of his mind. They bark with laughter. He's not giving him what-for at all, he's telling a joke while the surrounding people are searching for his missing son's body. What the fuck? I don't have time to seethe as suddenly, in one sweeping movement, everyone spans out across the park; beating the grass with their sticks as they go.

Fair workers line up watching them, judging the search party for judging them.

As casually as I can, I head towards the far side of the park. I don't want to hear someone yell they've found something. As awful as it is, at least I have hope; damaged and alive is better than damaged and dead, even if said damage was done by that pervert Greer.

My plan is to slip away just before the end of the search and meet up with Lawrence at Greer's house. This search party will be my alibi. With that in mind, I need to ensure people see me here. As I move through the park, I hear voices, so gravitate towards them. There are two women up ahead. I position myself behind them, ready to join in their conversation.

'You know, the poor boy played with my Declan,' one woman says.

Slowing my pace, I move to their right so foliage obscures me. I squint across and see it's Kristine with a K.

'We've met the family too.' It's Sharon from the school gates.

'Yes, but I met them only a few days before it happened. Declan and I were in the park when they crossed our path, you know how I like to ensure he gets enough fresh air. It was on the Sunday before it happened. Cherrie was so haughty; you'd think with her past, she'd play it more demure.' She pronounces *demure* wrong, but Sharon doesn't notice.

'But Robin is a sweetheart. He didn't deserve this to happen to him.'

'Do you think she did it?' Kristine asks.

'Probably. You heard about who she is, right? I mean if I'd known her son was at my daughter's school, I'd have complained sooner.'

Complained sooner? Does this mean I have some random parent complaint waiting for me at Robin's school? Could they expel him because of my dark past?

'I remember when the first murders happened. Her dad was so handsome; you'd have never thought he could do what he did.' Sharon whacks her stick over an innocent lump of grass.

'Yeah, and the wife knew, right?' Kristine whacks her stick out too, only harder.

'She must have, but I guess a handsome young husband was worth overlooking a few murders for, from her point of view. Me, I'd have never . . .'

312

I stop listening. History is repeating. Rumours keep coming back, like an antibiotic-resistant virus. Even when you think they're gone, they're just dormant, waiting to be rekindled by the fires of gossip.

As I move away from the women, a familiar voice sets my teeth on edge; beyond the tree line of the park is Jai. I should ignore him, and the fact he's crashing the search party, but I can't.

In less than a minute, I'm behind him. Too busy talking into his phone, he doesn't hear my approach.

'Take two.' Jai inhales and exhales. He rolls his shoulders and jogs on the spot like an athlete.

'Hello again, my faithful following. Here I am at the epicentre of the crime, as usual, putting the flesh on the bones. Robin was last seen here at Crazy Clive's Fair, so we will scour every inch of Black Friars Park hoping to find something, anything that could lead us to the poor boy. The search for Thomas Doncaster saw tears, anguish, and a family torn apart with grief. Will history repeat itself?'

Without realising I'm lurking behind him, within touching distance, he continues, 'This podcast has gone from strength to strength. We have had hundreds of tips and devised many theories on the gruesome events that have unfolded since Thomas Doncaster was reported missing. Too many questions we'll never know the answers to. Too many horrific events befell Thomas and now Robin. Helping a search party is an experience all in itself. I want to describe to you how I feel right now . . .'

How *he* feels? My hands curl into fists, but I keep them by my sides.

'Hope, horror and above all dread. The maniac responsible for these terrible crimes walked this same path;

breathed this same air, and right now could be within metres of me. I read that criminals often put themselves into the investigation,' he says, then in an annoying, breezy tone adds, 'Now let's go for a break.'

He fiddles with his phone, and almost turns around, but doesn't, instead he ploughs on with his recording. 'Welcome back! Now, let's dig a little deeper; Leigh-Ann's friends organised this search party. Why not Leigh-Ann? I haven't even seen Little Bones yet. If I had, she'd have probably attacked me,' he says and laughs.

If he only knew how close to Little Bones he is right now; how close he is to finding out what she can do.

'Most subscribers believe Robin never left this fair. I suspect we will find him today. I asked the police to bring cadaver dogs . . .'

That's it! I reach out, grab his shoulder and spin him round to face me.

'Whoa, snap, Leigh-Ann, you're here.'

'It's the search party for my son; why wouldn't I be here? And for the love of fuck, it's Cherrie.' My speech is slowed by each word fighting its way past gritted teeth.

'Okay, okay,' he says and lifts his phone, which is still recording. 'Can I get an interview? Get your side of things.'

I want to snatch the phone from his hands, throw it to the ground and grind it beneath my boot, but it would only make everything worse. Instead, I take a deep breath. 'Turn the phone off, please,' I say.

Jai clicks off his phone, but I've no idea if he's stopped recording.

'As usual, what you said was crap,' I tell him.

'Which part?'

'All of it. And you can't breathe the same air unless

314

you're next to someone. Your lungs are clean of maniac breath.'

'I'm not sure they are, Little Bones,' he says sniffing.

'Don't *you* dare call me that! You made up your mind about me before you started streaming your first episode, and you've been infecting others ever since.'

'I've brought much-needed publicity to your case.' He spins the phone around in his palm so the microphone is aimed at me, like the barrel of a gun.

'You accused me of killing my son.' I point at his chest, and Jai stumbles back. 'You poisoned the public against me.' My finger thrusts out, my nail grazing his padded jacket. 'You ruined my life.' One last stab of my finger and the force to his chest knocks him backwards.

'Please, Leigh-Ann, I'm only here to help find Robin. You want to find your son, don't you?'

'Yes! I want to find Robin, but you need to stop what you're doing.'

Jai grins. 'Or else?'

There's a butcher knife in my pocket. Sharp and solid, it sits waiting to fulfil its purpose, but there's a man who deserves its sharp edge more, and I can't let Jai distract me; in fact, this could help me cement my alibi.

'Can you record live?' I ask, motioning to his phone.

'Yeah, I recorded bits for the podcast to edit together later, but I'm about to Facebook live stream. My PR guru said . . .'

I put my hands up. 'Fine, I get it. Stream now.'

'You're giving me a live interview?'

'Yes, but only if it's quick. I'm here to search for my son, remember?'

Fumbling with his phone, Jai's grin widens enough

for me to see his unnaturally white teeth. This is his moment. I'm giving him what he's wanted all along. He'll get even more advertising money. I'm giving in, helping him and his career, and it's already nibbling at my soul like a rat.

I edge back; will guest-starring on his show look like I endorse it? That what he said about me being connected to the crimes is true? Is strengthening an alibi worth blurring this line? People will see me here at the park. Jai, under oath, would now have to say as much. I don't have to do this. I don't want to do this. Too many things are already out of my control. Taking another step back, I say, 'Please stop your podcast, you've caused enough trouble.' With that, I walk away, leaving Jai to live stream his reaction to my swift exit.

Turning, I double back on myself. I slip through the shadows of the park, an impressive feat considering there are over a hundred people waving torches around like wandering spotlights. I trudge up to the edge of the fair and find all the rides packed away. I go to the caravan with the green door and, for one final time, look around. Peering into each window like a ghoul hunting for a soul to drag down to hell. The rapist is not here. He's probably with his fellow workers, or maybe even in the hospital with an ice pack on his balls.

Lights appear, wielded by searchers making their way to where I am. I deliberately pop out to join them. I speak to a few people; random nonsense they should remember if the police were to ask if they saw me. I do this a number of times to ensure a plethora of witnesses for my alibi. Soon, walking on uneven ground in the cold starts to wear on me, so I slip away from the park.

Regardless of Mariah's prediction, the fair appears to be clear. Steadying my butcher knife in my coat, I sprint towards Greer's house.

Chapter 33

As I lurk by Greer's bungalow, a weird mix of guilt and excitement builds in my gut, like a big meal I can't digest.

Fuck, I'm way too early. Double fuck, I don't have Lawrence's mobile number. Probably for the best, avoiding evidence trails is a new thing for me.

Painful minutes tick by while I watch Greer's house. There are no lights on. He's not home. With all the attention, he could have skipped town; if he legally can leave town.

I look at my watch; it's fifteen minutes past seven. Lawrence is late. How long do I wait for him? It's cold and my anger isn't keeping me warm anymore. I'm shivering so much the knife nestled in my pocket is threatening to vibrate through the fabric.

Is he ever going to arrive?

A noise breaks my thoughts. I crouch down and see one of Greer's neighbours letting their dog shit on his front lawn. They don't even look up to see if anyone has spotted their drive-by poop drop. I recognise the dog walker as the old woman from the bus stop, the lady who told me where to find Greer.

I stare at the time passing by on my phone. Lawrence is now over a half hour late. He's not coming. Maybe he never intended to help me, he only pretended to; some bizarre revenge for what Mr Bones did to his family. Perhaps he's called the police in an attempt to have me arrested?

After another ten minutes goes by, I start to feel angry again. It's my second wave. Fuck Lawrence, I don't need his help. In my pocket is the weapon I need. I can do this without anyone else.

Quickly, I move to the edge of the back garden so I can look down the street. Nothing. Not even a neighbour's car is in motion; no police cars either. Hallow's Gate is quiet; the perfect place to keep an abducted eight-year-old boy. A flash of light streaks across my vision, making me squint. I step back to check both sides of the street. Just the headlights of a motorcycle. Greer's neighbour thrusts their foot down and the bike lets out an almighty rumble. They pull away onto the road and the night swallows them up. The cloying scent of diesel dissipates as the motorcycle's roar morphs into a distant purr.

My heartbeat thunders into a drumroll, making me feel like something dramatic is about to happen . . . yet it doesn't.

I should go. My nerves can't take this. I've trusted the wrong person and they've let me down. I go to leave, but what if I later find out Robin is in here? That he could have lived and been safe if only I'd channelled my inner criminal?

Shit, I can't wait any longer. I sneak behind Greer's

house, jump over a small fence, and find glass patio doors barricaded by wheelie bins. One by one, I pull the bins away. The sound of their creaking plastic wheels makes me feel even more conspicuous. I look up. Still no lights on in the house. I grab the small food-scraps bin, lift it up and swing it at the door. The first time the two surfaces collide, the bin bounces off the glass, the momentum almost knocking me over. The second time I swing it, the bin cracks the surface. The third swing breaks the door completely. The sound of shattering glass is too loud for such a quiet night. I hold my breath, waiting for someone to catch me, yet no one does. Letting the bin fall to my side, I step over the broken glass and into the paedophile's house.

As I move through the door, I catch my coat on the dangling glass shards. I reach across and pull the material free. As I do, I slice my finger. Blood wells up and drips onto the window frame. Great, I've left my DNA. I hesitate at this, but Robin's face appears in my mind's eye, and I find I don't care. Yes, I'm breaking into someone's house. Yes, I'm violating the law, a few commandments too – I just don't give a shit. To get my son back, I'll do anything it takes. Show me something to break and I'll crush it; smash it to powder under my boot. Show me the person responsible and I'll drain the lifeblood from them, one pint at a time.

It's dark inside the house, so I use the torch from the search party. A sick thrill that I'm using police equipment to commit a crime reinforces my nerves. The blackness retreats at the touch of the torch's spotlight, giving me snapshots of possible crime scenes, along with lacklustre furniture and fittings.

'Robin. Are you here?' I call.

No answer.

I move through Greer's living room, which only holds an old, heavy-looking TV along with a threadbare recliner chair. There's a hallway. The bungalow has rooms sprouting off this one main corridor, like a long plant reaching for light.

Quietly, I make my way to the farthest door; it's his kitchen. Small and as sparse as the rest of his home. A kettle, a microwave, a small countertop fridge, a gap for an oven, and a washing machine. I open the fridge expecting to see childish treats, but there is just a loaf of bread, a few packs of cheap meat, and a tub of fake butter.

I open the cupboards. Again, there is nothing any more damning than a packet of unopened Coco Pops, Robin's favourite cereal. The monkey on the box stares back at me with disappointment. I slam the cupboard shut.

'Robin?'

Still no answer. I spot another door to the right. A basement? A utility room? I open it to find it's a toilet.

'Robin?' My voice gets louder.

It's a strange feeling being in someone else's house at night. Greer could be somewhere in the house. I could burst into his bedroom and find him doing something terrible. No, if he were here, he would have heard me break in. He'd be confronting me by now.

I open the next door. It's as if I'm in some sick horror game show; ready to open door number two to find my son, or what's left of him. Worries like that will not help me. I need to stay positive. Empty rooms may not bring answers, but they take me a step forward to the right answer.

The next room is Greer's bedroom. His bed is one of

those inflatable mattresses, sagging across the floor. To my right, sits a clothes rail holding up a collection of bland shirts and trousers.

'Robin?'

Still no answer. I have no bed to look under, no wardrobe to search. It's hard and easy at the same time.

There's only one more door to open. I push it and find it locked.

Chapter 34

'Robin!'

No answer.

Shit, I've not got time to learn how to pick a lock; if only I'd paid attention when Gurpreet picked the extension lock. I've already been here too long. Greer could be back any minute, or the neighbours could have heard me break the glass door and called the police. No, I can't get this far and not check the one locked room in the house.

I lean on the doorframe. 'Robin,' I plead with it. I only want my son back. He's mine; he doesn't belong here. This isn't a home. There's no decent food. This is a prison and Greer is a horrible man who's done terrible things. These are all facts.

'Robin,' I shout, banging my hand onto the door. I dig down deep until I touch Little Bones. I wake her from where she hides in the darkest part of my soul. Feel her stir and surge forward. Stepping back, I kick out at the door. It doesn't budge, so I do it again and again and again, until the sound is deafening. Until I see the door-frame crack. Until the force of my boot makes the barrier between my son and me explode.

'Robin?'

I rush into the room, my torch scanning it.

It's a child's bedroom with bright blue walls. It has chunky wooden shelves covered with books. In the middle of the room is a perfect little bed draped in a duvet set featuring cartoon players chasing footballs; it even has a wicker Moses basket perched on top.

'Robin, it's Mummy, are you here?'

No answer.

There's a brilliantly coloured child's wardrobe in the corner. I hear a thumping, but it's not in the room; it's in me. My heart is beating so fast there's no discernible rhythm to it anymore. I've only ever felt like this once before. When I was a child, standing in front of a cupboard in Dad's studio, my hand hovering over the handle . . . I shake off the memory and move to open the wardrobe. I fling open its doors to find it stuffed with boy's clothes of all ages, all of which have the tags still on. On the floor of the ward-robe are three bulging plastic bags, each one big enough to fit part of a little boy. No, no. no. I don't want to look inside. I can't; my heart can't take it. My hand reaches out before I can stop it. Pulling down the handle of the nearest bag, I peek inside . . . toys. The bag is stuffed with baby toys, probably the ones Gemma saw him carry inside.

What the fuck has Greer been doing? Robin is not here. There isn't even a single clue pointing to the paedo-phile being obsessed by my dad and his killings, or even any other killer. No tell-tale shrine stuffed with crazy crap. Not even a hand-written diary to explain his exploits.

Nothing that books and TV have led me to believe would strengthen my suspicions about this awful man.

The butcher knife feels rigid in my pocket. Greer is smarter than I thought, and that would make sense with how he took my son; trading off my dad's identity to draw the police off him as a suspect. He doesn't fool me. I need to wait for him to come home. Forcibly convince him to tell me what he has done with Robin.

My phone beeps. It's a text from Gemma. An alien face emoji.

I look up to see her dining room backs onto this room. She's there in her window frame like a Hitchcock character. I point at my phone. She looks down. My phone beeps again.

Get out now! The text reads.

I go to the window and open it. Gemma grimaces at me and opens her window.

'My dad has called the police. You need to run.'

'Are these curtains always open?'

'Yes, he told us yesterday it's his son's room.'

'Does Greer have a son? Have you seen a boy here?'

'No, if I had . . .' She snaps her head around and then back to me. 'Please, you need to get out now.'

After closing the window, I sprint for the front door. As I get there, I realise it's not how I got in, so retrace my steps back to the broken patio door and leap out onto the lawn. Sirens whoop in the distance.

I run to the next street. Taking off my coat, I slow down to a pleasant stroll. The police car zooms past me, and I take a deep breath.

★

Once I'm home, I remember the cut on my hand. I've bled on my coat. I take it off and throw it in the hamper. I wash the wound under the tap; the pinkish water gurgles down the sink. I slap on a SpongeBob plaster, and then take off my boots; carefully placing them by the door. They are the only ones there now. I go upstairs, fetch a pair of Leo's trainers, and put them next to my boots. It makes me feel better, but only a little.

I text Leo that I left the search because I couldn't take it. He texts straight back, *It was a bust anyway*, then asks if he can come home. I didn't realise I'd taken that option from him. I text back, *Yes.*

Crime is exhausting, so I go to bed early. About an hour later, the bed depresses and a familiar arm finds my waist.

'Sorry I'm late, had to call Mum to tell her about the search,' Leo says.

'She wasn't there?'

'No, she's having issues with the deeds of her Spanish villa.'

I can't imagine much that Mrs Duffill couldn't buy her way out of, or into. 'Is there a Spanish clause about witches not owning property?' I say. Fortunately it comes out more of a joke than I meant it to.

'Very funny,' Leo says. 'She's trying hard to make the villa a second home for all of us.'

'Not much of an *us* anymore.'

'We will find him, I promise,' Leo whispers.

'I'm surprised you're not still blaming me. Everyone else is.'

'I'm sorry. I was angry. Those other people don't know shit. You could never hurt Robin. I know it above any doubt.'

As he pulls me close, I can smell cheap coffee and mud all over him. It's strangely comforting. His words roll around my mind, *above any doubt*. Easy to say, yet does he mean it?

I fall asleep and dream I'm in the old TV show *Lost in Space*. There's a robot protecting a little boy. He's waving his mechanical arms while saying, 'Danger, danger, Robin Duffill!'

As I wake with a start, I find Leo has given up on hugging me. He's now turned onto his back. Looking at my clock, I see I've only been asleep for an hour. I pull on my robe and go downstairs to make a drink. I need a new plan. Greer has to tell me everything he knows. I can't trust the police to do this. I'm sure they've gone through intensive interrogation training, but Robin isn't their flesh and blood. They didn't push him out after twelve hours of painful labour, and then watch him grow and smile and play. I'm much more qualified for this job, along with the dark deeds needed to achieve it.

I fetch my laptop and email Dad. He whispered to me about how easy it is to take a life. If anyone can help me with it, it'll be him. I ask for a VO form and am about to go back to bed when there's a knock on the door.

I answer it to find Patricia and DC Steadman. A police car behind them, silent but with its blue light flashing around and around.

My stomach rolls. 'You've found him?' I almost vomit the words.

'No, Ms Forrester,' DC Steadman replies. 'We believe you broke into Oscar Greer's house earlier tonight. You're under arrest.' He shakes his head at me as if I'm a naughty child and he's a parent opposed to discipline.

Patricia just looks at me with pure disappointment; like the monkey on the Coco Pops box.

As I go to follow DC Steadman outside, Leo rushes down the stairs.

'What are you doing?'

'Stay back, Mr Duffill. We need to take your wife into custody.'

'I'm not his wife.'

Leo pads down the stairs. 'What have you done?' he asks me.

'Nothing. I've just been looking for Robin.'

'In someone else's house,' Patricia adds.

DC Steadman raises an eyebrow. 'Cherrie Forrester, I am arresting you for burglary. You do not have to say anything, but it may harm your defence if you do not mention, when questioned, something which you later rely on in court. Anything you do or say may be given in evidence. Do you understand?'

Burglary? I didn't steal anything from Greer's house. Did I?

'Do you understand?' he repeats.

'Yes. Are you going to cuff me?' I raise my hands up, wrists together.

'We won't need cuffs if you are going to behave, Ms Forrester.' DC Steadman stares at me.

'We'll speak at the station, okay?' Patricia whispers.

DC Steadman grips my arm and pulls me down our drive towards the waiting police car.

'Wait, she hasn't even got her shoes on!' Leo grabs his trainers, the ones I put by the door. 'Take these.' He gives them to Patricia.

'Everything will be okay,' she tells him.

Leo nods with a weak smile.

DC Steadman helps me into the back of the car in full view of all my early-bird neighbours. My arrest will be all over the estate by morning. Everyone will assume it's for Robin's murder, rather than breaking into Greer's house. I know how these things work.

As I stare out of the police car window, I have two thoughts. The first is that men are idiots. Why did Leo give me his trainers when my boots were right by them? The second is what I will say when questioned. I should tell them about Greer's weird kiddie bedroom, but they must have seen it already if they searched his house.

And if I describe his house's interior it's as good as a confession.

Chapter 35

Wailing sirens and a blinding burst of light take me to the police station.

Patricia helps me out of the back seat. She puts Leo's trainers on my feet. They are too big, so they slop around when I walk, making me shuffle. Shit, I look down and see I'm still in my pink robe. Embarrassing, but lucky since my coat has a stolen butcher knife in the pocket, and is covered in blood.

After they escort me to the custody suite, I go through an alarming number of questions with the custody sergeant; who looks like a smiley comedian off the TV. I spend the whole time answering questions about medications I don't take and allergies I don't have. It's not until the end of it all I realise the comedian the sergeant looks like is an indifferent Michael McIntyre.

In a weird twist, they offer me a book to read called *The Code of Practice*. I'm then told I could call someone to tell him or her I'm here. Nodding, I hold the book in a limp embrace against my chest. They take the belt from my robe and the laces from Leo's trainers. Next thing I know, I'm in a cell.

Hours creep by; though, I can't be sure of the exact time since I'm not wearing a watch. Maybe I should read the book they gave me, but I feel like that would be giving in to them somehow, so throw it across the cell. It lands in a papery heap.

I remember sitting in judgement like this once before. Barely a teenager, my newest foster family locked me in my room. They spent hours asking me questions through the door about their dog. Bertie was a lovely collie-cross who never cared who I was, or what my father did; which was more than I could say about the Turners. They had already judged me before I'd walked through their door.

Bertie was old and affectionate. One night, I'd watched as he'd pulled himself off the floor to sit by the back door. I let him out; thinking he needed a pee. When he didn't come back, I went outside looking for him. When I saw his matted fur on the ground he reminded me of Trumpton. A still-cuddly toy sprawled across the ground. I'm not sure how long I stared at his body for, but it was how they found me. I was back to social services within a day, only this time there was a nifty new crime attached to my file: dog killer.

I hear footsteps and look up to see DC Steadman. Silently, he collects me and walks me to a small room, which is empty apart from a table and four chairs. I sit down. DC Steadman takes a seat on the opposite side of the table. DC Kimmings then comes in. Does this police station only have two working police officers?

They switch on a tape recorder, and DC Steadman states the date and the names of those present.

'Cherrie Forrester. We need to ask you a few questions. Hear your side of events,' says DC Kimmings.

'What event? I didn't burgle anyone.'

This may be all about Greer's house, but I need to be careful. I've committed multiple crimes: stealing the butcher knife, attacking the man in the Ghost Train, breaking into a private property. Oh, wait I've done that twice; technically, I also broke into the green-doored caravan. I doubt a strangled invitation from the rapist would exonerate me from rifling through his den of pot noodles and porn.

'We want to know what happened. Can we start at the beginning?' DC Steadman leans forward, tenting his fingers like Mr Burns from *The Simpsons*.

'You can contact a solicitor if you like, but it will slow things down considerably.' DC Kimmings gets comfort-able, sitting back in his chair like it's a sun lounger in Spain.

'Okay.' DC Steadman inclines back in his chair, mirroring his partner's relaxed demeanour. 'Where were you at around seven o'clock last night?'

I don't want to give anything away. You see those idiots on TV dropping facts like breadcrumbs for DCs Hansel and Gretel to follow back to their gingerbread house confession. I know that I'm not good at this. I remember my first visit to Mariah, the nervous chatter that had me answering all her questions. I need to calm down. Play this cool.

'I was searching Black Friars Park for my son. You remember Robin, who you are supposed to be out looking for.'

'Did anyone see you there?' asks DC Kimmings.

'Of course they did. There was Tracy and her gran, and

Patricia – doesn't she work for you? I'd hope she is a credible witness.'

DC Steadman taps his iPad, then shifts in his chair. 'Yes, but she only saw you once, before the search,' he says, wheezing from the movement.

'Jai saw me.'

'Who?' the DCs ask together.

'Jai Patel, that idiot who does the podcast. He recorded me talking to him.'

They exchange looks I can't quite work out and then DC Steadman asks, 'What time did you leave the search?'

'I don't remember.'

'Did you go home straight after?' DC Kimmings chimes in.

'I haven't been sleeping. I don't remember.' It's not much of a defence; however, I don't have a defence to speak of since I am guilty.

'Do you remember Mr Duffill coming home?'

'Vaguely, we spoke a little when he came to bed.'

'He came home later than you?' DC Kimmings asks.

Leo left the search at the end, if I'd have been there the whole time we'd have left together. I can see where these questions are going. 'You'd have to ask him that.'

DC Steadman purses his lips. 'We have a report that a woman matching your description was seen on the Hallow's Gate Estate near Oscar Greer's house. Can you confirm this was you?'

'No.'

'No, you can't confirm, or no, it wasn't you?' DC Steadman pushes.

'I'd like to go now. I'm in a robe. I'm tired. I want to go home.'

'You're under arrest, Ms Forrester. Just a few more questions,' one of them says, but I can't tell which one now, as it's getting harder to open my eyes after every blink.

Embarrassingly, my stomach growls, loud enough for all to hear. I also really need a pee. This is how they successfully interrogate prisoners; keep you for hours in a cell, then when they are ready for the interrogation, offer no comfort breaks between their questions. I'm not the criminal. Oscar Greer should be in my seat, answering their questions. Sweating under their stares.

'Do you remember getting home last night?' DC Kimmings asks.

'Yes, but I didn't look at my watch. The search was harrowing. It was cold, so I wanted to get home.'

'So you went straight home?' DC Steadman pushes again.

'I will not admit to something I didn't do, and you need to stop staring at me and search that bastard Greer's house. Paedophiles swap kids between each other.'

'Yes,' DC Steadman says. 'We know that.'

DC Kimmings brings out his iPad and glares at it for a moment. 'On the night of Friday 13th of October, you called 999 and said Robin was missing. Is this correct?'

Where is this going? 'Yes.'

'The emergency call operator claims you sounded calm on the phone. Would you agree with that statement?'

'No, I wouldn't agree with that statement. I'd just lost my son. I was just trying to keep calm so I could answer all the pointless questions she was asking me.'

'There was a gap of about twenty minutes between

when you lost sight of Robin on the Ferris wheel to when you called 999. Is this correct?'

I did waste time at the pathetic lost child stand near the Coconut Shy.

'Maybe, I thought I'd just lost track of him and he was still at the fair. I went to the old woman running the lost child stand. You interviewed her, right?'

'Yes, yes, we did. So you would agree that you waited to call the police?'

'Not waited to call the police. I searched the area myself. I waited to make sure Robin was actually missing.'

'But he wasn't with you from the time he ran towards the Ferris wheel?'

'Yes, but he could have been just around the corner. I didn't want to call the police without knowing I needed them. Everyone thinks like that.'

DC Kimmings taps on his iPad. 'Do you remember your movements at this time?'

'What are these questions about? Didn't you arrest me for burglary?'

'Please, just answer what you can.' DC Steadman leans forward in his chair.

Sighing, I quickly think through my response. 'When I realised Robin was not on the Ferris wheel, I asked the teenager running it to check the carts to make sure he wasn't still on there. When I saw he wasn't, the teenager told me to go to the lost child stand. I spoke to the woman there who said they found a little boy, but the boy was not Robin. I then called the police.'

'Did you text Mr Duffill at all?' DC Kimmings asks, not even looking up from the iPad.

'Yes, I was texting him before my son went missing. I then texted to see if Robin was at home.'

'You told us Robin doesn't run away, yet you thought he had?' DC Steadman narrows his eyes at me.

'You're twisting my words. Robin would never have run away.'

'Yet you checked to see if he had run off back home?'

The two police officers' questions are blending. I'm finding it hard to concentrate and not say something I shouldn't. They are now accusing me of doing something to Robin. Jai has infected the police with his vicious lies. It's becoming blindingly clear they have arrested me for burglary, but are fishing for a murder confession. Should I tell them what I found at Greer's house? Evidence he was keeping a boy there; and was planning on stealing another younger one who would fit in the Moses basket. Gemma is a witness. No, they searched the house, I remind myself. Surely, they would have found the room? Well, depending on when they searched. Greer could have decorated after they left.

'Ms Forrester, are you okay?'

My thoughts fall apart as I look at each of the DCs' faces to determine who just spoke to me. I can't tell, so I say, 'I love my son and would never hurt him, and if for some bizarre, unknown reason I did, why would I call the police? Why would I go through an appeal and a search party?'

'You mean the TV appeal where you made threats, the search party you left early and the calm call to the police?' DC Kimmings looks over at DC Steadman who has just accused me of a collection of seemingly trivial things, all of which could add up to me killing my flesh and blood.

'I'd like to leave now.' I get up.

'You are under arrest, Mrs Duffill. I suggest you sit down and answer our questions before we take you back to your cell.'

Again, with the Mrs Duffill, but I'm too tired to correct them.

'Just a few more questions,' DC Steadman adds.

I sit back down. 'I want to go.'

'We understand. Can you try to remember what time you came home last night?'

'I want to leave.'

'We interviewed people at the search party who said they saw you the first couple of hours, but there are no sightings of you after. Where did you go?'

'I'm not answering anything else. Take me back to the cells.'

DC Kimmings puts down his iPad. He looks different now, less like the man determined to find my son and more like an asshole looking to close a case any way he can.

'One more thing, Mrs Duffill. Did you coax Harry Doncaster into your car yesterday?'

What. The. Fuck.

I lean forward and slowly speak into the recorder. 'I was putting up flyers in the Rosemount Estate for Robin. I met Harry Doncaster in the newsagent. He was alone, so I gave him a lift home to keep him safe.'

'The same newsagent, which was the last place Thomas Doncaster was seen alive?'

'Yes, but by that logic, I've unknowingly visited many old crime scenes. Hey, wait a minute.' I lean towards them. 'You two show up at crime scenes a lot too. Is there something you want to confess?'

'Okay,' DC Kimmings says. 'We'll take you back to the cells.'

I get up and shuffle in Leo's trainers out of the room, flanked by the officers.

Suddenly, I'm alone again in the cell.

Everything is falling apart. If the police are looking at me, then they're not looking at Greer and certainly not looking for a Mr Bones copycat. I should come clean. Robin's safety is what's important, not mine. Standing up, I lift my fist to bang on the door, intending to grab the attention of a nearby policeman and gush out a confession. As I do, the Michael McIntyre lookalike opens my cell.

'Mrs Duffill, please come with me,' he says leading me to his desk.

'How many times do I need to tell you idiots, I'm Ms Forrester!'

'You can stow the attitude, Ms Forrester, or I'll throw you back in that cell.'

He bends down to fiddle with some paperwork. 'You've been bailed, but you must report back here to the station after your bail period on the 20th of November. Do you understand?'

Looking around me, I don't see anyone brandishing a wad of cash for my bail. 'Who bailed me out?' I ask.

'What country do you think you live in? This isn't the USA. No one has to bail you out here. You can go now, but you're still under arrest, so need to be back here at the police station on the 20th November.'

'Okay.'

'Sign here,' he says, passing me a form and a pen.

I scribble my name, but when I put the pen down, I

notice I've signed it Leigh-Ann Hendy. Inwardly seething at myself, I'm about to ask the custody sergeant for another form when he snatches it back. He then passes me a bag containing my robe belt and Leo's laces. After I shove the bag in my pocket, he shoos me away.

As I slowly walk through the police station, I see Patricia leaning over someone at a desk. I need to talk to her; perhaps she'll listen to what I found in Greer's house. I don't care that she's with someone else right now. The other victim can wait.

I march up to Patricia and tap her on the shoulder. As she twists around, I see who is with her; it is Mrs Doncaster. I recognise her from the online articles about Thomas's disappearance. She's even wearing the same tearful look on her face as she stares at something on the table.

'Patricia, I need to speak with you. Now.' I reach out to grab her elbow; a move she has done to me many times before. Seeing my hand thrust out, she jerks away.

'I'll come over to your house later, Cherrie.'

'Please, just a minute.'

Patricia motions for me to step away from her desk. Great, I don't even warrant the privacy of a room.

'If this is about Oscar Greer, I'll warn you not to say anything. I'm duty-bound to report back anything illegal.'

Shit! Okay, new tactic.

'Is there a copycat?' I ask. Greer may be my only suspect, but the police could have another.

'A copycat of what?' Patricia tries to look coy; but comes off looking guilty.

'Mr Bones, my dad.'

Tutting, she inches away from me. 'This isn't the movies. Real life is more obvious and far less dramatic.'

'Less dramatic than my son being abducted? 'Cause, that's pretty fucking dramatic.'

'Oh, no. That's not what I meant.'

Strangled silence spreads out between us. Patricia fills it with, 'I'm not saying what's happened isn't bad.'

'Just not as dramatic as a film.'

She moves back towards Mrs Doncaster. Fuck it, she's my only link to the police; I need her information. I reach out to grab her hand. She jerks back again, nearly falling over.

'It's not like I'm claiming the Blair Witch has my son. Mr Bones abducted boys around the same age, I'm his only child, and now my son is missing. It doesn't take a genius to see there's a connection.'

Visibly squirming, Patricia nods. 'I'll check it out but it won't do you any good thinking like that.' She glances at a non-existent watch on her wrist. 'Mrs Doncaster is waiting. I have to get on.' The last thing she does is pat my arm with patronising precision, before slinking back to her desk.

One thought rattles about my mind: if it is a copycat, Robin is probably already dead. Dad killed his abductees quickly; lack of artistic inspiration was never Mr Bones' problem.

I go to shuffle past Patricia's desk, and Mrs Doncaster looks up at me.

'Shine a light! You're fake Cherrie. That child killer's daughter.'

'My son is missing too,' I say to her.

'Thomas isn't missing anymore; he's dead.' Mrs Doncaster stands up to face me. As she does, I can see a pair of boy's white trainers in a plastic evidence bag on the desk.

'I'm sorry about your son,' I say.

'How dare *you* be sorry about my son!' she yells at me, poking her finger into my robed chest.

I step backwards out of her reach and almost trip over Patricia. 'My son is missing. Don't you have any sympathy?'

'You brought it on yourself. You and your defective killer genes. It's good your son is dead. Better that than he grows up like his . . .'

I pull my arm back and punch Mrs Doncaster in the face. Pain explodes across my knuckles where they collide with the bony bridge of her nose.

'Robin is not dead. Neither of us are anything like my dad.'

Patricia is rooted to the spot. She doesn't even try to separate us. Instead, she takes a few steps back to give us more room. Suddenly I'm back on the playground. It wouldn't surprise me to be walloped back to a chorus of *fight, fight, fight!*

Mrs Doncaster's palm flies to her nose, and she rubs it in disbelief.

'Want to say it again?' I ask her, my fingers uncomfortably curled into a fist, ready to hit her harder.

'Crazy bitch,' she whispers.

DCs Kimmings and Steadman flood out of the interview room and stop at the scene before them. A mother-fight in the middle of the station.

'What's going on?' DC Steadman asks.

Patricia looks over at him. 'Mrs Duffill hit Mrs Doncaster.'

'I'm not Mrs Duffill, you incompetent dumbasses!'

'You're not Cherrie Forrester either, are you?' Mrs Doncaster chimes in.

I step towards her. She backs away, hitting her butt on the desk behind her as she does.

'I legally changed my name. I have a passport to prove it. I am Cherrie Forrester. My son Robin is missing and yes, I have the unfortunate family fate of being the daughter of Mr Bones, but it was assholes like you lot who drove me to change my name to hide my past. I've not killed anyone. Although, I can see now why some people do it.' Pulling my robe protectively around my chest, I turn on my heels and stride out of the police station. I'm sure they all loved my outburst, and no doubt, they'll arrest me for assaulting Mrs Doncaster, but no one was in my corner. Patricia, for all her promises, did nothing. I can't trust her.

I walk down the street in a triumphant, violent haze like a gangster from a cheap film. People give me strange looks – I don't care. It's just over one mile from the police station to my house, so I keep shuffling forward in Leo's lace-less trainers, holding my beltless robe together for warmth.

Shine a light. I stop. That's what Mrs Doncaster said. I read that expression on the *Concerned in Rosemount* blog. Could she be the author? But then, why didn't she write something about her son's abduction and murder? Maybe I have it all wrong. Other people must use that expression; I've just not heard anyone use it around here.

An hour later, exhausted, cold, and with blisters all over my feet, I arrive home.

I open the door to find Leo in the living room, with Mrs Duffill. Great.

Chapter 36

Leo stares at me. 'The police let you go?'

'I'm out on bail for the burglary. Oh, but I also punched a woman in the face at the station, so I'm sure they'll be adding to the charges.' I plonk down onto the couch and push off Leo's trainers to air my throbbing feet.

'Who did you punch?' he asks.

'Mrs Doncaster.'

'You punched that poor woman who just lost her son?' Mrs Duffill flicks her palm to her head as if to swoon.

'She said Robin was dead and it was for the best, considering where he came from.'

'Robin's not dead.' Leo sits down beside me. 'We'd have felt it if he were.'

'Oh, my. Well, it sounds like she provoked you. You still shouldn't hit people, Cherrie. It's not ladylike.'

'There's a lot of things you shouldn't *do* to people, Mrs Duffill; doesn't stop everyone else doing them though,' I say.

Ignoring me, Mrs Duffill gets up. 'I have a room in the

343

villa for Robin. I've decorated it in his football team's colours, all blue. He was so excited about it last time I was here.'

'That sounds nice,' I mutter.

'He'll be safe and sound in no time, sipping Shirley Temples on the beach. I'm sure of it.'

'Thanks, Mum,' Leo says.

'Well, I will leave you two to get on with things here. I'll see you both real soon.' With that horrific promise, the monster-in-law drifts out of the front door on a breeze of Chanel perfume and better breeding.

'What did she want?' I ask.

'Mum's sorted out the Spanish deeds; she's moving next week. She wanted to say goodbye to you. It was nice of her.'

'Oh, didn't Tracy's gran shame her into coming over?'

'Yeah it was pretty epic. Can old ladies even say fuck?'

'Tracy's gran can. Hey, after all that, she didn't really say goodbye to me though; just threatened another meeting.'

'Don't be like that, Cherrie. She actually had a lovely speech for you all planned out. I think your entrance spooked her.' He rubs my arm.

'I spook a lot of people these days,' I mumble.

Leo looks down at his trainers. 'Where are the laces?'

I fish out the plastic bag from my pocket, throw it at him, then heave myself off the couch and make my way to bed. My head hurts, and I need to leave enough time between accusations and action to confront Greer. He knows I'm coming for him now; perhaps he'll make a mistake I can exploit.

I fall into bed, rolling myself up in the cold covers like

344

a Cherrie-burrito. My phone is still on the bedside table. I should have checked it, but I can't think straight. I need to sleep, just for an hour or two. I close my eyes to drift into a semi-conscious slumber. As I do, I hear noises downstairs. Leo is cooking.

Moments later, the bed depresses to my side. I feel someone lying behind me. I can't bring myself to look. I can still hear Leo in the kitchen. He's banging pans and arguing with the radio.

'What do you want?' I whisper.

Nothing.

An odd sensation shakes me. It may frighten Cherrie, yet Little Bones is curious. I turn around and find no one on the bed. I was dreaming.

I yell, 'Leo!'

Thundering up the stairs, he shouts back, 'What's wrong?' Then he bursts through the bedroom door.

'Bad dream,' I say.

Smiling, Leo crawls across the bed to hug me.

'I can't remember the last time you called out to me.' He kisses the top of my head, then leans over me to grab my phone. 'You've got two voicemail messages.'

I take my phone and listen to them.

As Leo scrambles off the bed, he says, 'Dinner in ten minutes.'

The first message is from Patricia, asking me to come back to the station at my earliest convenience. She's vague about why. The second message is from Mariah.

'Cherrie, I'm sorry I missed your call. I've been swamped. I had a vision last night. It was about footballs. Does this mean anything to you? I also saw a robot, which was odd. His name was Nostrom.'

The phone slips from my grip and bounces off the bed. There is no way she could have known about Nostrom, and there were footballs in the kid's room in Greer's house. The son no one knew he had, or has ever seen. My gut told me that sicko was guilty.

I call Mariah back, but she doesn't answer, not even her answerphone clicks on. She's probably with another client, but she has helped me. It's definitely Greer, and if he's not some sick fan of my dad's crimes, Robin could still be alive.

I change into a pair of dark jeggings and a navy jumper, which reaches my knees. I pull on my black leather ass-kicking boots and tie my hair up. I wrench my coat out of the wash basket. The butcher knife from Dawson's Food is still in there; I feel the weight of it in the pocket. With renewed energy, I hurry down the stairs.

'Just going for a walk,' I shout to Leo, who rushes from the kitchen to tell me something about dinner.

As I open my front door, I look down at the gap where Robin's shoes always used to be. It'll be full again soon.

Quickly, I jog towards Greer's house, each step taking me closer to Robin. Before I cross the road at the top of my street, I twist around to check for cars. As I do, I see a dark BMW gliding towards me. Moving slower than the speed limit, it slithers to a stop by the kerb. I see my face reflected in the tinted window. For a moment, I don't recognise myself. I look dangerous. It should scare me, but doesn't.

The window slowly rolls down. It's Lawrence. He gets out of the car and puts his hands up as if in surrender. 'I'm sorry for standing you up last night. I was at the police station. They questioned me for hours. They only let me go when they confirmed my alibi.'

'What was your alibi again?'

'I was in Wales at a conference when you took Robin to the fair. The organisers televised the whole thing. The police checked the footage. I've been officially cleared as a suspect.'

'Good for you. Now, if you don't mind, I have something to do.' I walk on. Lawrence follows me in silence, like a sad shadow. It should feel uneasy having a stalker follow you through the streets, but when you have a hole scorching your heart, burning deeper by the minute, strange can feel normal, even comfortable.

When we reach Greer's house, I look back at Lawrence and nod to him. He shuffles forward a few steps to stand beside me.

'This is his house? Odd, I didn't expect a bungalow,' he whispers. 'I'll search the front. You search the back?'

'I searched it last night without you. Robin isn't in there.'

'Then why are we here?'

'He has a boy's bedroom in there. Greer told the neighbours he has a son,' I say.

'He's setting it up for when the media dies down. He will have stashed Robin at a friend's house while the police searched his place.'

Hearing my little boy spoken of like an illegal object boils my blood. I wring my hands together and will myself to calm down.

'What are you going to do?'

I don't answer his question. I watch as Oscar Greer comes into view at one of his windows, gesturing as if he's talking to someone.

'Somebody is in there with him,' I whisper.

I move around the back of the house. Greer hasn't replaced the broken patio doors yet. Lawrence sees the plywood board covering the hole. He tries to move it, but it won't budge.

'Screw it; let's just knock on the door. Greer doesn't know me, he'll open it,' he says.

We run back across the lawn to the front step. I hide behind Lawrence. My fingers curled around the knife handle poking out of my coat.

Lawrence knocks three times. There's a scuffling sound. The door opens wide.

Chapter 37

Brandishing the knife, I leap out and see . . . Kylie. Her pregnant belly protruding from a corduroy pinafore dress.

'Cherrie? What the hell?' Her hands fly up in the air.

I lower the knife. 'Get out of there! The man in that house is a paedophile.'

Rolling her eyes, she yells, 'Oscar!' I watch Oscar Greer slink up beside her. 'You said some crazy mother broke into your house. Was it Cherrie?'

'Yeah,' Greer whines. 'Hang on; you know each other?' He looks from me to Kylie.

'Cherrie has been helping me with groceries. All those care packages from Dawson's came from her.' She sighs and then looks at me. 'Oscar doesn't have Robin; he's no kiddie fiddler. They convicted him for being with me.'

'What?'

'Oscar is my boyfriend. We met when I was sixteen and he was nineteen. I told him I was eighteen. When Mum found out about us, she called the police. We ran away together.'

'Next thing I know,' Oscar says, 'they accuse me of kidnapping and assaulting a minor; my name is all over the internet.' He purses his lips. 'I tried to tell you when you came here the first time.'

When the penny drops, it makes an almost audible splash in my mind. I hide the knife back in my coat pocket. 'The bedroom is for him.' I point at Kylie's belly.

'Yes, when Kylie turns eighteen, she can move in with me.'

'I was with him the night Robin went missing. I promise it's not Oscar. He would never hurt a child.' Kylie rubs her belly.

'I'm sorry, I'm so sorry,' I say, stumbling backwards to sit on their driveway.

'I get it, I do, but you're kind of scary, and you wouldn't listen.' Oscar moves forward to pick me up under one arm. Lawrence grabs the other. My two prime suspects are helping me to my feet.

'Why don't you come in? I owe you a cuppa,' Kylie says. Narrowing her eyes at Lawrence, she adds, 'Hey, isn't that the asshole who stalked you at the shop?'

'What?' Lawrence says.

'Sorry, Lawrence. You *were* kind of stalking me.'

'I understand,' he says. 'I shouldn't have scared you. I've not been thinking straight since my Tommy went missing all those years ago.'

'Again, I'm so sorry,' I say, then look at Kylie. 'No to the cuppa. I have to get home for dinner. I'm sorry about the patio doors.'

'It's okay. Leo does great work; you can send him round to fix them.' Kylie smiles, but her lips fall into a grimace. 'Is there no one else who could have taken Robin?'

Lawrence has an alibi. Oscar is innocent. The fair worker didn't have him; we've searched Black Friars twice now. Am I seriously back to the copycat theory? 'No, no one.'

My shoulders sag. A swell of tears threatens to cloud my vision, so I suck it up. 'I'm going home. I'm sorry.' I walk down the road, leaving Lawrence and Oscar standing together.

On the streets, flyers of Robin still flap on lampposts. They are worn by the weather now – his precious face faded.

I wander home on autopilot. I open the door and, not even bothering to take the knife from the pocket, shrug off my coat.

'You okay?' Leo asks as he fetches two foil-covered plates from the oven.

'No, I've no clue where Robin is.'

'If we knew where he was, he wouldn't be lost.' It comes out like a joke, but there's no hint of humour in his words. 'Dinner's ready.'

Leo sits down and starts to eat. I look down at my plate. He's made pasta with chargrilled vegetables and grated cheese. With a limp hand, I pick up the fork and push the food about on my plate.

'Bad news about the podcast. Jai Patel can openly voice his opinions, so can say anything he likes. He was also careful with his language too. It was always someone like you who did something nasty. That kind of thing,' Leo says.

I grunt back and keep eating.

'Mum hired a real shark of a solicitor, though. Hopefully, they'll get him on something else.'

'Uh-huh.'

Dinner tastes like dirt. I imagine it staining my insides black as it slides down my throat. Mum was a great cook. She would prepare special feasts for the boys who came to our house; those meals tasted like dirt too.

An image flickers across my memory. The vat; the hydrogen peroxide Dad used to whiten the bones. The image widens out to the whole studio; benches, easels, shelves holding tubes upon tubes of paint. Me, so small I couldn't reach the top shelf, even on tiptoes. It was Dad who lifted me up so I could find just the right colour, the shade *I knew* would make the bones sing.

When I close my eyes, I see a boy, little older than I was. Face ruddy and eyes wide. Mr Bones kept his victims in a cupboard in his art studio, the same place he used to hang up our aprons. As inspiration took him, he would kill them. I wasn't supposed to be in his art studio on my own, but one day I went down for some paint. The studio always felt different without Dad. The navy walls making it feel as if you were drowning beneath a dark, violent sea.

I was about to run back out without my paint, when I heard knocking coming from the cupboard. I hesitated before opening it. Dad never did hide anything from me, but my young mind wasn't focused on his evil deeds. I was just a little girl who wanted to spend time with her daddy. I was *his* little girl and he let me into his world, and told me his secrets. My hands were shaking by the time I reached up for the handle. When I opened the cupboard, I saw the crying boy, his limbs bound and a gag digging into his mouth. I untied him. He ran.

That's how they caught Dad. The twelfth boy escaped and brought the police to our door. It was my fault. I'd heard the knocking many times before, but it was the first time I'd been brave enough to open the cupboard door.

Dad must have known what happened, and that it was my fault the police arrested him, yet he never said anything.

Now, my only hope for Robin is that his abductor is the father of a little girl; one brave enough to open his door.

Chapter 38

Too many days slip by and all I can do is stare at my mobile. As my only lead, I call Mariah several times but she doesn't answer. I never mentioned Nostrom to her, did I? If I didn't, how could she know about him? Dad doesn't call either, and the police are oddly quiet. Each day I try to find more suspects, each day I fail miserably. Sleep is even more elusive than before and I vomit everything I eat, leaving me gaunt and almost skeletal.

Tired of pain and twisted thoughts, I sit in Robin's room. The mother of a lost child. I wonder what I'll do if we never find him, or if we do and he's not Robin anymore, just dead flesh and bone. Without my son, I'll die too. Strange, all this time I was worried I might be too much like my dad, that my DNA is cursed. Turns out, I'm more like my mum. Without the love of my life, I'll cease to exist.

'What are you doing?'

I look up to see Leo. I can't bring myself to speak. The

words are there, but they won't move from my mind to my mouth.

'Cherrie, come on. Let's go downstairs and watch some TV, eh?'

Scooping up my mobile, I get up and follow him downstairs.

'How about some chips? I could go to the Drunken Schooner,' Leo says.

The thought of eating anything makes me hurt more. I don't deserve food. I'm a shitty mother, and an even shittier detective. I was never going to find Robin on my own.

'Cherrie? Chips?' Leo repeats as if I'm a child.

Shaking my head, I sit down on the couch; curling my legs beneath me. Huffing, Leo takes the seat next to me and switches on the TV.

'You're not helping. I lost him too. We're not living in the *Cherrie Show*.'

I look down at my mobile. Still nothing.

After a few hours on the couch, my eyes ache. I doze, yet continue to take in what is happening on the screen. Leo is watching some DIY programme. I can't get my head around how he can watch something so mundane when our son could be anywhere, having anything done to him.

All this time, I've been clinging to suspect after suspect, trying to find Robin. That's how I've coped, but Leo has brushed it all aside. He's laying all his hopes on the police. The police who seem convinced this is my fault. That I've killed my son plus Thomas Doncaster to boot. They've bought what Jai Patel was selling, just like everyone else.

'Cherrie!'

My eyelids spring open. I bolt upright. 'What?'

Leo points at the TV; on it is a photo of a strangely familiar boy a few years older than Robin, dressed in a blue football shirt. 'Another boy is missing. Harry Doncaster, Thomas's brother.'

I wail. The sound snaps out of my mouth like elastic, then, too taut, it erodes and breaks away. I hear my screams bounce around my home as if they belong to someone else.

Leo puts his arms around me. I push him away. I know exactly what this means; whoever has taken Robin is now finished with him. They have a new toy. My son is dead, and I didn't feel the tug on my soul, the pull of flesh from bones as someone stole my only child from this world. I won't believe it. I can't. If he's dead, I might as well give up on everything.

I refuse to move off the couch. Leo goes to bed; tired of trying to encourage me upstairs. He still has hope. I watch the news item about Harry repeatedly, rewinding the live feed to pause on his photo. The grinning face I remember gobbling stolen crisps smiles back at me, as if he has a secret he's dying to share. Staring at Harry, I wonder about his connection to me. I gave him a lift; the police, for some reason, are aware of this. It's as if someone is trying to frame me. Not that it matters. Without my son, my life is over.

My phone rings. It'll be the police telling me they have found Robin's broken body. I won't be able to identify him; Leo will have to do it in my stead. I can't see what horrors the monster did to him. I'm not like Lawrence. Knowledge of my baby's murder will do nothing for me. Revenge, now that might be something to live for . . .

356

The phone is still ringing. I reach out and answer it without looking at the caller ID.

'Hello? Ma Cherie are you there?'

I cough out, 'Hello, Dad.' Hearing his voice, without the image of him in prison, sends me right back to the eight-year-old girl who needs her daddy.

'Ma Cherie, have you found Robin?'

'No, and there's been another boy taken now, Harry Doncaster, Thomas's brother.'

'The killer is done with Robin.' Unlike Leo, Mr Bones knows what another abduction truly means, and he won't pretend a happy ending is on the cards for me.

'I'm sorry you didn't get to meet him; my baby should have known he had a granddad.' I cover my mouth to stop from crying.

'Oh Cherrie, please. There's hope. I've been thinking a lot about Robin's abduction. When the police interviewed me, they showed me photos of boys I knew. Boys whose faces I watched shrivel in the garden and become clean and beautiful in the vat. You remember the vat, right?'

The vat was like a torture device, why is he bringing this up now? Although my anger simmers, I stay silent, to let him continue.

'But they also showed me photos of older boys who were missing. Ones that had not seen the inside of our studio. Why do you think they showed me them?'

'No idea.'

'Because they were making connections where there were none. They didn't know me well enough to realise that teenage boys were too old for my art. Their bones are less beautiful. I told them the truth and claimed all

357

my victims. I wouldn't claim the ones who did not belong to me.'

'What are you saying? Was there another killer back then?'

'No. My point is there are more fates than the end of a killer's blade. Boys run away. Boys hurt one another. Boys have accidents. Murder isn't the only reason for a child to be missing. Just remember, the police like to close cases.'

'They make connections where there are none,' I whisper.

'Perhaps all three cases are not related at all.'

'The other missing boys were brothers. That's too much of a coincidence. Those cases have to be related, but Robin had never met either Doncaster boy,' I say.

'Would Robin have ever gone off with someone he doesn't know? Someone he'd never met?'

'No, never.'

'The boys I took off the streets, I tricked them. You remember, don't you? You were with me most of the time. They would see you happy in the back seat and believe, as I was a dad, that they could trust me. Sometimes I'd pretend to be a taxi driver. Would Robin have gone with someone like that?'

'I doubt it.'

'Who does Robin know who could steal him away? Who loves him that much?'

I roll the idea around in my mind that someone I knew before this nightmare might have taken my son. Someone who wanted him but not me in their life.

'Mrs fucking Duffill,' I say. 'She's moving to Spain and asked to see Robin's passport, which is now missing. And

I caught her with an armful of Robin's clothes.' That bitch has always hated me. I bet the issues with the villa were some ploy not to waste her time at a search party looking for someone who is tucked up in her house awaiting their trip to Spain. Who knows what lies she told my son to set this whole thing up.

'You have work to do, Ma Cherie. I sent you a VO form. Let Robin visit me when you find him.' He hangs up.

Mrs Duffill must have heard the podcast, found out about my past. Hating me is one thing, but thinking I could ever hurt Robin. Fuck, she even knew we were going to the fair. She asked to come along and when I turned her down, she lay in wait for the right moment to snatch him. Told him lies and spirited him away until she could get him out of the country. After I'm convicted of killing him, of course. Wait . . . the skeleton. It definitely wasn't her dressed up, but she has money. She could have hired someone to do the abducting. On the other hand, she could have waved a wad of cash at some unconnected carnival worker.

I storm upstairs and wake up Leo with a shove.

'What?' he mutters.

'Your *mother*,' I spit.

'What?' Rubbing his eyes, Leo sits up.

'Your mother has Robin, doesn't she? The only question is: did you know? Has this all been some shitty act to look like the supportive boyfriend, when you're planning to steal away with our son to a Spanish villa with your bloody mother?' I push him.

'What are you talking about? Mum doesn't have Robin. Have you gone mad?'

'She has his passport. She asked about it at the dinner before the fair. And it's now missing.' I move around the bed and open the table drawer to show him it only contains our passports. 'And, she tried to take Robin's clothes.'

'Cherrie, wait one minute.' Leo gets up and walks across the landing into Robin's room. He comes back out holding a passport. 'Robin kept it in his room. He never put it back in our drawer.'

I grasp at the small book and check it. It is Robin's passport.

'The other day in Robin's room, she just missed him that's all. She was taking a T-shirt as a reminder of him, his smell.'

'Why wouldn't she just tell me that?'

'Because you did what you always do, exploded. And Mum doesn't like to show weakness, which is something you guys have in common.'

'Oh, really?'

'Yeah, and hey, I've been at Mum's house. I would have noticed if she was hiding Robin. She may not like you much, but she'd never do that to you. I wouldn't either. Still, nice to find out what you really think of me.'

Getting back into bed, he pulls the covers up to his chin. Our conversation is over. I don't even get the chance to apologise.

Deflated, I go back downstairs. Looking at the clock, I see it's four in the morning. I skim through the texts on my phone to find messages from Tracy, Gurpreet, Kylie and even Shania, yet nothing from the police. Guess they can't inform their prime suspect of how their investigation is going.

I need to straighten everything out in my mind. My

dad sent me on a brief wild goose chase, which may have just ended my relationship with Leo. I've no one left to turn to now. Lifting up my laptop, I click on *The Flesh on the Bones.* There's a new episode entitled *Thomas Doncaster and Robin Duffill.*

Listening to this will hurt, but I deserve the pain. I've acted less like Sherlock Holmes and more like Moriarty; accusing everyone around me and lashing out like a drowning woman determined to take down anyone stupid enough to reach out to save her. I play the podcast.

'I'd just like to take a moment to thank all my sponsors for their support and business, especially Dawson's Food who have a personal stake in what has happened to poor Robin Duffill.'

I'm not sure why I gasp at Jai's new connection to my ex-employers. No doubt, the roving reporter sniffed around where I worked to dig up more dirt, and then used his snake oil charm on Mr Dawson.

'Today we're talking about the two young boys who have already fallen foul of a monster stalking the streets of our town.'

It continues like this, recycling information given in earlier episodes. Then, when the time is right, he puts me forward again as the prime suspect.

'How can we trust someone who got a taste for killing so early in life? Evil children become evil adults, the only differ-ence is, as adults, they have more opportunities. My sympathy goes out to the Doncasters and of course, the Duffills; both lost their sons to a monster who hid in plain sight. But what a mask she wore! Helpful shop assistant, devoted wife, loving mother. Leigh-Ann waited for the right time to shed those masks and show her true face. She just didn't count on a podcast to shine such a bright spotlight on her. Who knows

how many other boys would be dead now if The Flesh on the Bones *hadn't stopped Little Bones, the Monster of Northants.'*

Well, this episode just got me a slander suit. No more *someone like me did something similar* or any other vague conjecture. Naming me as the *Monster of Northants* has to be something the solicitor can work with; that is of course if Mrs Duffill lets them after Leo tells her of my accusation.

I slip off my headphones and check the subscribers. The number is so large that I can't even bring myself to read it off the screen.

It's five in the morning so is still dark outside. I need a clue. Something to send me in the right direction. Shuffling into the dining room, I realise there is nothing left to go on; every clue exhausted, every lead dashed, and every chance to find Robin alive has disappeared just like he did at the fair. Lost and useless, I begin to build Robin's empty robot boxes into a tower. Midway through, I pull part of the costume to my chest and crush it to my heart. Robin was so excited to wear his costume for Halloween. Wait, is it the 31st today? I check my phone and see it is. The realisation my son will never again go trick or treating breaks me.

I'd always had hope that I could find Robin. Now, all I have is a psychic I'm still not sure I believe in. What she predicts sounds impressive at first until you realise you'd already told it to her, or she could have looked it up. But, no one knew about Nostrom, only me, Leo, Mrs Duffill and Robin himself. Did I say something about him on my first visit? I don't remember. If I didn't, that has to count for something. If all I have left is a faceless copycat, perhaps a psychic is my only hope to find him.

As the sun peeks up from the horizon, I jump into the car and drive to Mariah's house. I'm sure she'll be pissed off that I'm waking up her family so early, but I can't wait. I don't blame her for dodging my calls. I've not exactly been the easiest person to be around, but in all that time she has consistently tried to help me. I just hope she can help me this one final time.

I pull up behind their car and rush to the door. I knock. Nothing. I beat louder. Footsteps.

'I'm sorry,' I say through the letterbox. 'I need your help. Please.'

The door opens. Mariah stands there in a pale blue bathrobe.

'It's early,' she says.

The psychic looks different without her make-up; lacklustre and less imposing.

'I'm so sorry, Mariah. I need help. I have nowhere left to turn.'

Closing the door behind her, she says, 'Now isn't a good time.'

Thanks to that bastard Jai, she thinks I'm dangerous too. 'Please,' I whisper. 'I don't want to disturb Jon and Sarah, but I really need you.'

'Ummm, okay. Come in, but we need to be quiet.'

I walk in as quietly as I can. We sit in the living room together; the same couch I sat on that Saturday night, worried sick someone would reveal my identity. What a moron I was.

'I saw there was another boy taken yesterday. Poor Harry,' she says.

'Yes, does it mean what I think it means?'

'My gift doesn't work like that. I can't just answer questions. I need the cards.'

'Yes, let's get the cards.'

'I've just woken up, Cherrie. Look, perhaps we can talk later today. Meet at the coffee place in town?'

'The one by the pound shop?'

'Yes, the blue one.'

There's a myriad of blue coffee shops in town; she's not being very specific. Also, why would she want to meet me outside of her house? Is she scared of me? 'I won't hurt your family,' I say.

'Oh, that's not what I meant.'

Yeah, I get it. Mariah doesn't want her neighbours seeing me strolling into her home, again. An association with Little Bones, the Monster of Northants, would dent the house price.

'Please help me,' I say.

Mariah stares at me. Pity and slight worry dance across her face. I saw that face a lot in the parade of foster families, who all took a turn *caring* for my welfare. Mariah blinks a few times.

My feet are itchy. I get up and begin to pace. As I do, I see boxes behind the couch, empty cardboard boxes that weren't there before.

'Are you moving?'

'Yes, this place is much smaller than we first thought. Not big enough for the three of us. Damn new builds, who knew they would be so stingy with the square footage.'

One would be forgiven for thinking a real psychic would know they were being screwed on a real estate deal. Or perhaps have bothered to go on a walk-through before putting a deposit down? As if answering my internal question, Mariah blurts out, 'We moved in really quickly. Our old house had too many bad memories. We wanted a fresh start. I'm sure you understand?'

Guilt seeps into my thoughts. 'Is this because of me? Do you have to move because of who I am, and what they're accusing me of? Because you've tried to help me? I know everyone thinks I did something to Robin, but I didn't. I promise. You believe me, don't you?'

'I know you didn't hurt Robin or those other boys.'

'Could you tell everyone else, please?' I say with a half-smile.

'I can't do that.' She drops her stare to my boots.

'I was only joking, Mariah.'

'Yes, I know. I was just answering your question. Force of habit in my profession.'

A noise upstairs takes her attention. Offhand, she says, 'He's awake. I need to get on and make breakfast.'

'Sorry. Yes. I'll go. Shall we meet at nine at the coffee shop by the pound shop?'

'Yes, let's do that.'

She walks me out, and I wave as she closes the door. It's a small hope. Tiny. I'd cry, but it doesn't even deserve tears of sadness; maybe tears of anger. Sadness would mean I'm giving up on Robin, accepting his fate. I can't do that. I need anger instead. Anger so powerful it overrides my fear and common sense.

As I make my way down Mariah's drive, I see Jon walking up the street. I wave at him. He has a newspaper in his arms and, as he gets closer, I see Harry Doncaster's face plastered across the front page. Soon, they'll cover the Robin flyers with him too. Until the next boy is lost.

Robin is condemned to be one of many names forever trotted out every time someone examines the case for ghoulish entertainment.

Jon looks concerned that I'm at his house so early. I attempt a smile as I move towards my car. As I hear Jon go into the house, a weird feeling tingles over my brain, something Mariah said: *He's awake. I need to get on,* but Jon was out of the house and she has a little girl. As I look back towards their door, I'm so tired, I almost fall over with the movement. I put my left hand out to steady myself on their black car. As I do, I look through the car's passenger window. There's a pair of boy's trainers in the footwell. A sight so familiar it punches me in the chest, winding me.

Robin. They have him. And they own a dark car. I blamed Lawrence for stalking me, but it could have easily been Mariah and Jon in this car, watching my family, waiting for the right time to strike.

I reach into my pocket for my phone but hesitate. How long will it take the police to get here? Mariah and Jon could run in the meantime. Worse, they could kill Robin just to spite me for finding him. Wait . . . Is it this easy? It can't be. Why would they take young boys? Why kill them? They have no motive. Am I wrong? Perhaps their little girl wears boy's trainers, and Mariah didn't realise that Jon had left the house? Lots of people have dark cars. Shit, I've beat up rapists and accused innocent men of unspeakable things. Can I trust myself with this? No, I can't. Jon and Mariah are not child-abducting serial killers. They can't be.

As these doubts plant themselves in my mind and take root, my phone beeps. I look down to see a text from

Leo. It reads, *Where are you? You need to look at this*, then a link. I click it. It takes me to a news site with the photo of Harry Doncaster. Have they found his body already? However, that's not what the article is about; it's a confession. Harry is alive. He has confessed to killing his brother Thomas. He wanted his little brother's new shoes, those white trainers, and Thomas wouldn't share. Violently, Harry lashed out. Fearing the police were going to catch him, he ran away. There's no monster out there stealing little boys and giving back corpses, just one kid with a temper and a footwear fetish. Dad was right. None of this is connected. Jon and Mariah could have Robin. Taking one boy is more realistic than taking three.

I have to check. Even if I'm horribly wrong, Mariah will understand. I need to get back into their house.

Trying to barge in on Oscar went badly. Calm, I need to be calm. Little Bones unfurls in my stomach like a night bloom reaching for the darkness.

Casually, I walk back to their front door and knock.

Jon answers it.

'I dropped my car keys when I was talking to Mariah, sorry,' I say.

He glances behind him before fully opening the door for me. 'Okay, just be quick. We have a full day today.'

Smiling, I step inside.

'Where did you drop them?' he asks, his eyebrow twitching.

'They have to be in the living room. Perhaps down the back of the sofa, where I was sitting.'

Jon leads me towards the room.

It's a strange situation. Both of us pretending everything is normal. Both of us knowing it's not.

I don't follow him. Instead, I run up the stairs.

'Hey!' Jon yells after me. I hear him lumbering up behind me. On the landing, I see three doors. I choose the second one and open it. It's a girl's bedroom. There's a small bed in the centre of the room. A child-sized lump is under a mound of pink bedclothes.

'Robin?'

'Mummy!'

Chapter 39

Lunging forward, I grab my son. He wraps his arms around my neck and grips on to me. Feeling his breath on my shoulder, I burst into tears.

'Don't cry,' Robin whispers, which makes me cry harder.

My mind is trying to catch up with my emotions. I found him. He's in my arms and he's okay, or at least he looks okay. Quickly, I push back the pink frilly bedcovers and run my hands down his body to check for injuries, or signs of abuse, but there's none. They've not even tied him up with rope, or those painful-looking plastic zip ties.

'I'm so glad you're all right,' Robin says, sniffling into my cheek.

'That I'm all right?' I say. 'We've been looking everywhere for you.' Tears overwhelm my cheeks, but I can't tell if they're his or mine.

'I've been here,' Robin mutters.

I stare down at him. He's wearing Batman PJs and smells of baby shampoo.

'See, I told you she was all right, Jon. I'd have felt it if anything bad happened to my mum.'

Jon is standing in the doorway.

'Yeah, you were right,' he mutters.

I hear footsteps up the stairs. Mariah appears behind her husband.

'No!' she shouts. 'No, you'll destroy my little bird. He's meant to be with us.'

'It's over, sweetheart,' Jon soothes, as Mariah lets out a banshee wail and slips down onto the floor.

'I can still visit,' Robin says to his kidnappers. 'Mariah and Jon have been keeping me safe. They said I'd get a proper boy's room at their new house. I've been borrowing their daughter's room for now. She doesn't need it.' Grimacing, he whispers loudly in my ear. 'Sarah's dead.'

Gripping Robin, I stand up. 'We're leaving now.'

Jon sighs and moves out of my way. Mariah shrieks and reaches for Robin with desperate, flailing limbs; trying to grasp any part of my son that she can lay her thieving hands on.

Staring at the floor, Jon holds her back.

'No, she'll hurt him.' Mariah reaches out to Robin again. 'If he stays with her, he'll become a monster.' She pleads to Jon. He gives her no reaction, so she turns wildly back to me and says, 'Your son will be another Mr Bones. With us, he's fine, but with you, he'll change.' Looking back to Jon she pleads, 'Make her leave him here with us. It's best for everyone.'

I imagined when I was face to face with Robin's abductor, I would see red. Violence would erupt from me like a broken water pipe, drowning anyone foolish enough to cross its stream. Nevertheless, it doesn't. I do not need Little Bones here. Robin is safe.

I step closer to Mariah, Robin monkey-hugging my chest. Looking down at her, I say, 'I'm sorry your daughter died, but you can't have my son.'

'You don't deserve him; you're a monster,' Mariah splutters through anguished sobs.

'You have put me through a living nightmare. I came to you for help. You fed me false leads and lies. You're the monster.'

'Don't speak to my wife like that.' Jon focuses his hard eyes on me.

'Why don't you go put your skeleton costume back on and try your luck with another kid?'

'You were too busy on your phone to watch over your son. It was easy for me to take him. Swap his jacket, dump the red one, and walk him back to the car. If you'd been watching him, you wouldn't have lost him.'

'Fuck you!' I spit.

Robin cringes into me. I force myself to calm down. I don't want the situation to escalate, but I might not have a choice.

'He was perfect,' Mariah whines. 'He's so special.' Composing her sobs, Mariah looks at my son. 'Aren't you, baby? You're Mummy's special boy. My little bird.'

Shielding Robin from her craziness, I ease past them to stand on the landing. I feel Robin go to speak in my arms. He'll be kind to her; that's who he is. Fortunately, it's not who I am.

'Don't you ever call yourself mother to my son. I am his mum, I'm all he needs. The only thing you're right about is that he is special. But he will never be a monster.'

'With you, he will.' She looks up with big wet eyes, a broken woman losing another child.

'You pretend to be a psychic. You pretend to help people. You take their money and sell them lies. You're evil.' I walk backwards as I say this. When I see the railing for the stairs, I stop.

They both fall silent. I wait for retaliation with either words or fists. When I get neither, I carefully make my way down the stairs, out of their house, to my car.

While Mariah wails for her latest lost child, I help Robin into the car. Those bastards were moving house. They would have gotten away with taking my son if I hadn't come here this morning. For all my detective skills, dumb luck got me here in time.

I slide into the driver's seat and lock the doors. Robin's little fingers grip on to mine.

'Jon took me from the fair. He was the skeleton from the Ghost Train,' he says.

'I know. Why did you go with him, sweetie?'

'He told me you and Dad were hurt. That you asked them to look after me. I said Gran would take me, but they said she was too old. The next day they said you both died.'

'They lied, sweetie. We're fine. They wanted to take you for themselves.'

'They were nice to me. Most of the time, I liked them.' Robin looks down at his bare feet and flexes his little toes.

'I'm happy they were nice to you, but they did something wrong.' Starting the car, I look over to him. 'It's okay now. You're okay. I found you.' After the words leave my lips, my hands leap up to cover my face. I count to three and open my eyes. He's still there, grinning at me.

Robin squeezes my hand. 'I never believed you were dead. Nostrom said you were okay, but that I shouldn't try to escape, just in case they hurt me. He can be cautious, but that's robots for you.' He beams a killer smile up at me. I have to reach over to touch his cheek, to double-check he's real, that I've not fallen asleep and am dreaming this happy ending.

Driving home, I look over at Robin every chance I get. I still can't believe he's sat next to me now, after all this — healthy and safe.

As I pull up into our drive, Robin flicks off his seatbelt and launches himself towards the front door.

Leo must have been watching for me as he runs out to meet us. He drops to his knees and sweeps Robin into his arms, breathing him in.

Now I know for sure this is really happening.

Chapter 40

The police come to the house and interview Robin and me. They tell me Oscar went into the police station. Apparently, he was with a loud pregnant girl who demanded they drop all charges against me for breaking into Greer's house.

DC Kimmings and DC Steadman ask several annoying questions about how I found Robin. How I knew Mariah and Jon, and why I didn't call the police if I suspected the psychics of a crime. I shrug my shoulders at every question, my eyes never leaving my son, who sits at our dining room table showing DCI Jeddick his robot costume.

Four hours later, Leo shuffles them all out of the door. I'm alone with my family.

I call everyone, including Mrs Duffill, and tell them Robin is back home and safe. I shoot off an email to the prison to tell Dad he helped find his grandson – without the call about the connections, or lack thereof, I might have never put it all together quick enough. In my mind, like everyone else's, the Doncaster case and Robin were connected. He calls me later and asks me to visit soon. I'm so happy I even tell Robin he has a granddad who helped find him.

Two days fly by filled with visitors who want to see Robin; some even apologise for believing the worst about me. I should feel vindicated, but I don't, those feelings are swallowed by the happiness of having Robin back.

We spend the rest of the week watching films and sleeping in a puppy pile together on the couch. Robin never leaving Leo's eye line, or mine.

Strangely, my son is fine. He asks about Mariah and Jon as if they were his friends and had taken him on a weird holiday. He tells us they played games together, put cheese spread on his vegetables; they kept him safe. I don't have the heart to say anything bad about his abductors; people so much worse could have taken my son.

The succession of well-wishers who come to my door are in equal amounts odd and unexpected. A loud Kylie along with a quiet Oscar. Gurpreet dragging along a red-faced Shania. Lawrence, who admits it was he who gave most of the money to the Dawson Food's reward collection. Kristine, who apologises for thinking I'd hurt my son. Still, she does it in the most condescending way possible. Tracy and her gran who bring home-cooked meals. The most surprising person though, is Mr Dawson.

When I open the door and see him, a big part of me wants to slam it back in his face. Instead, I ask, 'What are you doing here?' I don't let him in. People who fire me get to stay on the doorstep.

'I'm sorry about everything.'

'Are you offering me my job back?'

'No.'

It's the worst apology I've ever heard. 'Then our business here is done.' I go to close the door.

'Wait!' His shoulders slump. 'Dawson's Food went into administration yesterday.'

Tracy was right. The rumours were true.

'I'm sorry to hear that.' It surprises me that I mean those words. I knew I'd miss working there, yet it feels worse knowing the shop will no longer exist.

'I stalled your P45, which means this is yours.' Mr Dawson gives me an envelope. 'It's your redundancy money. I hope it helps. I'm glad your son is safe.' He forces a weak smile before leaving.

I open the envelope to find a cheque for £20,000. Much more than standard redundancy pay. I stand still in the doorway and realise that, just for this moment, all my worries are gone. Everyone knows my identity, and I've not been run out of town with torches and pitchforks. Robin is safe. The police haven't pursued any charges against me. I have enough money to be a full-time mum for a little while. I've never felt like this before. Free.

'Cherrie, Patricia is on the phone!' Leo calls out.

I close the front door, then walk back into my living room to see Leo alone on the couch.

'Where's Robin?'

'He's playing with Nostrom upstairs. They're making a list of everything they want for Christmas.' Leo smiles.

'Cherrie, I'm glad you're there. I was just updating Leo on Robin's case,' Patricia says over the speakerphone.

I sit down and wait for her to say why she rang. Crap, perhaps they're summoning me back to the station.

'Jon and Frances Conway have been arrested.'

'Who's Frances?'

'She went by the name of Mariah.'

How apt – she'd changed her name too. 'What happened to their little girl?'

'Sarah Conway was killed in a traffic accident last year. Frances thought Robin was in danger with you. That's why they took him.'

'He's not in danger with me. How many times do I have to say it?'

'Neither were thinking straight. They were insane with grief over losing their child. Jon listened to the podcast about you and Mr Bones. When you visited them, they saw your name on the consent form and recognised you. When you told them you had a son, they were convinced something bad would happen to him if he stayed with you.'

'So the cases you were looking at, they weren't connected? Harry Doncaster killed his brother Thomas for a pair of trainers. Mariah and Jon took Robin to replace a dead daughter?' I ask.

I hear her tut. 'I can't discuss other cases with you, but what you read in the papers is true, for once.'

'Why did Mrs Doncaster write that stupid blog? Why'd she point a finger at Oscar Greer?'

Patricia sighs. 'I'm not supposed to talk about open cases, Cherrie.'

I narrow my eyes. If Robin had killed his sibling, I'd want to protect him, at least keep the son I had left. 'It was to draw attention away from Harry. She knew all along that Harry killed Thomas. Her perfect appeal was crap.'

'I can't confirm any of this.'

'Wait, there were trainers on the table at the police station, when you were with Mrs Doncaster. They were Thomas's, weren't they? You found Harry had them – it's why he ran.' I'm not asking; he was wearing them when we met. Another realisation slams through my head. 'Mariah said the Doncasters visited her too. She must have picked up on something they said. That's how she knew Thomas's body was shoeless.' The realisation that Mariah was a fake, and that at my weakest I believed her lies, all the while she was the cause of my pain, makes me want to vomit up all the good thoughts I had about her; clearing my gut so I can trust it again in the future.

'Cherrie, I've no idea what you're talking about, but if you'd like to come down to the station to give a statement . . .'

'No! I've had enough of the police station,' I say.

'Thank you for your help,' Leo suddenly says to her. I should say it too, yet I can't quite get those words out. I found Robin, they didn't.

As we hang up the phone, I realise I'll never see, or hear from, Patricia again; I'm good with that.

Sighing, I reach for the TV remote. 'Shall we watch the DIY thing you like?'

My boyfriend cocks his head. 'No, how about the medical thing you've been watching?'

'*Grey's Anatomy*?'

Leo laughs. 'You're kidding, right? That's what it's called?'

'Yeah, what's wrong with that?'

'I can see the headline already; Little Bones' favourite show is *Grey's Anatomy*.'

'Oh, perhaps we should watch something else.'

'No, I want to see just how dreamy this McDreamy is.'

Hiding my blushes, I find the next episode.

Before I start the show, Leo blurts out, 'I'm sorry.'

'You don't want to watch it?' I press pause.

'Not that. Just for a moment; I mean I thought it could have been you.'

I close my eyes. He'd said *above all doubt* to me; it was a lie, but I can't blame him for that. 'Yeah, you weren't alone. I forgive you. It wasn't a new feeling for me, being accused of crimes I didn't commit.'

Leo's arms snake about my waist. 'Knowing your past and how tough you had it, I love you more now. And you found Robin. You kept your promise.'

'It wasn't just me; Dad helped. Also, never underestimate the power of sleep deprivation.'

'None of that sounds helpful, but you can't argue with results.' He leans over and kisses my cheek. 'Oh, wait; I have a surprise for you.' Leo leads me to the dining room where my laptop is open on the table.

'Log on to your emails.'

There's an email from Jai. I look up at Leo. He grins at me as I click on it.

Dear Cherrie,

I apologise for The Flesh on the Bones. *I hope your family can get past all the unforeseeable events it created. I'm glad Robin is safe, and I have written an article for the local newspaper about your vindication. I will delete* The Flesh on the Bones *podcast. I have recorded one last episode as an explanation for the deletion and an update to the case entitled* Two Wrongs Didn't Make Me Right, *I hope you like it.*

Once again, sorry.

Jai Patel

'Mum's solicitor threatened not just to sue him, but

said he'd convince the police to file charges of reckless endangerment if Jai didn't take the whole thing down.'

'Really? Could they do that?'

'Probably wouldn't have gotten past the CPS, but Jai didn't know that.'

'Thank you. I need to thank your mum too.' This is the nicest thing she's ever done for me. We might not see eye-to-eye, yet Mrs Duffill stood up for me when I needed it.

'Want to listen to his apology episode now?' Leo asks.

It would be lovely to sit with my boyfriend and listen to a podcast that doesn't vilify me, but I can't guarantee Jai hasn't hidden some nasty rumour in there that could ruin the moment. 'Can I listen alone?' I ask.

'Sure,' he says. 'I need to do some quick measuring upstairs anyway.'

Leo jogs upstairs. Once he's out of earshot, I click on the handy link Jai put in his email and play the final episode:

'This apology podcast is sponsored by the Hungry Piglet Café where you are just one oink away from the best Full English Breakfast in the county.'

Fuck sake, that little weasel even managed to make money on his apology!

'Well, this is goodbye for now, lovely listeners. We've had our ups and downs on the show and it's been a ride to remember. I made some judgements that were not quite right, and I do apologise for any hurt they caused. As a journalist, you have to seek out the truth, and sometimes in doing that you can become blinded by evidence.'

Blinded by evidence? What evidence? Asshole.

'Cherrie did not kill Thomas Doncaster or her son. But I think, as you all were behind me in my theory, you all understand

why I thought what I thought and said what I said. What is fact is that Cherrie Forrester is Leigh-Ann Hendy. Her father was convicted of heinous crimes against young boys, and those are the foundation facts I built my theories on. Don't worry, I've enjoyed podcasting so much, that I'll be doing it again soon. Watch this space.'

Not much of an apology, but really, what did I expect? I turn it off.

'Did Jai behave himself on his final podcast?' Leo asks from behind me.

'I guess, but I still don't fully trust him.'

'Well, perhaps this will cheer you up. I'm turning the nursery into a playroom for Robin. Maybe we can talk about building another extension over the garage to add a room next to ours?' he says with a grin, which I suspect is not just for a new baby but for a new building project too.

'Okay, but you might need to take less than two years on this one, say more like seven months.'

Leo raises an eyebrow. 'Are you?'

'Nothing official yet, we need to go to the doctors, but I think so.'

Clapping his hands together, Leo dances a little on the spot, reminding me of Robin when he's excited.

'Let's not get ahead of ourselves. We all know what can happen when we make assumptions. We need to have it confirmed first, okay?' I say.

Nodding in agreement, Leo then lunges forward to hug and kiss me. 'Hey, let's forget about podcasts for a bit; and just watch all the *Strictly* episodes we recorded for Robin. Have a dancing marathon?'

'Sounds like a plan.'

Dropping to his knees, Leo kisses my stomach, then darts upstairs.

As happy as I am, I can't help but think about Jai. He said he'd be back. I click on to *The Flesh on the Bones* address to double-check it's been deleted. It should come up domain not found, but it doesn't. Instead, there's something new. It's Jai's replacement podcast, *A Bloody Neck Tie*. I scan the description. This series is about a teenage boy whose Dad strangled prostitutes somewhere up North. Jai has found a formula and although he's let me go, he's not letting his cash cow go so easily. It's not fair. The sins of the father dripping onto his children like bloody water over a bathtub.

An idea flashes across my mind. Odd, I hadn't realised just how much mental capacity my identity worries were taking up. I feel a clarity I've never known before. In the future I could start a support network. There have to be more people like me out there branded by our DNA rather than our actions. Innocent people born of bloodshed. I could help them grow from their past rather than spend useless energy trying to hide it. It could be my legacy for Robin and his baby brother or sister.

There's a familiar thunder of bare feet down the stairs. I look up to see Robin, Leo close behind him.

'Dad says we can catch up on *Strictly*, but can we go to the park first?'

'Sure.' I then remember something. 'Why don't you wear the robot costume for Nostrom? You didn't get your trick or treating this year.'

'Thanks, Mum!' Robin scoots off to pull on his cardboard boxes.

'You look happy. It's a good look.' Leo sits down across from me to wait for our son to turn into a robot.

'Why wouldn't I be happy? No more secrets, no more danger. And our family is whole again, and growing,' I say.

'We're a minority. Most parents never find a child missing beyond the twenty-four-hour mark.'

The change of topic is jarring. I close the laptop. 'I read the statistics too.'

'How did this all happen? How could one podcast change our lives like this?'

'I changed my name for a new beginning,' I mutter.

'I get it. I said I was sorry for how I behaved. I just needed time to process everything.'

I don't remember him using those exact words, but there's no point in arguing about it. Not now.

'Ready!' Robin shouts and awkwardly jumps out wearing his robot boxes.

'Come on then, tiger,' Leo says, then turns and adds, 'you too, Nostrom.'

Hand in hand, they step out of the front door, and wait for me on the driveway.

As I watch them, I realise that, even though my past is no longer hidden, the world is still turning. The people I love are beside me. Forgiveness for what I did with Mr Bones should never have been mine, but it is. I got my son back. Looking down by the door, I see Robin's school shoes are neatly nestled between my boots and Leo's trainers. He's such a good boy.

Mariah's predictions were crap. I didn't turn out like my dad – why should Robin? As I think this, I pull on my coat and feel the weight of the butcher knife shift in the pocket. No harm in leaving the blade in there a little longer. No one can predict the future. Someday, I might have to, once again, let out Little Bones.

Epilogue

With two mugs of tea, Lawrence sits down at our dining room table. 'Are you sure he'll talk to me?' he asks.

'Last time I visited, Dad said he would. I've never known him to go back on his word. I told him you helped me. He says you deserve the truth.'

'He said that?'

'Yes, but if you don't want to talk to him, I can just fob him off. He's my dad, but he's a terrible man. He saw little boys as objects that he could use and discard for his own amusement. He's sick, even admitted to me he'd do it all again if he got half a chance.'

Pursing his lips, Lawrence nods. 'I understand, but I still want to know how it happened.'

My mobile rings. I look down to see the prison number. 'Hello?'

'Ma Cherie, how are you?'

'I'm good. Lawrence is with me.'

'The stalker, yes.'

Moving away into the hall, I whisper, 'Dad, I really

385

need you to behave. Lawrence helped get Robin back – we owe him. *You* owe him more.'

'Of course, I understand.'

'Can I put you on speakerphone?'

'Yes, please do.'

I press the button, walk back, and place the phone on the table.

'Mr Hendy, thank you for speaking with me.' Lawrence bites his lip. The first signs of anger are already eating away at his gentlemanly veneer. He's exchanging pleasantries with the man who murdered his only child.

'You want to hear about your son?'

'Please.'

'I picked Thomas Edwards up outside a newsagent. He'd bought football cards. You remember, the ones kids collected back then. It was getting dark. I pretended to be a taxi. I did this a lot. Sometimes with Leigh, I mean Cherrie, in the car, sometimes alone. He was hesitant at first, not like some of the others. I laid on the charm pretty thick. Said I had a son his age and I wanted to make sure he got home okay.'

Lawrence trembles as he reaches for his hot tea.

Quickly, I place my hand over his and say, 'We can stop this now. You don't have to hear any more.'

Lawrence whispers, 'Thomas went out that night to show off his new trainers. Trainers I bought him.'

'It wasn't your fault,' I tell him.

'Should I continue?' Mr Bones asks.

Nodding, Lawrence tries to smile at me. Tears are in his eyes, yet there is also now a glint of completion. He is getting the answers he wanted, pain be damned.

'Yes, carry on,' I say to Dad.

'I took him home and used chloroform to knock him out. I did this to all the boys. I never wanted them to suffer. I put him in the holding cupboard while I made dinner for Cherrie. Afterwards, I became inspired to create a new sculpture. Quickly, I took his life. It was peaceful. He wouldn't have felt a thing.'

'Why him?' Lawrence asks. 'Why not another boy?'

'Luck and timing. He was the right boy, the one all alone. I am sorry, Mr Edwards.'

'Thank you,' Lawrence pushes out through gritted teeth.

'Bye, Dad,' I say, reaching to hang up the phone.

'Ma Cherie, when can I see Robin? You promised me you'd bring him here.'

I don't remember promising him anything, but I did many crazy things to find my son. I might well have given my word to facilitate a playdate of sorts; however, I'm not willing to jump down that dark rabbit hole just yet. Mr Bones will have to wait; it's not as if he's going anywhere.

'Soon,' I say and hang up.

Looking over, I see Lawrence's face contorted in a silent cry. I shouldn't have arranged the call.

'You wanted to know,' I whisper.

He nods at me and covers his mouth to stop from screaming.

I need to disrupt his reaction. 'Tell me about your Thomas. What was he like?'

Lawrence's face eases at the thought of his son alive.

'Tommy. He was so good at school; loved maths and science. He'd have grown up to become an engineer. He wanted to build robots.'

'What was his favourite food?' I ask.

'Sunday dinners, especially lamb.'

'Tommy sounds just like Robin.'

'He loved football too. He was going to try out for the school team that year. I used to play with him in Black Friars Park. He'd climb so high on those swings that I thought he'd hurt himself.'

'Tommy and Robin would have been such good friends.' Lawrence looks away. 'Thank you for setting this up.'

'Did it help?'

'No. Not like I imagined.'

'I am sorry.'

'You were a child. It was your dad's fault, not yours.' Lawrence pauses. 'Did your mum know? Did she help him?'

I think through my answer. Too many secrets and lies cloud the truth. 'She took the answer to the grave with her, but I doubt it. She didn't have Dad's cravings, she just craved Dad,' I say, but my words don't convince him nor me. Dropping my hand to my extended stomach, I silently promise my daughter that I will never treat her as my mum did me.

As Lawrence and I talk, he exorcises over twenty-five years' worth of questions about Mr Bones and his victims. I reply with what I can, all the while contemplating the answer to the question he's leading up to, *Were you there when Tommy died?* I ready myself to admit that, when Dad drove him to our house, we played football together. That his son's last meal was a Sunday roast on a weekday. And that the next time I saw him, I was helping my dad bury his body in the same garden we had played in earlier. But Lawrence doesn't ask the question I'm dreading.

Between teas, Robin runs over and gifts our guest with a crayon drawing of Nostrom. In the picture, the robot is holding Lawrence's hand and smiling.

'Thank you,' he says and ruffles Robin's already messy hair.

I'm then presented with my own Crayola masterpiece. I look down at the page and see my son has drawn me with my swollen belly, Leo, and himself with another man; a man who has his arm around my son's shoulders.

'That's lovely, sweetie. Who's that with us?' I ask.

Robin laughs. 'Come on, Mummy. Don't you recognise Mr Bones?'

Acknowledgements

The time and effort that goes into writing a book is massive. But it's not just down to the writer's efforts; behind every successful author is a team of publishing professionals, a longsuffering family, and a fantastic array of friends all offering support and help.

I'd like to thank everyone who stood by me while I wrote *Little Bones*; especially my friends Julie Kendrick and Karen Rust, who patiently listened to me talk about characters, plot and my research for hours. Both kept my worries and negativity at bay, when either could have easily halted my progress and stopped me achieving my dream. These incredible, patient, and talented friends came to me through my writing, so I have a lot to thank my books for!

Thank you to my family who understood when I couldn't spend weekends with them; as I was holed up with a laptop, a flask of strong tea, and a dream. The book you hold in your hands right now is the reason I sacrifice so much of my free time to my writing.

A huge thank you to the team at Avon; especially my amazing editor Bethany Wickington. Beth plucked my manuscript from an open submission pile and believed in it, and me, enough to offer me a contract – without her, you wouldn't have read this book. Thank you to the lovely PR guru Sabah Khan, without her you'd have never heard about this book. The Avon designers did such a fantastic job on the front cover that I almost cried when I first saw it. I hope my words are worthy of such an eye-catching and beautiful front cover.

Thank you to Rebecca Fortuin, Audio Editor at HarperCollins, whose excitement over the audio book of *Little Bones* was contagious. Together, we included extra content you won't find in this book, so if you can't get enough of Mr Bones et al., then download the audio book today.

I'd like to thank fellow thriller author and friend Jane Isaac, who writes gripping and dark thrillers, and is one of the nicest people I've ever met. Our conversations are always reassuring, intriguing and above all fun.

A big shout-out to all the members of my writers' group, Creative Minds. Through the years, the group has gone from strength to strength and grown to over 20 members. Writing is a solitary pursuit, so never underestimate the power of spending time with like-minded individuals and the motivation you can gain from a regular meet up. These people, and you know who you are, are some of the best I've ever spent time with. Creative, open and wonderful to talk to, writers are some of the most amazing people you'll ever meet and I feel so lucky to know each and every one of you.

A special thanks to my mum whose dream it was to

become an author herself and who has been a tireless cheerleader for my writing. She has read every word I've ever had published – I hope you enjoy this book too, Mum!

I had the astounding news during the UK's COVID Lockdown that HarperCollins, one of the largest publishers in the world, was interested in publishing my book; it was surreal. Without being able to see my friends and family in person, this amazing news only sank in a little – it wasn't until lockdown eased and I could share the success face-to-face that I had that pearl-clutching moment!

The world went through some unwanted radical changes in 2020 and the pandemic touched all our lives. So, I'd like to take a moment to acknowledge everyone who made a positive difference during this troublesome time, whether it was just a simple 'hello' to connect with a stranger, or risking their own life to save others – Thank you.

Finally, I'd like to acknowledge you. Yes, you, my lovely reader. Without you buying, recommending and reviewing my books, I couldn't do what I love. Writing is everything to me; I'm not sure what I'd do if I couldn't indulge in plotting and writing prose. So a big thank you to you too. I have so many books locked in my imagination that I can't wait for you to read!